Praise for *The Hours of the Night*

'*The Hours of the Night* is a wonderful contemporary novel, a story that draws you into the lives of credible interesting characters, as absorbing as village gossip. It is written with consistent clarity and at times the language rises to poetry . . . It transforms the stuff of life into art, without overwriting events or language, and it describes country life as a normal and interesting state, neither eccentric nor twee'
Philippa Gregory, *The Sunday Times*

'. . . moving and immensely readable. Sue Gee is a skilled craftswoman and her novel is full of understanding and passionate feeling'
Publishing News

Sue Gee's thoughtful novel examines the night of the soul, between the pain of experience and the dawn of discovery . . . The characters are engaging and the narrative profound yet amusing'
Classic FM – The Magazine

'Gee writes well about the co-existence of late twentieth-century life with an older rural existence. Her passion for literature, music and most of all the countryside lights up the novel . . . her writing achieves some startling effects'
The Tablet

'A serious novel, enjoyable and admirable simply by design'
Finetime

'I was left wanting more . . . wonderfully absorbing'
Home and Country

'Gee's sensitive use of pieces of seventeenth century writing . . . coupled with the lyricism of her own style, constitutes one of the delights of this book . . . It deserves many readers'
Hampstead & Highgate Express

'A poignant, perceptive and original novel'
Sainsbury's Magazine

'A novel of such brilliance and emotional complexity, it fair takes your breath away . . . The kind of book you just wish never ended and which, once over, is sorely missed'
Rasp

THE HOURS OF THE NIGHT

Sue Gee had a country childhood and an urban working life in book and magazine publishing before going freelance in 1983. She now writes, reviews and is an Associate Lecturer in Writing and Publishing Studies at Middlesex University. Her other novels are *Spring Will Be Ours, Keeping Secrets, The Last Guests of the Season* and *Letters from Prague*, which was serialised on BBC Woman's Hour. She lives in London with her Polish partner and their son.

ALSO BY SUE GEE

Spring Will Be Ours
Keeping Secrets
The Last Guests of the Season
Letters from Prague

THE HOURS OF THE NIGHT

Sue Gee

ARROW

Published by Arrow Books in 1997

5 7 9 10 8 6

Copyright © Sue Gee 1996

The right of Sue Gee to be identified as the author
of this work has been asserted by her in accordance
with the Copyright, Designs and Patents Act, 1988

First published in 1996 in the United Kingdom by
Century Books

This edition published in 1997 by
Arrow Books,
Random House UK Limited
20 Vauxhall Bridge Road, London SW1V 2SA

Random House Australia (Pty) Limited
20 Alfred Street, Milsons Point, Sydney,
New South Wales 2061, Australia

Random House New Zealand Limited
18 Poland Road, Glenfield
Auckland 10, New Zealand

Random House South Africa (Pty) Limited
Endulini, 5a Jubilee Road, Parktown 2193, South Africa

Random House UK Limited Reg. No. 954009

A CIP catalogue record for this book
is available from the British Library

Papers used by Random House UK Limited
are natural, recyclable products made from wood grown in
sustainable forests. The manufacturing processes conform to
the environmental regulations of the country of origin

ISBN 0 09 927461 2

Printed and bound in Great Britain by
Cox & Wyman Ltd, Reading, Berkshire

For Marek, walking
and
To the memory of Michael Wall

Who is this that cometh up from the wilderness,
leaning upon her beloved?

Set me as a seal upon thine heart, as a seal
upon thine arm; for love is strong as death;
jealousy is as cruel as the grave.

The Song of Solomon

The peace of God, which passeth all understanding.

The Book of Common Prayer

Part 1

The coming of autumn

1

Phoebe was fact and Gillian fiction: together, mother and daughter uneasily inhabited the damp, grey stone house which stood just over the border from Herefordshire to Wales. Just over, but within. They were in Wales, not England, and thus inhabited what would to Phoebe always be foreign territory, even though she might never want to move. Gillian was born here: there could never be any question of her moving.

In the autumn of 1957 Phoebe and her husband moved in with a handful of furniture and a baby on the way. The house had been empty for months: Phoebe, angular and tall, the swelling curve of her pregnancy outlandishly at odds with the rest of her, stood on the cold patterned tiles in the hall and looked up at bare stairs, brown-painted banisters, post-war wallpaper limp and stained with moisture. The air was chill; her footsteps were like gunshots as she moved from room to empty room; she stood in the sitting room with its rotting flowered carpet, surveying through unwashed windows an enormous garden, rankly overgrown with nettles, ivy, old man's beard. Phoebe mentally mowed it all down. She tore out weeds by the roots and had the decaying sycamore chopped to a stump, round which she planted primroses; she laid paths, sowed grass seed, dug beds for shrubs, for vegetables, for rare and mysterious flowers.

The light was fading: November dusk claimed the sky beyond the bare trees which, with a ragged hedge, divided the garden from farmland. The map had shown a river.

The baby kicked; behind her came the footsteps of her husband. Phoebe ignored them both.

Her husband flicked down a Bakelite switch at the door. A naked light bulb shone horribly on to the rotting carpet and ugly tiled fireplace someone once had liked: the unwashed windows went black.

He said: 'Do you hate me for bringing you here?'

'Of course not,' said Phoebe, whose view of the garden had been so abruptly shut out, but she did not say that she loved him.

And within her the vision of the garden grew: a chanting catalogue of Latin, handfuls of white labels, fine writing in black ink, more wonderful than any child.

Phoebe's baby was born in a snowstorm. The piercing stars which had hung above the garden at eight o'clock were blotted out by ten o'clock with whirling clouds of white. It was the middle of February: up on the hills sheep heaved and gasped and frozen wet lambs died within moments. Up in her bedroom, at midnight, Phoebe lay gasping and heaving in a black iron bed with brass knobs at each corner; downstairs her husband dialled and dialled. He put down the heavy receiver and opened the front door. Snow roared in and he banged it shut again; he raced up the bare brown stairs to the bedroom.

'What shall we do? What can I do for you?'

Phoebe clamped her teeth on a fistful of sheet and turned away from him. Sweat poured down her, though the room was bitter. He fumbled to turn up the oil stove and the little blue circle went orange and yellow: too high. He ran down to boil a kettle and dialled again. If not the doctor then the vicar, the vicar's wife. Phoebe was three weeks early: he found he was crying.

The vicar's wife reached them at one in the morning, leaving a message *en route*. At five the doctor hammered on the door; at six he drew a slimy white-coated creature from between Phoebe's legs and pronounced it a girl.

Phoebe's husband, pale and pacing, came up from the hall to see her; he kissed Phoebe's face, smoothing back soaking dark hair, saying he knew not what.

The doctor gave Phoebe the baby, wrapped in towels.

'Put it in the crib,' said Phoebe, and turned her face to the window. The snow had stopped falling; the sky was an unearthly colour; the whole of the land was silent and still.

'She's perfect,' said her husband, bending over his daughter.

Gillian followed her parents round the garden. It was spring, she was three, and the trunks of the trees were dark above her, leaves silken and tender, a mist of green. A spade sliced into damp earth and turned it; boxes of plants stood about, waiting their turn. Down at the far end drifts of daffodils swayed as the wind went past: the air was fresh and the sky light, streaming with young clouds. Lambs bleated across the other side of the hawthorn hedge, sprinkled over the farmer's field. Gillian's hair was unbrushed, and her face had traces of breakfast upon it. She wore a print dress and Wellingtons, and carried a doll in a vest and a trailing shawl.

Her father came up behind her, pushing a barrow of compost.

'Mind,' he said gently.

She stood aside.

Phoebe was digging hard, wearing a headscarf. She pushed it back impatiently at the approach of the barrow.

'I must get on,' said her husband.

'With what?'

'Phoebe –'

'Go on, then.'

He made to kiss her; she let him.

Gillian followed him back to the house.

'Can I sit with you?'

'If you like.'

She sat in a brown, uncovered armchair with sagging springs, and her doll slept in her lap. Her father moved along the shelves: he took down books, and sniffed the pages. He stood there reading, marking, slipping them back again. He showed her a book bound in black, with gold on the spine.

He read to her.

' "Orient and immortal wheat, which never should be reaped, nor was ever sown. I thought it had stood from everlasting to everlasting." '

He turned the pages.

' " The World is not this little Cottage of Heaven and Earth ... It is an illimted field of Varietie and Beauty..." '

Gillian smoothed the trailing shawl. Her doll was having a dream.

' "Lov is the true means by which the World is Enjoyed. Our Lov to others, and Others Lov to us." '

Her father put the book back. He went to sit at his desk, with a pile of paper, and a pen. A wicker basket stood beside him, filled with scrunched-up balls of white. He lifted his pen, he turned to look at her.

'Your face needs a wash, my darling.'

'It doesn't matter,' said Gillian.

A fire smoked in the grate; the hearth needed sweeping. Later the scrunched-up balls of white would be consumed: she would help him to throw them, one by one.

Beyond the window, faraway Phoebe dug in the compost. She

looked like a clothes peg, Gillian thought. Her father wrote something, and crossed it out. He sat looking out of the window: lambs
bleated, catkins shook. He lit a cigarette and went on sitting there,
looking out, looking in.

After a while Gillian left the room with her doll; he did not hear her.

Gillian's father died in a flood.

In the autumn of 1961 it rained for a week without stopping, and
the banks of the river burst. The field below the hill behind the house
became a lake; the house, on high flat ground, was safe, though much
of the garden was ruined; down in the village, where the river came
snaking round, where children, in summer, floated boats and sticks
and fished for things, water now swept and swirled along the main
street, drowning doorsteps, pouring through gaps at front doors into
small front rooms, rising, rising.

Gillian's father, who could not swim, clung on to the back of the
farmer's tractor. They did what they could to ferry beleaguered
families out to high ground, up to the church; wrapped in blankets, a
soaking congregation filled the pews, and listened to the rain pound
on the roof and against the leaded windows, shaken by the wind.

Gillian's father, on the third trip back to the village, saw a black
dog swimming weakly towards them and shouted: in his cab, in
driving wind and rain, the farmer did not hear him. Gillian's father
bent down and reached for the dog, and slipped, his hand missing
the collar, his foot missing the footplate. The tractor drove on, the
water closed above him; he and the dog went down together.

This was the autumn of Gillian's fourth year.

The poems her father had sent off to London in the summer were
published, a posthumous second volume, and well received. People
in universities admired them, and forgot them. Years passed.

These days Phoebe rarely spoke of her husband, and Gillian could
not remember him: not his voice, not his face. There were
photographs, but they were different from memories.

Those days had been locked away by these days, in which mother
and daughter, both without men, though for different reasons, had
come to an accommodation.

Gillian remembered an armchair, a man at the bookshelves, the
scratch of a pen.

2

The villagers were used to Gillian; strangers thought her odd. She was odd. Odd is unmatched, unpartnered, out on its own: Gillian, at not quite seven o'clock on a morning in late September, was out on her own in the garden, her overcoat over her nightgown, slippered feet flapping on damp brick paths. It was Sunday: church bells rang. Gillian's hair was a cloud of fuse wire: she combed it down and tied it back in the day, but at night it floated out across her pillow, and it floated out now, as yet unrestrained, on to the collar of the grey tweed overcoat. Gillian's hands were worker's hands, with bitten finger-nails, prone to chaps and chilblains, prone to go blue with cold; they clasped a mug of hot tea as she walked through the garden.

Cobwebs beaded with dew hung on the hawthorn hedge which bordered it, and the neat box hedges which in places divided it. Phoebe had wrought a miracle here, and won a reputation. Gillian had other names for the plants which her mother so carefully catalogued in midnight-blue notebooks: she walked around the garden talking to the companions of her childhood. Then, they had towered above her; even now, even before she came to the trees in the farmer's field, there were places where she stood gazing up at mighty spreading leaves, branching from enormous fleshy stems with hairs on. Such plants encroached, and had to be conquered; others were nurtured, and cuttings were taken, put into pots and put into the greenhouse.

The greenhouse stood to the side of the house, built by a local firm to Phoebe's specifications with a small legacy from an aunt. That was in 1968, when Gillian was ten. She walked home from school and stood watching the men with her drink and her sandwich: a wooden frame was hammered, glass panes lifted from a stack against the wall of the house swung dizzily before her, reflecting the grass, the flagstones, the summer sky. They were slid into place in perfect grooves; blood trickled from the thumb of one of the men and he swore. It took just under a week, and then the slatted shelves went in,

9

and Phoebe stood inside, looking out through the glass to her garden, planning. Gillian watched her, sealed away.

'Go and do something useful,' said Phoebe.

Now the white frames were peeling and flaky. They had been painted and repainted: by Phoebe, who no longer had money from a legacy left to pay for it, and by Gillian, clumsily, dangerous up a ladder on spring afternoons, splashing the flagstones.

'"And behold a ladder, set up on the earth, and the top of it reached to heaven,"' she said aloud, recalling Sunday school, and Scripture, and Jacob's dream. '"And behold the angels of God –"'

'I'll do it myself,' said Phoebe.

The greenhouse stood to the side of the house; a dovecot hung from the wall at the back. It had been there for ever, was there when Phoebe arrived with her husband, though she did nothing about it. Only Phoebe, thought Gillian, could ignore a dovecot. A gift of doves was the gift of a lover: Gillian, who had never had a lover, knew that. But these doves came from a woman in the village whose brother kept some, and sometimes sold them. Phoebe and Gillian drove over to see him one Sunday, when Gillian was twenty, and at a loss. They bought two – for breeding, said Phoebe, paying the man. Gillian clasped the box with its air-holes and raised it and turned it towards her: the two doves were silent, tapping the cardboard sides with their beaks, sliding about, their toes scraping the bottom. Gillian, peering, could see whiteness, and brightness of eye.

'You have nothing to fear,' she told them.

At home she took them out of the box and held them in turn against her; she pressed her face to feathers of snow and ran her fingers down the sweet and perfect curve of the head and neck. When she released them they did not know where to go: they fluttered to the roof and walked along broken slates with jerky and uneasy footsteps.

'Come down to your house,' said Gillian, and scattered a handful of corn.

The doves came down and ate, and found the dovecot; the next day they began to murmur and coo, and the ground was splashed with white. Now there were over a dozen, and sometimes Gillian and Phoebe sold a pair to visitors.

Visitors came to the house to buy plants, travelling sometimes from some distance. Articles had been written about Phoebe and her garden: they were known to people up and down the country.

Gillian's name was known also, but to a smaller circle, and her visitors were rare. Her poems appeared in small magazines at infrequent intervals; she gave readings in the upper rooms of pubs.

High on the hillsides, sheep cropped toughened autumn grass; on lower and more gentle slopes the woods were yellow and still, sheltering ploughland. Winding grey roads and quiet lanes connected isolated cottages and farms.

Gillian had been walking these lanes all her life. As a girl she had cycled, also, riding an old black bike with a basket, ticking on cold October days between trees and hedgerows, the soundless fields beyond. Fallen dry leaves danced before her; sometimes a curlew called. Gillian, at ten, eleven, twelve, was writing on these cycle rides, though she did not know it, and what went into her diary then was only a record of days. But the landscape, silent as a church, sank into her. In winter, storms and rising water filled her dreams; in spring and summer she leaned the bike against a tree and flung herself down on the grass, gazing up, up, feeling herself detach from herself and look down upon outstretched girl, black bicycle, rippling grass. Later the bike was abandoned, with one flat tyre too many for Phoebe to bother about: it was parked in the shed with a quantity of spiders and forgotten. Gillian went walking.

She went walking still.

Early morning in late September. Sunday: the bell for early communion. The mist rose from the valley beyond the garden and the sun rose, touching Gillian's hair. There were no visitors at such an hour, and the doves were still in their dovecot. Phoebe was still in the house.

Gillian came to the end of the garden, where a great pond lay. Phoebe had dug it and filled and planted it: in spring, kingcups spilled into it, bulrushes and tall yellow iris rose around it; now, with the approach of autumn, the glossy green waterlily leaves were yellowing also, beginning to curl.

Gillian stood in her tweed coat and nightgown at the water's edge. The mist rose from the valley beyond the hawthorn hedge; spiders dropped from the glass-beaded webs; the sun rose and the surface of the water shone with holy light.

'Breakfast,' called Phoebe. 'Come along.'

Gillian went. She hung up her coat in the dark tiled hall. Glimpsing Phoebe in the kitchen, moving between range and table in paisley dressing gown, she had a thought and trod on it.

11

The man on the kitchen wireless was talking about what the papers said. Phoebe and Gillian took the papers intermittently, according to budget; they read them according to mood. The man on the wireless described varying reactions to summit meetings; civil war; the sordid fall of men from office. Gillian reached for the teapot and refilled her mug from a height.

'Don't do that,' said Phoebe. 'Did you sleep well?'

'I think so.' She lowered the teapot. 'What about you?'

'Very well, thank you.' Phoebe passed her a pale green plate: watery lumps of scrambled egg sat on a piece of toast.

Gillian took the plate. Alistair Cooke was writing to her from America: he wrote every Sunday, it bored her to death. Across the table Phoebe was eating briskly, looking at the headlines. Outside, the doves began to coo.

'My angels,' said Gillian.

'What did you say?'

'Nothing.' She looked round the kitchen, swallowing lumps. A window overlooked the lane, another the garden at the back: both windows were small enough to mean that they often needed the light on, and it was on now, a single bulb in a shade the colour of fly-paper, hanging above the table. If Gillian had had her way there might have been other lights, illuminating corners, but the budget did not run to other lights.

Overall, the furniture in the room – the range, the moquette chair beside it, the scratched worn table and dresser against the wall – had the same disconnected air which pervaded much of the house: of objects put in a place on first arrival and never since thought about, much less rearranged. Gillian rarely visited other people's houses, but she sensed when she did so what was missing here, even if other people's furniture was not to her taste.

'Toast?' she asked, rising.

'Thank you.' Phoebe turned the pages of the paper and pushed up her spectacles. Gillian took up the breadknife. The review section lay untouched by her plate: you needed a lot of energy to keep up with all those goings-on. She sometimes read the books pages, but she rarely read the books: it was Phoebe who took out three or four a month from the market-town library, and filled in request cards, and sat up in bed to all hours of the night with her specs on.

Gillian lay beneath the bedclothes and listened for her poems, a broken urgent whispering which had to be given silence.

12

The bread, sliced too thickly, could not get out of the toaster, and was going black with rage. The kitchen filled with smoke.

'Oh, for heaven's sake,' said Phoebe, pushing her chair back.

Later, in recompense, in bilious green cast-off jumper and brown trousers, Gillian stood at the sink and washed everything up. She had made her bed, she had brushed back her hair and tied it, she had switched off the fly-paper lamp. The kitchen was lighter, now; she looked out to the garden where her mother was on her knees. Last year's bulbs were spread on a sack beside her: Phoebe, with her trowel, opened up the earth and overturned it; she cast out stones.

A cast-out devil, ragged and black, hobbled along the lane at the front of the house: Gillian, in her cast-off jumper, rinsing the plates and putting them up in the rack beside her, saw him, limping and scratching at bits of himself, searching for sanctuary. Bread was cast upon the waters. A man had a cast in his eye. He stood on a street corner, moaning in the rain. Ah. There. The devil leapt into him, turning round and round, settling down in his new home.

Gillian, writing, went for potatoes. They stood in a heavy paper sack behind the larder door and were covered in earth. She carried them back to the sink in a bowl and water gushed on to them. She peeled them and put them round the joint in the big black roasting tin on the table, as Phoebe had told her to do, and opened the oven door. Good morning, said Gillian, here you are. She pushed in the roasting tin and went upstairs, writing, leaving the oven door open.

Upstairs was chilly and damp. She went to her room, her desk.

On a morning in spring, some years ago, she had entered her father's study, and knelt before his desk, and pulled all the drawers out, one by one. She had piled them up and carried them up the stairs; a man, summoned from the village, had helped her to turn the poor empty thing on its side and carry it up with her. The desk was strong, and had withstood everything. Its drawers were slid back into place again; it was set before her window, where it belonged. That was immediately clear. It had been her father's, and then it had been no one's, and now it was hers.

And now she stood before it, unscrewing her marbled fountain pen. Some things were male and some were female: white sheets lay beneath the fountain pen, waiting to receive his touch.

Gillian sat down. Her room was at the front of the house: she could not see the garden. Across the lane beneath her stood a hedgerow:

13

beyond it, visible only from up here, hill and valley rose and fell beneath a soaring sky.

Bells rang.

Gillian lifted her pen.

3

A blackboard stood outside the house, advertising produce. Visitors might come from a distance for plants, but locals, and passers-by, called in for vegetables: greenhouse tomatoes; cauliflowers, carrots, beans and winter greens from the walled area across the garden from the pond.

Phoebe had not, in her long-ago vision, planned this area, but produce became an economic necessity. In the early spring of 1962, six months after her husband's death, she ordered stone from a discount merchant advertising in the local paper, and made a request to the travelling library.

The travelling librarian was used to giving out romances: he stamped the City Library's copy of the book on dry-stone walling and handed it down to Phoebe, waiting with Gillian in the cold.

'This for your husband?' he asked, having no other customers yet, a long round to make through the valley, and only the dog in the cab for company.

'No,' said Phoebe shortly. She looked at the book jacket and turned to the contents page. A sharp spring wind blew across the fields: Gillian pulled the shawl round her doll and shivered.

'Looks like rain,' said the travelling librarian.

Phoebe agreed.

'A book for the little one?'

Phoebe glanced at Gillian. 'Do you want a book?'

'Yes, please.'

They climbed the steps, into the warmth of the van. Phoebe leaned against the door frame, turning pages; Gillian and the doll looked about them. The children's section was small. Gillian, who had just begun to read, chose a book about cavemen. Comfortable women with shopping bags climbed the steps. They discussed the imminent rain, and Catherine Cookson; they recognised the child in the corner, and were kind.

'That's a nice story you've found there. You'll be starting at school with the other children soon, I expect.'

Gillian, afflicted with shyness, shrank.

'Come along,' said Phoebe. She nodded to the women and snapped her book shut. They hurried home.

In the afternoon, when the rain had stopped, Phoebe dug a trench. She laid plumb lines. Gillian sat at her father's desk and looked at pictures of sabre-toothed tigers and mammoths, printed in yellow and black. She made out some words and guessed at others. The doll had her afternoon sleep. 'I can read,' Gillian told her, when she woke up.

Two days later, an articulated lorry dropped the stone off, tipping it up on the verge. Phoebe, mindful of accidents, coated a couple of planks with whitewash and set them up against the pile, to warn the occasional passing car or tractor. She carted the stones, barrow by barrow, along the path at the side of the house, and across the garden. Gillian took those stones which fell off, and built caves, down by the pond. Phoebe's full attention had not yet been given to the pond, which was still a wild place. Gillian made Plasticine cave men and women, a Plasticine mammoth. The wall grew, spit by spit, and was finished just after Easter. After Easter, Gillian started school.

Phoebe, before it was fashionable, grew her vegetables organically. She piled up compost, and avoided pesticides. The greens had holes in the leaves, and the carrots were pale and of varying sizes, but they tasted well. She chalked up prices on a blackboard bought at the school bazaar, and sat it outside, with a couple of pots of thyme. Gillian had thought the blackboard was to be for her. When people called to buy, she took them down the path, and pointed to Phoebe, planting and pruning. Twine and secateurs stuck out of Phoebe's pockets; she was always carrying something – flowerpots, a trowel, boxes of cuttings. The visitors were an interruption, but grew used to her brisk manner. Phoebe kept the money in jam jars, and let Gillian count it, until the day when she dropped a jar, and broken glass and coins were scattered and mixed up all over the kitchen floor. Phoebe cut herself, trying to separate them. Gillian hid.

It was late afternoon. Phoebe, after an undercooked lunch, had raked up the first fall of leaves, piled them on top of the summer's weeds and deadheads, and lit a bonfire, down by the pond. She had retired to the vegetable garden, to pick the last of the runner beans and sow spring cabbages.

Gillian stood watching the bonfire. Frail smoke rose from the centre and drifted across the garden, where dahlias were aflame. On the other side of the dry-stone wall she could see the last scarlet flowers of the beans, and Phoebe moving amongst them, in her knitted hat. It was growing cold, and the light was beginning to go.

Rooks cawed, doves flew up to the dovecot. Footsteps came round to the side of the house, and stopped on the flagstone path. Gillian, after a moment or two, registered this, and turned, and saw a man.

He was tall and spare, wearing a weatherproof jacket and Wellingtons: neither were new, but she knew straight away that he was not a local, not born and bred, as she was. He saw her, and came down the path.

'Good afternoon.'

Gillian nodded, and turned back to the fire. She prodded the leaves with her foot.

'I'm sorry to disturb your Sunday. I was passing and I saw the blackboard. I've heard of your garden.' A cultured English voice: a new arrival, or a tourist, right at the end of the season.

'It's my mother's garden.' Gillian turned to look at him. 'That's her.' She nodded towards the lean figure in knitted hat, moving amongst the canes and scarlet flowers. 'It's no use talking to me,' she said.

The man smiled. He was older than her, with an open, outdoor face: quite a nice face, she supposed, if you liked men. Gillian knew nothing at all about men.

'Well – I'll go and talk to your mother, then, if I may.'

She did not answer. He glanced towards the pond, at the glossy leaves of the waterlilies, beginning to curl, and the dense variety of reeds and rushes all round the edge. A warbler was darting in and out. Yellowing leaves from the ash trees bordering the farmer's field fell in the still cold air and spun slowly on the water.

'That's a wonderful pond.'

'It is the altar of the garden,' said Gillian, who had never said this to anyone.

The man looked at her curiously.

'Hello?' said Phoebe, over the wall. 'Can I help?'

'I'm going to get my coat.' Gillian left the bonfire, and the visitor, and walked back up to the house. Doves were fluttering round the dovecot. She took her coat from the peg in the hall. The larder door

17

was open, and she could hear the faint scritch of a mouse. If Phoebe heard it, she would set the trap. Gillian went in to the dim chilly room and switched on the light. 'You'd better go,' she said. 'You'll be given no quarter here.' A deathly silence. She stood sniffing the earthy smell of the potatoes in their paper sacks, and the damp wood of the spider-infested beams. Strings of onions hung from nails, a perforated zinc meat safe stood on the shelf in the corner, imprisoning the undercooked joint. 'You have been warned,' said Gillian to the silent mouse, and went outside again.

Phoebe and the visitor were visible over the wall of the vegetable garden, deep in conversation. Gillian returned to the bonfire and stood poking it with a long stick of ash, disturbing it, as Phoebe had told her not to. She listened to the fall of leaves and twigs inside it, and the rise and fall of voices. The grass in the field beyond the pond was grey as the afternoon drew in. She squatted close to the embers, struggling to rekindle the morning's opening lines.

Phoebe and the visitor were no longer talking: she had left him to look round while she carried a cardboard box of runner beans up to the house. Gillian, straightening up from the fire, rubbed at rheumatic aches in her knees and observed the visitor, walking along the paths, looking at labels, pausing by the roses, over now, waiting for Phoebe's secateurs. Lavender bushes grew beneath them, alongside the brick path; he stopped to crush a dry spike between his fingers, sniffed, and walked on.

Gillian considered the bonfire, and wondered if she had killed it. Her opening lines were elusive, and would not come right: she consigned them to burning, deep within the fire.

'Tea,' called Phoebe, from the house. She had switched on the hall light and stood framed in the open back doorway: a bulrush, straight and tall.

'Coming.' Gillian made her way up towards her. She thought of her fragments of poems, and their terrible death, and felt a stab of pity. Well. Sometimes you had to be ruthless.

The visitor fell into step beside her. 'I'm glad I came.'

'Everything's dying,' said Gillian.

'It's still beautiful.'

'Yes. It's all my mother.' She turned, and they walked on.

'And what do you do?' he asked her.

'Get in the way.'

They came to the house. From somewhere in the lane came a dog's intermittent barking. Heads looked out of the dovecot; there was a murmuring from within; feathers spun to the ground.

'How very nice.' The man stood looking up at the flutter of white, as one or two birds came out to the ledge, and followed each other in again.

'Fantails,' said Gillian. 'They're mine – I bought the original pair.'

Phoebe stood at the open door. 'You left the larder light on.' She offered the visitor tea: he shook his head.

'Very kind of you, but I think my dog's had enough. Hear her? I left her shut up in the cab.' He nodded to them both. 'I'd better be off.'

He did not say to where, and neither of the women asked. People round here did not ask questions of strangers.

'Don't forget your beans.' Phoebe nodded towards the cardboard box by the door, and he paid her and picked it up. 'Do call again,' she said briskly. 'We're always here.'

'Thank you. I'm sure I shall.'

His footsteps faded round the side of the house. Phoebe and Gillian went indoors.

'Someone who knew about gardening,' said Phoebe, putting the kettle on.

Gillian, through the window, glimpsed a Land Rover, pulling away, a black-and-white sheepdog up in the cab, alert beside the driver.

Phoebe put mugs and a bottle of milk on the table. They drank their tea listening to *The Natural History Programme*.

In the evening Gillian went to church. She closed the front gate behind her, and walked down the darkening lane in her tweed coat and headscarf, knotted beneath her chin, much as Phoebe knotted her own. It looked well on Phoebe; it did not look well on Gillian, thirty years younger, thirty-five years old and unattached. She did not care. She came to the church, where bells were ringing.

There were places in the valley where fifty houses were served by three chapels. Here, in the Church of Wales, Evensong was held once a month. The vicar had other churches in the parish to attend to, and if lay or retired clergy assisted in covering the weekly Matins and early Communion, they did not always stretch to the day's third service, whose sparse attendance grew sparser still as the days grew shorter and colder.

Gillian and Phoebe sometimes attended Matins: Phoebe was a mainstay of the flower rota, and had also, over the years, made a number of tapestries for hassocks. She did these things in secular spirit: it pleased her to attend a service and observe her larkspur and scented stock in tall green jugs beneath the pulpit, her Chinese lanterns on the whitewashed windowsills set deep beneath stained glass. It pleased her to kneel on a hassock she had worked all the previous winter, sitting in the kitchen, listening to *Science Now*, or *Bookshelf*, or the classic serial. Some of the patterns she copied from books and some she designed herself, tugging sky-blue and cream and gold and crimson wools into lambs and crosses and fleur-de-lys, as Brontë and Dickens and Thackeray filled the kitchen, and Gillian sat listening in the red and grey chair by the range.

Gillian had no talent for tapestry, nor for flower arrangements. She came to church to pray.

She walked through the lych gate and up the smooth path between graves and yew trees, passing, at a distance, her father's grave, set in the shelter of the right-hand wall, beneath another yew. Many of the more recent stones were carved in shining black granite, and some had elaborate inscriptions, and floral designs in the corners, inlaid with gold. Her father's memorial was simple: a slab of grey stone, his name, his dates. And a single word. Poet. It was one of the first words Gillian had learned to read, there in the churchyard on a cold spring morning six months after the accident: the same spring in which Phoebe had built the dry-stone wall, and she had started school. The earth above the grave had settled, the stone had been set, she and the vicar and Phoebe stood before it, and the vicar said a prayer.

'Our Father, Which Art in Heaven,' he said.

'Poet,' said Gillian, when he had finished, and felt the word sink into her, as certain and sure as if it had always been waiting to do so.

The wind blew over the churchyard, rippling the tender new grass. Most of the daffodils which grew beneath the wall or in clumps between the graves were still in bud, but a few were opening, bright and fresh.

'"In sure and certain hope,"' she said aloud, and Phoebe and the vicar looked at one another, over her head.

'She remembers,' said the vicar.

'So it would seem.'

'Yes,' said Gillian. She remembered the flood, and the lashing rain, and hearing the telephone ring in the hall as she played beneath her father's desk, with the scrunched-up balls of white, and crossings-out. She remembered finding Phoebe in the kitchen, sitting there, white as paper, not doing anything at all: unheard of. She remembered being taken to somebody's house, through rising water, and having to stay there, and she remembered the coffin in the church, and flowers and people everywhere, and standing by the open grave as the coffin went down, down. She had not known that a hole could go so deep.

'"Ashes to ashes, dust to dust,"' read the vicar; '"in sure and certain hope of the resurrection to eternal life..."'

The wind blew, the heads of the early daffodils tossed. Phoebe and Gillian were led across the churchyard for hot drinks in the vicarage, and talk of other things.

'Evening, Gillian. Keeping well?'

'Very well, thank you.' She walked past Gwen Jones in the porch, past the notices of missions, and parish council meetings, and the flower rota, and took her place in the church. Her place was on the far right of a pew in the middle, beneath the brass plaque raised by subscription in the village. Her father's name, and dates. Words from a psalm.

> *The floods are risen, O Lord, the floods have lift up their voice...*
> *The waves of the sea are mighty, and rage horribly:*
> *but yet the Lord, who dwelleth on high, is mightier.*

Would it not, Gillian had once asked the vicar, have been more fitting to have lines from one of her father's poems?

The vicar, who was seventy-six, and retiring to live with his sister in Tenbury, thought about her question. Gillian, who was thirteen, had gone to say goodbye to him. It was a fine autumn morning, a Saturday. She stood in the hall on bare floorboards, amidst tea chests and cardboard boxes, holding a bunch of bronze chrysanthemums, wrapped in newspaper.

'Come in, come in,' said the vicar. 'I'm all at sixes and sevens.' He led her through the open door of the front room. The sitting room, he and Phoebe called it. Gillian, like the villagers, called it by its place in the house. The removals lorry was calling on Monday: there were only two chairs left. The vicar took the chrysanthemums into the kitchen, and returned with them in a milk bottle, which he set on the mantelpiece. Gillian was sitting in one of the chairs, by the fireplace. They looked at one another. He had buried her father. His wife had gone for the doctor the night of the snowstorm, when she was born. His wife had died the year Gillian had turned eleven, and started at the market-town comprehensive, travelling each day by bus. The vicar had no children. Tomorrow was his last service here. He sat on the opposite side of the empty fireplace, and admired the flowers.

'My sister has a garden in Tenbury,' he told her. 'Very nice. But small. Not like your mother's. There was never a gardener like your mother. How is she keeping?'

Gillian said she was well. The high-backed chair was not unlike the one in the kitchen at home. She shifted a little, not knowing, now she had come here, what she should say.

'Well,' said the vicar. 'How are you getting on at school?'

Gillian thought of the concrete buildings, whose windows streamed with condensation in winter and glared in unbearable heat in summer. She thought of the noise: in the corridors and cloakrooms and the enormous classes, and of the loud, confident girls who wore rings, and put on eyeliner in the cloakrooms before they went home, and shunned her. She thought of the clever ones, with their As for Physics and Maths, who put up with her. She saw herself as the others saw her, something she had only just begun to do and later would abandon: a girl with a nondescript body and frizzy hair, an only child with a dead father, who read on the bus and talked to herself –

'I don't.'

'You do, I've seen you. Walking up and down in the playground. Muttering.'

'Writing,' said Gillian, before she could stop herself, and blushed to the roots of her hair.

'*Writing?* What do you mean?'

'Her dad was a writer,' said Bethan, who had been at primary school with her, and was loyal. 'There's a plate up to him in our church.'

'Oh.' And the girls drifted off again, in their twos and threes.

'You mustn't mind them,' said Bethan. They walked round the playground, arm in arm, till the bell went.

But Bethan had other friends, and then a boyfriend. Gillian knew nothing at all about boys. Then Bethan's father got a job in Birmingham, and they moved away. Gillian hadn't had a letter since Christmas.

*

'Well,' she said to the vicar now, 'I don't really like school much.'

'Not everyone does,' he said kindly. 'A wider world awaits.'

Gillian did not want a wider world. She wanted to be left in peace. She said: 'I wanted to ask you – about the plaque to my father. Why did my mother choose the psalm? I mean – I wish she'd used one of his poems.'

The vicar considered. 'I don't think we could have had something secular, you see. Your mother was grieving: I helped her to choose. I felt that a psalm was more fitting.'

'Oh.' She tried to imagine Phoebe, grieving.

'Could you not have asked her about this yourself?' he said, watching her.

She shook her head. 'Not really.'

'You're not close?'

'Not really.'

'I see. Well. I'm sorry you don't approve.'

'It isn't a question of disapproval.' Gillian looked at the bronze chrysanthemums, lighting up the empty mantelpiece, and the dusty squares on the wall, where pictures had hung. There were almost no pictures in her house. Everything colourful and nice was in the garden, and on the tapestry hassocks. She thought about Phoebe and the vicar choosing a psalm, because her father's poems were secular, and of the mighty Lord, presiding over the floods which had taken him away. She said:

'My mother doesn't believe in God.'

'Is that so?'

The vicar had the tips of his fingers pressed together. His hair was white and his glasses tortoiseshell. Today he was wearing an old, sage-coloured cardigan, which needed darning. He had known her all her life, and now he was leaving.

'I'm not sure if I do, either,' she said. 'Believe.'

'Is that so?' said the vicar again. 'Does it trouble you?'

'Sometimes.'

'Would you like to say a prayer?'

'No, thank you.'

Prayer was like poetry: solitary, private, deep within. It was different in church, when everyone recited the responses. But to pray aloud with another person? Unthinkable. Even with him.

'A cup of tea?'

'No, thank you.'

They smiled at each other, in perfect understanding. He saw her to the door.

'My best regards to your mother. Thank her for the flowers.'

'I picked them,' said Gillian. 'They were from me.'

She got on her bicycle, propped against the railings, and rode away.

Vicars came and went after that, and for a long time Gillian stopped going to church.

She came in from the wilderness on the twentieth anniversary of her father's death. Few people remembered him, nobody spoke of him. She and Phoebe never spoke of him. She sat beneath the plaque on the wall at Evensong, smelling wood and stone and polish for brass. She listened to the organ, plaintive and slow. She joined in the collects and responses, unfamiliar for so long, but coming back to her, words from her childhood, gone deeper than the grave.

I believe in the Holy Ghost; the holy Catholick Church; the Communion of Saints...

Give unto thy servants that peace which the world cannot give...

By thy great mercy defend us from all perils and dangers of this night...

Outside the stained-glass windows the November sky was black. It began to rain.

'The fellowship of the Holy Ghost,' said Gillian, under her breath. 'The grace of our lord Jesus Christ.'

She was twenty-three years old, and had no place in the world.

The church was unheated until October, when the Calor gas stoves were lit. Gillian, in her place, in her tweed coat and headscarf, knelt on one of Phoebe's hassocks and felt the chill go straight to her knees. She bent her head, listening to the bells. She had been taken up to the belfry once as a child, by her teacher, following Bethan, holding on to the rope slung between brass rings on the wall, feeling giddy. There were six bells, and six bell pulls, crimson and gold, and a picture of the Queen, with the names of those who had rung at the Coronation. She and Bethan had stood crammed up with the others watching the ringers and covering their ears. Now, she listened to the peal grow slower, and fade away, and become the single, summoning note: Come, come, come. The organ made quiet intercession; she closed her eyes and tried to pray, and could not. The morning's visionary moments had left her – the opening lines of her poem had burned to death, and she was disturbed and unsettled.

The visitor had unsettled her. Visitors got in the way. She had disclosed to a stranger the place where the altar of the garden lay and something had slipped away from her, as if she had read out lines from a poem before it was complete. You should never do that. He had made her do it – something in his face had made her, not even thinking. They had stood in the fading afternoon light, as the smoke from the bonfire rose towards heaven, and yellowing leaves from the ash trees spun on to the still clear water. And she, as if a flickering flame had been lit within her, had perceived: I can say anything to this man. And spoken.

'Hello? Can I help?'

Phoebe, over the dry-stone wall, sharp as a beanstick.

Around her, in the church, Gillian could hear the footsteps of the last arrivals, taking their places in the pews. Prayer books were passed and opened, comfortable greetings exchanged in low voices. The notes of the organ slowed, changed key, announced: the vestry door opened to reveal the vicar, robed in white and black. Gillian, rising to her feet, looked past him, to where, on the altar, candles burned.

'Accompany me with a pure heart and humble voice unto the throne of the heavenly grace...'

Gillian, with the handful of people who made up the congregation, knelt once again, seeking that shining place.

4

Who is this that cometh up from the wilderness –

Edward, driving home with the dog beside him, thought about the woman in the garden, and then forgot her. The road climbed, and wound round the hillside, leaves blew over the windscreen, a few spots of rain came and went.

Back at the farmhouse, he went to shut the hens up. Already a note of frost in the air, and the gate to the yard felt cold to the touch, the latch stiffening, in need of oil. The dog followed him about, chivvying hens from their places beneath the trailer, behind the hay bales, under the hedge in the back field.

'Here, girl, here.' He whistled, high and thin.

Tarn worked close to the ground, crouching still, moving swiftly, working the hens up the field. They squawked and ran towards the hen house, lifting pale legs and glossy wings, tuk tuk tuk, heads darting, quick quick quick over the rough grass, this way and that.

'Better than the fox,' said Edward. He closed the gate to the run behind him, shutting Tarn outside. The hens climbed the little ridged plank to the door, splashed with droppings, into the smelly warmth of roost and straw and nesting box. A lantern-torch hung from a rail: he switched it on and checked the boxes. One or two, but the season was almost over. The birds were erratic, unreliable, laying in places you had to search for, the kind of thing a child would enjoy, peering under the hedges, in gaps between bales in the barn. He put the eggs in his pocket, carefully, and the hens took their places, up on the roosting perch, fluffing up, bright eyes blinking in the light, waiting for him to go. He turned off the lantern.

Outside the run, Tarn was waiting. She followed him down towards the house, at a distance, stopping to sniff and pee, checking the hedgerows. This field, next spring, would be used for the new lambs, his first. Now, his eighty ewes were scattered high on the hills, moving amongst yellowing bracken, alongside the neighbouring

26

farmer's sheep, bleating as night approached. Edward stopped for a moment, hearing the first low note of an owl in the dusk, but it didn't come again. He walked on, Tarn at his heels, a shadow, always beside him.

'Good girl.' First dog, too.

Inside, he opened a can for her, mixing the meat with scraps from lunch and biscuits from the paper sack in the cupboard. He poured himself a beer and sat at the kitchen table, looking at the papers, waiting for the phone. Tarn went to her basket by the Rayburn and lay down, her tail thumping. She gave a sigh. The clock ticked, the basket creaked, Edward turned the pages. The papers were full of news from London, which he had been glad to leave. He scraped back his chair, feeling hungry, and remembered the cardboard box of runner beans, left out in the jeep.

He went to fetch them, thinking again of the mother and daughter in the garden, so difficult with one another. He had some of the beans for supper, with cold meat and a couple of slices of bread, listening to the end of a repeated concert from St John's, Smith Square, first broadcast last winter.

Last winter, he had still been living in London.

Tarn slept in her basket, occasionally whimpered, dreaming. The phone call did not come. Edward spent a half-hour sorting out books still in boxes in the room across the passage, where he had put his old dining-room table, and begun to put up shelves. He switched all the lights out; he climbed the stairs to the landing and stood in the darkness, looking out over the farmyard, hearing, quite clearly now, the hunting owl. Stars came out. He went to bed, and lay reading, craving his lover's return.

They first saw the farm last November, leaving London still sleeping, locking up the flat and driving out at daybreak through the orange-lit tunnel at the Barbican, past St Paul's and along the river. Rowland drove, because he liked driving, and the car was new: a plum-coloured Peugeot, sleek and fast. They sped along the Embankment, his belly close to the wheel, his face still heavy with sleep. Beside him, Edward looked at the map and directions. Miles from bloody anywhere. The advertisement was clipped to the map: he'd found it last weekend in the paper, and phoned first thing on Monday, as soon as he got to work.

'It's been on the market a while,' said the agent. 'Needs quite a bit doing to it – but of course that's reflected in the price.'

'Of course.' Edward, in his Civil Service office, his black swivel chair, swung round so that he could see the skyline. Clouds hung low over spire and office block: he pictured rain soaking into bracken, streaming down slate, and he and Rowland watching it, from their farmhouse kitchen. He listened to the agent, asked questions, made a provisional date. He rang the rehearsal rooms, leaving a message for Rowland King, with the London Consort. When Rowland rang back, he sounded amused but tolerant.

'You're serious?'

'I think so. Are you free?'

The pages of Rowland's diary turned; Edward could hear tuning-up in the background. Rowland was booked up months ahead. But Sunday was OK, so long as they came and went in the day.

'We'll be there and back in an hour if you keep this up,' said Edward now, as they hit the motorway past Oxford. 'Coffee?'

'Please.'

He unscrewed the flask. Rowland switched off *Record Review* and slotted a tape in. The motorway was still almost empty. They raced past fields where the mist was clearing; cows stood on wet grass, their breath in clouds, coats steaming. The car was filled with Schubert.

Edward said: 'When you're not there, I can listen to you.'

'You won't last a month,' said Rowland.

'You flatter yourself.'

'I don't mean because of me. I mean the country. It's hell. Creation expires before teatime. Who said that?'

'Sydney Smith. You forget I grew up on a farm. It'll be like coming home.'

'That's what you said about me.'

'Yes.' Edward looked at the big body, heavy face, dark beard. He reached out a hand.

'Not when I'm driving,' said Rowland.

They finished the flask of coffee, crossing the Welsh border just after eleven, climbing the hills with Edward frowning over the map and Rowland sounding the horn on corners.

'If anything comes down, we're done for.'

A tractor came down, and he rolled back into a passing place.

'Fuck –'

The driver of the tractor raised a hand.

They climbed on, looking out of the windows. The valley grew broader, the sky higher, filled with cold sunlight. A buzzard soared over the hills.

'How much further?'

'Nearly there.'

The agent was waiting in the yard.

They followed him, in his sheepskin coat and boots, into the barn and outbuildings, piled up with rusting junk, and freezing. Years of house martin nests clung to the rafters, crumbling to the touch. Webs festooned the corners. They followed him back across the yard, past the pump, hearing distant sheep and somewhere the sound of water.

'That's the spring,' he said, unlocking the front door. It needed a shove; dust fell. Inside, they stepped over cracked linoleum, and smelt damp. The kitchen had an electric stove, mottled grey, and ancient cupboards. There was a table, a ladder-backed chair.

'The son took most of the stuff when the old boy went.' The agent rubbed at the window panes at the back, revealing a nettle bed, and sloping field. 'Not that there was much to take.'

'How long did he live here?'

'Eighty years? And his father before him. I think the only time he left was to go into hospital.'

'There's a phone?'

'There was.'

They looked about them, saw a black Bakelite receiver on the floor, knotted pink flex, frayed at the plug.

'I'll keep that,' said Edward.

They went into a sitting room, across the hall. Yellowing copies of *Farmers' Weekly* lay about, chewed at by mice.

'This could be a study.'

Rowland shook his head, tolerantly amused. There was a bathroom down here, too, with a bath on claw feet and green and white tiles.

'I'd keep those, as well.' Edward turned on the tap and a trickle of brownish water came out, and stopped, with a banging of pipes.

'Needs a bit of work,' said the agent.

'You're telling me,' said Rowland.

They climbed dark stairs to the landing, and the sun came out, watery and uncertain, but lighting a stretch of bare floorboards, through dusty windows at either end, and one in the wall. Rowland raised an eyebrow, pacing.

'You could sing up here,' said Edward, realising it was true. You could walk up and down and let rip. He thought of it, and of himself downstairs, listening. He could get a dog.

Rowland said nothing. He walked into the bedrooms, one by one. There were three, all in a row, the second interconnecting with the third, which was tiny. A box room? A guest room? asked Edward, following.

'They'd freeze to death.'

'A music room.'

'It'd rot.'

'From London, are you?' asked the agent. 'You could put in a Rayburn downstairs, oil-fired. It's expensive, but it does the trick.'

'I'm chilled to the bone,' said Rowland, beating his arms round his chest.

The agent looked at him, thinking. 'You don't mind me asking – your face is familiar, somehow –'

'I sing,' said Rowland, crossing to the window. He blew on a cobweb and brushed it away.

'He's sometimes on the box,' said Edward.

'Ah. That must be it. Hope you don't mind –'

'Not at all.'

They walked from room to room again.

The agent went out to the landing and waited; he looked at his watch.

'We mustn't keep you.'

'No hurry. Take as long as you want.' He rubbed his hands.

'A Rayburn,' said Edward, as they went downstairs.

Out in the yard again, they stood back and looked at the house with a new perspective.

'It's the roof that needs immediate attention,' said the agent. They climbed the back field and looked down at missing slates, moss, broken guttering. A wind blew across the field, rippling the grass. Edward, turning, saw a hawthorn hedge and oak and ash trees, lichen creeping along grey limbs. There were woods which needed clearing.

'Well?' he asked Rowland. 'What do you think?' He put an arm round his shoulders, unthinking; Rowland drew away, and the agent coughed. They climbed higher, surveyed the grazing for sheep and cattle, discussed the possibilities of leasing land from the neighbouring farmer.

'I'm pretty sure that's what old Evans used to do.'

They walked back down to the farmyard. Edward said they would talk it over; he'd phone in the week.

'No rush.' The agent checked that he'd taken the key and shook hands with them both. They watched him pull out of the gate.

'I'm sorry,' said Edward, putting his arm round Rowland's

shoulders again, when the car was out of sight. 'I got a bit carried away.'

'You always do. I have a reputation to think of.' But Rowland drew Edward close. 'You really want to live here, all by yourself?'

'You're away so often. I'm all by myself in London.' Edward rubbed at the beard. 'It could be wonderful, when you were here. Peace. Just us. You need it.'

'Mmm.' They walked across the farmyard, arms round each other, thinking.

'And when I'm not here?'

'I could get a dog.'

'Or another man.'

'Never. Anyway, where would I find one? You're much more likely, in London –'

'True.' They had come to the yard gate, which the agent had left open. They crossed the lane, to a verge and a ditch and a hedge, and looked down. The sun came and went behind heaps of cloud, drifting over the sloping fields, the hedges and dry-stone walls and post fences. Far below was a river, far above the buzzard, searching bare land.

'They can see mice at a thousand feet.'

They looked at the scattered farms and houses, the scalloped telegraph wires all across the valley. A delivery van wound down the road on the far side. They made out church spires, a viaduct, a creeper-covered house and courtyard and a white, octagonal roof.

'There's a garden here, too,' said Edward, remembering.

'No doubt there are many.'

'No, I mean a garden I've heard of, or read about. I'm sure there is. Oh, well, it'll come to me.' He leaned against Rowland's dark head. The wind blew on their faces. 'What do you think?'

'You want it, don't you?'

'I think so. Yes.'

'Well, then. There we are.'

They searched for each other's mouths.

'Christ, it's cold.'

On the way back to London, Edward said: 'It's true, what I said. If we have all this time apart, there's plenty of chance for you, down there –'

'There's plenty of chance on tour. There was quite a nice chance in Rome, if you want to know.'

'I don't. Please.'

'Only joking. What shall we do about lunch?'

31

They stopped in a pub outside Hereford. Edward sat in a corner seat, looking at Rowland, up at the bar, ordering, smiling, unrecognised. Or perhaps there was a woman over there who saw, and frowned for a moment, trying to think where –

Rowland brought back two pints. 'Food's coming. They gave me a little ticket.' He put it down on the table, next to the beer mat. 'Cheers.'

'Cheers. To us.'

'To the farm.'

A microwaved lunch arrived. They ate making plans, talking of mortgages, of roofers, and Rayburns and septic tanks. It was probably the most practical conversation they'd had in more than a year, since Edward had sold his flat in Kentish Town and moved into Rowland's flat, in the Barbican, investing the proceeds.

'There's a hell of a lot to do.'

'There's no rush. I can do a lot of it myself. I'll enjoy it.'

'You always were out of place in London.'

'I know. Twenty-five years, and I never belonged. I never belonged anywhere till I met you.'

'Ssh.'

Back on the motorway, Edward said: 'If you did meet anyone else – I mean, while I was up there –'

'Getting cold feet?'

'No, but –'

Rowland turned to look at him, driving at eighty, glancing in the mirror for speed checks. 'You'd better not do this unless you're sure. Giving up the day job, starting again as a sheep farmer. It's madness unless –'

'I'm as sure as I've ever been of anything since I met you,' said Edward. 'But if it meant losing you – If anything happened to us –'

The traffic was building up, and Rowland looked back to the wheel.

Careful, Edward told himself. Careful. He's here, you share everything, you're buying this place together. Let it be.

The phone was ringing. Edward, deeply asleep, woke, hearing it, saw the sky was light, just. He stumbled downstairs.

'Hello?'

'I'm at Heathrow,' said Rowland. 'I thought you'd like to know.'

'I would.' He shivered: even in the kitchen it was cold. Tarn rose from her basket: she came to him, tail beating, nose in his hand. He stroked her, kneeling beside her steady warmth. 'When did you get in? How was it?'

'We've just landed, I'm waiting for customs. I'm bollocksed. Metaphorically speaking, of course.'

'Of course.' Edward fondled Tarn's ears, knelt down beside her, feeling a wave of happiness. He could hear canned voices in the background, announcing departures. But Rowland was home.

'What about you? How is it up there?'

'A bit parky.'

Rowland laughed. 'And the livestock?'

'All well. I'm checking the sheep this morning. Tarn's wonderful, do you want to say hello?'

'I think that's pushing domestic bliss just a tad too far, don't you? What time is it?'

Edward looked at the clock on the wall. 'Just after five. Where's your watch?'

'My God, I must be worse than I thought. Behold, it is upon my wrist. Right. I'll come up then, shall I?'

'You don't want to go to the flat?'

'Not as much as I want to see you.'

Edward shut his eyes. 'Drive safely.'

'Will do.'

He put the phone down. Tarn made her way to the door, wanting to be let out. He followed, unlocking the door to the yard, watching her race to the pump, and lap at the puddle beneath it. That was another thing that needed doing: it squeaked, and dripped. Mist hung over the trees in the lane, and the sky was pale as milk. One or two stars were still hanging about. He closed the door quickly, and went back to the kitchen, turning on the radio, moving the kettle on to the hot plate, leaning against the rail.

The weather forecast spoke of rain, and wind on high ground. Drinking his tea, feeling happy, with Tarn indoors again, under the table, Edward gave a thought to the poetry of weather forecasts: simple vivid phrases, betokening drama. He gave a further thought to the poetry still in boxes, waiting for more bookshelves. Another task for a rainy day.

Tarn rested her head on his feet.

5

It grew colder. Leaves blew along the lanes and up in the hills the bracken was turning. Gillian, up at her desk, wore fingerless woollen gloves and felt a chill at her back. When Phoebe was out, she came down to the kitchen with her pen and paper, brewed tea, and worked at the table, listening to the settling coke.

One day, she went walking, and met someone she had never seen before.

It was mid-week, mid-morning. You might see a farmer out with his dog, but on the whole this was not a time for seeing anyone out on the hills: locals were at work, or shopping down in the village; weekend walkers had gone back to the city. And this was late October: only the hardy went walking.

Gillian had completed a poem. It had survived the night. Thereafter, it had survived a period of critical assessment; so had another. She typed them out, on the upright black Remington, and addressed two envelopes, one to herself and one to a magazine in London, where she had never been. She licked two stamps, curling with damp on the desk: red, to speed the poems on their journey, and regretful blue to bring them back to her. She did not think these ones would come back: they both felt strong and ready for anything. She expected to see them next on a quarto page, on fine paper.

Good. Now then.

From out in the lane came the whine of the milkman's float. Phoebe had gone to the market town, and left money in a small brown envelope, with instructions. Gillian went downstairs to look for it.

The milkman knocked on the door and stood waiting in the porch, in his donkey jacket and knitted hat, shifting from one foot to the other. On Saturdays, and in the holidays, he had a boy.

Now, everyone was at school. Gillian found the envelope in a sensible place on the hall hatstand, beneath the mildewed mirror, and the map.

'Frost last night,' said the milkman, drawing a pencil line through a column of figures. 'Right then, thank you very much.' He snapped his book shut and picked up the empty bottles.

Gillian watched him walk to the float, across the lane still wet from the frost. The sky was slate and the air was bitter. She took her tweed coat from the peg and set out for the letterbox.

The letterbox was set in a wall, by a telegraph pole. Gillian slipped in her envelope and pressed her gloved hand on the little enamelled plate in the slot. She slid it up and down. She had been doing this since she was a child, and it was still just as satisfying. Up, down, click, click. Second post. As good as any. Beside her the telegraph pole hummed contentedly. A few weeks ago swallows had sat twittering and preening all along the wires. Now they were gone. Quite right. She was filled with energy and satisfaction. She would walk up Bryncarnedd and lay a stone. There were stones on that cairn for every one of her poems completed. No one knew that. Well. No one had any need to know.

The sky was lightening. She walked along the lane, meeting no one. Leaves lay in heaps along the verge beneath the hedgerows, and invisible birds rustled amongst them. A flash of russet and white darted into a ditch; a pheasant croaked in a ploughed field and picked his way over the furrows, gleaming. Another flew up from the hedge at her footsteps and out, over the field with a whirr of wings. Bare earth, bare trees, a lightening sky, a sudden flock of migrants, the last to leave. Gillian spoke her poems aloud, rejoicing. She came to the five-barred gate which led to the track up the hillside and set off, over rough ground.

Hillocks and tussocks and mole casts. Sorrel, in rusting clumps. The ground sloped down, then rose again, and then she was on the track, and the hillside grass on either side was coarse and springy. Sorrel gave way to bracken: sheep grazing here and there looked up and moved quickly away at her approach, mud-caked tails bouncing against spindly legs. They bleated for a moment, then lowered their heads again, and she could hear their steady cropping of the grass. Crows stepped amongst them, stabbing the ground; they hopped and flapped up as she drew near them but were bold and unafraid, returning quickly. Gillian knew about crows. They pecked out the eyes of the dead, and gobbled entrails. In springtime, she feared for the trembling lambs. Now it was autumn, an hour of daylight soon to be taken away, but a poem completed.

Crows cried, sheep bleated, the buzzard wheeled over the hills. Gillian walked on, rounded a bend, saw someone ahead of her.

She was tall and straight and narrow, and she walked with purpose: an easy, graceful stride. She wore a long grey mac, and a beret on cropped hair.

The convention amongst walkers was simple: you greeted, you passed. It was a code which suited Gillian perfectly. The woman, hearing her approach, slowed and turned round. Gillian saw skin as pale and opaque as piano keys, a fleeting glance of enquiry. The hair was hennaed, there were long silver earrings.

'Hello.'

'Good morning,' said Gillian.

Ahead was the *carnedd*, dark on the skyline. She strode past the woman and began to climb, her coat feeling heavy as the track, once a drovers' road, grew steeper. Her shoes crunched on pieces of shale and slate, and small stones. It was weeks since she'd added a stone.

Who dared to intrude upon her?

She came to the top and a sheep, startled, bounced from behind the cairn, and trotted away down the hillside. The summit was exposed and windy, but the exertion had made her warm. She opened the wings of her coat and flapped them. Beneath was a loosely knitted green cardigan, with big flat buttons, bought in last year's jumble sale and proving useful. Beneath that was an open-necked shirt. The air cooled her face and neck. She peeled off her fingerless gloves, and cast about for a stone.

Plenty to choose from. She found one small and sharp and acceptable in His sight. She turned it over and over, made her way back to the cairn and stood looking out over the valley. Her valley, every place known to her: the viaduct, the convent, the winding river; each hill on the far horizon, each chapel and church and distant farm. Some of these places were unvisited, but all of them were known: by name, by their place on the framed map next to the mirror in the hall at home. The map was worn and faded, with rust marks from pins, but it showed everything.

The air was cold on her face. The watchful buzzard soared and fell. She took her small sharp stone and dedicated it, and slipped it into its place.

There.

Footsteps behind her. She turned.

The woman smiled at her: a hesitant, sensitive smile.

'It's very steep.'

'Yes,' said Gillian. She watched, feeling the morning taken away from her, as the woman bent to pick up a stone and placed it carefully on the top of the cairn.

'It's like an altar,' she said, stepping back. 'Don't you think?'

'No,' said Gillian, filled with anger. 'Not in the least.'

Trespass. Invasion. She made to pass, to go straight back down the track and home again, her exaltation ebbed away, robbed from her by a stranger. She had spoken rudely: it was the kind of tone and remark which brought a rebuke from Phoebe. Well. Phoebe was not with her now.

The woman did not seem put out. She asked, with caution, if Gillian lived near here.

'Yes,' said Gillian flatly.

'I'm sorry – I feel I've intruded on you.'

She shrugged.

'I'm new,' said the woman. 'I've only been working here since September. I'm still finding my way about.'

Another *arriviste*. Like that man – that visitor. Well – she hadn't seen him again. Good.

'Where do you work?' she asked grudgingly, because that was the kind of thing you were supposed to do: not encroach upon strangers with questions, but respond to information.

'At Cadair Hall.' The woman pointed. 'The school.'

Gillian followed the outstretched hand. She saw trees cloaked in scarlet and gold, a lake, a creeper-covered house and courtyard, a white-painted octagon roof.

She said 'Cadair? But that is the convent.'

White robes whispered on cloistered stone, a heavy key turned in a lock. High walls, high windows, pages turned in silence. Ice broken in bowl and pitcher, breath streaming on the cold dawn air; feverish coughing in the night; a cell, a single bell –

'It was,' said the stranger. 'Now it's a school.'

Gillian frowned. 'I know nothing about it.'

'It's a special school – I suppose you might not know, unless you had a child who –'

A bus, rumbling along the lane. Figures strapped tightly into their seats, rocking, rocking. Arms flailing, mouths open, a lopsided face

37

with round pink spectacles pressed to the glass, grinning, squinting. Gross heads, and twisted little hands –

'No,' said Gillian. There was a hole in one of her pockets: her fingers moved this way and that.

'Well. That's where I work, anyway. This is my day off.' The woman hesitated, held out her hand. 'Nesta Frank. In case we meet again.'

Gillian nodded, ignoring the hand.

'May I ask –'

'Gillian Traherne.'

It meant nothing. The woman's face registered no recognition. Nobody knew. Her family, her father, she herself –

'We are all invisible,' she said aloud, and laughed abruptly.

The woman looked at her.

'You must take no notice,' said Gillian.

'But I'm interested,' said Nesta. 'May I ask – do you work round here – are you –'

'Work?' said Gillian. 'No. I am a burden on the community.'

Crows cried, sheep bewailed their fate. She turned and stalked down the track.

Edward lay in his lover's arms and watched him sleeping. The farmhouse was quiet: the deep, undisturbed peace of a Sunday afternoon, with the light fading at the window on to the yard, the covers heavy, love complete. Down in the unlit kitchen Tarn stirred in her basket, whimpered, settled again: it was so quiet he could hear the wicker creaking, and the steady tick of the clock, which drew breath, and struck the hour.

Rowland, sleeping, heard it, and shifted, and opened his eyes.

'Ssh. Don't move.'

He shook his head, reached for the watch on the table. Four o'clock.

'Time for me to go, I'm afraid.'

He kissed Edward's head, and made to get up.

'Not yet,' said Edward. 'Please, not yet.'

'I must.'

'Once more.'

'You can't mean it.'

'I can. All this time without you –'

'It's only a week –'

'Only? Only?'

They were teasing, mouth against mouth, still drowsy. Then Edward moved, and knelt up before him, pushing back the bedclothes.

'It's freezing.' Rowland stretched up to retrieve them.

Edward pushed him back. 'Sssh. I'll warm you. Lie back.'

Rowland lay back against the pillows and raised his arms. He lay upon the rumpled sheet, a great naked giant of a man, with his barrel chest and torso, his full fleshy belly and spreading hips. His legs were long and his penis was dark and thick and powerful, swelling and rising as Edward knelt over him, not touching, not speaking, waiting, breathing, his lips apart.

Then the lightest touch.

Rowland closed his eyes.

Another. Another.

'Go on. Go on.'

'Wait.'

He knelt up again. Rowland groaned.

'Do it. Do it.'

'I will, I'll do anything. I love you, I love you.' His fingers moved gently, just the lightest touch, stroking, feeling the hardness. 'Yes? Yes?'

'Yes,' said Rowland. He moved on the pillow, back and forth, back and forth.

Edward lowered his head.

Sometimes it was like that. More often, especially at the beginning, it was Rowland, who had had many lovers, who took control and command. As day broke, as day ended, in the dark hours of the night –

'I love you –'

'I love you –'

'You want it like this? Like this?'

'Yes. Yes yes yes yes do it do it do it –'

'I'll do anything, I'll die for you –'

'Don't die, don't ever leave me –'

'You are my one beloved –'

'And you are mine –'

Now, when they had finished, the afternoon light had gone. They lay in each other's arms, drifting towards sleep again. Then Rowland made an enormous effort, and rose. He sat on the side of the bed, his head bowed.

'How am I supposed to drive after that? How am I supposed to do a decent run-through?'

'You'll do both all the better.' Edward pulled the bedclothes round the naked shoulders, and leaned against him. 'All right?'

'Mmm. Thank you.' He turned to kiss Edward's cheek. 'How did you get so good?'

'You showed me. Poor virginal thing that I was.'

'Mmm.' Rowland reached for the light switch. 'You'd think you'd been doing it all your life.'

'I've been doing it all my life with you. That's what matters.'

They sat blinking in the lamplight.

'Barn owls.'

'Have you seen one yet?'

'A couple of nights ago, before you got here.'

'It would be. I want one in our barn.'

'I'll try and arrange it.' Edward got up, and pulled on his dressing gown, throwing Rowland's over from the back of the door. The room smelt of sweat and sex, of musty wood, old carpet, plaster. From somewhere in a beam or skirting board came a swift, skittering sound.

'Better get a trap. Several traps.' Rowland was pulling on his dressing gown. Edward's was towelling, long and dark; his was a heavy patterned silk. He pulled the tie round his belly. 'It's still bloody cold up here, Rayburn or no. What are we going to do when it snows?'

'Hide in the barn and keep ourselves warm. We can light a fire up here, can't we?' Edward was at the door. 'How about a bath?'

'Just the ticket.'

'And tea?' He was walking down the landing, over the creaking floorboards, switching the lights on, bringing the house to life again.

'Good man.'

Rowland rubbed his face. He went to the mirror propped up on the mantelpiece and looked at himself. Shagged out. Heavy. In need of a shave. He crossed to the window and looked out on the darkening farmyard, at the outbuildings and the barn, the trees in the lane, where the last leaves still clung, the pale stars rising beyond them. From downstairs he could hear the bathwater running, Edward lifting the lid of the Rayburn, putting the kettle on, letting the dog out.

Rowland went back to the mirror, looked again. Thick dark eyebrows, heavy-lidded eyes: a European, operatic face, passionate and powerful. That was how Adam described it. Well – agents were paid to go on like that.

'Rowland?' A shout up the stairs. The bath taps were turned off, the pipes were banging, he could smell the hot steam.

'Coming.' A last glance in the mirror.

Steam drifted up the stairs from the open bathroom door. Rowland considered the face which looked back at him, and what lay behind it; he listened to the domestic sounds of the house: the dog let in again, a dish set down, Edward moving about the kitchen, secure and content.

As Rowland was, now; as he hoped to remain.

They bathed, they got dressed, they sat at the kitchen table drinking hot tea, having a look at the Sunday papers, bought after breakfast down in the village, abandoned in the access of desire after lunch. Rowland, in the Arts pages, ran his fingers down the columns of concerts. He and the choir were listed for two in London – Tallis and Byrd at the Barbican, Purcell in the Festival Hall. Then to York. Then to Leeds. Then – he rubbed his face, thinking. That was it, before they left for Sydney. The autumn Australian tour: the Consort booked for Sydney, Melbourne, Perth. Six concerts in ten days.

'Jesus.'

'What?'

'Australia.'

'When you come back,' said Edward heartlessly, 'you should do something here. Hereford Cathedral in the spring. That would be nice. What are you doing in the spring?'

'At the moment,' said Rowland, draining his tea, 'I could hardly tell you what I'm doing tomorrow. Or did last week.' He pushed back his chair, and stood up. 'Time I was off.'

'You said that an hour ago.'

'I know.' He glanced at the clock. 'You seduced me shamelessly.'

'But it was nice.'

'It was. And I'm going to be late. Think I'll make it by nine? I'd better phone.'

Tarn was out of her basket, crossing the room, tail beating slowly.

'She knows you're going.'

'Good dog, good dog.' Rowland rubbed at her ears, and picked up

41

the telephone. 'You couldn't get my bag, could you,' he said, dialling. 'I really think I'm cutting this a bit – hello? Damian? It's me. Listen –'

Edward climbed the stairs again, and fetched the bag from the spare room. Clothes lay on the floor. The spare room just had a bed in it; a bare bulb hung from the ceiling. One day they'd –

He heard the ting of the phone, and Rowland calling.

Tarn was waiting at the foot of the stairs. She followed them down the passage to the front door, her claws clicking on the boards. Edward had pulled up the linoleum, cutting himself on a rusty nail and wondering, briefly, about tetanus. He hadn't sanded the boards yet. Or perhaps he might stain them. Well. That was something else to think about: he could have it done by the next visit.

Out in the yard their footsteps rang on the frosty concrete. Rowland slung his bag in the back of the Peugeot and slammed the door. From somewhere came the two low notes of an owl.

'There. Just for you.'

'"Then nightly sings the staring owl –"'

Edward put his arm round him. They embraced in their heavy jackets.

'It's been heaven. Drive safely, won't you?'

'Don't fret. I'll phone.'

'Even if it's late.'

'Even if.'

From across the yard came a squawk and scuffle. 'You'd better get those hens in.'

'Christ. How could I have –' Edward turned, saw Tarn crouching low by the trailer, tongue lolling. 'Lucky not to have lost one already.'

'You may have done. Go on. Go and be a farmer.' Rowland was pulling the car door open.

'I'm thinking of getting some ducks.'

'The fox'll be glad to hear that.'

The engine was running, the headlights lit up the barn door. Edward bent for the last kiss. The yard gate was open. He walked over and stood beside it, watching the long sleek car reverse and swing round towards him. Rowland raised a hand, came through slowly, pulled out into the lane and turned. A last look back. Then he was going: slowly down to the bend, the tail lights shining, and round it, sounding the horn. And gone.

Edward lifted the gate from the verge and swung it to. With oil, it moved now with a satisfying smoothness, clanging shut on the catch.

Behind him, Tarn was racing wildly about the yard and the hens were frantic.

'Here!' He was sharp, and she knew she was in the wrong, and sank to her haunches, panting. 'So I should think. Come on, now.' He fetched the black rubber torch from inside the door and flashed it over the yard. The birds were dazed and frightened – by the dog, by the swinging beam of light. It took twenty minutes to get them all up to the hen house, and count them, and find that one had, indeed, been taken. A Leghorn, a beautiful bird. He felt ashamed.

The owl called again, as he made his way back down the sloping field towards the house. So low, so clear. He looked about: at the woodland, at the trees near the house, one of which was too close, and too old, and would have to come down before the storms. He hoped for the tall rounded shape of the owl on a branch, but saw nothing. How could they lure him into the barn?

Inside, he pulled his boots off, and drained cold tea, standing in his socks in the kitchen, listening to the silence.

'Rowland,' he said aloud.

He climbed back up to the chilly bedroom, and stripped the rumpled bed. He put fresh sheets on, unironed but clean, feeling for once secure in parting, and the desire to start the new week as himself: not sleeping with the sweet stale smell of his lover but as a man alone, getting on with it. There was much to do.

This feeling lasted most of the evening, as he put the sheets in the machine, made supper, finished the papers. Afterwards, he went into the study, as he had begun to call it, and stood at the shelves again, sorting. Books he had owned all his life found a new home here – childhood Kipling and Grahame and H. G. Wells, books from university and a useful working life in the Civil Service, and now a new batch, for a new life. A shelf for sheep and country matters: *I Bought a Mountain, British Sheep, Hedges, Walls and Boundaries, Modern Farming and the Countryside, The Poultry Keeper*. There was all that, much bought in London before the move, some found since on visits to Hay, where you could find anything. And then the library he was beginning to build about the Shropshire/Hereford borders – from Hay, from local sales: maps and guides and history. Poets. A whole shelf for the poets. He was shelving them, as organised here as he had been in his Civil Service office, in alphabetical order.

Herbert, born in Montgomery Castle at the end of the sixteenth century: his parents had an effigy in the church, that was somewhere to visit. He'd already been to see the plaque to Housman in the church wall of Ludlow – Edward's grandfather had known *A Shropshire Lad* by heart.

'In summertime on Bredon the bells they sound so clear –'

Edward could hear him now, his steady Northumbrian voice making a lonely childhood tolerable.

He turned the pages, sniffed them, slipped books into their places. Masefield, another Ludlow man. Thomas Traherne, from Hereford. Another, more recent Traherne he'd picked up in a sale in Ledbury. Wilfred Owen, born in Oswestry, dying in France; Henry Vaughan, buried on the road to Abergavenny; Wordsworth, walking through the ruins of Tintern Abbey.

Up they all went, taken out of their boxes, the dust blown off and the pages mended. Some needed more than a strip of Sellotape: he had put aside those which were decent editions, needing spines or loose pages properly glued again, or stitched. Might be nice to do a book-binding course one day, he should look into it. Sure to be something in Hay.

The clock struck ten, then eleven. There was no phone call. Edward's contentment dissipated, then turned to anxiety. He came out of the study, turning the lights out. He rang the flat. No answer. He let Tarn out for the last time, and stood at the door to the yard for a moment, looking up at the starry sky. The Milky Way flung out its canopy, he made out Orion, and the Bear. Beyond the farm, the fields and hills lay in the deepest silence.

No owl.

No Rowland.

He went back into the house, ordering Tarn to her basket. He rang the flat once more, and then, in a flood of longing, he turned on the hi-fi and slipped in a disc.

Rowland. The house was filled with his voice: tender, powerful, soaring.

Edward leaned back in his chair in the kitchen, his eyes closed, and let this man take him: now, always, body and soul.

Phoebe had got out the sewing machine. Gillian stood beside her, watching. Long white sheets with rents in trailed to the floor from the kitchen table. Phoebe gathered them, straightened them, flattened them beneath the stab of the needle, her foot on the treadle moving quickly. The sheets submitted: were stitched and restored and made new, and fell at her feet in gratitude.

'You're blocking the light.'

Gillian moved, and took up her place against the smooth rail of the range, warming her back. She had not felt like Evensong tonight. Outside the window the sky was starry black.

'Why don't you draw the curtains?' said Phoebe.

She drew them, with a sharp rattle of hooks. Phoebe bent low over the machine. The gleaming needle rose and fell between the clamp which held down the sheet. She went faster.

Gillian stood watching. So fast, so fast, the cotton reel on the spike on the top rattling and spinning, too fast, too fast, help help the life is being drawn out of me –

'Damn.'

The snap of a frail white thread. Phoebe stopped. The cotton had come out of the needle's eye: she bent over it, her glasses pushed up her nose, licking the broken end, feeding it through. She set off again, at a gallop, but the machine did not take up, and the sheet lay crumpled and torn.

'*Damn*.'

'It's the bobbin.'

'I know it is.' Phoebe drew back the slim silver plate which covered it. Gillian crossed the room.

'You're blocking the *light*.'

'I just want to look –'

'Well, stand back, then.'

She stood back, waiting. Beneath the silver plate was darkness, and a silver boat, wherein the bobbin lay, fitting perfectly: click click at each end. The boat, which Phoebe was easing out, had a thin complicated plate on its side, for the thread from the bobbin to wind into, and from thence up up through the darkness, into the machine. Gillian did not understand its passage. She could not thread it, or do anything useful. She watched as Phoebe prised the empty bobbin out, and threaded white cotton into it, and bound it to its rack at the side of the machine and began to tread again, her feet pumping the treadle. The machine hummed, the cotton reel spun wildly, the empty spool was filled: brrrrrrr round and round so fast, the thread running back and forth, back and forth, growing thicker and thicker, until it was full and complete –

'There.' Phoebe lifted the bobbin from the rack and snapped it into the shining boat. She bent over the place of darkness, sliding the boat into place. An experimental movement of the foot. 'That's it.' She picked up the silver plate.

'Don't put it back.'

'What?'

'Don't put the plate back. I want to see –'

'What are you talking about?'

'Please. I just like watching the –'

Phoebe sighed. She picked up the heavy fall of sheet and began again.

'Slowly. Go slowly. I want to see –'

'Just like when you were little.'

The treadle slowed. Gillian hung over the machine and looked down.

Deep in the darkness of the underworld the little silver boat was ferried over the Styx, bearing the souls of the dead. They were left on the dark far bank, and Charon rowed back again, for more. Pale shapes huddled at the water's edge, the sky was starless and the river so deep so deep and bony fingers went to gaping mouths, wailing, wailing –

'Are you ill? What on earth is the matter?'

'I'm sorry.' She returned to her place by the rail.

A sigh. The machine whirred and clacked and Gillian stood there, watching the gimlet eyes behind the glasses, the gathering and releasing of the torn white sheets, their sigh as they fell to the floor, like the souls of the dead, abandoned to the lapping blackness of the water beneath the world.

6

The ground was hard and the air was biting. Birds hopped about the hawthorn hedge and in and out of the ivy on the back house wall, tugging at berries, scarlet and black. In the mornings, the doves stayed late in the dovecot. The full round leaves of the winter cabbages were white with frost, and frost rimed the grass and the brick paths laid between it; the last leaves in the shrubbery fell in silence. The lanes were heavy with misted brown and grey tendrils of old man's beard; mistletoe hung from bare branches, berries as pale as the moon; the moon of approaching winter was a flat bright coin, rising over ploughed fields.

Phoebe, beneath her lined leather waistcoat, wore a shirt, two sweaters and a vest.

Now that the clocks had gone back and the mornings were dark as the early evenings, she read for an hour upon rising, taking a tin tray with mug and milk jug and the green enamel teapot up to the bedroom, sitting up in her dressing gown with a good biography, thoroughly enjoying herself. It was her one concession to age. Along the dark landing Gillian's door was shut; it often remained shut as Phoebe, dressed and filled with interesting information, made her way past it with the tea tray again, giving a brisk knock, then descending the stairs for a single slice of toast with the eight o'clock news and weather forecast.

'Gillian?' She called up the stairs. 'It's after eight.' Silence. In spring and summer Phoebe did not have to deal with this, and would not have stood for it. In spring and summer and well into autumn Gillian rose as early as anyone could wish for, out in the garden at sunrise, getting in the way. As winter approached she went to earth, like an animal, and Phoebe allowed it – more accurately, had given up trying to change it.

She washed up, hung the wooden-handled brush on its hook by the sink, and turned off the wireless. She took her waistcoat from the

47

hall peg, the good fork and secateurs from the back room, pulled on her boots by the back door. And out into the garden, closing it firmly behind her.

The bulbs were long in; the wallflowers, curling and yellowing in the frost, had their roots well established. The herbaceous borders had been dug and planted and fed with bonemeal. Down in the vegetable garden Phoebe propped her fork against the dry-stone wall. She took up the long grey ashpoles, pulled away the last of the runner bean plants and stood the poles up in bundles, ready for store. She fetched the fork and dug steadily, breaking up the frozen clods, ready for a spring planting. Starlings and blackbirds followed her progress, and flew down for writhing worms and insects: they snapped up incubating pests.

'Keep it up,' said Phoebe.

She trundled her barrow of limp wet weeds and beans along to the compost heap. On a brick path a thrush was smashing a snail shell, chip chip chip. When he had finished he flew up into one of the trees at the edge of the farmer's field, singing high as the morning wore on and the frosty air warmed and thinned a little, perhaps for the last time of the year, and weak sun dispersed November cloud.

'"That's the wise thrush: he sings each song twice over,"' said Phoebe, recalling childhood Browning, digging in mulch and manure.

Inside the house, Gillian, who had risen from her bed at the sound of the back door closing, sat at her desk in three jumpers, scraping at spiky-leaved patterns of frost on the window pane, dissolving them in the blessed silence with the breath of the living God.

Manure came from a stables three miles or so down the lane. Phoebe patted black and chestnut heads looking out of the looseboxes and greeted the girl.

'Freezing, isn't it?'

'Nice and bright now, though,' said Phoebe. She shovelled manure from the heap in the yard and bagged it in heavy green gardening plastic; she heaved the bags into the back of the van.

'Need a hand?'

'I'm fine, thanks.' She slammed the doors.

The girl was leading a hunter out from his box: his hooves rang on the yard and he tossed his head.

'Aren't you a fine beast,' said Phoebe. Once, in the absence of anything more suitable, she had hoped that Gillian might find employment up here: girls came and went, and why should she not – But Gillian had been afraid, and the animals sensed it.

'It's something you need to have a feel for,' said the owner, not unkindly, calming a restless mare, moving Gillian out of the way. 'Not something you can force, now. If you don't feel comfortable –' She looked at Gillian, standing awkwardly in the yard with a brush and curry comb, not knowing what to do. 'Not really a horse person, are you?'

Gillian shook her head. Phoebe sighed. They drove home in silence.

'I can't help it,' said Gillian, as they drew up.

'It's a job,' said Phoebe. 'Occupation.'

Gillian did not answer.

'Independence.' Phoebe gave another sigh. 'Go on. Open the gate.'

That was years ago.

'Steady now,' said the girl, and looped the leading rein through a hoop in the wall. 'Nice and easy.' She got out her brush from her apron pocket and began to groom the hunter with long, regular, confident strokes. 'Going to take you out in a little while, aren't we?'

'I must be off,' said Phoebe. She climbed into the van and drove slowly out of the yard.

The van was due for a service: the clutch was worn, and the gears slipped in and out too easily. And then there was all that weight in the back: the exhaust had come loose, and banged, and must be seen to. Phoebe did not believe in paying other people to do what she could do herself, and could, she had proven, do most things. But the van, bought years ago for five hundred pounds, and on which she depended, must be properly maintained or become dangerous. She would book it in at Gareth's for Monday.

Gareth had two pumps and a workshop, just across the bridge, and had not yet been taken over. He sold crisps and chocolate but no canned drinks, and when he wasn't working he leaned against the worn blue doors of the workshop reading the paper and watching the birds on the telegraph wires. He was born and bred and useful, charging a fair rate for a decent job. And there weren't many people you could say *that* about.

Mist rose from the fields. Much brighter now. Phoebe hooted greetings to passers-by: Huw Williams, sixteen stone hunched over his wavering bike, who dared not raise a hand in answer, and, nearer home, a couple of women from the village, carrying shopping home in red-checked nylon bags. She drew up at the house.

The side gate, closed when she had left, stood open. She parked along the verge, and went to fetch the wheelbarrow.

'Gillian?'

The lean-to shed by the woodpile had been opened. The door stood wide and the bicycle had been taken. Phoebe fastened the door shut and went indoors.

'Gillian?'

Cups stood draining by the sink, perilously close to the edge of the board. A teatowel drooped on the back of a chair, there were crumbs all over the table.

'Gillian!'

Now where had she got to?

Gillian, taking the bicycle out of the lean-to shed, had found that the tyres were soft. She unclipped the pump and gave them new life. Cobwebs trailed over the saddle: she wiped them away with her sleeve, unbuckled the bag at the back and put in her sandwich in greaseproof paper. She sounded the bell. It was rusty and faint, and the brake blocks were worn and squeaking, but the machine was, as Phoebe would put it, perfectly serviceable. She wheeled it up the glistening path, and rode away.

Phoebe dragged the bags out of the van, and on to the barrow and pushed them down to the vegetable garden. She heaved them out and leaned them up against the dry-stone wall. Tomorrow she would dig in. You should never cover the ground at this time of year, but digging in was useful. She straightened up from the last bag and felt her back, which was lean and strong and reliable, give, for a moment, definite discomfort. She stood there, her hands at her waist, bending back and forth to ease it, hearing the birds, smelling the freshly forked earth, the manure on her boots, the wintry air. There. That was better. Perhaps enough for one day. Not often she thought *that*.

She lunched with *The World at One* and after *The Archers* rang Gareth, and had a sensible conversation about the worn clutch and loose exhaust. She booked the van in for first thing on Monday and went outside to the greenhouse.

The greenhouse was warm and calming. A pleasant afternoon lay ahead, potting on annuals, raised from seed in September: antirrhinum, calendula, larkspur and nemesia, nicotiana and love-in-a-mist, all of which went well at the front gate in the late spring and early summer.

Black plastic seed trays stood all along the shelves: Phoebe used her finger and a teaspoon to lift the fragile seedlings, blew cobwebs from three-inch pots and filled them with compost. She worked quickly, her thumbs pressing each seedling in with practised sureness, setting the pots in empty trays, lightly spraying them with water. There. That was that done. She swept up the crumbs of fallen compost and brushed them back into the bag, sealing it tight; stacked up the seed trays and stood looking with brief satisfaction at the rows of little pots, neatly grouped, ready for labelling.

The light was fading. She felt in her waistcoat pocket for her marker pen, and could not find it. She looked in the pot of white plastic labels, but it wasn't there. Phoebe searched patiently, then irritably. No doubt Gillian – She found it, at last, fallen down between slats right at the back of the geraniums. She straightened up, and felt again the deep, definite discomfort in her back. Damn.

Where had Gillian got to?

Mist rose from the fields. Gillian cycled past the churchyard, past the school, and down to the village. Chimneys were smoking and women stood gossiping outside the shop with bags and pushchairs. Gillian knew nothing at all about gossip. The shop window was stuck over with notices: WI meetings, sheepdog trials, items for sale. Phoebe set store by this window, through which she had, over the years, largely furnished the house. Gillian passed the little knot of women and slowed for Bron Morgan, thin as a beanpole, crossing the street.

'Thank you, Gillian. Keeping well?'

'Very well, thank you.'

Cotton lace curtains patterned with birds hung at the windows; the last geraniums stood on the sills, with china cats and dogs. Gillian saw a Land Rover parked hard up against the pavement outside the ironmonger's. A border collie sat in the back, tongue lolling. An everyday sight, but Gillian, for a moment, wavered.

The visitor.

In summer the ironmonger's door was propped open with a solid black doorstop. Now, though the buckets and rakes and watering cans still stood outside on the pavement, the door was closed. Gillian knew the smell of the paraffin stove behind it, and the bare wood floor; she knew the panel of wooden drawers, with their brass plates and labels and copperplate writing, but the Land Rover now obscured the glass, and she did not know who stood beyond it, purchasing nails and hooks and rope and packets of seed.

Her feet on the pedals were heavy as sin.

She rode on, the chain dark with grease, which would not wash out. Phoebe used to scrub at her socks when she came home with long thick marks on them, holding them down on the wooden draining board, the bristles so hard that holes came, which had to be mended. Gillian was set to mend them, and did it badly. The chain needed a mudguard: Gareth looked out for one, and then forgot.

'You'll just have to be careful,' said Phoebe. 'I shouldn't have to keep telling you.'

Gillian rode on, and the trails of smoke from the village chimneys rose to the cold morning sky and disappeared, like ghosts. Behind her the bell of the ironmonger's pinged. She did not look back.

Two old boys in flat peaked caps were pushing open the door of the Fox, where she sometimes gave her readings, in the upper room.

Blackened oak and smoke-stained curtains, hiss of the taps and thud of the darts and the bar wiped down with a damp cloth and visitors greeted –

He was taking his pint to a corner table, his dog beside him, the paper to read and a list of chores ticked off –

Gillian cycled to the end of the street, across the stone bridge over the river, and out past Gareth's, where tyres stood in a pile, and banging came from the workshop. The ground sloped upwards: the street became a winding lane between high hedges. She pushed down hard on the pedals but they would not yield. She got off and pushed, drawing in to the verge as a vehicle approached.

The Land Rover went past her: the driver raised a hand.

Was it him? Was the gesture a simple acknowledgement, such as all drivers made? Or was it a recognition?

Well. He had gone.

Good.

She wheeled the ticking bicycle beneath a vault of bare branches. Cows stared from the gateways, black and red and mushroomy grey. Their noses were wet, their coats were splashed with mud. The sun was rising, a tractor was descending. The farmer lifted his hand; Gillian nodded: simple, satisfying gestures.

What need of more?

She had reached the summit. She climbed on again, and went down, freewheeling, everything silent and open and free, only the sweet tick tick of the bike, the drift here and there of leaves.

Freedom and release from fear.

Ahead, the broad wet valley, gleaming in the sun. Frost melted, mist risen, the slow progression of cattle across the autumn fields, their breath streaming out before them. Beyond, the sheep-sprinkled hills, patchworked with walls and hedges on the lower slopes, thick with bracken, then bare of all but stone, as they rose to meet the skyline. Bryncarnedd, Bryncarreg, Penmynydd, Maen and Moel. She knew every one of them, the sun shone on each of them, pale but glorious.

Jubilate deo.

She flew down the hillside.

Gillian cycled past churchyards where sheep grazed between the headstones; past war memorials, laid with scarlet wreaths; she rode through quiet villages and out past noisy school playgrounds, where children ran about. She knew all these places from her own childhood, but she did not come cycling out here often now, and she had not known that the convent of Cadair Hall had become a school.

Nose in a book – head in the clouds – dreaming – miles away– I've just *told* you –

The hailstone of Phoebe's reproaches came rattling down the years.

They were at the kitchen table, she was doing her history homework, she was fifteen. It was winter, there was a power cut, Phoebe had lit the oil lamps and was reading to her out of the Shell *Country Book.*

'"The Cistercians, or White Monks, came to England after the Conquest, in 1128. The object of their order was to live a life of reformed purity and loneliness..."'

Gillian sat gazing at the shimmer of heat above the white moon of the lamp, and her eyes burned. Yes, she said under her breath, yes yes –

'What?'

'Nothing.'

'"They removed themselves from the neighbourhood of men and settled in distant undeveloped valleys – particularly in Yorkshire and the north, and in Wales – where they could turn the level floor into rich hay and farm land, while pasturing their sheep on the surrounding moors and hills ... They changed Welsh and English scenery, not always for the better, since their thousands upon thousands of sheep slowly destroyed the aboriginal woodland of the hills ..."'

'Aboriginal?' Gillian frowned, seeing spears, and bodies caked in mud.

'Native,' said Phoebe. 'Concentrate.'

She read on, her clipped decisive voice leading Gillian across the valley to Cadair Hall, and amongst the roofless ruins of Tintern Abbey, where sheep grazed and the wind blew through empty tracery.

> '"And I have felt
> A presence that disturbs me with the joy
> Of elevated thoughts; a sense sublime
> Of something far more deeply interfused,
> Whose dwelling is the light of setting suns ..."'

'Well?' asked Phoebe. 'Who wrote that?'

> '"And the round ocean and the living air
> And the blue sky, and in the mind of man ..."'

said Gillian. 'Wordsworth.'

'Yes. I see they have taught you something.' Phoebe cleared her throat. '"Nuns were no less familiar in medieval England than monks, and were also distinguished in common speech by the colour of their habits ..."'

White robes whispered over cloistered stone, a heavy key turned in a lock. High walls, high windows, pages turned in silence. A cell, a single bell –

'"Often a nun was called a minchen, a word which was the feminine of monk, and which frequently occurs in minor place-names."'

Phoebe looked at Gillian. 'What have I just read?'

'Sorry?'

'*Concentrate.*' She snapped the book shut, she rose from the table. 'If you could only concentrate,' she said, riddling the Rayburn, 'you could do quite well.'

But Gillian missed out all the dates in her History O-level, and failed it.

'What on earth –' Phoebe looked at the self-addressed card with its dismal record of Es and Fs. It was high summer, the garden full of dappled shade.

'I'm sorry,' said Gillian. She pointed to the radiant A, the comfortable B and C.

'But no maths,' said Phoebe. 'No biology. No physics, no chemistry. And as for your history – what on earth did you *do*?'

'I wrote about nuns,' said Gillian.

Phoebe was exasperated. 'What is to become of you?'

Gillian did not know.

She came to a crossroads, slowed down, and checked the signpost. A milk tanker passed her, and the grass on the roadside trembled. Cadair lay to the right, a mile beyond Minchen Crib. She rode towards it.

Crimson creeper clambered round the windows. The double doors were heavy polished oak, studded with iron, painted black; flagstones led to outbuildings round an open courtyard up to the left; a sweep of lawn to the white head-dress of the octagon roof of the chapel, all new brick and narrow windows. Beyond the slope of the lawn was the gleam of the lake; leaves lay in drifts across the grass, scarlet and russet and gold and burnished gold. The trees were bare now, and shadows fell on the grass.

Someone was sweeping, and someone was banging a drum.

Gillian, with her bicycle, up at the tall iron gates, stood watching and listening.

She had come here after her failure, seeking sanctuary. She had stood where she was standing now, in a hand-me-down summer dress, her hair tied back, her hands on the handlebars wet with apprehension. She had rung the china bell in its circle of gold, set into the high brick wall, and gazed at the tall iron gates and the towering yew trees beyond them, dark as death.

The bell rang, and after a little while a door could be heard to open. Quiet footsteps sounded on a path; a grille in the straight black gate slid open. A nun in white robe and veil looked out at Gillian, and her gaze was steady and clear.

'Yes?'

Gillian could not speak. The nun waited.

'You are troubled.'

She nodded.

'You are seeking spiritual guidance.'

Her face burned.

The nun unlocked the gate. 'You may come in.'

Gillian shook her head. Her cotton dress drooped, there was oil on her bare legs.

The nun made a gesture. She made to unlock the gate. 'Please.'

Gillian could hardly breathe.

'If I come in I shall never come out.'

'Perhaps that is God's wish.'

Sweat streamed down her. 'No, no.' She swung round her bicycle and clambered on, banging her shin, wincing, turning the wheel.

'We shall pray for you,' said the nun.

Larks sang, and the fields were golden.

Gillian rode away, belonging nowhere.

And now the solid gates with their square of a grille had gone, and straight iron bars had replaced them.

Gillian watched, and listened.

The sweeping came from the side of the house: its rhythm was patient and sweet.

The drumming came from the chapel –

Its rhythm was wild and unsteady –

Other sounds: shakers, and bells, and a piercing ugly whistle –

Silence. A spatter of clapping. Laughter.

Gillian waited.

After a while the door of the chapel opened.

Out came the halt and the maim.

Wheelchairs in the autumn sun –

Grimaces, twitches, gaping mouths –

Staggering footsteps, dragging hands –

Huge heavy heads, and legs like sticks, like tree trunks –

Sounds without consonants, sounds without words –

Shouting and laughter.

Gillian, shrinking, watched, and looked for Nesta Frank and saw her, tall and straight and narrow, her hennaed hair bright in the sun, her silver earrings swinging.

She drew in the breath of God and pressed the bell.

Heads turned, and Nesta saw her. Other adults accompanied the children; Nesta came down the path.

'Hello,' she said through the tall iron bars. 'I remember you.'

'I was passing,' said Gillian. 'I –'

'I'm delighted to see you. Will you join us for lunch?'

'No. No, no. I must –'

Nesta smiled at her. Up at the house the last of the children were wheeling or stumbling in through the doors. Leaves danced over the grass, and across the courtyard. The patient sweep sweep of the broom had stopped.

'We quite often have visitors. There's always room.'

Her hands on the handlebars were clammy: she clasped the rubber grips and felt each finger find its place: there, one by one, so.

'Do stay.'

To eat amongst strangers, to sit with those children –

If I come in I shall never come out –

'I should like to get to know you.'

'Yes, yes, but I –'

Nesta swung open the gate. The path to the house lay ahead. She put a hand on Gillian's hand: a warm, fleeting touch. Gillian shrank.

'Listen. Why don't you come and have lunch with us, now you're here? Afterwards I have to take another music group, and then I'm off duty. You could come back to my cottage for tea. I'd like that. Or do you really have to go back?'

She had left the side gate open.

Phoebe did not know where she was.

'No,' she said. 'I don't have to –'

'Well then.' Nesta's hand was on the bicycle, leading Gillian away from the sanctuary of the lane, up the smooth path. Lawns stretched away on either side. The gate clanged shut behind them. Gillian gripped the handlebars until her nails dug into her palms.

'I feel I'm being brutal,' said Nesta, with a smile. 'Forgive me. I just feel you must have come here for a reason. People usually do.'

What a lot of nonsense, said Phoebe. I can't bear that kind of talk.

Gillian walked alongside Nesta, looking straight ahead.

Sunlight shone at leaded windows; the children were assembled; someone had said a kind of grace. Gillian, with Nesta beside her, sat at the dark oak table.

'Let us be thankful for our family of friends, and for the meal we are about to share...'

Home-made loaves on smooth round breadboards, a platter of

cheeses, fruit on a stoneware dish. Hot soup on a trolley, ladled into bowls and handed round. And also –

Beakers with closed lids and flexible straws. Tubes which led from bottle to nostril. Mouths which grimaced and sucked and hung open, drooling. Eyes as dark as the eyes of an animal, long shut away, rolling, and showing the whites. Plastic spoons with curving handles, stabbing and missing and dropping things, guided to gaping faces –

Gillian sat stiff on a high-backed chair. The bread was passed on the smooth round breadboard, butter on a dark green dish; soup from the trolley was ladled and set in a plain white bowl before her. She was poured water, and bidden to help herself, to begin, please. She was told by people with clear pale skins, nice clear voices and calm expressions that they were so pleased she was able to join them. After lunch there was music again, in the chapel. She must stay for that.

Gillian listened, breaking her slice of brown bread into pieces. She rubbed at the pieces until they were crumbs, until they were dust, and could not be saved.

She lifted a spoonful of soup to her lips.

Eat up, said Phoebe, down the long dark tunnel of her childhood. Come along, now.

Gillian lowered her spoon, and sipped her water. Beside her, Nesta asked kindly:

'You okay?'

'Yes, yes, of course.'

Every muscle was tense with effort and discomfort. On her left sat Nesta, silver earrings glinting in the wintry light. Everything about her indicated vitality, generosity, contentment; she spoke to the children near her, the young boy next to her, with gentle matter-of-factness; she cut up bread and cheese and helped to feed the children with deft, easy movements, making everything light and possible.

'Want a drink? Here we go – you take it, that's it, well done.'

On Gillian's right sat a child with a heavy square body and hair cut short and blunt, held back with a thin pink slide. Her glasses, too, were pink, round and thick in their frames, and her hands were not unlike Gillian's hands – square, with bitten fingernails, reddened from poor circulation. She ate steadily, managing everything, turning now and then to smile gapingly, and lean against Gillian, or stroke her sleeve. Gillian sat rigid. She had been told this child's name, and could not remember it. She shifted uneasily as the girl turned towards her again, so large and cumbersome, and began to pick, with slow but intent curiosity, at loose bobbles of wool on her sleeve.

'Maureen. Our visitor might not like that.'

Gentle reproach, not from Nesta but another woman across the table, to whom Gillian had been introduced. Sadie, in her forties; with shining skin and hair tied in braids round her head. Another stranger.

'It's all right,' said Gillian stiffly. 'I don't mind.'

Sadie smiled at her. Something in Gillian wanted to hit her. Beyond Maureen was a grossly misshapen child she could not look at, and a boy who lolled in a wheelchair. Dark tufts of hair stuck out from a bony head, his lower eyelids drooped, his hands were stiff and immobile. He waggled one finger, and made awful sounds.

'More soup, Steven?'

A man with a beard was beside him, offering a beaker with a straw. Steven lowered his head and sucked. His hand shot out in a spasm; the beaker flew.

'Whooah!' shouted a boy across the table. Gillian jumped. 'Whooah!'

'It's all right, Dominic,' said the man with the beard. 'You eat your own lunch. Steven's fine, aren't you, Steven?' He bent to retrieve the beaker. 'Shall we try again?'

Steven gargled and jerked his head. Gillian looked away. She gazed at Dominic. Anger and danger hung about him.

'Cheese?' asked Nesta, next to her.

'Or more soup?' suggested Sadie.

'No. No, no, I –' Her face was burning. Horrible noises were all around her, strange wild sounds like honking geese, or squeezeboxes. Soothing voices rose and fell amongst them. Dribble was wiped away.

'Whooah!' roared Dominic, getting to his feet. He picked up a spoon and banged it against his head. 'Whooah! Fucking arse!'

Gillian pushed back her chair.

'All right, Dominic,' said Nesta. 'We all know you're here. Sit down again, please, or leave the room.' She waited. Dominic glared and sat. She turned to Gillian. 'I'm sorry, he can be –'

Gillian rose unsteadily. Maureen plucked at her sleeve.

'Stop it!' She knew she was scarlet. She turned to Nesta. 'Where is the lavatory?'

'Just across the hall.' Nesta looked at her sympathetically. Gillian

ignored the look. She marched stiffly across the acre of floor towards
the doorway, out past the strange wild thread of sound and the
murmuring voices, out to the huge quiet hall. Blessed emptiness. A
great slate fireplace. A polished piano. A sign on a lavatory door. She
pushed it open, banged it behind her, sank against cool white tiles.
Her hair sprang out from its tight elastic band and the sweat poured
down her. She closed her eyes and left this house of grotesques and
outcasts, seizing her bicycle, racing towards the gate.

Gillian! said Phoebe. Come out at once! Unlock the door!
    Never, said Gillian, in the long dark tunnel of her childhood.
Never, never, never.
    Gillian!
    I'll huff and I'll puff and I'll eat you alive –
    'Gillian?' Someone was knocking. 'Are you all right?'
    Nesta, glinting and calm and generous.
    'I'm fine,' said Gillian, cherishing darkness and silence.
    'The music starts at two,' said Nesta quietly. 'You don't have to
stay.' She went away again.
    Gillian opened her eyes. She saw she had come to the wrong place.
There was a hoist, a seat raised high, a handrail. This was for
children who had to be helped to do everything. It smelt of
disinfectant. Soon it would be needed.
    She used the strange high bowl and ran water over her hands in
the basin. There was no mirror. That was of no consequence. She
smoothed back her hair with more water, and went outside again.
Lunch was finishing, lolling adolescents came wheeling out to the
hall. Gillian pressed herself away from them. She made her way out
to the chapel, to wait and see.

Holy shafts of sunlight pierced the octagon walls, but this was no
longer a chapel. Sacrilege and desecration had stolen the cross and
the altar, ripped out the pews. A few chairs, and a number of
cushions, were arranged round an empty wooden floor, whose
boards were smooth and pale and polished. They soaked up the
afternoon sun. Underfloor heating warmed them, and what had
been a place of prayer and contemplation was now –
    A dance floor.
    A disgrace, said Phoebe.
    Gillian could not argue. She sat hunched up on a cushion between
two slits of windows, her arms round her knees. This had been her

position in the lavatory, but here she could not hide her head. She looked straight in front of her as the children came in through the door with their helpers, gaping and lurching and leaning on frames. Those who could walk unaided pushed other children in wheel-chairs; those who could wheel themselves spun out to the centre of the floor, liberated by this smooth and shining openness.

'Right,' said Nesta. 'Let's make a circle. Everyone find a space.' She spread out her arms, she made smaller signs, to individual children. Gillian, watching from her cushion, realised she was using another language. Gestures embraced the world. Some of the children answered her, awkward but engaged.

'Hello,' signed Nesta. 'The sun is shining. We're going to make some music.'

Phoebe shuddered.

Gillian did not know what to think.

A girl in a long rust-coloured skirt, with hair to her shoulders, walked round the circle, giving out shakers and bells. The children who could take them took them. Drums and tambourines followed. There was a shimmer of sound.

The girl in the rust-coloured skirt brought the box to Gillian.

'Would you like to join in?' She offered a drum, small and light. Gillian shrank. 'No, thank you.'

'I'm Claire,' said the girl. 'I'm here in a gap year, before university.' She smiled encouragingly.

Gillian nodded, willing her to move on. The girl crossed over to a piano. She began to play. The chapel was filled with rhythmic sounds.

'Are you all ready?' signed Nesta, saying the words aloud.

Drums beat erratically, tambourines shook. Gillian observed that a number of the children could do very little. She watched the man with the beard, and another, much younger, hold these children in an embrace, and help them to lift their instruments, to tap or beat upon them. She watched Dominic waving a drumstick, banging upon a hollow wooden box, trying to break it.

'Careful,' said Nesta.

Maureen was enjoying herself. She put down her tambourine and moved out to the middle of the circle. She stood swaying from side to side, now and then clapping, or making noises.

'Lovely,' said Nesta. 'Who wants to dance?'

A wisp of a child, who at lunchtime had plucked at the air, sat looking straight ahead.

'What about you?' said Nesta. 'Nadine? May I dance with you?'

Nadine quivered. Nesta sank down beside her. She took her frail hands and held them; she moved them from side to side. Nadine gave a tremulous smile. Nesta helped her up to her feet; she took her inch by inch towards the centre, swinging her arms; they smiled at one another. Nadine, out in the middle of the floor, allowed herself to be moved round at arm's length, a long, slow-motion spinning with the music. Her face broke into a radiant smile, and Nesta, when they had finished, hugged her.

Gillian, hunched on her cushion, drew her arms tight round her knees. She turned to look out of the window. Leaves danced over the lawn, and clouds were gathering. Soon she could leave.

The session had ended, the instruments were packed away.

'It's finished, now,' signed Nesta, and spread her hands on emptiness. The music fell into a void. Where had it gone?

Claire played the children out again, leaving with their helpers. When the chapel doors were open a wind blew in the coldness of autumn. Gillian felt glad. Nesta came over.

'Thank you for staying.'

Gillian shrugged.

'I know it can be difficult.'

She did not answer, getting to her feet in ungainly fashion.

'Well.' Nesta regarded her. 'I have to write a report, then I'm off.' She hesitated in the face of Gillian's silence. 'Would you still like to come back? Do you have time?'

Gillian thought of Phoebe, wondering. She would be irritable now, and irritable later.

'Yes,' she said flatly. 'Where do you live?'

They walked towards the doors. Claire had stopped playing, and was putting chairs away.

'I could give you a lift,' said Nesta. 'Your bike could go in the boot.'

Gillian shook her head. She must draw breath.

'Give me directions. I'll ride around for a bit.'

Nesta gave them. Gillian listened, and tried to concentrate.

She rode through the lanes and the wind rose all about her. A pub sign swung, creaking. The Feathers. They needed repainting. So did the blue door, tightly closed. Across the road was a hedge, and a pond in a field. She saw ducks in the reeds and then ducks ahead of her, crossing from just beyond the pub: two muddy white Aylesbury and a Muscovy drake, his pendulous scarlet flesh wobbling. They were anxious at her approach and she slowed: they quacked through the hedge and the reeds.

The sun had gone, and the sky was high and pale. Gillian took the turn-off, and saw the cottage.

Two up, two down, a smoking chimney; a car parked to the side of a rutted track ending in a gateway. The cottage was set down from the road, beneath a hedged and sloping garden of rough grass and apple trees. Windfalls and unraked leaves lay in the grass: a beehive stood by a hedge on the far side; a blackbird hopped amongst the leaves. He flew up, with a sharp alarm call, as Gillian got off the bicycle and wheeled it down the track. A wicket gate was set in the hedge: it stood open. She went through, and parked by a waterbutt. The door of the cottage opened.

'You found it. I'm so glad.'

Nesta held the door wide, as Gillian came up the path beneath the window. She saw a reflection: a wild-haired person in a worn old coat, with a pinched cold face and nervous manner.

She said: 'I'm not really used to visiting –'

'Then I am honoured. Especially after this afternoon. Well – come in.'

A bootscraper stood by the step, and a pair of boots stood beside it. Nesta was tall and straight and smiling: beyond her, Gillian made out a dark interior, flickering flames.

She went inside.

A flight of narrow stairs, a stride from the entrance, an old flowered carpet, a door to the right, ajar: a chair, and a glimpse of boxes. A door to the left, wide open. A log fire, brightly patterned furnishings, a mantelpiece crowded with photographs and cards and candles and bits of this and that, with a long piece of burnt-orange fabric tacked all along it, scalloped and beaded with glinting pieces of mirror. A little brass burner, stuck with sticks. Threads of blue-grey ash fell on to the hearth, threads of scented smoke rose towards the ceiling.

Chanting voices, altar candles, the Cross held high –

The burner swung on its chain, the clouds of incense drifting –

Procession, confession, bowed heads –

Agnus Dei, qui tollis peccata mundi, miserere nobis –

Incense was holy and high –

There was nothing like that in Wales.

'I'm just an old hippie at heart,' said Nesta. 'Tea? Shall I take your coat?'

Gillian, unused to the niceties, or to being in strange places, stood in the crowded sitting room, with its Indian bedspreads flung over the chair and sofa, the faded wallpaper hung with pictures, a piano jammed up in a corner and a low table littered with books and letters and felt as out of place as a bullock: a wild, lumbering, awkward creature, breathing heavily, hungry and cold.

She said: 'I'll keep my coat on,' and sat, uninvited, on a corner of the sofa, knocking a pile of books from the table, looking helplessly about her.

She sat in her corner, drinking scalding tea from a chipped mug. The chip was a reassurance: there was nothing at home that had not a chip or a crack or a rivet. Across the fireplace, Nesta stretched long legs out from an old armchair and regarded her. The fallen books were back on the table, the logs burned comfortably, the room was full of incense.

Sickly, said Phoebe.

Gillian ignored her.

'So.' Nesta leaned forward and picked up a tobacco tin. 'Do you mind if I –'

'It's your house,' said Gillian. 'You must do as you wish.'

Phoebe frowned.

'Thank you.' Nesta opened the tin, and took out a packet of papers. 'I'm trying to give up, but when I'm off duty –' She rolled deftly, licked the paper, reached for a match. Gillian, still in her coat, sat watching. Nesta lit up. 'That's better.' She threw the match into the fire. 'So,' she said again. 'Where shall we begin?'

Gillian had no idea.

'When I met you,' said Nesta, 'up on the hill –'

'Bryncarnedd.'

'Is that what it's called? I find all these names unpronounceable – say it again.'

'Brincarneth. Bryn is a small hill. Carnedd is a cairn.'

'I must write it down.' Nesta inhaled. 'Are you Welsh? I wondered about you, when we met – you know how you do. I wondered where you lived, and if you lived by yourself –'

'I live with my mother,' said Gillian flatly. 'She's English, but I was born in Penglydr.'

'Penglyder. That's how you say it.'

'Yes.'

Nesta waited. Gillian drank her tea.

'Tell me about you and your mother.'

'Why? What do you want to know?'

Gillian, said Phoebe, with a note of warning.

'I'm sorry.' Nesta drew a strand of tobacco from her tongue and flicked it into the fire. Disgusting habit, said Phoebe. Silly girl. She should give up.

'Too many questions?'

'It's all right. It is how people go about things. You must take no notice of my manners.' Gillian looked at the carpet, faded and worn. That, too, was something of a reassurance. 'No doubt it comes of too much solitude,' she said boldly. 'Ask away.'

'You said you're not working.'

'Did I?'

'Up on the hill. Don't you remember? You said you were a burden on the community – it was one of the things that made me like you.'

Gillian flushed. 'I don't remember.'

'Are you looking for work?' Nesta stopped. 'I'm sorry – that sounds like a Job Centre question.'

'It does. Do I look employable?'

They looked at each other. Nesta laughed.

'How do you spend your days?'

'I write,' said Gillian. 'It is all I know how to do.' She bit at a fingernail. 'And please don't tell me you have always wanted to write.'

'I haven't,' said Nesta. 'I enjoy what I do. So there.' She drew on her rolled-up cigarette. 'What do you – ?'

'I am a poet.'

'Are you published?'

'Intermittently.'

Nesta sat thinking. 'Gillian Traherne. I'm afraid I haven't heard –'

Gillian recalled the windswept summit of the hill, the dark stones of the cairn, the bitter sky, the questions. No one had heard of her, nor of her father, nor of the family name. Only in universities, and even they had forgotten.

She said: 'There is no reason why you should have done.'

'But will you let me read something?'

'Perhaps. I give readings sometimes – you could come to one of those. If you'd like to.'

'Yes. Yes, I would.' Nesta had finished her roll-up; she threw it into the fire. 'More tea?'

'Yes.'

Yes, please, said Phoebe.

'Please,' said Gillian.

Nesta reached for the heavy brown teapot. Gillian looked at the photographs on the mantelpiece, all crowded together. A pity, said Phoebe, looking round the room. She should have a good clear-up. Have you tidied your room?

Gillian took her tea from Nesta. On the mantelpiece were children, gaping and grinning, like those she had seen this morning. There were people who looked as if they could be Nesta's parents. There was a man.

Perhaps it was time she showed an interest.

'Who's that?' she asked abruptly.

Nesta followed her gaze. 'That is my husband.' She put another log on the fire.

'Oh.' Gillian felt herself flushing. 'I didn't realise –' She stopped.

Nesta reached for the tobacco tin. 'He died three years ago,' she said calmly. 'Almost exactly three years.'

There, said Phoebe. Now look what you've done.

'I'm sorry.' Gillian scarlet, did not know where to look.

Nesta opened a cigarette paper and dropped thin strands of tobacco on to it. She rolled it and licked it and shook out the match. She stood up, and took down the photograph. 'Here.'

Gillian took it, and looked at it. A street, parked cars, terraced houses, a man coming out of a gate. He was tall, wearing jeans and a sweater; he had dark curly hair, he was laughing. There was a van, with open doors and boxes.

'That's our house,' said Nesta. 'That's the day we bought the flat. It was nice inside. Here.'

She passed another frame. A man and a woman lay stretched out on a couch, their arms round each other, bare feet propped up on cushions. Plants, pictures, clutter, a door to a garden. The woman had long red hair and a long print skirt; the man's clothes looked loose on him, and his face was thin. Nesta, young. Nesta and –

'He was called Hal. There's lots more photos, but I don't suppose you want to see them now.' She took the picture back; her fingers lightly touched the glass. 'This was four years ago, before he got ill. Well – he was ill then, but we didn't know it. I'll just show you one more. Where we worked. May I?'

Gillian made a gesture. She had no idea whether it was appropriate. She took a photograph of this man – Hal – kneeling upright, opposite a boy of ten or eleven, his arms outstretched. The boy had a strange closed look beneath dark brows, a shambling, uncoordinated appearance. He was big for his age – Gillian did not know how she knew this, but she did know – a large, uncontrolled, perhaps uncontrollable child, making uncertain progress across a room. Towards this man. Hal.

The boy made her think of the children at Cadair: a misshapen, outcast thing, a grotesque, shut away –

'He was autistic,' said Nesta. 'That boy. Like some of the children I work with now. Like Dominic. I'm sorry – he was quite disturbed today. I know it can be distressing. Sometimes he's more reachable –'

Gillian did not answer. She gave back the photograph. The light was fading. Nesta switched on the lamp. Gillian thought of her bicycle, with its single reflector, and of the darkening lanes. Phoebe would be –

'My mother will be –'

Nesta sat down again. 'I'll run you home, if you like. I'm sure we could put the bike in the back.'

'No, no. There's no need for that.' She picked up her mug and drained it, and put it down, and did not know what to do next. She could feel Nesta watching her, waiting for some comment or question. For conversation. 'I'm sorry,' she said again. 'I told you – I'm not used to –'

Nesta said calmly: 'There's no need to say anything. We hardly know each other.'

'Thank you. Well –' She rose to her feet, and knocked against the table. Nesta drew it away. 'Can I go to the bathroom?'

'Of course. Upstairs, straight ahead on the landing.' Nesta knelt down to tend to the fire; she reached for coal.

Gillian climbed the narrow stairs in her heavy coat, and went into a small cold bathroom, feeling for the switch. More photographs lined the walls. Nesta in the bath, with her hair up, leaning back in the water, reading; Hal in the bath, sitting up, soap on his shoulders, reaching for a sponge. Nesta washing her hair, pouring water from a china jug; brushing her teeth, turning to laugh at the camera. Hal in his half-open dressing gown, sitting on the edge of the bath with the newspaper, while the water ran. Water and nakedness and casual, everyday intimacy. Gillian, in her heavy coat, looked from one to another, shrinking away to nothing.

67

When she came down again, Nesta had piled up the fire with fresh logs.

'Are you sure I can't give you a lift?'

'No, no, it's kind of you, but I must –'

She was at the front door, she must go, she must go –

Nesta took a jacket from a peg and accompanied her down the path.

'I hope you'll come again. You know where I am now.'

'Yes. Thank you.'

She wheeled the bicycle up the track. The air smelt raw, the ground was hard, the moon was rising. The first few stars hung above the apple trees.

'Well. Goodbye.'

'Goodbye.' Nesta reached out to touch her arm. 'Thanks for coming.'

Thank you for having me, said Phoebe.

'Thank you for having me,' said Gillian. She climbed on to the bicycle, she rode away quickly, the saddle creaking.

Nesta watched the faint red glow of the reflector as the bicycle passed the lights of the pub. She pulled her jacket around her and walked back down the track to the cottage. Silence and starlight. Her first winter in Wales. The third winter of widowhood.

Frost shone on the path. She picked up her boots by the door and took them inside. The fire leapt up to greet her, threads of ash from the joss stick fell to the hearth. The room smelt of wood and incense and herbal tea and looked, through Gillian's eyes, as she saw it now, a desperately cluttered and poky place, full of bits and pieces. Gillian had lumbered about like a farm animal, penned up for the winter months, used to the field. But I like you, thought Nesta, rolling another cigarette. You interest me.

The fire crackled and spat. Nesta sat smoking and thinking. She stretched out on the sofa and closed her eyes.

When she woke, the fire had died down. She lay for a while, her face turned to the window, watching the moon rise. She must draw the curtains, she must make something to eat, she must write letters to London. London felt further away than Africa. She must do this and she must do that, and she must have an early night because tomorrow she was on night watch, and that could be hell. She went on lying there, pulling the Indian bedspread over her, watching the moon.

Hal used to sing that, he often sang snatches of this and that, it
came from his mother. She was nice, a lovely woman, and now her
heart was broken.

'You are my sunshine, my only sunshine . . .'

Nesta got up. The moon rose beyond the window frame. She went
to the door and opened it. The moon was sailing far far away through
the winter clouds, but the silence felt deep and safe.

She pulled on her jacket. She pulled on her boots. She walked
through the apple trees, up the rough ground, turning to look out
over the valley. Somewhere in the darkness cattle breathed. There
was a dog, there was a beam of light from a car in the distance, then it
was gone. Nesta, growing cold, reached out her arms in the
moonlight.

'Where are you?' she said aloud. 'Hal? Do you not know I'm here?'

The porch light was on. The light was on in the kitchen, and the
curtains were drawn back. Gillian got stiffly off the bicycle and
wheeled it down the path. The moon was high: the moon had saved
her. The lanes and the hedges and hills were winter-black but the
moon had risen high above them and she had felt no fear, only the
cold, going deep: into her bones, into the empty fields.

The door of the lean-to shed was shut. She fumbled with the icy
metal catch, and could hardly move it. There. Her fingers were
painful and raw; she wheeled the bicycle in and leaned it against the
wall. Moonlight showed moisture on the brick. She closed the door,
but could not manage the catch.

Shut it properly, said Phoebe.

She found a stone.

Now to receive her reproaches.

Gillian walked down the path. The moon was high and the garden
glittered: silver-white, grey-green, each still leaf, each blade of grass
thick with frost, stretching away before her towards the pond, where
the reeds and the water were frozen.

Winter's grip.

In winter the holy light which shone on the surface of the water
met ice, not its own reflection, and the plants and the creatures
beneath it were close to death.

An owl hooted. Gillian turned away. She looked at the back of the house. Where the moonlight touched it, the ivy gleamed. The kitchen curtains were drawn back here, too, and the light spilled on to the clumps of lavender beneath the window. She could see Phoebe, bent over her tapestry, tugging the thread up; she could hear the wireless.

Her footsteps sounded on the path. She looked up at the dovecot, quiet and still. She listened, shivering: a faint sleepy murmur, a shifting of feet on the icy boards, deep within. So cold, so cold –

'How can you bear it?' she said aloud.

The coming of winter

7

A dusting of snow lay on high ground, a shimmer of frost on field and hedge and garden. As the pale sun rose behind the hills an unutterably beautiful winter light suffused the valley.

Gillian lay shivering beneath the bedclothes. On the long ride home from Nesta's cottage she had caught a chill, which became a fever. At night she lay tossing, and coughing, and streaming with sweat, and her dreams were wild. At daybreak she slept deeply, and woke to a sweet piercing sun through the gap in the curtains. Behind the curtains the window panes were thick with ferny patterns of frost, but she was too weak to draw them. She coughed, and her breath streamed out before her like the breath of cattle moving slowly across the whitened fields.

A rattle of coke as the range was fed. Footsteps along the tiled hall, up the creaking stairs and along the landing. The rattle of a teacup, a brisk knock.

'Good morning. How have you slept?'

Phoebe set down the teacup and drew back the curtains. The room was filled with sunlight: Gillian closed her eyes, which were dazzled, and hurt, and shrank down into her pillow. Her hair was tangled and damp. Phoebe felt her forehead.

'Not more than a hundred, I shouldn't think. Sit up now.'

She struggled; Phoebe plumped the pillows. 'There.'

Gillian leaned back and was given the teacup.

'Drink up.'

She raised it to her lips and spilt tea in the saucer.

'*Careful.*'

'Sorry.'

'Never mind. Try again.'

Gillian tried, and drank.

Phoebe crossed the room and bent down to light the paraffin stove. Up here, in winter, the Rayburn took the chill off, but no more. She lifted the lid, struck a match; Gillian, from the pillows, watched the orange flame race round the wick, and turn to blue as Phoebe adjusted the knob.

'There.'

The burning paraffin shimmered through the cut-out leaves in the top; the room was filled with a smell familiar to Gillian since babyhood. At night, still, she liked to lie and look at the soft yellow leaves stencilled on the ceiling; Phoebe, still, checked last thing to make sure the flame was out.

'There,' she said again, straightening up. She was always saying it. Tick, tick, tick: the day's tasks accomplished, and on to the next. So.

'So.' She came back to the bed. 'More tea?'

Gillian nodded, and her head swam.

'I'll bring you some toast.'

'I'm not sure if I –'

'And then you had better get up and sit in the chair. Your bed is a terrible mess.' Phoebe took the teacup. 'Your whole room is a mess,' she said, making for the door. 'I don't know how you can bear it.'

Gillian lay back on the lumpy pillows. She looked at her desk, and the scrunched-up balls of white all round it. She must tear them to pieces, and save their souls. The fumes of the paraffin shimmered and swam, her eyelids felt heavy and full. She looked at the rest of the room, at the dust, and the clothes half-dead on the chair.

'It is a pauper's room,' she croaked, and her eyes closed.

When Phoebe returned she drank a few sips of tea but could not eat.

'Do you think I should have some medicine?'

'I'll see if there's an aspirin,' said Phoebe, but there wasn't. 'The body heals itself,' she said, drawing back the bedclothes, brushing the sheets. 'All you have is a chill from a foolish excursion. I don't know what you were thinking of.'

'It was interesting,' said Gillian, as she had said two nights ago, shivering down in the kitchen, sheltering against the Rayburn. The flames of Nesta's fire leapt up before her, the scent of woodsmoke and incense clung to her, voices went to and fro. 'She was interested in me.'

'Your hair needs tying back,' said Phoebe, and reached for the brush. 'Come along, sit up properly.'

Gillian submitted to the comb's sharp teeth and the harsh black bristles of the brush. Phoebe tied it all back with a fabric-covered elastic band, sold from a card by the till in the village shop. 'You had better go to the bathroom while I do your bed.'

'Don't touch my desk.'

'I have no intention of touching it.'

Gillian swung her mottled blue feet to the dusty floor and slowly made her way to the door. An ancient dressing gown hung on a hook. She put it round her shoulders and shuffled out.

'For heaven's sake,' said Phoebe, shaking out the eiderdown, straightening the sheets. 'It can't be that bad.'

The bathroom was an icebox. A candle of warmth came from the upright paraffin stove set against the wall by the towel rail. Gillian rubbed condensation from the mirror and beheld a thin, feverish, red-eyed creature, such as no one might wish to know, or take an interest in. She brushed its teeth, and washed its face in warm water, and took it to the lavatory. She rubbed at the window pane, and let it look out on to the garden, cold and still. A crow flapped low across the farmer's field and up to the bare trees, cawing hoarsely; bluetits swung on the coconut Phoebe had hung from the bird table.

'I must feed my doves,' said Gillian, but the feeble creature began to shiver and shake, and she led it back to the bedroom, feeling her way along the landing.

Phoebe was setting the bedroom to rights. The bed was freshly made, the sheets turned back; the drooping pile of clothes on the chair had been picked up and folded. She had brought up the Hoover, and was plugging it in. Gillian crept over the trailing flex and into bed. She lay against the worn pillows while the Hoover roared at the trembling dust and fluff and gave its dreadful punishment.

'There.' Phoebe switched it off, and bent to take the plug out. She straightened up slowly, and made a sound.

'What's the matter?'

'Nothing. Just a twinge. So.' She wound up the flex and came across to the bed. 'Feeling better?'

'My head's a bit – are there really no aspirin?'

'Nature will take its course,' said Phoebe. 'Your body has its own resistance. Rest and fluids will do the trick. Would you like a glass of water?'

'No.'

'No, thank you. Something to read?'

She shook her head and liquid sloshed about inside it. Downstairs the letterbox banged.

My poems have come back to me, thought Gillian, who had checked the post each day with diminishing hope. I shall comfort and succour them, and keep them safe.

'That'll be the Notcutts catalogue,' said Phoebe.

The milkfloat whined along the lane and drew up; they could hear greetings exchanged on the frosty air, and the slam of the post van door. Milk bottles rattled and chinked.

'Well, I must get on.'

'Thank you for doing my room.'

'I don't know how you have left it for so long.'

Phoebe wheeled out the Hoover, squeak squeak squeak.

Paraffin shimmered in the morning sun, the milkfloat floated away, the Hoover was left alone on the landing. Footsteps down the stairs and over the tiles and a sudden sharp sound as Phoebe bent down to pick up her catalogue and tug the front door open. In came the draughts of milk and cold air. Bang. The house and Gillian trembled, and lay still.

'Lunch.'

She swam to the surface.

'Had a good sleep?'

'I –'

'Come on, sit up, you'll feel better with something to eat.'

Gillian struggled. She saw the green tin tray, a bowl of tinned tomato soup, bread and butter. She saw a square of white.

'Is that for me?'

'It is.'

'Did it come in the post?'

'How else? Can you manage now?'

Gillian took the tray. 'Why didn't you tell me?'

'I can't come up and down all day.'

'But it's –' It was not her self-addressed envelope, with its blue stamp full of regret. The name of the magazine was on the outside, in a pleasing and distinctive typeface.

'Careful, now, you're going to –'

She opened the envelope with shaking fingers.

'Mind the soup –'

Her eyes raced down the quarto page.

'Mind the *soup* –'

'I have had two poems accepted,' said Gillian. 'He wants to see more.'

'Who does?'

'The editor.' The bowl slid gaily over the tray. 'The editor!'

'Gillian!' Phoebe leaned across.

'Sorry.' She let the letter fall, she drank her soup.

'It's a good magazine?' Phoebe was looking at the envelope.

'Very good. Radical and well respected. They published Father –' Gillian put down her spoon. 'You don't remember?'

'No,' said Phoebe.

Edward was up in the hills. Far across the valley he could see two figures, a farmer and his dog, a mirror image of himself and Tarn, working the ewes, tough Welsh Half-breds, down the cold slopes towards the winter grazing of the fields.

'Feee-oh! Feee-oh!'

The high, piercing whistle, thin as a blade of grass, clear as footsteps on an icy road, sounded from hillside to hillside.

'Feee-oh!'

Tarn raced, crouched low, leapt up again; her eyes were everywhere, her tongue lolled; he felt the connection between them like elastic, springy and taut, going from gut to gut, going deep.

'Come by, come by, come by!'

But she knew far more than he could call on from childhood memories, she had been working sheep for two years before he bought her, and sheep were in her blood: their crowding together, their panicked eyes and bleating, their rushing this way and that, encircled by her, terrified by her, bouncing out of the bracken and trotting down the stony slopes, their fleeces swaying, caked in muck.

'Feee-oh!'

Edward was a boy again, up in the hills of Northumberland, following his grandfather, and the dog Ben.

'Good lad.'

His grandfather turned to wait for him, leaning on his stick; ahead, a river of sheep, white-faced Cheviots and the long-coated, horned and mottle-faced Rough Fell, swirled and turned and spilled down over the rough grass, Ben racing and panting alongside.

'You've kept up well.'

'Thanks.' Edward stood beside him, feeling the winter wind on his face, smelling snow. The cries of the sheep were everywhere.

'Enjoying yourself?'

'I always enjoy it here.'

Far below were the clustered buildings of the farm; he could see the tractor and trailer, and his tiny grandmother, crossing the yard, passing the cowshed, where the cows, brought in for the winter months, stood close and still on the slurried ground; passing the milking parlour, and the covered pen across from it, where the bullocks were. He could see the curl of smoke. He would be here for Christmas. He had been here through most of the summer, though he'd had to spend Easter at home.

Home?

This was where he belonged.

They followed the dog and the sheep, down to the fields left empty by the cows; the ewes would graze them now, until they were taken into the lambing sheds. He thought of the frail skinny little one they'd had to rear with a bottle last year, of holding her close as she sucked and sucked, draining it all in a moment, set back in her pen of hay bales in the barn, bloated and warm beneath the lamp. This last Easter he'd had to miss all that, staying in London, and his grandmother had written to say there were two motherless lambs, Katie and Will, and she could do with his help.

'I wish I lived here,' he said, as they made their way down the hillside.

His grandfather grunted. 'Mum and Dad would miss you, wouldn't they?'

'No, they wouldn't. If they missed me, they wouldn't be sending me off to board.'

'They do that because you're an only lad, you know that. And they're working. Better for you to be with the other boys, isn't it?'

'I'd like it better if I were here with you and Gran. I could go to school on the bus –'

For years he dreamed of it: miles away in chapel, in Maths, in Latin, down in the deep on the cricket field, though he enjoyed cricket. He did not belong: he felt that at eight or nine, though he could not work out why. Perhaps it was being an only child. Perhaps it was having older parents. Perhaps it was just how things were, and you had to get on with it. He got on with it: with the prep, the letters home, the intermittent bullying and continuous noise. Most of the time he supposed it was all right. When it wasn't, he planned his future, up on the farm.

'Feeling a bit homesick?'

'No, sir.'

'Well, come along, then, Sullivan, wakey-wakey, there's a kit check in five minutes.'

'Yes, sir.'

He stuffed his rugby and gym kit into his bag, he went to line up in the quad. He answered the roll call, he showed them his socks and shorts and vest in house colours, but he wasn't here: he was down in the hay bales, out in the hills, he was coming home on the bus at the end of the day and hugging Ben in the yard, having tea before milking, and driving the cows down the lane with a stick, the dog at his heels.

One day, he said to himself in the noisy corridors. When I grow up, he said in the choir, though he enjoyed the choir. At night, in the dorm, they ragged and beat up the new boys and made them drink cocktails of toothpaste. Everyone talked about money, and cars, and the Common Entrance. He passed the Common Entrance, and went on to more of the same.

Three things happened before O levels.

The dog Ben died, and it felt like losing a brother. He could tell no one this.

His grandfather died, and he discovered that the farm, where he had always assumed he would one day be living, was a tenancy only. His grandmother, after a while, had to leave, and go to live with her daughter in Alnwick. A new tenant farmer moved in.

Soon after this, on a crisp autumn morning at the beginning of the fourth year, Edward looked at the fair dreamy face of the sixth-former ahead in the breakfast queue, and acknowledged, at last, what he had always, in a deep, secret, awful place, known to be true. It wasn't the school; it wasn't his home, or his parents. It was him.

I love you, he said, in a secret, silent, glorious and terrifying part of himself, as the boy ahead of him turned round, and gave him a smile which felt as if it could have been given to no one else.

And: *I'm queer*, he said to himself in the mirror, up in the empty dormitory, during the lunch hour. That's what it is. Oh, Jesus, Jesus, Jesus.

The face that looked back at him was as white as the neatly turned back sheets on the rows of beds stretching away from him to the open window. Outside, he could hear the raucous lunch-hour noise from the quad. He should be down there, but he wasn't. He should belong, but he didn't. The face in the mirror was his face, and the face of his father, of whom he had always been afraid – that, too, was a new acknowledgement, a half-truth half known, pushed aside, now brought out into the open.

This wasn't something lots of boys went through. This was for ever: he knew.

'Sullivan?'

'Yes, sir?'

'What are you doing up here?'

'Nothing, sir.'

'Well, take a conduct mark. You know it's out of bounds.'

'Yes, sir.'

'Everything all right? Not sick, are you?'

'No, sir.'

'Then go along.'

Out, and along the corridor.

Autumn sun lit crimson creeper, yellow stone. Polished oak boards and panelling gleamed, the sky through the open leaded windows was a dazzling blue. A perfect September afternoon.

Edward descended the polished oak staircase.

The future yawned open, dark and unthinkable.

That was a long time ago.

'But this wasn't the Dark Ages,' said Rowland, years later, listening. 'People were coming out, there must have been other boys there who felt okay about it –'

'If there were, I didn't find them.'

'And the lovely boy in the sixth form didn't –'

'He didn't.' Edward smiled, turned in Rowland's arms and kissed his cheek, thick with stubble. It was four o'clock in the morning, it was their second night together.

'Do that again.'

He did it again.

'Here.'

There. And there.

Time passed. Dawn broke. In the long narrow gardens bordered by the Barbican apartments, the lamps which burned all night went out. Light at the curtains, birdsong, the slam of a taxi door. It was Sunday. They slept.

Over breakfast, which was lunch, Rowland said:

'So if I hadn't –'

'I should have left that party after your concert, as I have left many parties, and gone home alone, end of story.'

'But you would have thought about me?'

'I would.'

'With desire and longing?'

'With desire and longing.' Edward put down his toast, and looked across the table. The kitchen was a six-foot square. He had never felt so out of proportion in a room. He had never felt so happy. 'With more than that,' he said slowly. 'I knew from the moment I saw you.'

Rowland looked back at him. 'Yes. And so did I.'

'After all your many lovers?'

'After all my many lovers.'

They had come to the lower back field, where the hens were kept. A bit of a wind had got up. Tarn was flying back and forth, as the ewes crowded up to the gate, and one or two strayed, in a hopeless, helpless sort of way, trotting off along the hedge by the next field, which belonged to the neighbouring farm. They bent to graze, and as the dog came after them made for the hedge, got in a muddle, and struggled out again, swerving wildly. Tarn swept them back with the flock; more scattered.

'Come on, come on, away to me –' His grandfather's calls.

Edward moved quickly towards the stragglers, his stick outstretched. He pushed his way through the heaving fleeces, lifted the hook on the gate and swung it wide. The wind blew, the sheep streamed through, Tarn raced after the last two or three and drove them in, panting.

'Good girl, that'll do.'

He closed the gate, he told her to lie down now, good girl, and she sank to the grass, still watchful. Within moments, the scattered ewes, trotting this way and that, had lowered their heads and begun to crop at the winter grass. In a while, it was as if they had always been here.

Edward stood by the gate, watching it all. Tarn rested, breathing more calmly, the sheep moved slowly over the field and the hens picked their way amongst them, clucking enquiringly, lifting cold yellow feet, pecking at tussocks of grass and scattered grain and scraps. The empty fields of the neighbouring farm, whose buildings lay some two miles distant, stretched away on either side towards woodland; rooks and pigeons flew over the bare trees, calling. Edward could smell sheep and earth and dog. Next year, with a bigger flock, he would talk to the farmer about renting one or two of those empty fields.

For now, there was the lambing to think of, the outbuildings to see to. The roof of the house was okay. So it should be: it had cost enough. The barn and outbuildings' roofs he must patch up himself, before the winter rain rotted the timbers still further. Lambing sheds, that was what his grandfather had had. He could wire the buildings up to the generator. He pictured newborn lambs beneath a lamp, safe in a pen of hay bales, warm and dry. Better make a list. Plastic sheeting, nails, measure up for new timber, measure up for flex –

Coffee first. Then down to the village, the dog in the back.

'Tarn?'

On her feet in a flash. Ears pricked, nose forward, ready to go.

'Heel. Leave those poor beasts be.'

She followed him over the rough ground.

'I must do the Christmas arrangement,' said Phoebe. 'Come along.'

Heaps of greenery were piled up by the back door: holly, mistletoe, sprays of winter jasmine and trailing mounds of ivy, scarlet-berried cotoneaster and the last of the honesty and Chinese lanterns, sprayed with glycerine.

'You'll need to wrap up well. Have you got your gloves? It'll do you good to get out and about.'

They carried the greenery out to the van. Holly leaves protruded from the newspaper; they scratched and pricked through Gillian's woollen gloves and caught on the worn tweed overcoat.

'There.' Phoebe slammed the doors. 'Jump in.'

Gillian came round to the side. They drove away. Phoebe sang snatches of carols.

'"The holly and the *i*-vy, when they are both full *grown* –"' She changed gear as they approached the village. 'I must say Gareth did an excellent job on the clutch, can you feel it?'

'Yes,' said Gillian. 'Much better.'

'What are the roots that clutch, what branches grow / Out of this stony rubbish?'

Eliot, in his horn-rimmed spectacles, reading in his cracked dry voice on an old cracked record. She had taken it out of the library, when she left school, with her single A-level, and never taken it back. Cards came for it, Phoebe searched for it –

'You *must* know where it is.'

Gillian couldn't think.

She played the record when Phoebe was out, on the blue-and-white Dansette beneath the bookshelves in her father's study. That was before she took the desk to pieces and took it upstairs. The room smelt of damp and dust and old books: she took them down from the shelves and sniffed them, and read bits of them, and put them back.

The corn was orient and immortal wheat, which never should be reaped, nor was ever sown. I thought it had stood from everlasting to everlasting.

The volume had been read and reread; her father had marked passages in pencil.

Spiritual things are the Greatest, and Spiritual Strength is the most Excellent, Usefull and Delightfull –

She could remember him, just, standing up at the shelves while she played in the corner, or drew at his desk, or sat in the armchair, her doll in her lap.

. . . orient and immortal wheat –

Scarlet combines moved across the valley. Gillian slipped the black volume back in its place. She took down Eliot, in his ochre jacket.

Lady, three white leopards sat under a juniper-tree –

Someone, at a reading, once asked what he meant by that line. Eliot looked at the questioner, over his horn-rimmed spectacles.

'It means: *Lady, three white leopards sat under a juniper-tree.*'

The scratched LP went round and round, the voice was as dry as the dust on the shelves. People at school had hated it.

'It's so *bor*-ing.'

She played it again and again.

> *In my beginning is my end . . .*
> *In my end is my beginning.*

Eliot's wife was mad. She walked down Knightsbridge with a piece of paper pinned to her hat. It said: MURDER IN THE CATHEDRAL.

Well. Good for her.

Gillian put him back in his place. She took down her father's poems, in worn green cloth.

'Right.' Phoebe drew up at the church. The lych gate was open, the grass on the verge was wet. There were one or two people tending the graves, and a light shone from the vestry.

'Gwen must be here already,' said Phoebe. 'Out you get.'

They opened the doors, they hauled out the piles of greenery. Berries fell to the ground. Gillian pricked her finger, and swore.

'Gillian!'

'Sorry.'

You swear, she said to Phoebe's back. I've heard you.

'Morning, Phoebe. Morning, Gillian. Want a hand?'

That was Gwen Jones, in her wine-coloured winter coat, bulging over Crimplene skirt and twinset, coming down the path from the west door.

'I heard the van. Really bitter now, isn't it? Oh, now isn't that all lovely?'

They gave her bundles in paper; more berries fell.

'Careful,' said Phoebe.

'It's just what we need, to brighten everything up. I've done out all the vases.' Gwen's breath hung on the air in cloudy puffs. 'And how are you, Gillian? Keeping well?'

'I've been a bit –'

'You look a bit peaky.'

'She's much better now,' said Phoebe.

They carried it all into the porch, and set it down on the oak settle. The inner door was open, propped with an iron stop.

'Mind, we could take it inside, and work from there,' puffed Gwen.

'Better to leave it out here,' said Phoebe. 'Some of it's horribly wet.'

She went back to close the van doors.

'Been a bit under the weather, have you?'

'I'm better now, thanks.' Gillian pushed her straying hair back beneath her headscarf. She looked at the notices of missionary work in Africa, and forthcoming Youth Club events.

'Mind, our Sally's been terrible this winter, her and the little ones. Off school for almost a fortnight, she was at her wits' end. There's a lot of it about this year, don't you find?'

'An awful lot.'

They stood and waited.

'Still doing the writing?'

'Yes,' said Gillian, and then, fiddling with a loose thread of wool on her gloves, 'I've just had two poems accepted by a good magazine in London.'

'Have you really, now? Well, isn't that lovely for you? Going to give one of your readings?'

'I might.'

'Lovely.'

Phoebe was back, wiping her feet on the mat.

'Right. Let's make a start.'

Gillian spent the morning doing what she was told. She carried in the heaps of greenery, and set them on the flags. She filled and carried vases; every now and then she held up a branch of mistletoe, or a spray of winter jasmine –

'How about here?'

'I don't *think* so,' said Phoebe.

The church was cold, and their voices echoed. There were Calor gas heaters, but only for Sundays and special occasions.

'They had them on for Dai Griffiths' funeral,' said Gwen. 'Last Wednesday week. A lovely service, just took the chill off. Terrible in here now.'

'Pass me those lanterns, Gillian,' said Phoebe, up by the pulpit. 'Careful with them. And another lot of ivy, I think.'

'Should've brought my Thermos,' said Gwen, snipping at holly stems. 'Ouch.'

Gillian's limbs were heavy and tired. She walked to the back of the church. Watery sun shone through the stained-glass windows, on the flagstones, the pews, the brasses, all polished up for Christmas. Someone had left a smear of polish just in the corner of her father's plaque. She made her way along the pew, and rubbed at it with her sleeve. The west door opened: she turned, and a man came in.

The visitor.

Cold air followed him. He shut the door.

His footsteps sounded on the flags, he looked about him, he saw her. Gillian's cheeks were burning. He did not recognise her. Then he did.

'Oh. Hello.'

She nodded curtly. He walked past. The church was full of the smells of spruce, and cut greenery, of polish and wax and the underlying musty chill. Gwen had gone into the vestry: there was the sound of water, running into a bucket. Phoebe, up in the pulpit, trailed ivy in and out of the fretwork; she looked down upon the aisle, and the new arrival.

'Oh, hello,' she said brightly. 'I remember you.'

'Good morning.' Edward walked towards her, crossing the transept. 'I was just passing, I've kept meaning to look in, I hope I'm not disturbing –'

'Not in the least. Now you're here, you can pass me that ivy – there, down on the step – thank you.'

Edward smiled. He bent down to the chancel steps and passed it up to her.

'Gillian's supposed to be – Gillian?'

The vestry door stood open: Gwen came out with a bucket.

'We'd better put what's still waiting in here, don't you think? Keep it fresh –' She saw the visitor. 'Morning.'

'Morning,' said Edward. He looked at the bucket. 'Can I help –'

'No, no, don't you bother.' Gwen set it down by a pew, and straightened her arm. 'Heavy, mind, water's always heavier than you think, isn't it?'

'You could go and give Gillian a hand,' said Phoebe.

Edward turned. He saw Gillian struggling with armfuls, flushed and slow.

'Of course. Here –' He strode up towards her. 'Let me –'

'Thanks.' She did not look at him. They walked side by side down the aisle in silence.

'Thanks so much,' said Phoebe, from the heavens. 'Just put it there –'

'Where do you want these, then, Phoebe?' asked Gwen.

'The lanterns must go in a window.' Phoebe was climbing down.

'Like last year, I remember. Lovely.'

Edward looked at the deep stone windowsills already filled with profusions of glossy dark ivy and moon-white mistletoe, at the sprays of jasmine and clumps of holly in tall green metal vases on the chancel steps, the ivy weaving in and out of the choir stalls, trailing over the pulpit. Scarlet berries burned against gleaming green –

'Perfect,' he said. 'You've made it look beautiful.'

'She always does,' said Gwen. 'You should see when she does a wedding.'

'It's a very nice church,' said Phoebe, wiping her hands. 'Now, then. Gillian, if you could put everything that's left in Gwen's bucket –'

He left them all to it, walking slowly round. The church was simple and well-kept: stern Norman pillars, whitewash between exposed timbers in the roof of the nave, Victorian glass in good repair. There was a small chipped effigy of a woman called Agnes, with a lamb at her feet. He should have brought Pevsner: next time he would; this had been an impulse, something he had meant to do for months. He looked at a stone in the floor, to the memory of Ann Ellis, who in 1765 had died in childbed; at a stone on the wall to

Thomas Bowen, killed at Ypres. On his way up to the font, he saw a couple of brass plaques, and the woman from the wilderness up beside one of them, rubbing at it again with her woollen gloves.

He was not conscious, or only barely conscious, of thinking of her like this. Only later, a long time later, when he looked back – on a garden in autumn, on a wintry morning, moments in an icy church – did he realise that this, from the beginning, was how he had always thought of her.

To the memory of
Edward Traherne, 1921–1961
The floods are risen, O Lord, the floods have lift up their voice…
The waves of the sea are mighty, and rage horribly:
but yet the Lord, who dwelleth on high, is mightier.

He stood there, frowning, thinking. He ran his mind's eye along the shelves of poetry up at the farm. A yellowing volume, long out of print, bound in worn green cloth –

'Excuse me –'

The woman from the wilderness turned. Her headscarf had fallen and hung about her neck; her hair, in the chill of the church, was a mad damp frizz. She looked feverish and on edge.

'Yes?'

'I'm sorry to disturb you,' he said again. 'I'm just wondering – Edward Traherne. The name is familiar to me. He was a poet?'

'Yes,' said Gillian. And then: 'He was my father.'

'Your father.' He shook his head. 'How extraordinary.'

A couple of footnotes, lines in a reference book. Buried in the churchyard in Penglydr. Descendant of –

– *orient and immortal wheat…*

'Thomas Traherne,' he said slowly. 'Does he have anything to do with –'

'Yes,' said Gillian, and something deep within her moved, and fell into place, and settled there. He had heard of them. He knew. 'We are descended from his brother.'

'Well, well, well.' How had he not made this connection? He had been to book sales, and spent long evenings reading; he had been to the village, buying provisions, ironmongery, papers. And still he had not visited the church, nor made the connection –

Well. He had had a great deal to think about, a lot to do. That was all you could say, and it was true.

'My father is buried in the churchyard,' said the woman from the wilderness.

'Yes. I must go and look.'

'I'll show you, if you like.'

'That would be kind.'

She came edging out of the pew: he stood aside for her.

'Gillian?' called Phoebe from the altar steps.

'I'm just going to show –' she turned to him, her face aflame. 'I don't know your name.'

'Edward,' he told her. 'Funnily enough. Edward Sullivan.'

Of course. Of course it would be. She looked back at Phoebe, and her hands shook. 'I'm just going to show Edward Sullivan the grave,' she said, and her voice was shaking, too.

'Oh?' A flicker of a frown.

'He knows about it.'

'Oh.'

Edward took a step towards the altar. 'Is that all right? I've read about your husband, just a little – I hope I'm not –'

'Of course. Go ahead. I must finish in here, I'm afraid.'

'Such a shame,' said Gwen, lifting dripping stems. 'He was a lovely person.'

'He is never spoken of,' said Gillian, rediscovering what she had known from the moment she and the visitor had met, out in the garden on an autumn afternoon, the smoke from the bonfire rising in a thin blue spire to heaven: she could say anything to this man.

'Mind, it's a long time ago,' said Gwen.

'Well,' said Edward. 'Shall we –'

'Don't forget to sign the visitors' book,' called Phoebe.

'What? No, no, of course not.'

It lay with the prayer books on the table at the back: large, black, open. Signatures from far afield: he added his, and the name of the farm. Gillian glanced at it, walked to the door, held it open, shivering.

The morning's mist had risen, but the grass was still wet and moisture clung to the yew trees. They walked down the path towards the right-hand wall, covered in ivy and moss. Somebody cycled past, but the churchyard was empty, now. People were having their lunch.

'There,' said Gillian.

He saw a tall plain stone, and simple lettering. He saw the single word. Lichen crept round it. He looked, once again, at the dates. He looked at Gillian, standing next to him, her headscarf pulled up against the raw air, her face pinched and bluish, now they were outside.

'You were –'

'I was three. Three and a half.'

'I'm sorry.'

'There was a flood. He drowned.' She bent down and brushed a few leaves from the grass. There was a place to set flowers, a round metal lid with holes, but there were no flowers.

'Can you remember him?'

'Yes. Some things.' She straightened up. 'I remember the day he died. I write at his desk.'

'You write?'

'Oh, yes. His mantle is upon me.' She smiled, wryly.

They had come to the place where the paths met: ahead was the lych gate; beyond, she could see the Land Rover, and the dog in the back, waiting.

'Well.' Edward stopped, and took a last look at the church. The watery sun came in and out behind the spire, a magpie flew up to the weather vane. 'We must meet again. You must come up to the farm one day.' He realised he had told her nothing about himself, and she had not asked. They didn't, round here, it was one of the reasons he liked it. 'I've been here about a year,' he said. 'I'm busy doing the place up, getting it going. I have a few sheep, there's a lot to do –' He did not mention Rowland: you had to be careful, still, in the country. People talked, and people were wary. He said: 'I go to book sales sometimes, that's how I came across your father. I just didn't make the connection, it was foolish –'

'And Thomas Traherne? How do you know about him?'

'I've always known about him – since university, anyway. The country parson from Hereford. The visionary poet.' He smiled, he held out his hand. 'Tonight I shall reacquaint myself with both of them. And I hope one day with you.'

'Thank you.' They shook hands: even through the worn green wool, he could feel how cold she was.

'Bad circulation,' she said drily. 'I've written a poem about it.'

'I shall look forward to reading it. Well: goodbye.'

'Goodbye.'

He turned and walked to the gate. Someone was coming along the road, up the hill from the village; a car went past. Gillian said suddenly:

'Edward?'

He turned to her. 'Yes?'

'I might give a reading. Will you come?'

'Yes,' he said. 'I should like that.'

And then he had opened the lych gate, and then he was gone.

Gillian stood watching him greet the dog, and go round to the front. She watched him clamber in, and drive away. A hand came out of the window, raised in farewell.

She was frozen. Her feet were frozen. She walked back along the smooth grey path to the grave, and she stood before it. The churchyard was quiet and still. She could hear the river, distant but insistent, making its way behind the village. The water was cold, the water was icy, the water had risen and risen –

'Gillian!' called Phoebe, out at the west door. 'What are you up to? We have to clear up, come along.'

8

Frost glittered in patches on the path leading up to the Hall, on the grassy sweep of the grounds, the smooth trunks of beech trees. Inside, oil-fired radiators sent up a shimmer of heat beneath the mullioned windows, the narrow glass of the chapel. No ferny patterns for the children to gaze at, or etch with fumbling fingernails when they woke up, but they had to be warm.

Nesta, just on duty, on night watch tonight, was helping the Blue Room to start the day.

> 'This is the way we brush our teeth,
> On a cold and frosty morning.'

Heads lolled in turn over the basin, saliva and toothpaste and water swirled away.

'Good girl,' said Nesta, as Nadine, new and afraid, brought her scarlet toothbrush wavering towards her open mouth. 'That's it, can I give you a bit of a hand there? Good girl. And spit. And rinse. Well done.'

Steven, in his wheelchair, flailed a hand and grunted. Dominic wouldn't let Nesta near him. He squirmed and twisted and made incoherent noises.

'I know,' said Nesta, trying again. 'Had a bad night? Come on, Dominic, let's get it over with, hey?'

Dominic made roaring sounds, picked up his sweater and hurled it across the room.

'Everything okay?' Martin, sharing the shift, looked in at the doorway. 'Good morning, Dominic. How are things?'

'Give us a hand.' Nesta threw him the sweater.

'I heard sweet singing,' he said, catching it. 'Right, Dominic, let's have a go.'

Dominic tolerated Martin, and let him. Nesta brushed Steven's tufts of hair.

'This is the way we brush our hair, brush our hair –'

'Sweet,' said Martin again.

'Shut up.'

From open doors all along the landing came the sounds of running water, cupboard doors opened and shut, children calling and groaning. The busiest time of the day, the whole house engaged in it, an hour of tasks to accomplish before descending to the refectory: by the chair lift, humming up and down the broad staircase; by the main lifts, holding one chair at a time; or by the stairs themselves, which some of the children, clutching on to the banister, could manage alone.

We are a special community, serving children with special needs, with a wide range of abilities, and disabilities . . .

'Right, then,' said Nesta, straightening up from the last pair of shoes on the footplate. 'Who wants breakfast?'

Some of the children could wheel themselves, Rachel not at all. Dominic could help to push her, but often wouldn't; like others who were quite capable of dressing themselves and helping others, but who threw their clothes around the room or trailed toothpaste all along the carpet, or pulled people's hair or pissed down the side of the toilet.

Some of our children have psychological or emotional difficulties. Cadair seeks to integrate, to create an atmosphere of warmth and trust and purpose where each individual can reach the fullest potential . . .

Nesta wheeled Rachel out along the corridor, and up to the first lift, where others were waiting. Some of the children – those who often woke in the night – had rooms to themselves, the old single rooms of the nuns, simple and bare. There were changes: each nun had a chair and a table – these went, from the rooms needing space for a wheelchair. The nuns had white walls, no pictures. The children had bright colours, posters and prints. There were bears and soft toys, bitten and chewed and flung about, clumsily caressed. There was an alarm system wired to every room, pitched for the slightest cry. The nuns slept in solitude. A number of children, like those in the Blue Room, slept in groups. Cells had been knocked through, three or four together, making small dormitories, filled with light from the windows overlooking the grounds or courtyard.

We seek to create an atmosphere where each of our children can enjoy the warmth and benefits of a family life, when perhaps their own family can no longer give as much as they would like . . .

The chair lift hummed up the staircase, empty, and came to a halt. Maureen, from the Yellow Room, clambered clumsily into it, and jabbed the button. She could have walked down the stairs, but she loved the ride, and when she was strapped in went down smiling, holding on, passing the Christmas tree set in the stairwell. The tree was sixteen feet tall, and had gone up yesterday. The hall smelt of pine, strong and sweet, and today they would string on the lights.

'And today,' said Nesta, wheeling Rachel into the lift, 'we're going to put up the decorations.'

They sat around tables in the art room, or worked on the plastic trays clipped to their wheelchairs, cutting and daubing and sticking: paper and card and scraps of felt and fabric, phials of gold and silver glitter, spillproof pots of glue. They made angels and animals and stars and bells and candles, stuck with red ribbon to hang on the branches. They dropped coloured pasta and pulses on to paper plates smeared with glue, and shook out the glitter. Blunt-tipped scissors sawed laboriously at sugar paper, tongues protruded, lentils and beads and buttons fell to the floor and scrunched beneath moving wheels.

Some of the children did some of these things. Others were in the kitchen, cutting out biscuits, shaking on sugar, pressing stars. Those who could do none of these things sat beside those who could, making noises. They banged on the trays on their wheelchairs, they clutched at shakers and rattlers and dropped them, their hands hit their faces and the arms of their wheelchairs, their feet jerked off the footplates. Nesta and her fellow workers moved from child to child. Outside the frost was melting, the sky light. Sparrows and starlings and blackbirds flew to the bird table down on the lawn, tits swung from coconuts and pecked at pots of fat. 'Look,' said Nesta, going to the window. She wheeled Rachel to see them; Maureen came lumbering over. She stood by the garden door, shifting from foot to flat foot.

'Robin. Robin come.' Her slanting eyes behind thick glasses lit up with pleasure. She was almost sixteen and looked twelve, short square body in skirt and jumper, short straight hair fastened back with a hairslide. She responded to everything: music and painting and birds in the garden. 'Robin come, robin come.'

'Do you want to make a robin?' asked Nesta. 'Shall we put it on the tree?'

They finished him just as the gong went for lunch, a bird the size of a duck, and rather resembling one.

'Very nice,' said Nesta. 'Let's write your name.'

Maureen leaned over the paper, breathing hard, grasping a thick black pencil. Uneven letters dug into the paper, deep in the robin's breast.

After lunch the children rested, and Nesta, on night watch since ten, was off duty. In the afternoon the tree was to be decorated; at dusk they would switch on the lights, and sing carols.

'Wake me,' she said to Martin, leaving the table. 'I don't want to miss it.'

She climbed the stairs, and went to her room. The night-watch room, furnished chastely as a nun's: bed, chair and table. Along the landing, murmurs came from open doorways, then it was quiet. Nesta slept.

She was woken by a tap at the door, and sat bolt upright, ready to go.

'Yes?'

'It's all right,' said Martin, opening the door. 'It's only me.' He set a mug of tea on the table. 'Four o'clock.'

'Thanks.' Nesta sank back to the pillows, reached for the light.

'Had a bit of a rest? You sounded on red alert.'

'Mmm. You know what it's like.' She picked up the tea. 'What's happening?'

'We've done the tree, we're gathering, but there's no rush. See you down there in about ten minutes?'

'OK. Thanks.'

He went out, closing the door. Nesta drank her tea, slowly coming to. From downstairs she could hear unsteady footsteps, the squeak of wheelchairs, rising voices. She turned to look at the window; the sky was black. She switched off the light for a moment, blinked, and saw the first stars. She finished her tea standing at the window, pulling herself together, looking down on the courtyard, lit by the outside lamps, where the frost had formed again, sparkling on the dark slate roofs. Already it felt like night, and a whole broken night lay ahead.

We are looking for an experienced therapist willing to enter into every aspect of our shared life . . .

Nesta, in Camden Town, had sat reading the job description in her empty flat.

I qualified in 1986 ... I have wide experience ... She had spent two evenings after work filling in the application form.

I have been bereaved and broken. I am recovering. I need to change my life –

Rain fell on the square of garden, where the bulbs were coming up. She and Hal had planted them, the first autumn. This was the first year he wouldn't see them.

I was used to sharing my life with my husband. We both shared our work with our colleagues, as part of a team. Now he has gone I have had to learn some independence, and perhaps am reluctant to let it go entirely. Might we discuss the possibility of my living outside the community? I should need to sell my flat ...

She yawned and drew the curtains, shutting out the frosty darkness. When she got back to the cottage after her nights on duty she'd sleep and sleep. She thought of the leafless garden, the path leading up to the front door, warping with winter weather. The cottage would be freezing at first. Tempting to stay here, with central heating and companionship –

The voices from downstairs were growing louder. On the piano, someone was trying out 'Hark the Herald', someone sang loudly, out of tune, and there was laughter. Nesta went out to the bathroom, and down the broad staircase.

'Just in time,' said Martin, looking up.

The children and staff were gathering round the tree, which was hung with the morning's decorations. Paper stars and candles, animals and birds and lanterns stirred with every movement. Maureen's bird was a triumph. Tall white candles had been lit, but the hall lights were still on.

'Everyone here now?'

'Sorry I'm late.' Nesta found a place beside a wheelchair. Rachel, within it, rocked back and forth.

'Not at all. Right, then. Sssh, everyone. Claire?'

Claire, by the door to the kitchen passage, nodded, and switched the lights off. Darkness, and murmurs and noises.

'Look at the candles.'

High on the stern slate mantelpiece, and across on the piano, the candles stood straight and white and beautiful, haloes of light shimmering round each flame in the dark. There came a perceptible hush.

'Jonathan?'

Jonathan, kneeling down by the tree, nodded, and reached for the switch on the skirting board. Flick. On came the lights of the tree. They were pale and starry and they shone all the way to the top: from deep within the bushy lower branches, out to the tips of the spread at its widest, winding through the upper branches and all round the rough bare stem, ending in a single, shining light.

A murmur of pleasure. The children craned their necks, moved forward, reaching out. The paper decorations twirled and swung.

'Claire?'

Claire, at the piano, nodded and began to play. The first notes of 'O Little Town of Bethlehem' sounded into the quietness. Then the staff, and some of the children, began to sing.

> ' "O little town of Bethlehem,
> How still we see thee lie.
> Above thy deep and dreamless sleep
> The silent stars go by..." '

The voices of the grown-ups were steady and sure; the children joined in, tuneless and enthusiastic. Tambourines and shakers sounded, hands beat on trays; as the verse ended, Maureen lurched over to the piano, stabbing joyfully at the keys.

Night watch. Nesta, fully clothed, daring to doze beneath the eiderdown, woke with a start.

A cry, loud and disjointed –

'I'm here.'

Legs swung off the narrow bed, feet into shoes, out along the landing, dimly lit. The cry became a rhythm –

'Ba-ba, ba-ba –'

'I'm coming.'

The doors to each room stood ajar, all night; lights, very low, were kept on all night. But Nesta knew, without checking, who was making those sounds.

'Ba-ba, ba-ba, ba-ba, ba –'

'Here I am.'

Rocking, rocking, beating on the bedclothes, heavy head with pudding-basin haircut going back and forth, back and forth –

'It's all right, Rachel. It's all right.'

Rachel: a grave, sensible name, betokening competence and grace. Nesta sat down on the side of the bed and took disconnected, overweight, brain-damaged Rachel into her arms.

'There we are, there we are...'

'Ba-ba, ba-ba, ba-ba –'

'Ba-ba, ba-ba, ba-ba.' Nesta held her close.

They rocked back and forth in the glow of the nightlight. Nesta felt carefully beneath the bedclothes. Rachel's nappy was dry: it wasn't that which had woken her. A sound? A dream? How did disconnected, ten-year-old Rachel dream?

Back and forth, back and forth.

'Slowly,' said Nesta, after a while, resisting. 'Slowly, slowly, ssshh, ssh –'

'Ba-ba-ba-ba –'

'Sssh, sssh, sssh –'

Slowly and more slowly. The heavy head lolled against Nesta's shoulder.

'Better now?'

Asleep.

Nesta, yawning, disengaged herself, and gently laid Rachel down. Rachel's mouth was open, full lips slack; she breathed thickly, and her limbs twitched. Nesta smoothed the bedclothes, smoothed the blunt dark hair. She looked at her watch. Just after two-fifteen. She crept from the room.

In the staff bathroom, a gaunt woman with messy hennaed hair stared back at her from the mirror.

You wouldn't much like the look of me now, she told Hal, pouring a glass of water.

I didn't look too good myself, last time you saw me.

True. She drained the glass. Christmas is always the worst bloody time. Why couldn't you have died on a Bank Holiday Monday, or something? Wouldn't feel it so much then.

Yes you would.

True.

Out on the landing she stood for a moment, listening.

Snores and irregular breathing; the whole house sunk in sleep. The scent of the Christmas tree hung in the air; she leaned on the balustrade and looked down on the shadowy hall. Pine needles dropped to the floor in the silence; she could see, through the fanlight over the oak front door, stars in an inky sky. She thought: I am the only person awake in this house, perhaps in the whole valley. She moved, and the floorboards beneath the carpet creaked. Below, the hall clock struck the half-hour, a single mellow note. Nesta thought: in another hour, when the nuns were here, they would have been

97

woken, for Matins and Lauds. Doors would have opened, all along the corridors, full of damp and draughts. She thought of the cold, the silence broken by the rustling procession of white to the chapel, the shimmering candles and shivering women, the fine high voices, chanting the hours of the night.

The house was centrally heated now, there were carpets and curtains and piping hot water, but it could still be cold, and in places draughty, and hearing, now, a creak from the floor above her, where the staff bedrooms were, it was not hard to imagine a ghostly footfall, a lost and wandering spirit.

Nesta, listening, knew that some people awake in a sleeping household, hearing noises, would be fearful, but she felt no fear, as she walked back to the night-watch room, logged Rachel's waking in the open book on the table, lay down on the narrow bed. The worst thing that could happen to her had happened.

She slept, fighting sleep, and was woken, moments later, by a cry.

She drove home two days later through the frozen valley. The fields and hills lay white in the morning sun, and the sky was a hard and glittering blue. Nesta drove slowly, because thin patches of ice still lay in the lanes, but she wanted to drive fast, because the light was so beautiful and strong. She played a tape. Her fingers beat on the wheel and her silver earrings swung.

She looked out across the valley as the road climbed high, at glistening barn roofs and square-towered churches, at the fine straight line and pleasing arches of the disused viaduct, the dry-stone walls and clumps of trees. The river wound through the valley floor, as brilliant this morning as the sun, and somewhere on the other side was the place where Gillian lived.

Nesta, in the mirror, could no longer see Cadair Hall. She came down to level ground, and drove through the village which was now her village, where she bought essentials. And out, on towards the cottage, passing the Feathers. She came to the turn-off and bumped down the lane, rutted and hard, to the gate ahead, overlooking farmland, and the wicket gate in the hedge, which was hers. She pulled up, and switched off the engine, and the tape.

'Here I am,' she said aloud, getting out into the frosty silence.

Sheep crowded up to the field gate, bleating hard. 'I have nothing for you,' she told them, and clicked her own gate open, surveying the sloping garden. In the far corner stood the beehive, and within it the bees, which she had not yet seen, and did not know how to handle. Well. There was plenty of time. The beehive was silent and still, and the boughs of the apple trees leafless and black, but in the spring –

She went up the path to her door, and unlocked it, hearing the brush of the wood against letters and cards on the mat, as she pushed it open.

She could feel, even before she went over the threshold, the chill of the place. It might have been daunting, but it was not. There was no one waiting for her, and she wanted no one. There were the children and her colleagues at Cadair: this was her quiet retreat.

She bent to pick up her post, pushing the door to; she carried it through to the sitting room, which smelt, faintly, of incense, and cold ash in the hearth. Cards from London: she knew the writing on almost all of them. And a card posted locally, the envelope written in black ink in a cramped and spiky hand she did not recognise. Still in her jacket she went through to the little kitchen at the back; turned on the boiler, filled the kettle. The floor was quarry-tiled and the room so cold she could see her breath. The window here, as in the bathroom, had a metal frame: beyond, she could see the hungry sheep, returning from the gate to their empty hayrick, bending their heads to the winter grass. The farmer came each afternoon at about three, before it began to grow dark. Nesta looked forward to his visits, the days she was here, almost as much as the sheep: her farmer, from whom she had bought the cottage; her beehive, her place in the local scheme of things.

You're doing nicely, said Hal, as she made her apple and rosehip tea; she carried it through to the sitting room and picked up his paper knife. The scent of the steaming tea was cheering: she sipped it, slit open her letters and cards. Who was this cramped and barely legible person? It was Gillian, she suddenly knew it, even before she had slipped out the card, and read the invitation.

Nesta Frank. You are invited to a reading of recent poems, in the upper room of The Fox, Penglydr, on 4 January at 8 p.m. I regret that I am unable to provide refreshment.
Gillian Traherne

Nesta smiled. She opened the rest of her post and read the news from London. She put all the brightly coloured Christmas cards on the mantelpiece, and Gillian's card, a square of white as plain and uncompromising as a nun, leaning against a candlestick amongst them.

'I like you,' she said aloud. 'You interest me.'

You've said that before, said Hal.

Then it must mean something, said Nesta. And don't you think I'm right?

I often think you're right. And yes, I agree.

Nesta smiled again. She swept up the ash from the hearth and laid a new fire, she made another mug of tea and carried it up to the bathroom, where she lay in piping water, looking at the photographs from another life.

Christmas approached, and the weather was sharp and bright. Then came one or two days of unaccountable mildness; the sky pale, the ground damp from the melting frost, the air smelling of earth again, and full of birdsong.

Gillian stood in her coat in the hall, looking again at the map. Tremynydd. The name had once been any name, the small grey print and faded lines of fields and footpaths like those marking a dozen farms, between worn creases, and rust marks from pins. Now, as her eyes went straight towards it, the single word said calmly: I am here. I have always been here. She traced the route with her finger. Down to the village, out and up the lanes towards Llanfonen, climbing high above the valley. Then left, passing only fields, leaving behind all human habitation, until, with a couple of twists in the lane –

'Gillian?'

She crossed the tiles to the front door. Flop came a Christmas card on to the mat. She pushed it aside with her foot.

'Where are you off to?'

'Just for a walk.'

Phoebe came down the hall from the kitchen, holding a mug of tea. 'You're up early.'

'I couldn't sleep.'

'Whyever not?'

Gillian did not answer. She pulled the door open.

'There's a Christmas card.'

'What?'

'A card. Down by your foot.'

Gillian looked.

'Pick it up.'

She picked it up, and passed it.

'And do shut the door.' Phoebe slit open the envelope. 'Who's this from?'

Gillian went out to the porch and pulled on her Wellingtons. Sparrows flew in and out of the hedge across the lane, full of energy and hope. The door behind her opened.

'You haven't had any breakfast.'

'I'm not hungry.'

'Are you going down to the village?'

'No.'

'Because, if you are, there's a list.'

'I'm not.' She made for the wooden gate. 'Sorry.'

The door closed sharply behind her.

And now it was mid-morning, and now she was almost there. The walking had done her good: not too much exertion, as bicycling, after her illness, would have been, but a good steady pace, her footsteps a quiet rhythm in the empty lanes. When she looked to her right she could see all the familiar places of her childhood – the village and church and winding river, the neighbouring farms, the viaduct and white octagonal chapel roof of the distant convent, which was no longer a convent, but Nesta's school – and when she looked up she could see the buzzard, as she had always seen him, circling high, watchful as the eye of God.

She rounded a bend, and heard hammering. She slowed, and stopped.

She knew every place on the map, every house in the village, but this farm she did not know: her walks and bicycle rides had taken her along the straight and narrow, and out across the valley, but rarely up high to the west. Around the next bend lay unfamiliar territory, and perhaps she should not be there, would not be welcome.

The hammering stopped, and started again. On the telegraph wire running along to the right above her, a jackdaw lifted his tail and dropped a grey-green splash to the grass. He looked at her with sharp metallic eye. Beyond him the buzzard soared higher, became a speck, was gone.

The jackdaw raised his wings and left her.

There was no one to know what she did.

She rounded the bend, seeing through bare trees the slate roofs of

101

the farm to her left, and Edward up on an outbuilding, rolling out blue plastic sheeting, banging in nails. She walked on, she came to the gate.

Tremynydd, on a metal plate. The Land Rover, parked in the yard. And a dog, barking wildly, racing down towards her.

'Tarn!' The hammering stopped. There was a ladder, propped against the wall. Gillian, long ago, tilting a ladder, had smashed into pieces a pane from the greenhouse: long broken shards of glass and drops of blood lay on the ground and Phoebe had come running.

Jacob had dreamed of a ladder, laying his head upon stones in the field –

The dog at the gate was racing back and forth, tongue lolling. Gillian stood and waited.

'Tarn!'

Edward was climbing down. He came through the yard towards her.

'Hello. What a nice surprise.' He bent to hold the dog's collar with one hand, lifted the latch with the other. 'Come on in.'

'You're busy –' she indicated the ladder, the roof, the plastic sheet.

'No, not at all, I could do with a break.' He straightened up, and the gate swung wide. 'Please.' She came in over the mud, and he said, 'Don't mind the dog, she's just excited.'

'That is what all dog owners say,' said Gillian. She walked through the open gate to the farmyard. The dog strained towards her, wagging her tail.

'You're not afraid? She just wants to get to know you.' Edward kicked the gate to, and it clanged shut. Gillian held out a fist in woollen gloves. The dog smelt it, grew calmer, was released.

'Go on, off you go.' Edward looked at Gillian. 'Well. Can I offer you a coffee?'

'Thank you.' She walked up the yard beside him, her hands in her pockets, looking about her.

'Much warmer today,' said Edward.

'Yes.'

'Have you walked all the way here?'

'Yes.' Her hands in the woollen gloves were uncomfortably warm; she took them out and did not know what to do with them. The dog was following, nose to the ground in her footsteps; sheep called from behind the house.

'I'm so pleased you've come – I've been looking at your father's poems.'

'Oh. Good.' She felt a rush of pleasure.

They had come to the front door.

Edward opened it, and stood aside. 'Please. Go on in.'

Gillian did not know how to precede a man into a house. Beyond the coconut matting and the coat-hooks was a passage of bare floorboards, laid with rugs. Doors stood open, the walls were lined with pictures. She had the fleeting impression that she was entering a town house, though she knew little about town houses, and wiped her feet on the mat repeatedly, not knowing where to go.

'Straight ahead,' said Edward behind her, pulling his boots off.

'Shall I –' She gestured at her own boots, and the dog went past her, tail moving slowly from side to side, making for a door on the left.

'Well. Yes. And let me take your coat.'

Gillian bent down, and pulled her boots off. She took off her gloves, and her coat, which was a part of her, and stood in her socks on the floorboards as Edward hung it up next to his jacket. Sunlight fell on the polished boards and the rugs from the open doors; she glimpsed, as she went nakedly down the passage, bookshelves and a polished table.

'To your left,' said Edward. 'Follow that dog.'

She went into the kitchen, and the clock on the wall struck ten.

'My grandfather's clock. Truly. Basket, Tarn.' Edward pulled out a chair at the table, and Gillian sat there without boots or coat or gloves. She pulled at a long thread of wool in the sleeve of her cardigan, and felt it unravel, and make a hole.

The clock struck the last notes. Edward put the kettle on. Beyond the kitchen window, high ground made the room quite dark. Sheep and hens moved over the sloping field; there was a hen house, a hayrack.

'How do you like your coffee?' asked Edward, shaking beans into the grinder.

'We always have instant. Well – we don't drink much coffee.'

'I'm sorry – would you rather have tea?'

'I suppose I would.' Gillian looked at him. 'Is that rude?'

'Not in the least. I should have asked you.' He reached for a tin from the shelf beside the Rayburn: a smart, modern-looking tin in black and gold. There was nothing like that at home. At home, there was a box of Tetley's tea bags. She looked round: at the table, where

103

spectacles rested upon a pile of papers; at the mantelpiece, full of Christmas cards, the dresser, full of china, and more cards. Newspapers were neatly stacked in corners, there was a shelf of cookbooks, the floor was swept.

'Do you approve?'

Gillian flushed. 'What do you mean?'

'Just that. Do you like it?'

'This room?'

'This room.' He was smiling, pouring boiling water into a pot.

'I do not have opinions about rooms,' said Gillian. 'I am not that sort of person.'

'I see.' He set down the pot on the table, brought mugs and milk and sugar. 'But you're observant.'

'Am I?' She pulled at the thread in her sleeve, and the hole grew larger.

'Aren't you?' He sat down, and looked at her easily. Behind him, the dog stirred, and her basket creaked. 'You're a poet. Aren't you required to observe?'

'That's different. I don't go to people's houses and make judgements.' She wound a long thread of wool round her finger. 'Well. I don't go to people's houses very often.' Just Nesta's house, full of clutter, and attar of roses.

'Then I'm honoured.' Edward nodded towards her finger, and the widening hole. 'Alas, you are undone.'

She looked down at the sleeve. 'Oh dear.'

Tie a knot, said Phoebe. Tie a knot, quickly, before it goes any further.

Gillian unwound the length of wool, and looked at it, and did not know what to do with it. She poked the end into the hole, and left it.

She said: 'I'm pleased you've been reading my father's work. I came to invite you to a reading.' She felt in the pocket of her cardigan, and placed a white envelope on the table between them. 'I have made out a card.'

'Well. How very nice.' Edward reached for the glasses resting on a newspaper. He opened the envelope. Gillian watched him do these things, and took pleasure in it. Then he began to read the card aloud, and she looked down at her tea and stirred it round and round.

' "Edward Sullivan. You are invited to a reading of recent poems, in the upper room of The Fox, Penglydr, on 4 January at 8 p.m. I regret that I am unable to provide refreshment. Gillian Traherne." '

He looked at her over his spectacles. 'How charming. Thank you. I am delighted to accept.'

'Good.' The spoon continued its progress, all round the rim of the world.

'May I ask – since I am still fairly new here, and don't know many people – who else might be there?'

'Local people. Anyone in the Fox that evening who shows an interest. I would invite the vicar, but he's dead. Our old vicar, I mean, who knew my father. The one we have now is different. He is a man of the cloth, but not of the spirit.'

Edward raised an eyebrow. Gillian drank her tea.

'I have invited my new editor, but it seems foolish to expect that he might wish to come all the way up from London in midwinter.'

'He might well. It is just the sort of thing he should be doing.'

'We shall see. And I have invited one new acquaintance, a woman called Nesta Frank. She works in a school on the other side of the valley, near Minchen Crib. I don't know if you have come across her.'

He shook his head.

'Well. I have sent her a card. She is a person of intelligence, with attractive qualities.' Gillian paused. 'I am unused to mixing with people.' Another pause. 'The school where she works – Cadair Hall – was once a place of significance to me –'

'Because?'

'It was once a convent.'

Edward waited. 'Perhaps you will tell me more about that on another occasion.'

'Perhaps I shall. So.' She finished her tea and put down her mug. 'Not a very large gathering. If there is anyone you would like to bring –'

'Well – yes, I was wondering if that would – if I might bring a friend. The person with whom I share the house.'

Gillian frowned. 'I did not realise –'

'He's not always here, he spends most of his time in London. I'm not even sure if he'd be able to come –' Edward pushed his chair back and rose to look at a calendar, hung on a nail by the phone. Already, Gillian observed, next year's lay beneath this one, and was full of engagements. Edward lifted it down. 'January 4th – yes, I think that's OK. Good. Would that be all right?'

'Of course. Is he – does he take an interest in poetry?'

'He takes an interest in many things, but he is a singer. Rowland

King.' Edward paused, waiting for some recognition. 'With the London Consort. They're sometimes on the television, I don't know if you've ever –'

Gillian's face was blank. 'We do not have a television,' she said. 'My mother listens to the radio a great deal, it is possible that she –'

'Well, never mind. I'm sure you will meet him in due course.' He put back the calendar. 'More tea?'

'No, thank you.' In the field beyond the window the sheep were tugging at the hayrack, winter fleeces caked in mud, bodies heavy and full. She said: 'Will you be lambing?'

'Yes. That's why I was up on the roof – patching up before they're brought in.'

'It's a lot of work. I mustn't keep you –' She made to rise.

'You mustn't go yet. I want to talk to you about your father, your family – will you come and have a look at my library? As it is laughingly called. I'm building up a collection of local writers – if I had had my wits about me I should have made the connection between your father and Penglydr long ago. Please.'

He made a gesture.

She followed him out of the room.

The narrow farmhouse corridor was darker, now that the front door was closed, but gleams of sun from the upper landing, and from the library, fell on the threadbare rugs, biscuit and blue and orange, faded tapestry colours.

Rather nice, said Phoebe.

Go away, said Gillian. You have no business here.

Edward, ahead of her, had pushed the door wide: she stopped to look at a print, the kind of brooding landscape of Wales which the English liked to buy. When she went in, he was up by the bookshelves and the room now was full of the morning sun. She looked round: at the table, the shining windows. Out in the yard the blue tarpaulin lifted and flapped in a sudden gust of wind, but in here was stillness, and order, and peace.

He pulled out a book she had known since childhood, bound in worn green cloth. He smiled at her, as she approached.

'So, Gillian. Here.'

He said her name; he put his hand on her shoulder; he drew her into the sun.

They sat side by side at the polished table, the books before them. Edward picked up the volume bound in worn green cloth.

'*The Eye of Understanding.* This is your father.'

'Yes.'

His study smelt of damp and dust; a fire burned in the grate, consuming discarded lines. He moved along the bookshelves, sniffing the pages, marking passages; he sat smoking at his desk, looking out of the window. Lambs bleated, catkins shook –

Edward opened the book, and turned the pages. 'He has taken the title from – here it is –

' "The prospect of the Feilds or silent Heavens . . . the Skies adorned with Stars, and the feilds covered with corn and flocks of sheep and Cattel . . ." '

' "When the Ey of your Understanding shineth upon them, they are yours in Him, and all your Joys," ' said Gillian.

He looked at her.

'You know it by heart.'

'Of course.'

'It's very beautiful.' He turned back to the page. '*Centuries of Meditations.* Thomas Traherne, 1637–74. And here he is.' He picked up another book from the table. The jacket was old and blue, and had been torn and mended, in yellowing Sellotape. Slips of paper marked the pages. From the front, Edward took out a sheet, covered in fine black writing. 'I was making a few notes the other evening,' he said. 'Refreshing my memory. After we met in the church.'

Gillian looked, and saw names and dates. Her name.

' "Thomas Traherne: son of a Hereford shoemaker," ' Edward read aloud. ' "Orphaned at an early age, but writes of infant happiness. Oxford 1653, ordained 1660. Rector of Credenhill, outside Hereford, until 1669. Metaphysical poems, visionary meditations: *The Centuries.* 'Orient and immortal wheat, which never should be reaped, nor was ever sown. I thought it had stood from everlasting to everlasting . . .' " '

He turned to her. 'Those are the lines which are best remembered?'

'Yes. But he's mostly forgotten.'

Edward turned to his notes again, pushing up his spectacles. ' "Chaplain to Sir Orlando Bridgeman, Lord Keeper of the Great Seal, 1669–74. Household in Teddington. Died there, aged 37." '

'Of the smallpox,' said Gillian.

A morning in late September. Autumn sun at leaded windows, the gardener sweeping leaves. A house by the river. A fire in the grate and a glass upon the table, smeared with half-dissolved powders.

A thin sick man in a linen nightshirt, propped against the pillows. John Berdo, gentleman, is seated at the bedside, taking down the will –

'"I desire my Lady Bridgman and her daughter the Lady Charlott should have each of them a Ring . . . and to Mary the Laundry maid ffyve shillings and to all the rest of the servants half a crowne apeece . . ."'

'I didn't know it was smallpox,' said Edward.

'There is a great deal about Traherne that is not known. The date of his birth is uncertain. So is his parentage. It is possible that the shoemaker was his half-brother John, who brought him up after the father's death, with his little brother Philip.'

You see? said Phoebe. You were always quite capable of absorbing information when you chose.

'Philip,' said Edward, turning back to the book. 'The brother to whom Thomas left all his books. I like his will.'

There are others present in the sickroom, servants of the house who will be witnesses. A stray beam of sunlight touches the medicine glass, there is the rustle of skirts –

'"My best Hatt I give it to my brother Philipp And sister [speaking to Mrs Susan Traherne the wife of his brother Philipp, which Susan was then present] I desire you would keep it for him. And all the rest of my Clothes that is worth your acceptance I give to you . . . All my books I give to my brother Philipp . . ."'

Edward's finger skimmed down the lines. 'It's touching, don't you think?'

'Yes,' said Gillian, 'but Philip was not a worthy beneficiary. He got above himself when it came to the poems. He rewrote and tampered.'

'Yes, that's in here, in the Introduction.' Edward tapped the book. 'He lived to a ripe old age, I gather. He travelled, he became Minister of Wimborne Minster, he had a family – it is from him that you and your father are descended?'

'I believe so, yes. Thomas never married. I should like to be able to claim a more directly poetic descent.'

'Philip tampering with the work – you would find that unforgivable.'

'Most people would find it unforgivable.' Gillian looked at the volume held in Edward's hands. 'It is *The Centuries* which are so fine. Where did you find that copy?'

'On a bookstall near the Barbican, I think. Do you know that part of London?'

'I don't know any part of London. I have never been there.'

'Are you serious?'

'Yes.'

Edward shook his head, smiling.

'Well, how very refreshing. I couldn't wait to leave it, I must say. But Rowland still has his flat there. I go down at weekends sometimes, if he can't get here.'

'You must be very good friends.'

He looked at her. 'Yes.'

Clouds had gathered, and the sun was fitful now. A window pane rattled in a gust of wind; out in the yard the blue tarpaulin lifted again, and flapped about. Edward cast an eye towards it.

'I am detaining you,' said Gillian.

'How nicely you speak. No. Not at all. I am enjoying myself. So long as the rain keeps off. Well. Where were we?'

'On a London bookstall. Leaving the city.'

'Yes. And I found such a nice passage here the other night.' He turned the pages, looked at his notes, found a slip of paper. 'Here we are. It spoke to me directly. See if you like this – or perhaps you know it already.

'"When I came into the Country, and being seated among silent Trees, had all my Time in my own Hands, I resolved to Spend it all, whatever it cost me, in Search of Happiness, and to Satiat that burning Thirst which Nature had enkindled, in me from my Youth. In which I was so resolut, that I chose rather to live upon 10 pounds a yeer, and to go in Lether Clothes, and feed upon Bread and Water, so that I might have all my time clearly to my self: than to keep many thousands per Annum in an Estate of Life where my Time would be Devoured in Care and Labour..."' He looked at her over his spectacles. 'Not that running a farm is devoid of care and labour, you understand.'

'Go on.'

'"And God was so pleased to accept of that Desire, that from that time to this I have had all things plentifully provided for me ... through His Blessing I liv a free and Kingly Life, as if the World were turned again into Eden, or much more..."'

Edward had a fine, steady voice. When he stopped reading, there was a silence, which filled the room.

'Well,' he said at last. 'Do you like it?'

'Yes. Very much.' Gillian reached for the book. 'May I?' She turned the pages, searching. 'I like this, too. It is not unrelated.'

'Read it to me.'

She read it to him.

' " The World is not this little Cottage of Heaven and Earth. Tho this be fair, it is too small a Gift ... it is an illimted feild of Varietie and beauty: where you may lose your self in the Multitude of Wonders and Delights ... " '

'An illimted feild,' said Edward. He made a gesture: yes, it is just so. And then the door, which had swung to, swung slowly open, and Tarn came in, her claws clicking on the bare boards. He held out his hand towards her. 'Since I came into the country I even have a dog,' he said, smiling. 'My cup runneth over.' He bent down, fondling the black-and-white head. 'Good girl, good girl.'

Gillian watched him, observing the pleasure given by his caress. She said: 'My father drowned in trying to save a dog.'

Edward looked up. 'Is that so?' He stopped stroking; Tarn sank to the floor at his feet. 'I'm sorry - I didn't realise - it must be distressing for you to -' He made another gesture, to send Tarn out again, but she said:

'It's all right, I am only telling you. I am quite used to dogs - everyone has them.'

'But you do not.'

'No. We have the doves.' She lifted Traherne again, with a smile. 'The gift of the Holy Spirit. The dove descending.' And then: 'Spiritual Things are the Greatest, and Spiritual Strength is the most Excellent, Usefull and Delightfull.'

He looked at her thoughtfully, picking up the book in the worn green cloth again, *The Eye of Understanding*. He said: 'There is a line like an umbilical cord running between Traherne and your father.'

'Yes,' she said simply.

'There is this moment of vision - this man steeped in the landscape, and the life of the spirit. Then there is a silence, for generations. And then there is your father. A fine poet. He is lyrical, and tender and spiritual -'

'And out of fashion.'

Edward raised the book to his face, he turned the mildewed pages, and sniffed them.

Gillian said: 'My father used to do that, I can remember him doing that. I do it myself, but have never seen anyone else -'

He smiled, sniffing again. 'The true bibliophile.' He ran his finger down the contents page: 'Stiper Stones ... Burning the Stubble ... On Bryncarnedd ... Canonical Hours ... To Gillian.' He stopped, he found the page. 'I was reading this the other night. You were born in a snowstorm.'

'I was. In the lambing. I was born in a snowstorm, my father died in a flood. Who knows what fate may befall my mother?'

Gillian, said Phoebe.

Only joking.

Edward said hesitantly: 'Do you mind my asking – you and your mother –'

'We are inseparable.'

He looked at her quizzically; he turned back to the page.

'May I?'

'Please.'

'"To Gillian. And to Phoebe."' And he read aloud again: of the whiteness of knuckles, and a twisted sheet; of fleece and snow and stars, of whirling flakes and a flickering flame; of a face, beloved, turned away, and a slimy, white-coated creature drawn out of her, drawing breath. Of a new, beloved face on a candle-white pillow, the sky an unearthly colour, and of a limitless peace, stretching between crib and silent field, the last snow fallen, and a falling into sleep.

'"We are cold, we are cold.
Hold, hold."'

Gillian sat listening. Edward stopped reading. They looked at each other, and the quietness of the house lay all around them.

'So,' he said gently. 'There was Thomas. There was Edward. And now there is Gillian.'

'Yes.'

'And where is her book?'

'Deep within.'

He walked with her across the yard, and the dog followed them, nose to the concrete, cracked by the frost and filled with runnels of water. The clouds were piling up, the air grown cold again, and a wind beginning to rise. The tarpaulin up on the roof flapped harder: Gillian watched its fight for freedom.

They came to the gate.

'Are you sure I can't give you a lift?'

'Quite sure.' She pulled her scarf from her pocket, and tied it round her neck. 'I am used to walking, it helps me think.'

'And what will you think about?' he asked gravely, looking down on a thin cold face with broken veins, yellow-green eyes like stones beneath water, the fine corrugation of hair tied tight.

'Of our conversation,' she said. 'Of the pleasure of it.'

He smiled. 'I shall think of it too. Thank you for coming.' His hand was on her shoulder again; he bent to kiss her cheek: once, twice, as Londoners did. 'Happy Christmas. I shall look forward to the reading.'

Then he opened the gate and swung it wide, calling sharply to the dog to stay at heel. In her heavy tweed coat and her Wellington boots Gillian walked out to the lane, where fallen twigs lay scattered. Rooks cawed, and the gate clanged shut behind her. Edward raised his hand.

She walked straight ahead. Twigs snapped beneath her feet, and happiness and hope welled up within her until she could hardly breathe. She quickened her pace, she broke into a run, gasping, her hair in the rubber band loosening, springing out wiry and wild.

She came to the bend in the lane, she slowed, she stopped. She listened to the cries of the sheep and birds across the illimted fields of her childhood, and to her own breathing, deep and fierce. She pushed back her hair, she turned, and walked slowly up the slope of the lane towards the farm again, quietly, so as not to disturb him. At a place by the hedge, before the iron gate, she stopped, and looked.

He was up on the roof again, and the ladder rested against the wall beneath him.

Gillian, from the reading of her childhood, recalled again Jacob, dreaming, his head upon stones in the field –

and behold a ladder set up on the earth, and the top of it reached to heaven, and behold the angels of God ascending and descending on it –

Edward straightened up, and walked slowly over the rooftop, from beam to beam. Gillian, beholding him, beheld the angels, the silent Heavens, the Skies adorned.

9

Christmas approached. The brief mild days had come and gone, the wind had risen, and now the sky was thick with implicit snow, and the air, once again, was freezing. The scent of the snow was everywhere: already, on high ground, patches lay beneath a pewter sky; everyone talked of it, down in the village, and lorries from the council, brushing the hedges of the narrow lanes, stopped at crossroads and corner verges to tip coarse sand and salt into council bins.

Behind the milking parlours cows slipped on icy slurry, waiting their turn on the machine, the rattle of nuts into metal bowls. Bullocks fed on silage, in barns where icicles formed on the rim of iron roofs; they shifted in damp bedding, backing into corners, eyes white and rolling, as fresh bales of straw were cut, and forked in, and the gate in the railings clanged. Lengths of orange baler twine lay about; sparrows flew into the darkness, and out again. In fields close to the house the sheep, heavy with lambs, huddled together beneath the hedges, moved over the stiff cold grass to the daily delivery of hay, soon trampled, and scattered about.

Down in the village, the shops were bright, and hung with decorations, and the Fox was always busy. There was a darts match, a quiz night, only the second year they'd run one, a great success, and bound to be won, as last year, by Phoebe's team. She had Bron Morgan, another reader, on her table, and Gareth, from the garage, who did the sport, and Huw Williams, because somebody had to have him.

'Here you are, Huw,' said Phoebe briskly, as he lowered his enormous bulk on to the settle. 'Got your pint? That's it.'

'Not sure I'll be much use to you,' he said, loosening his collar, sweating already. 'Still, I'll have a go.'

'That's the spirit.'

Across the room, Gillian had been teamed up with Gwen, who had brought her knitting, and with Gwen's husband, who could answer rugby questions going back fifty years.

'Have to watch Ted,' said Gareth. 'He's sharp.'

'Nonsense,' said Phoebe. 'No flies on you, Gareth.'

'A few on me, I'm afraid,' said Huw, draining his glass.

'You finished that already?' Gareth was genuinely astonished.

The room was crowded and bright, and full of good humour.

'It does him good.' Bron Morgan, thin as a stick, with horn-rimmed glasses, was setting out pencil and paper for their own score.

'We're looking forward to your reading,' Gwen told Gillian. 'We saw the notice, didn't we, Ted? In the shop. Very nice.'

'Thank you.'

Ted drew on his pipe. 'We'll be there.' He looked at the clock above the bar. 'Time we were starting. Just waiting for Evan, now.'

Glasses and mirrors winked the reflections of fairy lights all along the bar. A collection for multiple sclerosis was building up well in a giant glass jar; the raffle would be drawn in a fortnight, for a doll in pink nylon, with glossy brown hair and white shoes and socks. 'Our Sally would give anything for her,' said Gwen, casting off. 'She's bought a yard of tickets.'

'Here's Evan,' said Gillian, as the door swung open.

'Sorry to be late,' he said, taking off his cap. 'Calf came at five o'clock, bit of a surprise.' He blew on his hands. 'Cold as it's ever been, snow on the way, that's certain.'

'Just in time for Christmas,' said Gwen. 'Your calf I'm talking about. Very nice.'

'Better get a drink quick.' Ted was tamping down his tobacco. 'We're just about ready for the off.'

'Will do.' Evan nodded to Gillian, pulling off his scarf. 'Keeping well?'

'Very well, thank you.' She was looking at Evan's dog, who had followed him in through the door. A big dog, much heavier than Edward's, and older.

'Seen better days, haven't you, Flash?' said Ted, scratching the dog's head. Flash sank stiffly to the floor.

'You let him be,' said Evan, making for the bar. 'He's good for another while yet.'

A bell rang loud, as he reached it.

'Are we all ready now?' Pat, behind the bar, had his box of cards before him, 'Jenny's keeping the score – all right, love?'

Jenny, across at the blackboard by the darts, gave a cheery wave. 'All in order.'

'All the bells working? Give 'em a go. That's it, very good. Right then.'

And they were off.

What is the capital of – what sea lies between – what river flows through – what straits divide – what is the tallest, the smallest, the oldest and rarest, the deepest, and who won the cup?

What do these initials stand for – who captained England – which horse won the – who is the president of – who wrote, who invented, who painted, who said – and what is a, where is a, why is a –

Ping ping ping. Over here, over here. That's ten to Table One, and thirteen to Table Three, come along, now, and here's an outsider, Table Five coming up fast, and it's neck and neck, and who played and when was and why did and which was the odd one out –

How did people know all these things?

Gillian, scarlet with effort, looked across the room at Phoebe, flushed and triumphant. Phoebe knew everything, ping ping ping.

'Didn't your mother do well?' asked Gwen, as they all came out into the night. She called out to Phoebe, striding ahead. 'I'm saying to Gillian, Phoebe, didn't you do well? You should be on *Mastermind*, I thought that last year.'

Phoebe gave a little laugh. 'Oh, I don't know about that. We all did our bit. Now, then, Huw, how are you going to get home? Not on that bike, I hope.'

'Well, I –'

'Nonsense. We can put it in the back of the van, and Gillian can – Gillian?'

'What?'

'You can squeeze in with Huw's bike in the back, can't you?'

'No need for that,' said Ted. 'She can come with us.'

'No, no, it's all right, I can –'

'No trouble at all,' said Gwen, pulling gloves on.

'No, really, I –'

'Or you can come in the van with Flash and me,' said Evan. 'It's on my way.'

They were all out in the street, breath coming in cold puffs beneath the lamp, feet stamping, car doors slamming, footsteps up the pavement, calls of good-night, good-night.

'If you don't mind,' said Gillian firmly, 'I'd really rather walk.'

'It's *freezing* –'

'You've just been *ill* –'

'But I'm better now.'

'Oh, for heaven's sake.'

Better be off, then, all the best then, good-night, good-night, lovely evening and Happy Christmas.

Gillian walked away from all of them, slowly, until the last car had pulled out of the car park, and Phoebe and Huw had rattled past her, the bike in the back and he, enormously, in the front. She walked towards the end of the street which led round to the church, and up the hill towards the house, but when she came to the corner she stopped, and after a moment turned back again, scarf wrapped round her mouth against the cold, walking back through the village.

Lamps glowed behind drawn curtains; she could hear voices, and the television. But now there was no one about, just a few people left in the Fox having one last round. She walked in the lamplit quiet beneath the blackness of the night, the starlit hills, and she walked right out of the village, to where the river ran.

The river ran cold and swift and deep: beneath the stone bridge, where the children played in summer, and on between low-lying banks, where the reeds were glistening and still. Inky clouds moved over the moon, and took its face away. The sky and the river were racing, but the air was as still as ice, waiting, waiting.

'"In the bleak midwinter / Frosty wind made moan..."'

Christmas Eve. Rowland had just arrived, pulling up in the yard, singing as he got out of the car and held out his arms to Edward, coming to greet him, the dog at his heels. The two men embraced. Mid-afternoon, thick cloud, the first fine, freezing flakes, stinging their faces.

'You just made it, well done. Let me give you a hand.'

Rowland opened the boot of the Peugeot, passed out bags.

'What have you got in here, bricks?'

'Bottles. Presents. Dog biscuits. Hello, dog.'

'Don't say you've missed her.'

'Haven't missed anyone, least of all you.'

'Thanks. Look, here she comes.'

Tarn was greeted and fondled, the bags carried up to the house.

'Jesus, it's cold.'

'I've made up a fire.'

'Where?'

'Where do you think?' Edward pushed open the front door with his foot. Light and warmth greeted them; the house smelt of polish and wood and a joint in the oven. They dropped their bags, held each other.

'Let's have a look at the home improvements.' Rowland inspected every room, climbed the stairs to the landing. More rugs. Books on the sill by the windowseat, a fire laid in the bedroom, everything shipshape and pleasing. 'You've been busy. Well done.'

'And outside, too,' said Edward. 'The roof's better now – lambs should be okay in there. Want to have a look before it gets dark?'

'Tomorrow. Too cold. Let's have a drink.'

They went back downstairs to the kitchen.

'A beer? I thought we might mull some wine tonight.'

'We should be having people in. Getting into the community. Shouldn't we? Or having people up from London – Adam and Damian. Poor old Gerry.'

'Plenty of time.' Edward was getting cans from the fridge.

'You really think we'll survive a whole Christmas up here with only the two of us?'

They had had this conversation before.

'It's our first,' Edward said again, closing the fridge door. 'Last year we were still in London because nothing was ready here. Now it's a home. Isn't it? Please stop making me feel guilty. We don't need anyone else. Not this year. Here.' He passed a can and a glass. 'Welcome back.'

'It's good to be here. Cheers.' Rowland was still in his heavy winter coat, a London coat, lined and expensive and out of place. 'I'm sure you're right.' He drank looking out of the window, at the sheep, the lowering sky. 'You've done very well,' he said again. 'And you were right – you can cope up here on your own.'

'So long as I know you're coming.' Edward went up behind him. He leaned against the expensive shoulders. 'Anyway,' he said, kissing Rowland's neck, 'I'm getting into the community a bit. We even have an invitation. Here.' He moved away, and took down the square white card from the shelf above the Rayburn. 'Might you enjoy this?'

Rowland's glasses were still in his bag. He held out the card before him. 'Recent poems. Regret no refreshment.' He raised an eyebrow. 'Tell me.'

Edward said: 'She is –' He stopped, realising that he did not know how to begin to convey this woman: Gillian's history, her strange plain looks, her intensity and eccentricity. 'She is extraordinary,' he said at last.

Christmas Eve. Phoebe, unaccountably, felt unwell. Shivery. Pains in her chest. Perhaps she had caught it from Gillian.

'You said it was a chill.'

'Perhaps it was a virus.'

'Can I get you anything?'

'There is nothing to get for a virus. It has to take its course.' She sat by the range in the moquette chair. 'I shall have to miss Midnight Mass. What a damn nuisance.'

'Do you mind if I go by myself?'

'Of course not.'

Gillian left the house early, at twenty-past ten. She walked down the hill to the church, where lights were burning behind stained glass; Matthew, Mark, Luke and St John the Divine, brilliant in the darkness. She walked up the path towards them.

The church was unlocked, her footsteps echoed on the porch flags; she pushed open the inner door. The flames of candles stirred in the draught, and were still.

She was the only one here.

The church smelt of winter pine and greenery, all Phoebe's holly and ivy and jasmine and lanterns massed up and trailing and fine. The candles, tall and alabaster-white, had been set everywhere: in niches, on ledges, high upon the altar.

The silence was absolute and pure.

Gillian walked round slowly, looking, as Edward had done. She came to the polished plaque to her father, and stood before it; she turned, and walked on, and stood before the altar, laid with gold and snow; she knelt before the shining Cross.

In Him, the fountain, in Him the End; in Him the Light, the Life, the Way.

That was from the *Fifth Century*. Edward, and her father, had marked the page.

She knelt, bowed her head, was possessed by radiance.

Christmas morning. Nesta took her children to the window, and then, with a crowd of others, to the open front door, to see the miracle: the grace and stillness of the trees, the sweep of the lawns, the muted outline of the chapel roof – whiteness thick and soft and silent, covering the grounds, the lane beyond the gate, the distant hills.

Shrieks, and staggering footsteps.

'Sssh. Listen. Sssh, now. What can you hear?'

They clung to one another.

Sssh.

Not a sound.

The sky was heavy and full and promised more. Then into the stillness a solitary pigeon, grey against grey, flew towards the chapel. A breath, a moment, faces turned to the beat of wings, the silence broken. Then it was gone.

Nesta had no feeling for the rituals of religion, and no belief. None the less, sitting up late by the fire on Christmas night with the others, she found herself thinking of this moment as a glimpse of benediction.

Edward and Rowland lay in one another's arms and looked out through the window beneath the eaves of their bedroom on to the new, fresh fall: hesitant at first, then coming thickly. The room, which had been filled with reflected light when they drew back the curtains – sensing, at daybreak, that deep silence and change in the air which only snow brings – now was darkening again, the sky blotted out, the fall hypnotic, endless.

'And a white Christmas,' said Rowland. 'You even managed that.'

'Of course. The barn owl's next.'

'Good man.' Rowland drew the bedclothes up round his neck: a duvet, two eiderdowns, a rug. They needed all of it.

'Supposing the pipes burst.'

'They won't. I've lagged them.'

'Of course you have.'

They turned back to the window. Snow piled up against the panes made scalloped heaps in the corners of the sill.

'How can anything so dramatic be so quiet?'

'Sssh,' said Edward. 'Stop talking. Let's just be.'

They moved nearer to one another, fingers interlocked, naked limb against naked limb. They lay quite still.

And little that had passed between them in all their time together came close to the intimacy which grew between them now: deep, erotic, wordless.

The snowflakes fell and fell.

They turned to one another, they took one another in perfect silence.

Phoebe, by Christmas morning, had shaken it off.

'Don't know what that was. Nothing much, anyway.' Carols were on the kitchen radio, dazzling whiteness lay beyond the window. 'Happy Christmas.'

'Happy Christmas,' said Gillian, alight with joy.

They brushed each other's faces, poured their tea.

The snow settled, and lay thick upon the ground for days. Late on the day after Boxing Day a snow plough came, clearing a single road between the village and the market town, banking up deep-packed snow along the hedgerows. Most of the lanes remained impassable, and for mile upon mile the whiteness of hills and fields was broken only by the line of hedge or wall or snow-trimmed gate. Now and then a farmer tramped across, delivering hay to his ewes and leaving a line of footprints; now and then freezing rooks flapped low across the fields, calling; for hours the countryside was sunk in quietness.

Up at Tremynydd, Edward and Rowland read, and made love, and listened to music. Rowland practised. He walked up and down the landing, running through scales and songs and tenor lines. At Easter the Consort were taking the *St John Passion* on tour all round the country, performing last in London, in St Bartholomew the Great. Edward would be going down for that. They would be coming up to Hereford, going on to Cardiff, and then St David's. A lot to look forward to. Now, Edward checked the ewes each morning, and came in stamping, sent Tarn to her basket and made coffee, listening to the creaking floorboards above, and to the voice of his beloved – not in a church, or concert hall, not on the radio or on a disc, but here, in the heart of the house, stone amidst snow, with fires lit and deep, undisturbed contentment drawing the days together. He had never been so happy.

'"And behold, the veil of the Temple was rent in twain..."'

Rowland stopped, put a disc in, filled the house with sound: the choir, the chamber orchestra, the solo – his own voice rising, rising – singing against it, a double concert –

Edward, taking coffee into the study, felt the hairs on his arms, and the back of his neck, prickle and rise. He set down the mug, stood listening; then, when Rowland switched the disc off, he looked along the bookshelves. He took down the Trahernes again, Thomas and Edward. He took down George Herbert, who had died in 1633. Had Traherne, up at Oxford, thirty years later, read, and admired him?

The door was nosed open. She never left him for long.

'Come on, then, lie down.'

She found a patch of snow-reflected light, she settled, nose on her long black paws, ear cocked towards the music.

'Like it? Listen to this.'

He turned the pages of Herbert's collected poems.

> ' "And now in age I bud again,
> After so many deaths I live and write;
> I once more smell the dew and rain,
> And relish versing ..." '

He read the perfect lines aloud; he thought of Gillian, who relished versing: the only person, other than Rowland, to whom he had ever read aloud: of her rapt plain face and nervous manner, which became, when they talked, so concentrated and engaged.

' "Oh heart, melt in weeping, and pour out thy dolour ..." '

That was the soprano, Rowland had the disc on again, and the sound, almost unbearably pure, sent, as Rowland's voice did, sensations of awe and delight through every hair on Edward's head.

Was Gillian musical? He leaned back in the chair at the table, the books lying open, and closed his eyes, letting the voice upstairs possess him.

By mid-morning, a few days later, the trees had begun to drip, and the top layer of snow to sink, and turn to glassy crystals. The sky, its burden lost, was pale and high again, lit by a cold and distant sun, which today was perceptibly stronger. Down in the village the pavements had been cleared: it began to be wet underfoot as the piles of snow in the gutter softened, and people trod over torn-up cardboard boxes laid down in the shops, where stocks were low. There had been no deliveries of bread or fresh milk for a week. Phoebe made a foray, returning with cartons of UHT, medium-sliced Mother's Pride and tinned tomato soup.

She spent days on her tapestry, a hanging for the church at Easter, yellow and white and blue; she gave Gillian a box full of skeins and odd lengths of wool and silks to sort through and tidy, and make herself useful.

Gillian sat at the kitchen table, winding and unwinding. Holy colours lay before her: she drew them through her fingers like a rosary – the blood of Christ, the wafer of the sacrament, the blue and gold of heaven – as the wireless talked of this and that, and Phoebe expressed her views. The house itself, beyond the warmth of the kitchen, could not have looked less colourful, more uninviting. Damp patches had appeared on several walls, and bowls had been set in the bathroom beneath disconcerting drips.

'We need a complete programme of maintenance,' said Phoebe, snipping a thread.

The thaw, and cautious traffic over salt and sand into the market town, made the lanes passable, just. If Nesta had spent Christmas in her cottage she would have been snowed in. As it was, the days spent at Cadair had been warm and full; she drove home for New Year feeling content.

Getting dug in, said Hal, as thick slush splashed the wheels. You've made the right move.

I think so, said Nesta, crawling up to the crossroads. So long as the pipes haven't burst. That wouldn't be very funny.

No. But you'd cope.

Thanks, Hal.

She inched over the crossroads, drove past lacy hedges. The car windows were steaming up: she rubbed at them, envisaging, despite Hal's reassurance, an unpleasant homecoming to sodden carpets and general ruin. Who, realistically, would help her?

No one you like the look of, up at the Hall? There isn't, is there? Mates, but no soul mate.

He was right, as usual.

Never mind, he said gently, as he used to say to the children, no matter what they had dropped or broken or failed to do. Time enough.

She came to her village, and stopped to shop. When the snow had really gone, she must go over to the market town and stock up at the supermarket. Now, she went into the post office and village store, wiping her feet, greeting the thin young man in nylon overall stacking the shelves. Radio One burbled from behind the till; in the queue to the post office counter people were coughing, getting out pension books and Giros. Nesta, going round the shelves with her basket, nodded to people she knew by sight: young mothers with pushchairs counting child benefit into plastic purses, young men pulling income support books out of their inside pockets.

Rural poverty. In London, in many quarters, poverty was immediately apparent on the streets: in the beggars in doorways, the rundown estates, the sixties schools with stained concrete buildings and scruffy playgrounds. Here, because the beauty of the landscape took you over, it was easy at first to forget, or not discover, that many families lived from week to week, that jobs were hard to get and farmers lived on overdrafts, crippled by quotas and debt. Nesta, taking her basket up to the queue at the till, and waiting, thought for a moment of Gillian, to whom she had not given a thought for days, with her ancient old coat and Wellingtons, her unemployable air. Tomorrow night was the reading, and perhaps a new perspective on living out here, with an audience of who knew who.

Might be a kindred spirit, said Hal, as she came outside to the car again, and opened the boot. You never know.

You do realise, said Nesta, driving out of the village and on towards the Feathers, that no one will ever replace you. She put on a tape of Elton John, because Hal had loved him.

We talked about that, said Hal. You know I don't want you to mourn for ever.

Yes. But I didn't know then – nothing can ever prepare you – I'm fine, most of the time, it's just now and then –

She drove past the Feathers, all lit up for lunchtime, came to her turn-off, drove slowly down the track.

Hey, said Hal, you're crying. Please don't cry.

I didn't mean to – I don't know why, just now – but I miss you, I miss you –

She pulled up at the field gate, right in the middle of 'Your Song'; she put her head on the wheel and wept.

It thawed, then froze again.

The layers of crystals on top of the hard-packed snow turned to ice, and the lanes, even a path to the front door, could be dangerous. At night, the stars were like glass.

> ' "Blow, blow, thou bitter wind,
> Freeze, freeze thou bitter sky..." '

Rowland, crossing the yard to the Land Rover, let his voice ring out through the cold air. 'Look at those stars.'

> '"Though thou the waters warp,
> Thy sting is not so sharp
> As friend re-mem-ber'd not,
> As friend re-mem-ber'd not –"'

The windows of the outbuildings were black, the roofs and tarpaulins shrouded in white. Here and there a patch of slate shone dark, where the snow had melted.

'"Friendship is feigning, most loving mere folly..."'

'Don't say that.' Edward, letting Tarn jump up to the back, slammed shut the tailgate.

'Why not? It's a fine song, don't you think? Shakespeare.'

'I know exactly what it is. Almost unbearably sad. Will you do the gate?'

Rowland's feet scrunched towards it, swung it wide. Edward drove slowly through, Tarn moving about in the back, excited.

'Down!' Rowland swung the gate shut and came round, climbing into the front seat with an effort. 'Damn silly, taking a sheepdog to a poetry reading.' He drew the strap across his belly. 'Taking any dog.'

Edward let off the handbrake and slipped slowly down the hill. 'Dogs go everywhere up here,' he said. 'You know that. Anyway, she's like us – she needs an outing.' He glanced in the mirror. 'It's all right, she's lying down now.'

The headlights beamed on to banks of snow; he took it carefully round the bend. The trees were pale and ghostly, but lights from the farms and cottages shone all across the valley as they descended.

'And you think she'll be good?' asked Rowland, looking out of the window.

'The dog or the poet?'

'Both. But I meant the poet.'

'I hope so. I'll be surprised if she isn't.'

'And disappointed?'

Edward hesitated. 'Yes.'

They came to lower ground, turned left at the T-junction, and then they were approaching Penglydr, the snowy churchyard far up the hill.

'That's where her father's buried?' Rowland asked.

'Yes. We should have gone to church at Christmas. I could've shown you. And the plaque.'

'Plenty of time.'

'I thought you wanted to get into the community.'

'I do. But going to church –'

They had come to the main street. Frozen snow lay along the gutters; chinks of light came from behind drawn curtains. There wasn't a soul about. Ahead were the lights of the Fox. They drove into an empty car park.

'Oh, dear.'

'We're early,' said Edward, pulling up.

'Do you honestly think, on a night like this –'

'Who knows? It'll be an experience.'

Gillian picked up her sheaf of poems, and one of them fell from grace. She bent to retrieve it, then stood, pale as paper, to face her audience.

The room held perhaps twenty people, seated in rows of wooden chairs. Beside her stood a standard lamp with an ancient parchment shade; there was a table, a bible, a glass of water. Before her was semi-darkness, the scraping of chairs, glasses set down on the floor, a general settling. Gillian sipped her water. She was wearing Bri-Nylon trousers, lace-up shoes, a long black jumper and a paisley cotton scarf at the neck.

Those clothes do not become you, said Phoebe. I've told you before.

This is my reading, said Gillian. Go to hell.

Her hair was scraped back from a central parting, and tightly tied; tendrils escaped at the temple, wilful and wild.

She cleared her throat. 'Well. I should like to begin.'

Thank you all very much for coming, said Phoebe.

Gillian and her sheets of paper shook.

She said: 'I shall begin with a short sequence of poems with a domestic setting.'

This reading must have form, and shape; she must lead them carefully, her listeners, like sheep down a lane – safe within high hedges, following a familiar path, then to the gate, then to the windswept field, the view of heaven.

So.

'The first is called "The Milkman's Consort" –'

She could feel, in the darkness, somebody smile.

And she began. In a high strained voice she read of milkfloats and

125

mousetraps and bad circulation. She read of presentiments of violence, of the roaring Hoover and trembling dust; she moved on to 'My Mother, Sewing' – the merciless machine, the linen rent in twain, the spool of the thread of life unwinding and unwinding, faster and faster –

She read of the garden rake, sweeping up sins, of a garden which contained both altar and the slow-burning fires of hell, and of the heaps of greenery hacked down to decorate cold stone, all the wild life taken out of it, thirsting for water –

She stopped, she sipped from her glass. She said, in a voice which had grown stronger, 'Now I shall read you some lines from the Book of Revelation.'

A ripple of enquiry in the dark.

She picked up the bible; a slip of white marked the page.

So. Let them have it.

'"I saw four angels standing on the four corners of the earth. Holding the four winds of the earth –"'

She read, she broke off, and looked for a place in the darkness to gaze at, and found it, just above the door. She told this place clearly that she did not believe in explanations, that poetry should stand up for itself.

'I read those lines from St John the Divine to set my work in its spiritual context. I am a servant of God. It is my inescapable destiny to write.' She coughed into the silence. 'Well. Now I shall read some more poems. The first is called "In Penglydr Churchyard".'

Frost-hardened earth heaped up at a graveside, the churchyard empty, save for the footsteps of the dead. Yew trees dripped, a thread was snipped, a soul descended to darkness –

The water beneath the world was rising, lapping at doorsteps, seeping through cracks, sweeping a child away –

The hills and the fields were engulfed and swallowed, it rained and rained, and when it had stopped the earth lay flat and still and shining, waiting for the sign, the dove descending.

There came instead an eagle, mighty and cruel, magnificent –

Gillian, lifting her eyes from the page, saw in the darkness a glance exchanged, a nod.

She finished her poem. She shook. She said:

'When I was young, I was tormented. The dark night of the soul. It seemed to me that I should seek sanctuary within an order, that discipline and prayer might save me. One day I rode across the valley. This poem is called "At Cadair Hall".'

A summer afternoon, the lark ascending, the holy blue of the sky, immortal wheat –

A grille, an opening, a pathway up to God – whisper of white on cloister stone – a cell, a single bell –

If I come in, I shall never come out –

Gillian had taken possession of the room.

She read of redemption, and grace, and prayer. She read of the consecration of poetry, up in the hills; of walking the lanes in winter, of the combine harvester peeling back the fields in autumn, of the cries of sheep and crows on the wind, the unrelenting eye of the buzzard, caught between heaven and earth. She read of the visible and invisible, weaving lines from the Psalms, from the Litany, from Revelation, in and out of her verses, a thread as fine as a silken hair and as strong as steel.

'This poem is called "The Psalm Appointed" –'

'This poem is called "Holy Communion" –'

She read of a seeking of salvation; she was in a trance: no longer reading but declaiming, the sheaf of white sheets no longer glanced at, but held aloft as she paced up and down.

' "I sleep, but my heart waketh: it is the voice of my beloved that knocketh, saying, Open to me, my sister, my love, my dove, my undefiled –" '

And then she stopped, and looked about her, at the figures in the darkness before her, and the white sheets of paper fell to the floor at her feet like snow, and she said:

'Well. I think I have finished, now –'

The room had become a cathedral of quietness. Then the applause began. She bent down, gathered up her poetry, stood before her audience, dazed and flaming.

'Gillian.'

The room was emptying, but he stood before her, he said her name. She was pierced by emotion, lifting her face to his.

'You are completely wonderful.' His hand was on her shoulder, he bent to kiss her: once, twice on her burning cheeks. 'I knew you'd be good,' he said, 'but that was –'

She could not speak.

'May I introduce you –' He was turning to a man at his side, someone she had never seen before, and had not noticed. 'Rowland King. Gillian Traherne.'

The man held out his hand: it was fleshy and warm.

'Congratulations. That was very fine.'

'Thank you. I –' She looked round the room in a dream. One or two people were waiting to speak to her: most were going downstairs to the bar.

'May we buy you a drink?' said Rowland.

'Yes. Thank you. I –'

Someone was approaching, light of foot. Silver earrings glinted and swung, cropped hennaed hair shone by the standard lamp.

'Nesta –'.

Nesta smiled, and kissed her. Once, twice on the cheek.

'Hello, Gillian. I'm so glad you invited me.'

'Well, I –' She turned towards the men. 'I –'

Introduce them, said Phoebe. Surely you can do that.

She introduced them, faltering at Rowland's name.

'I'm sorry, I'm not very –'

'Please. You must be exhausted.'

There were greetings, smiles of interest exchanged between people who knew how to conduct themselves.

She said: 'I need safe conduct –' and broke off, covered in confusion.

'Of course you do.' Edward put his arm across her shoulders. 'Come on.'

They all made their way to the open door. A young man stood waiting: there were nods and glances. He said, in a light soft voice: 'That was great. I really liked it.' He was tall and slender and pale; fine hair of an indifferent colour fell to his shoulders.

'Thank you,' said Gillian, rallying. 'Thank you for coming.'

'I've heard you before,' he said. 'Last summer. I like poetry readings, I go to quite a lot.'

'Well –'

'Come on,' said Edward again. 'Let's all talk downstairs.' He looked at the young man enquiringly. 'Can I buy you a drink?'

'That's very nice of you.'

They clattered down the narrow stairs. Gillian could hardly walk. The bar was crowded: she saw Gwen, and Ted, and Bron Morgan – everyone was there, and a mass of strangers. Phoebe was drinking cider. She raised her glass, and came over.

'Well done. Want a drink?'

'I think I'm –' She glanced towards Edward: he and Phoebe greeted each other with warmth. 'And may I introduce –' he said.

Rowland King, and Nesta Frank, and Phoebe Traherne, and –

'I'm afraid I don't know –'

'Phil,' said the pale young man, and brushed his hair back. 'Phil Dryhurst. Hi.'

'How do you do,' said Phoebe.

They sat in the snug, crowded together on seat covers worn and mended, printed with hunting scenes. It was months since Gillian had been amongst so many people, except at the Christmas quiz, and in church; and then she was amongst people who knew her, and made allowances. Now, the group drawn together by her poetry, drinking and making interesting conversation, contained significant strangers, new acquaintances with whom she must engage, and discuss her work, and sound intelligent.

One thing to preach, to declaim in the darkness, uninterrupted and on her own.

Another to sit, and keep on sitting, and try to answer, and take a returning interest.

Or perhaps she need do none of these things.

'She's done her bit,' said Edward kindly, taking charge. 'She doesn't want to be quizzed about it now, do you, Gillian?'

'Well –' She leaned against the covered settle, uncomfortable and hot. 'I'm just not very – I'm not really used –'

'But you were good,' said Nesta, rolling a cigarette at the far end of the table. 'You were inspired. For someone shy you were pretty amazing.' She licked her paper, drew strands of tobacco from between her lips. 'I'm sorry, I should've asked – does anyone else want one of these?'

'I thought you were going to ask if anyone minded,' said Rowland, only half-joking. 'Passive smoking, and all that.'

'Oh, sorry.' She stopped, and looked at him. 'Do you really mind?'

'It's just not very good for the voice, that's all. Never mind, you go ahead, I'll avert my gaze.'

'I'll have one, if I may,' said Phil, from across the table. 'I like a nice roll-up now and again.'

Nesta smiled – such a sweet and gentle smile, thought Edward, observing her. 'Here,' she said to Phil, passing the cigarette over. 'You have this one, then.' She turned back to Rowland. 'Why do you have to worry about your voice?'

Rowland was looking at Phil. 'I sing, that's all,' he said, to both of them.

'Professionally?' Nesta was licking the next paper.

'Yes.'

'Who with?' asked Phil.

'Something called the London Consort.'

'Do you really?' Phoebe was leaning across the table. 'I must say that's rather thrilling. I often hear them on the radio.'

Rowland smiled and nodded. 'Yes, we're fortunate to be played now and then –'

'Such modesty,' said Edward, finishing his pint. He glanced around the table. 'You should hear him.'

'I have,' said Phil, lighting up. He looked back at Rowland.

'I knew I'd heard your name somewhere. You're the tenor, aren't you? I've got you on CD.'

'Well,' said Phoebe. 'Isn't this exciting?'

Rowland was smiling at Phil. 'I'm delighted to hear it. And what about you? Are you in the music world?'

'Yeah,' said Phil, 'but not your kind of music. At least, not entirely. I compose, but it's more New Age sort of stuff. Mind you, I like to blend in the classical.' He turned to Gillian, who was looking at Edward. 'Your kind of thing, if you know what I mean. The old and the new.' He drew on the roll-up which Nesta had given him. 'The way you blend the Bible in with your own work – it's very powerful.'

Gillian was looking at him vaguely. 'Sorry – were you talking to me?'

'For heaven's sake,' said Phoebe, but there was general laughter.

'Time for another drink,' said Edward.

'I should get them.' Gillian flushed again. 'I'm sorry, I –'

'Not at all.' Rowland was feeling in his pocket, pulling out his wallet. He passed it to Edward. 'My shout, but you're nearest. Do you mind?'

'Of course not.' He got to his feet.

'Where's Tarn?' asked Gillian.

'Who?' asked Phoebe.

'My sheepdog.' Edward was gathering glasses. 'I've left her out in the Land Rover.'

'She'll be freezing,' said Gillian.

'Poor thing.' Nesta lit up.

'Yes, do bring her in,' said Phoebe.

'Are you sure?'

'Of course. Everyone brings their dogs in. She's trained, isn't she?'

'She's practically human,' said Rowland.

A murmur of laughter, everyone enjoying themselves.

'Right, then.' Edward took orders. 'Same again, everyone? Can you pass that tray, Nesta? Thanks. And I'll go and get her.'

'Well done.' Rowland turned back to the table.

Edward took the tin tray of glasses up to the bar, nodding at someone he knew by sight, who turned out to be Gwen. They talked of the weather, the reading, the dog he had left outside. Gwen introduced her husband, and their old friend Bron, bright as a button. Edward ordered the drinks, and found Nesta beside him, offering help.

'Thank you.' He smiled down at her, noting the earrings, the lovely face. 'And what about you?' he asked her. 'Are you in the music world?'

'Not at all. I'm a therapist. Learning disabilities. Special needs.' She told him, briefly, about her job, and he listened attentively. 'Mind you, I try to do a lot of music with the children,' she said. 'They really respond.'

The tray of drinks was full again; Edward reached for Rowland's wallet.

'I'll take them,' she offered. 'You go and get your dog.'

'Sure?'

'Sure I'm sure.' She smiled, easy and graceful. 'See you in a minute.'

'Thanks.' He went to the door.

Outside, the street was deserted, the cold fierce. Poor Tarn. He walked round to the car park, his footsteps loud; he looked up at the stars, as brilliant as he had ever seen them. Long before he had crossed to the Land Rover she had heard him, and leapt to her feet, bounding about and barking madly.

'Here, girl, it's all right, I'm back.'

He dropped the tailgate open and she was out in a flash, fast as a cat, racing round and round him, tail beating, nose in his hand and dancing off and back again.

'Silly girl, come on, now.' He bent to embrace her. 'Will anyone ever love me as much?'

They set off together across the car park, back to the welcoming lights.

'Have to behave, now,' he told her, and then, as they reached the door, more sternly. 'I mean it. Heel. Obey.'

She was calm at once, steady and at his side. 'Good girl.' He pushed the door open.

After the darkness of the night, and the distant brilliance of the

131

stars, he had to blink to see the table where everyone sat, laughing and talking. Then he made his way towards them, Tarn so well behaved that no one turned or noticed them approaching, and so he could see exactly how everyone was placed: Gillian, drained of energy, leaning back against the settle with her eyes closed; Phoebe, talking to the lovely Nesta Frank; Phil, across the table, looking at Nesta with open appreciation, and Rowland, on the other side, gazing – yes, that was not too strong a word – gazing, with unmistakable interest and desire, at long-haired, languid Phil.

Part 2

The coming of spring

10

In the middle of January, a thaw that lasted. Slush on the main roads, and down in the village; shrinking maps of white on the hills. Snow heaped up along the verges sank into itself in caverns, and trickled into ditches clogged with leaves; by the third day, little was left of it: a patch here and there in field and garden, a scallop by a gatepost, the last wet trails in lonelier and less visited lanes.

It was still cold, though not quite as cold. The sun came and went: diffuse and misty, piercing and bright.

Gillian was afflicted with restlessness.

'That reading has gone to your head,' said Phoebe, turning out a cupboard on the landing. 'Time you did something useful. Here. Take these.'

Gillian held out her arms for a pile of worn towels and tablecloths. Downstairs the letterbox banged.

'What shall I do with all this?'

'Check it for mending.' Phoebe was inside the cupboard again, clattering about with a brush. Clouds of dust and shreds of newspaper hung about her. 'Moth,' she said, emerging. 'Mildew and damp.'

Gillian carried the drooping pile of linen down the stairs. A thick quarto envelope lay on the mat. She hurried towards it, dropping ancient napkins.

The Mandrake Press. There on the left-hand corner.

She left the yellowing damask on the hall stand, bore the envelope into the kitchen. The magazine, on good-quality paper, had printed her poems first. They looked like interesting strangers. There was a compliment slip, a compliment written upon it. The editorial spoke of her father.

Gillian sniffed the pages, pulled out a chair.

Melting snow dripped from the gutters into the farmyard. Edward, in the empty barn, stood listening to it, looking up at the roof. Chinks of light shone here and there, and he'd left out two or three half-bricks at the top of the wall for returning swallows, but the place was secure and weatherproof now, the rafters repaired, the rusted and broken roofing replaced. Quite a job, but he'd done it, got it all wired up to the outhouse generator, whose hum was a background noise he no longer noticed. Kept going all through the snow, thank God.

Drip, drip. Good sound guttering. He paced about. The broken furniture and rusting bits of machinery had gone to the scrapyard; he'd sold the tractor for fifty pounds to a dealer. Now the filled-in concrete floor was swept, and straw and hay bales were piled in a corner. It was cold out here, but the place smelt pleasantly of fresh timber and the hay: a good place for lambing.

'You've done a decent job,' said Rowland, at the door.

'Thanks.' Edward looked at him, his back to the light in the doorway, not coming in. 'You off?'

'Think I'd better be.'

'Got everything?'

'Think so.' He moved aside as Tarn put her nose round his legs and slipped past. 'What do you want?' he asked her.

'She's been nosing in and out since breakfast,' said Edward. 'And the other buildings.' She came up beside him, and he put his hand on her head. 'Haven't you, girl?'

'Getting excited?' Rowland addressed her, from the door. 'All geared up for the lambs?'

Edward thought: We are talking to each other through a dog. Like walkers meeting in a London park, making dog conversation.

Christ.

Tarn sniffed about, and went out again. Rowland moved aside for her.

'Right, then,' he said.

Edward stood for a moment in the emptiness and sudden light, as Rowland turned and walked across the yard. A sparrow flew into a half-brick gap, alighted and chirruped. Then it was gone.

He thought: What is happening now is of no consequence. Say nothing. Do nothing. It will pass.

He went out into the yard.

Wetness was everywhere: in the air, in the patches of melted snow on the concrete, on Tarn's damp coat, on Rowland's sleek, plum-coloured car. He stood with his hand on the door.

Edward said: 'Rowland, do you –'

Rowland said: 'It's been wonderful. I'll phone.'

Edward moved towards him. 'Kiss me goodbye?'

Oh dreadful, despicable question mark, hanging in the morning air. He could almost see it, begging.

Rowland gave a laugh. 'Come here.'

A brief warm hug, a swift warm pressure of mouth on mouth.

Rowland, since the evening of Gillian's reading we have not been right –

Rowland moved easily away and opened the car door.

Don't go, don't go –

He did not say these things. He managed not to say them.

He said: 'Have a good journey.'

'I will.' Rowland leaned down and gave Tarn a pat. 'Look after your master.'

'She will.'

Listen to it.

'Right, then. Talk to you tonight.'

'Or tomorrow.'

'Oh, right. Sure.'

And then Rowland was in the car, and reversing, and turning, and driving away, a hand raised through the open window, a sound on the horn, and out to the lane and gone, with Tarn racing after, barking, hurtling towards the gate.

'Here!' shouted Edward. 'Come back here!'

Sheep bleated from behind the house. A jackdaw up on the chimney gave a clipped, metallic call. Then the emptiness of a home without a lover began to spread everywhere: over the muddy yard, across the fields.

Nesta, in her dressing gown on Sunday morning, received a phone call.

'Hi,' said Phil. 'Remember me?'

She remembered. She sat on the corner of the sofa by the unlit fire and looked out of the window at the dripping apple trees. The room smelt faintly of damp, more strongly of charred wood. She must re-lay the fire for the day ahead, and get someone in for the roof.

'Have you had breakfast?' asked Phil.

'Not yet. Just making coffee. What about you?'

'Yeah, I've had mine. Cornflakes in bed with the cat.'

Nesta smiled. 'Male or female?'

'Male. Ex-male. Tabby. Very friendly. That's enough about him. What are you doing today?'

'Gathering my wits for the week ahead.'

'D'you want to come and listen to some music?'

Nesta considered.

Go on, said Hal.

'Okay. Thanks. When?'

'Whenever. When you're ready. I'll make you some lunch if you like.'

Sounds all right.

'Okay, that would be nice. Tell me again where you live.'

He told her; she reached for a pen.

When they had said goodbye, she went to the kitchen for coffee, and carried it back to the sitting room. She sat stirring, thinking. Charred logs lay on a heap of ash in the fireplace; above, on the mantelpiece, the severe white square of Gillian's invitation was still propped up against the candlestick.

> *I saw four angels standing on the four corners of the earth*
> *Holding the four winds of the earth –*

A revelation. The awkward manner and unease had fallen away, like a dark cloak on the floor; the wavering high voice had drawn power, grown strong. Gillian had taken possession of the room until she herself was possessed: declaiming, abandoned, free.

Filled with the Holy Ghost.

Nesta drank her coffee. She thought of the close of the reading, of Gillian's feverish exhilaration, lights coming on and congratulations, the room emptying, introductions amongst those who stayed. Someone waiting at the door.

Downstairs they all crammed in round a table. Nesta sat rolling a cigarette, and was reproached for it.

Do you mind – I have to look after my voice.

The tall young man had heard of the voice, and the voice had shown an interest. Nesta had noticed. She was trained to notice. She had liked the look of the man and his dog; she had been curious about the brisk, enthusiastic mother. There had been nobody who interested her as Gillian did, but she could, as they all sat talking, see various possibilities for friendship.

'Do you think – could I phone you?'

Musical Phil had followed her to the door. That had been

unexpected. She tore out a page from her notebook, scribbled her number, had another look at him. Much too young. She drove slowly home through the frozen valley, banked-up snow in the lanes glittering in the headlights.

Nesta licked her Rizla paper and looked out on to the garden. A heap of wet leaves she'd raked up in the autumn lay in the far left corner of the hedge; across rough grass stood the beehive, white paint peeling. Snow had lain thickly on its sloping roof: she had gone out and wiped it away, on the morning of the reading; she had stood there in the silent garden considering the winter stillness of a thousand bees within. Now, as church bells began to ring along the valley, she considered again, picturing layer upon layer of them, dormant and cold.

Bloody cold down here, said Hal, now. You should go back to bed.

I was going to light the fire, said Nesta, lighting her cigarette. She threw the dead match into the hearth. I was going to light the fire and spend the day catching up on things –

What sort of things?

This and that. Letters, ironing, domestic life –

And now you're going to a strange house to listen to music.

Yes.

She took her coffee and cigarette over to the piano, and put them on top, where an ashtray perched on a pile of books. She lifted the lid and picked out a tune with one finger.

You are my sunshine, my only sunshine –

The keys were damp and stiff. Sometimes it was freezing in here, and sometimes, with the fire, much too hot. Poor old piano: not right at all.

You make me happy, when clouds are grey –

You hardly ever play, said Hal. You can't play, let's face it. I wouldn't have minded if you'd sold it.

No, no, I couldn't do that.

You'll never know, dear, how much I love you –

She drew on her cigarette.

As the morning drew on, the sky began to darken, threatening rain. Nesta, frowning over the map in the car, looked up, and looked from right to left. Was she lost? She had grown used to her beat between Cadair and home, she had got to know the route to the market town, and the route across the valley, towards Penglydr, where Gillian lived. But here was unknown territory, even though she couldn't be more than four or five miles from any of these places.

You were never any good with maps, said Hal. Brilliant at lots of things, but geography was never –

You do it then, said Nesta. Behind her a tractor was approaching; she waited until it had rumbled past, then pulled out again from the verge and drove on, between tall laid hedges, past field gates. She could not see the river, and she could not see the sign Phil had told her to look for, between Nant-y-Coed and Mynydd. What was she doing out here?

'Oh, I wish –' she said aloud, and then she came to a bend in the lane and rounding it saw a sign ahead: Long Betton. That was it. She drove on, she took the turning, she saw, as Phil had said she would, a small plain cottage set by itself in a field, as if it had been put down for a moment, and then forgotten. Trees stood to the left, alongside a ditch and a hedge; jeans and a couple of shirts hung on a washing line round the side. There was a porch, a waterbutt, a pile of logs beneath a makeshift lean-to; there was a beat-up van.

Nesta drew up, and pulled on the handbrake. She got out and opened the gate. Rainclouds were moving over the hills; much of the land surrounding this field had been ploughed and she could see that in summer the cottage would be bordered by cornfields, that the trees would provide a deep and softening shade and the verges of the lane be filled with wild flowers. But now –

She returned to the car, and drove through the gateway; she got out again and closed it, feeling the first drops of rain, feeling cold and apprehensive. As she bumped slowly over the ground the door of the cottage opened, and Phil appeared in the porch, young and tall and graceful – yes, he did have a graceful walk, as he came down the field towards her – and she became, for a moment, Gillian, arriving at her own cottage, filled with clumsiness and apprehension.

The sky was pewter. Rain hit the windscreen.

'What the hell am I doing here?' she said aloud, and gave Phil a sweet and gentle smile, winding down the window as he came forward to greet her.

'You found it.'

'Eventually.' She switched off the engine.

'I knew you would.' He held the door open. Rain fell harder. 'Come on – quick.'

They hurried towards the porch. Through the rain, through the open door, Nesta heard music, a clear high pipe, tune of a wanderer, up in the hills. She thought: I like the sound of that, and raced for shelter.

Inside, through an open door to the left, she glimpsed speakers, a piano, trailing wires. The clear high pipe was joined by a violin, tuneful and inviting.

'That's nice.'

'Yeah. It changes – you'll hear. Come and have a coffee.' He indicated the kitchen, across the dark hall. Nesta went through, and sat down at the table. She pulled out her tobacco tin. Phil ran water from a tap at a stone sink, overlooking the field at the front. 'Lunch is in the oven. Nothing grand.'

'It's nice of you to do anything.'

She could smell baked potatoes; a saucepan stood on the stove.

Phil put the kettle on. He sat down across from her, pushing back light fine hair; he watched her lick her paper, and flatten it out. 'What are you putting in there?'

'Tobacco,' Nesta said drily, taking some out of the tin.

He felt in the table drawer, and pulled out a pouch. 'Shall we have some of this? Home grown.'

'No, thanks.'

'Oh, come on.'

'No, thanks.' She sprinkled tobacco on to the paper. 'But you go ahead.'

'Not so much fun on your own.'

'Well, sorry.' She brushed the last threads from her fingers. 'Do you not want this one, then?'

He hesitated, turning the pouch over, watching her deftly rolling and licking. 'Not used to this,' he said, as she offered it. 'Oh, well.' He leaned forward, let her light up, inhaled. Behind him the kettle came to the boil.

'How come you don't indulge?'

'I used to,' she said, rolling another. 'Now and then, in the old days in London. Not here – as you say, it's not so much fun on your own. Anyway, I've got out of the way of it.'

He got up to turn off the kettle. She lit up, watching him make coffee, moving about the kitchen, opening the fridge. It was raining steadily now, a downpour upon the fields, against the casement window. Across the hall the music was changing, as he had said it

143

would, the folk tune interweaving with something deep and electronic. 'Did you write this?' she asked.

'Yeah. It's a demo tape. Like it?'

'I think so.'

They sat listening, smoking, drinking coffee.

'Tell me about it,' said Nesta, as the track came to an end. She put out her cigarette, and watched him lean back in his chair. 'Does it have a name?'

'Mmm. I've called it "Carreg". That's Welsh for rock.'

'Are you Welsh?'

'Born and bred,' he said with an exaggerated lilt, and she smiled. 'It's true.' He got up from the table. 'My grandparents have always lived in this valley. My parents moved away, and had a shop down in Abergavenny, but when I left college I came back here.' He was by the stove, turning the ring on, stirring. 'Couldn't keep away. I've rented this place for years now. Most of the cottages round here get tarted up for holiday lets, but so far I've been lucky. Owned by an old boy who can't be bothered.'

The saucepan began to bubble; the smell of tomatoes and wine filled the room. 'Can I do anything?' Nesta asked.

'Not much to do. I told you it was simple. There's knives and forks in that drawer; I've got the plates warming.'

'How very domesticated.' She rose, took out cutlery, pushed aside the pouch; she carried the mugs to the sink. 'This is the first rain for ages,' she said, looking out at the soaking grass. 'Before I came here I thought it would rain all the time.'

'It often does.' He took out some cheese from the fridge, grated it into a bowl. 'OK, I think we're ready.'

They ate, and at her invitation he talked: about a musical mother, he and his sister at piano and recorder early, a guitar for his fifteenth birthday. Playing about with a folk group in Abergavenny, saving up for a keyboard, then everything changing with the new technology.

'Liberation.' He leaned over the table, ladled more tomato sauce on to her plate. 'I went to college in Swansea, started composing, had a good tutor – I've been at it ever since. Like I was saying in the pub, I go for this mix of sounds, the old and the new.' He sat down again. 'Like Gillian Traherne – you know, all that biblical stuff in with her own verse.'

'Yes,' said Nesta, wincing at the way he spoke of her. Biblical stuff. 'And you've heard her before, you said. Do you really go to poetry readings a lot? Is that what people do around here in the depths of winter?'

Phil smiled. 'You did it. It's more in the summer, with festivals, but yes – people go.' Again the exaggerated lilt: 'It's in the blood, see: Wales is full of poets. Gillian Traherne has a bit of a local reputation. Her mother, too – she has this garden, opens it up in the summer. My grandmother used to talk about it. Phoebe Traherne's garden.' He finished his plate, gestured at the table. 'More? Another potato?'

She shook her head. 'I couldn't, thanks.' She thought about Gillian, walking up in the hills, so rude and offhand when they met.

Work? No. I am a burden on the community.

'What about earning a crust?' she asked him. 'Apart from composing, what do you do? Is that an insulting question?'

'Not in the least.' He was reaching for her tobacco tin, as if they had known one another for years. 'May I? I teach, on supply. Not that there's much demand.' He grinned wryly, rolling up. 'And you? You're getting to know people, yeah? You work at this school, you said in the pub –'

'Cadair Hall. Yes. It's a good place, I'm glad I came.'

'Go on.'

'Well – what can I say? It extends what I've always done. I trained as a special needs therapist in London, and I worked in a school as part of a team –' She broke off, taking the roll-up he offered her, letting him light it.

He said, rolling another one: 'It's such a naff question, but how come someone like you is on your own? I wanted to ask you in the pub, but –'

'I'm a widow,' Nesta said calmly, and drew on her cigarette.

'Oh, shit.' He put down the packet of papers and looked at her. 'I'm sorry.'

'Thanks. It's okay.'

'Is it?'

'Well –' She made a gesture.

'How long were you married?'

'Six years. We met at the school in London. He was very gifted, the children responded really well to him, he taught me a lot. And then –' She inhaled again, looking out at the rain. 'Then he got ill.'

Phil hesitated. 'How old was –'

145

'He was thirty-two.'

The rain came and went: drifting across ploughed fields towards the hills; returning. Phil made more coffee; they took it into the sitting room. Nesta stepped over the trailing wires, and a couple of unwashed mugs, and looked around her. The piano stood against the wall beyond the fireplace, a keyboard beneath the window overlooking the fields at the back. There were two sagging armchairs, a hi-fi, racks of CDs and cassettes, a general scattering of papers. There was a fire, in need of attention.

Phil threw a log on, and poked about. He added another, gesturing to a chair. 'Meet the cat.'

The cat took up much of the seat.

'What's his name?'

'Abraham.'

She smiled, and squeezed in alongside. Abraham opened his eyes, a clear and perfect yellow, and stretched. He rose, and made himself comfortable upon her. 'You're very nice,' said Nesta, settling down.

Rain fell, the fire crackled quietly. The woodsmoke made the room smell like her own sitting room, and feel pleasantly familiar. Phil was standing up at the piano, humming, improvising on the theme he'd played earlier – a few chords here and there, a pause for thought, a run, long graceful fingers assured and easy. Nesta sat listening. Abraham slept.

Phil glanced across at them. 'Okay?' He left the piano and stood at the keyboard flicking switches. He played about with the theme again, bringing in strings, bells, a drumbeat. 'I've got this on the brain, I keep coming back to it.'

'Even though it's on tape already?'

'Yeah.' He switched off the strings, let in South American pipes, breathy and soft. Everything changed.

'You could go on for ever,' said Nesta.

'Yeah, I do.' His hair had fallen over his face, he pushed it back, and smiled at her.

'And do you – I mean, it's none of my business, but do you make any money from all this?'

'Not a lot. I've done this demo tape. The recording studio cost a fortune, and I've sent it out everywhere, but so far nothing's happened. Local radio, but –' His hands ran over the keyboard. 'Still waiting for the phone call.'

'I'm sure it'll come,' said Nesta, and realised she meant it. 'I mean, you are good, I think. I do like it.'

'Thanks. I'll play you something else now.'

'Something of yours?'

'Yeah, some friends are playing. It's on a different tape, hang on.' He turned to look along a shelf.

Nesta shifted in the chair, feeling in her pocket for the tobacco tin, and Abraham made a sound. 'It's all right,' she said, stroking him again. 'I'm not going anywhere.'

'Are you musical?' Phil asked her, still looking. 'I mean you've obviously got taste –'

'Obviously.' She was licking a paper, raised an eyebrow at him. 'I don't know if I am. I can hardly play a note, but I do use music with the children all the time. Percussion mostly, very simple, but we all enjoy it. You should come and listen one day.' She rested the paper on the arm of the chair, sprinkled in tobacco. 'Hal was the really musical one,' she said, as Phil found his tape, and slotted it in. 'He played the piano, he was always singing –'

Phil pressed the button: the sound of a harp filled the room. Swift-flowing water, wind in the trees. He turned to look at her.

He said: 'He's always with you, isn't he? Hal. All the time.'

She glanced up, feeling the music run through her, meeting his gaze.

The rain fell away. Nesta, listening to harp, violin and piano, fell asleep. She woke, and saw through the window the sky above the distant hills grown light. A struggling sun lit shapeless clouds. She looked at her watch. Soon it would be dark again.

Across on the other side of the room Phil was stretched out in the other chair, long legs before him, feet in Doc Martens crossed. He, too, had his eyes closed. The music, accomplished and tender, came to an end. Abraham stirred. She said quietly:

'Phil?'

Eyes open, a lazy sweet smile.

She thought, for a sudden, surprising moment: we could be waking after making love.

He looked at her, and she knew, instinctively, that he was thinking the same.

'Mmm?'

'I must go soon.'

'Not quite yet.'

The fire had died down; he leaned forward, put on the last couple of logs. A few little flames began to grow round them. He looked beyond her to the window.

'It's stopped raining.'

'It has.' Nesta felt Abraham stir again.

'Tea-time,' said Phil, getting up. 'Yes? Would you like a cup?'

'I would.' She looked at him, tall and graceful and easy.

She said: 'This has been very nice.'

'Yeah. It's still very nice. I'm going to play you one more thing before you go.'

'Thanks. I like the harp. Really.'

'Yeah, everyone likes that. Back in a minute.'

He went out of the room. Abraham leapt from her lap and followed.

Nesta sat on in the sagging chair. She watched the fire growing again, beginning to crackle. She heard Phil banging about in the kitchen, putting the kettle on, opening cat food. She heard him go down the hall to the back, and a chain flush.

She thought: We fell asleep together.

He came back, put mugs on the table beside her.

She said: 'That singer, Rowland something. In the pub. You said you had a CD –'

'I have. Rowland King. That's what I was just going to play you. Here.' He passed her a mug; he rose, looked through the CDs. 'OK. Listen to this.'

An unaccompanied tenor, pure and clear.

'*Domini nostri, Jesu Christi . . .*'

The room was full of him. An answering bass, a company of voices, tender and clear. Rowland again.

Nesta listened, and found she was full of awe. 'He's –'

'He's the best,' said Phil.

'What is this?'

'St Matthew Passion. Lassus.'

It meant nothing to her: not the composer, not the Passion of Christ. But Rowland's voice –

'And there's this,' said Phil, putting on something else. 'The Christmas Story – a bit late, but I think you'll like it. Schütz – seventeenth-century German.'

'Can I just see –' Nesta got up, reaching for the CD case. She stood by the fire, looking at the photograph.

The London Consort. They stood in some church interior, evening dress against stone pillars, the women in silk and taffeta. The soloists, presumably, stood at the front, and there was Rowland, heavy and dark and smiling to the camera. She thought: I don't know anyone like you.

'Here,' said Phil. Strings and organ sounded. Nesta listened. 'Rowland King's the Evangelist.' He passed her the notes.

The strings died away, in came the cello. In came Rowland's extraordinary voice.

'*"Es begab sich aber zu derselbigen Zeit..."*'

Nesta frowned, and found the translation.

'And it came to pass in those days that there went out a decree from Caesar Augustus that all the world should be taxed...'

Christmas and the snow had come and gone. She thought of the pigeon, soft and grey, the moment of silence with the children, whiteness everywhere.

She sat down again, listening.

'*"Aber das Kind wuchs und war stark im Geist..."*'

'And the child grew and waxed strong in spirit, filled with wisdom, and the grace of God was upon him.'

Nesta sat smoking, thinking.

The grace of God –

A line which Gillian might use. She thought once again of the reading, of Gillian on fire before her audience; of them all downstairs afterwards; of Rowland, so clearly, watching Phil –

Triumphant brass. The music ended, the fire spat. Nesta looked at Phil, leaning forward to tend it, hair falling over his face again. He was musical and young and careless; perhaps he was beautiful. She said slowly: 'Did you realise that –'

'What?' He looked up at her.

'That Rowland King liked the look of you.'

'Yeah?' he said, and the languid smile returned. 'Fancy that. My hero.'

'Is he?'

'One of them.' He gestured round the room. 'I like all sorts of things, I'm interested in music, full stop. King's a hero, so's Bach, so's Eric Clapton, so's Orb.'

'Isn't that unusual?'

He shrugged. 'I don't know. I just know music is what matters. King probably likes a wide range, too, he wouldn't be a real musician if he didn't. Anyway –' He leaned forward for the case; like her, he studied the photograph. 'I suppose I'm quite flattered.'

'It doesn't bother you?'

'No, why should it? We're not living in the Stone Age, even out here. Anyway –' He took another look at the photograph. 'I don't suppose I'll ever see him again.'

'You might. You might well.' She threw the end of her cigarette into the fire, with a sudden thought. 'I suppose he could help you, couldn't he?'

Phil looked at her, considering. 'Yeah,' he said slowly. 'Yeah, I suppose he could.'

It was growing darker. They went to the cottage door. Abraham, with a little sound, slipped past them in the porch, and out to the field.

'Hunting,' said Phil. 'He brings dead things back in the morning.'

'Even though he's been fed?'

'Some cats are greedy. God, it's cold.'

The ground was soaking, the trees dripped. Nesta glanced at sodden shirts and jeans on the line.

'You forgot your washing.'

'So I did.'

Their feet squelched in the coarse grass. They came to her car.

'Well,' said Nesta, feeling for her keys. 'Thanks for a lovely afternoon.'

'Thanks for coming.' He leaned forward, gently kissed her cheek. Light soft hair brushed her face; for a moment she could think of nothing.

He said: 'May I phone you again?'

'Yes. Yes, of course.' Clouds were gathering; she opened the car door.

His hand touched an earring. 'Bye, Nesta.'

'Goodbye.' She smiled at him quickly, climbed into her car. Phil walked alongside as she bumped over the field; they came to the gate and he swung it open. She flicked on the lights, seeing the lane wet and shining, and something dart into the hedge. In the mirror, as she pulled out, she saw Phil waving, closing the gate.

Well.

She drove home slowly, following the signs, turning over the afternoon. An owl on a gatepost stared into the headlights, the fields stretched away in a deep, midwinter quietness. She came to the turning to home.

Well? asked Hal, waiting. How did you get on?

*

'"Quomodo sedet sola...
How doth the city sit solitary
that was full of people.

How is she become as a widow...

Jerusalem, Jerusalem, return to the Lord thy God..."'

Edward sat listening in the darkening farmhouse. The rain, which had eased off in late afternoon, had begun again: in the pause between verses he could hear it, soaking into the field behind the house. The ewes, imperturbable, stood grazing alongside the hedge.

The music ended. He said aloud: 'I shall do nothing.'

The rain fell for days, and the river ran fast and deep. It carried winter debris from up the hills – fallen twigs and branches, fallen birds. The water rose higher. It bore the skull of a sheep, picked clean by crows, a mangled rabbit, bloody-furred and eyeless, remains of a buzzard's kill. There were things left behind by walkers; a woollen glove, a beer can, silver paper. Flotsam and jetsam swept past the clumps of dead reeds, were darted at by ducks.

The rain fell and the water rose and council surveyors parked on the road by the bridge and walked over the spiked marshy grass in boots and anoraks. They looked at the water-level post and made notes. Rain trickled down their spectacles: they went for a warming drink in the Fox. The water rose and the spikes of the marshy grass disappeared. Low-lying fields were lakes, and ditches gurgled. The red-painted mark on the water-level post was reached, and passed, and now everyone was talking of it, a few recalling the autumn floods of 1961, when Edward Traherne was drowned.

Gillian could not sleep. In the long drowning hours of the night she lay on her lumpy mattress, listening to the incessant fall of water, craving the silence of the snow. The rain overflowed the blocked and broken guttering and spouted from cracked and loosening pipes. It splashed and poured on the glossy dark leaves of ivy and leaked through the bathroom ceiling, into a bowl. Gillian rose from her lumpy mattress and climbed out of bed. She went to her window and watched the rain driving against the glass, sweeping along the lane and down the hill to the churchyard, soaking the bones of the dead.

She went to her desk, where the quarterly magazine from the Mandrake Press lay on a pile of notebooks. When the rain stopped, she would take it to show him: he must be the first. She would walk up the empty lanes to the farmyard, and lift the gate –

'Gillian.'

'Edward.'

She gave him the magazine, she received his kiss. Once, twice on the cheek, and then –

Into the quietness of the house, the warmth of the kitchen, the tick of the clock. Into the library, side by side at the polished table. He put on his spectacles, turned the pages, began to read. The dog slept. Around them everything was still.

Gillian picked up the magazine and held its coolness against her burning cheeks. Along the landing Phoebe coughed in her sleep. Rain beat against the windows.

The village was threatened with flooding. Edward thought of Gillian and Phoebe, hearing the talk in the shops, driving the Land Rover out to the bridge to look at the rising river, the heavy slant of rain on the marshy banks. Wild swans and water birds made for the reeds, and shelter. He drove back through the village, sending up swishing sprays of water; he imagined it all, over thirty years ago, swirling over doorsteps, rising to windows, and upper windows, the tractor with Edward Traherne upon it, ferrying families up to high ground, and the church.

And then the drowning dog, the hand extended, the slip on the footplate, the sudden gasp –

When he got home again, Rowland phoned; he had heard the weather forecast and sounded solicitous.

'Seen anything of anybody?' he asked lightly. 'Been to the pub?'

Edward said it was too wet to see anyone. Except for essential forays, people kept indoors. He'd had to drive out to the market town for vaccine from the vet. Other than that, and checks on the hens, he and Tarn were confined to the house. He was reading a lot.

He listened to the news from London: of rehearsals and concerts, a good recording, somebody's party.

'You should come down,' said Rowland.

His heart leapt.

But he couldn't, so close to his first lambing: it felt irresponsible, foolish.

'You couldn't come up?' he asked, holding the telephone close to his ear, watching the endless rain.

Pages turned in the diary. Not quite yet.

They said goodbye with casual affection. It didn't feel right. Edward rang back again, half an hour later. The answerphone was on. He wanted to leave a message, but he didn't.

He went out to check on the hens, cooped up and silent. No eggs. Rain pattered hard on the roof. He returned to the house, the dog at his heels; inside, he rubbed at her soaking coat. He tried to read.

In the long aching hours of the night he lay thinking, recalling the two of them at Christmas: so close, so deep, watching the silent fall of snow.

The rain fell, and a moment of danger was reached. The news spoke of gales on the coast, coming inland. But the moment passed. The gales blew away to the north, and never came over the Cambrian Mountains, nor the Black Mountains or Brecon Beacons, closer to home. The rain, in the middle of the fourth night, slowed, and stopped. In the morning, the sky was clear.

Over the next few days the water subsided. Talk in the village turned to other things. It grew colder. The talk turned to lambing.

Phoebe, unable to get out in the garden for days, was out there as soon as the rainfall ended. She walked in her Wellington boots down the paths, gathering up drowned snails in a bucket. The herringbone brickwork was dark, still holding water; the beds were full of stones, washed up to the surface, but the rain, though relentless, had been steady: the gales had not crossed the mountains, and her stakes stood firm. Nothing had been uprooted or lost. The bulbs, just poking up, were loose in their moorings of earth, but would soon settle down and be none the worse for a soaking.

She squelched between fruit trees, down to the pond.

The water had risen; the surface was thick with duckweed. The reeds, so tall and thick in summer, were wet pale parchment. Beneath the ash tree the first sweet shoots of snowdrops were appearing, amidst tufts of unkempt grass. A nice wild place: the reeds needed cutting, but nothing much else to be done. Another few weeks, and the ground would be full of kingcups and aconites, the first spears of yellow flag iris knifing upwards.

Phoebe stood for a while, observing things. Across the hedge in the farmer's field the grass was alive with starlings, making a racket, stabbing at the ground. Iridescent plumage shone against the wet grass; they were after the leatherjacket grubs washed up by the rain: that was a useful job.

Another few weeks and the cows would be back, let out to pasture, moving over the lush new grass.

Phoebe stood watching, listening to the birds. Beyond the field, though the sky was clearing, the hills were still misty, low cloud drifting over the highest peaks.

How it had rained.

For a moment she saw herself, thirty years younger, out in the garden after the floods, looking out over the hills, Gillian silent and white beside her; finding herself in the strange new country of widowhood.

Single again. A stab of relief.

But then there was the white and silent child.

'Mother?'

'Yes?'

'What's going to happen to us?'

'Nothing,' she said firmly. 'Everything will stay the same.'

Phoebe carried her bucket of snails to the compost heap, and threw them out. They scattered and landed with small wet sounds. She noticed, swinging the bucket again, walking across to the dry-stone wall, the queer tight feeling in her chest which came and went.

Well. It came, and it was fortunate that it went. Nothing to make a fuss about. There had been the brief, unheard-of fever at Christmas: not a day's illness since. She set down the bucket and walked through the gate to the vegetable garden, up and down the paths. Slugs were everywhere. Back for the bucket. Lots to do.

Up in the house, at the leaking bathroom window, Gillian watched her stalk about.

The ewes, as always, scattered at his approach. Tarn, invisibly leashed beside him, waited the command. The morning air was cold: raw, February weather, a succession of dark days following the last dramatic weeks of snow and rain. Now the rain had been swept away. It returned now and then in sharp flurries, but mostly there was only this cold: dark nights, dark mornings, sunless days. He read books about lambing, and talked to the vet.

'If there's a way of dying, sheep will find it.' The vet, small and wiry, took boxes of booster vaccine down from the shelves, protection against lamb dysentery and other diseases. He talked about enzootic abortions, infections, mastitis, watery mouth.

154

'Not doing this all on your own, I hope,' he said, writing out the bill.

'So far.'

'Well, you know where we are.'

Edward drove home again, the boxes on the seat beside him. The ewes were on a high protein feed now, supplementing the hay: heavy sacks of pellets from the feed merchant, taken out to a field in the trailer, tipped out into a trough.

On his return he watched them crowd around it, the great fleecy bulk of them, heavy with lambs. He tried to remember things his grandfather had told him, remembered only the extraordinary moments of seeing his first lamb delivered: drawn out with baler twine, coated in muck, lying limp and ugly in the hay, and the ewe transformed: licking, snickering, unimaginably active and vocal, nudging the long trembling legs and pointed face, the lamb up in minutes, tail wriggling wildly, nose in the heavy fleece, hungry and seeking.

The dog Ben was gulping something bloody and full.

His grandfather's hand was on his shoulder. 'All right? Quite a sight, eh?'

'Yes.' He watched the lamb's urgent struggle for the teat, the moment of satisfaction. He thought: Now I know about these things.

'Okay, Tarn. Not too fast.'

She was crouched low beside him: now she sprang away, running in a great sweep round the field, circling the bleating ewes, drawing them in, ears pricked to his whistle and call.

'Steady, steady, get on, that's it, away to me now –'

He was up there with his crook, moving round the animals, driving them down towards the pen. The cold air was full of their cries.

He strode down the field again, lifted the latch of the first gate. The boxes of vaccine were there in a carrier bag, hung over a post. He felt in his pocket for the syringe, capped and ready. He'd done this once before; shown by the vet on a visit last November: this was the booster. He stood there opening the first box, stripping off the foil round the row of ampoules; he snapped off the top, filled up the syringe, held it up to the light. He was watching his grandfather, all those years ago: the practised eye, the steady hand, calm voice.

'That's it. Good lad.'

'Right, Tarn.' He could hear himself echo the easy tone he'd loved as a child. 'Let's be having them.'

In came the first ewe, looking nervously about her; he grabbed her, held her fast between his knees, parted the thick oily fleece.

'Good girl, good girl.' A quick sure movement to aim for: his fingers shook. He drove into invisible skin. The ewe made a desperate movement. 'Wait!' He let her free, but kept the pen shut. He knelt beside her, feeling her condition: he tried to feel for breech, for twins, running his hands down the fleece, over the swollen belly, checking between the back legs for any indication of prolapse. Sometimes half the uterus protruded; then the ewe had to be strapped up, lumbering about in the last weeks in harness. This one felt all right: only one lamb, and everything in place.

'Okay, off you go.'

And he released her, lifting the latch of the second gate, letting her bounce away and swerve up the field.

'Tarn?'

In came the next. This time his hand was steadier.

The morning wore on, the sky lightened. He managed the lot of them, one by one, without a single accident: no spills, no broken needles. For an hour or so he thought of nothing but the job in hand: catching, holding, injecting, and inspecting; releasing through the gate. The pen was well made; the task well accomplished. For a moment he thought of Phoebe, her competence and briskness.

'Tarn? Last one.'

The last one was frantic, separated from the flock.

'Steady, steady, that's a girl, easy now.'

The last ampoule empty; he ran his hands over her vast bulk. This one could be tricky: twins for certain, and maybe, tucked deeply, a tiny third. He pulled out the can of spray from his pocket, gave a quick burst of scarlet down by the tail. Have to keep an eye.

'Right.' The stink of the spray hung in the air for a moment. Could get high on this if you weren't careful, especially down in the barn. 'Off you go.' Up with the latch on the gate, and out she trotted.

'Lie down,' he told Tarn. 'Leave them now.'

He went round the pen, picking up the empty ampoules, dropping them into the bag. And out, clicking the latch behind him. He walked down to the field gate, thinking of help he would need. Eighty-five ewes he'd have down in the barn. Even if it was easier there, having them all penned in, he still wouldn't manage it all on his own, night after night. He wondered if he had left it too late to ask around, and decided he probably had. He'd better ring Pritchard, see if there was anyone he knew. Again, for a moment, he found himself thinking of Phoebe, so lean and energetic. In a difficult moment she might come in useful, could probably turn her hand to anything. Perhaps he should drive over, have a word.

The air was sharp and fresh. Clouds moved swiftly, rooks made a din in the trees. As he came down through the field gate, leaving Tarn nosing about in the hedge, he saw ahead on the farm roof the solitary jackdaw, heard its quick harsh call. He remembered the morning of Rowland's departure, and his desolation; he wondered why now, with a useful task accomplished, and plenty more to do, he should feel it again, such an ache of absence, and realised it came from thinking of Phoebe, which made him think of Gillian, and recall again the reading: her brilliance, and his delight in it, and then, coming in from the cold with Tarn beside him, his moment of shock and fear.

'Rowland,' he said aloud.

Rooks called, the jackdaw suddenly rose from the roof. He came into the farmyard, saw Gillian: closing the gate to the lane behind her, crossing the yard. She looked up and saw him. Her face was aflame.

Who is this, that cometh up from the wilderness –

'Hello,' he said gently, feeling her terrible shyness. 'I was just thinking of you.'

They sat side by side at the polished table. He opened the magazine, he sniffed the pages.

She watched him. How nicely he did things: receiving the magazine with a kiss, setting it aside until he had washed his hands from being outside with the sheep, had made her tea, and brought her in here. Everything done at a measured pace, everything right. Now he could give the poems his full attention. He had put on his glasses: it gave her such pleasure to watch him do that.

'So.' He ran a finger down the contents page, he read the editorial.

'Edward Traherne, descendant of Thomas ... a fine lyric poet whose reputation has been too long in the shade ... tragic death ... his daughter, Gillian, a striking and original voice ... should reach a wider audience...'

He looked at her over his spectacles. 'This is very nice. Are you pleased?'

'Of course.'

He turned to the poems. '"In Penglydr Churchyard" – I'm glad they took that. And "Cadair Hall" – yes, I remember. You read them both, didn't you?' He ran his eye down the verses, nodding; he leaned back in his chair. 'Why don't you read them again to me now?' He passed the magazine to her, still open.

'Oh, no, I –' She shrank from the thought. Up in the farmhouse, miles from anywhere –

'Go on,' he said gently.

Such a beautiful voice –

How close they would be. How intimate –

'I don't think I –'

'Please.'

A shaft of winter sunlight, struggling through cloud, glanced in at the window to the yard.

'There,' said Edward, indicating its fall to the floor. 'Your spotlight.'

Well. There was no one to know.

She rose, trembling all over. She walked to the window, stood with her back to it. Hesitant sun lit the quarto pages.

She began to read.

Doves ascended, daffodils blew, a coffin went deep, deep –

The pages shook, but her voice grew stronger.

The water beneath the earth had risen, a child had been swept away –

There came over the still and shining waters an eagle, mighty and cruel, his wings beating through the skies of Wales –

Inside the church, a bible rested upon his back, open at one of the psalms:

The floods are risen, O Lord, the floods have lift up their voice . . .

Gillian was alight. She read to the end of 'Penglydr Churchyard', she drew breath, leaving a moment's silence. Within it, she felt Edward's eyes upon her.

'"At Cadair Hall",' she said to the holy shaft of sunlight. She read of vows, and a door swung shut for ever. Voices chanted through the canonical hours of the night; at daybreak the mist rose from the fields; in the heavy stillness of noon larks sang, and the fields were golden.

The corn was orient and immortal wheat, which never should be reaped, nor was ever sown. I thought it had stood from everlasting to everlasting –

She finished reading.

The silence of the house fell upon her.

Edward said quietly: 'Gillian –'

'Yes?' She was trembling all over.

'You are inspired,' he said simply. 'I have no other word for what you are.'

I am in love, she said to the sacred winter light, feeling the rapture of those extraordinary words rising from deep within her, filling her, taking her, body and soul. I am in love.

She could not look at him. She could not speak.

The dog came down from the back field and made her way round to the yard. She barked, once. Edward rose to let her in; she followed him along the passage. Gillian could hear her claws click on the boards. She moved from the window, sat on the high-backed chair at the table, waiting for Edward's return.

'Kitchen,' he said to the dog in the passage. 'Basket. Go on. You've got muddy feet, you shouldn't be coming round to the front.'

The dog was obedient: Gillian heard her go into the kitchen. She heard the lapping of water from a stone dish, the creak of wicker. She sat quite still, the magazine before her on the table, her heart hammering.

'So,' said Edward, returning. 'Here we are.'

He sat down again, shifted his chair back so he could look at her. He pushed up his glasses. 'Well, now. What are we going to do with you?'

Gillian gazed at a place in the middle of the table. Someone once had scratched at it, gouged it, even: a bored little boy, leaning across, digging deep, forgetting everything else –

'*Thomas!*'

He jumped up, dropped the penknife, was sharply scolded. He fled, banished from civilised people, in tears and scarlet –

'What do you mean?' she asked the scratched-out place.

Edward tapped the magazine. 'It's true. What they say of you. You should have a wider audience. We must think.'

She shook her head. Her cheeks were still flaming. 'No. No. This is quite enough.'

Edward looked at her. She could feel it. He said to her: 'Where have you read? I mean outside Penglydr.'

She tried to think.

'Brecon once. Abervale and Chapelbrook. Just villages.' She picked at a corner of the magazine. 'Nowhere, really.'

'But you are known locally – yes? You have a following.'

'I'm not sure I would call it that.' A quick wry smile: she looked away.

'Well.' His fingers drummed on the table. 'We need a plan. A wider world awaits.'

Who had said that to her, all those years ago? The vicar, in his sage-coloured cardigan, in a house full of tea chests, waiting to move away. She had gone to say goodbye, taking chrysanthemums wrapped in newspaper; resting her bicycle against the wall, clicking open the gate. How quiet everything was.

The floods are risen, O Lord, the floods have lift up their voice –

'I wanted to ask you – about the plaque to my father. Why did my mother choose the psalm? I wish she'd used one of his poems.'

Gillian bent the corner of the magazine back and forth, not looking at Edward. Moments in a lost and difficult girlhood had been waiting for these moments, she could feel it: an arc drew together the child adrift and the woman who had come home.

She said, not looking at Edward: 'A world in a grain of sand. My place is here.'

He saw her to the gate. It was time for lunch, but she would not stay and he did not press her, sensing her sudden withdrawal, as if he had pushed her too hard. And he must be off to see Pritchard, sort out some help,

'Tell me,' he asked her, lifting the latch, 'does your mother know much about lambs?'

'My mother?' She frowned, stepping back as the gate swung wide. 'I expect she knows something, yes. She knows about most things.'

'That's what I thought. It's just in case of emergency –' He explained, filling in a little of his background, his childhood dream, and inexperience, swinging the gate back and forth. She listened intently, her eyes on the ground.

'I'm talking too much,' he said at last. How cold she must be, waiting for him to finish.

'Not at all.' Her colour rose: she glanced up at him. 'I am always talking about myself – I know almost nothing about your life.'

'Well.' He made a gesture, thinking how true that was. 'There's plenty of time.'

'Yes.' The cold damp air had loosened her wild mass of hair; she looked suddenly happy again. 'Thank you for looking at this.' She tapped the magazine in her tweed coat pocket.

He bent to kiss her. 'Thank you for showing me. Thank you for coming.' His hand rested a moment on her shoulder: her eyes shone. 'I'll see you soon,' he said, feeling their deepening engagement with one another, the growth of his affection for her.

'Yes,' said Gillian.

And then she walked out through the wide-open gate, and down to the corner of the lane, turning once, quickly, to nod a goodbye as he swung the gate back to the latch. He raised his hand; the gate banged shut; she was gone.

Edward walked back up the yard. Rooks called from behind the house; he noticed a wagtail, walking up and down by the pump: it flew off, came down again in a corner. Up and down, up and down. Another few weeks and the place would be alive with birds, seizing stray stalks of hay and fallen twigs, nesting in the eaves, in the trees, all down the lanes. Well. That was something to look forward to: that and the lambs.

He must do something about the lambs. Make a phone call, talk to his neighbour, Pritchard.

He came to the door; feeling how cold it was again, the coldest day since the snow. What a long way Gillian had to walk. He stood pulling his boots off, thinking of her, tramping the empty lanes in her Wellingtons, coming to bring him her poems.

'A wider world awaits.'

'A world in a grain of sand. My place is here.'

He turned over the times they had spent together: the meeting in the garden, smoke rising thinly from the bonfire, into the autumn sky; moments in an icy church, a wintry churchyard; quiet hours here of books and conversation. He thought of her reading just now, her incandescence.

Sheep bleated, clouds passed over the farmhouse roof. He went indoors. Rowland's weatherproof jacket hung on the rack in the passage; he hung his own next to it, touched them both. He heard himself saying to Gillian:

'There's something I'd like to talk to you about –'

Then he saw her strange virginal face before him, the face of a woman inspired and reclusive, who went nowhere, knew only local people, who shrank from the wider world. No, he thought. No. Not yet.

'Where have you been?' asked Phoebe.

'Walking.' She hung up her coat, left her boots in the porch.

'I do wish you –'

'Sorry.'

Gillian climbed the stairs. She walked along the creaking landing to the bathroom. When she had finished, she held her cold hands beneath hot running water, hearing the pipes bang.

Put in the *plug*, said Phoebe. You're wasting it all.

She turned off the tap and stood looking out at the garden. Snowdrops, the nuns of winter, grew in abundance: along the brick paths, down by the pond, in clumps beneath the trees. Their petals were closed in prayer: soon they would open, pierced by the sharp spring sun, and give thanks.

She put her hands to her face, hardly breathing.

'Gillian!'

She pushed open the window. Below, from the dovecot, came a movement, the flutter of wings, the scratch of long feet on the lichened ledge. Then out flew a dove, and another, beating down over the garden, just on the edge of greenness. They flew high over the empty flowerbeds, the herb and kitchen garden, the long herringbone of the paths, over the orchard, towards the winter-dead reeds, and the first shoots of spring, down to the altar of the garden. They alighted in the ash tree, they settled themselves in the kingdom of heaven.

'Gillian!'

'Coming.'

She walked back along the threadbare runner, past Phoebe's unheated bedroom and the cupboards of unused linen.

'Lunchtime,' said Phoebe, down at the foot of the stairs. 'Long past lunchtime.'

'Coming.'

She went to her bedroom, she closed the door. She stood at her desk with its piles of paper, sheet upon sheet. Some things were male and some were female: white sheets lay beneath the fountain pen, waiting to receive his touch. She picked it up, stood motionless.

'*You are inspired –*'

'I am in love,' whispered Gillian, into the dusty emptiness of her room.

She heard his voice within her, so deep, so deep.

'I am in love.'

The scratched, unpolished desk, the sagging bed and weary low rush chair stood listening: she held out her arms to embrace each one.

11

Nesta and Phil were out walking. It was a Saturday afternoon: tonight she was on night watch again, and up at the Hall till the following weekend, covering staff shortages: Martin, off sick with flu, and Claire, who was visiting her family. Nesta had spent the morning tidying up, ironing, packing her bag for the week ahead; she had eaten the last of the bread and cheese, and made a list of everything she would need to shop for, on her way back. Then she had locked up the cottage, and walked up the path to the car.

Beyond the field gate the sheep glanced up as she started the car; she drove up the rutted track, still thick with mud from the rains, turning left to drive past the Feathers, as usual, and then, at the junction, left again, heading towards Long Betton, a route she knew now, after a couple of invitations, with no need to look at the map.

She drew up by the verge at Phil's gate, saw him already at the cottage door, coming down the field towards her, ready to help.

'Hi.'

A kiss on the cheek through the open window; she bumped across the grass, seeing him, in the mirror, closing the gate, walking up behind her.

'Coffee? Or shall we just go?'

They stood together, looking at the sky. The last two visits had held music and a great deal of rain. This was their first walk. The sky was light and high: wind blew the clouds to the west.

'Let's just go,' said Nesta. 'Where's Abraham?'

'Somewhere about. I'll get my jacket.'

She waited for him; the cat came round from the side of the woodpile, carrying something.

'Oh, Abraham –' She reached out towards him; he fled.

'Abraham's got a mouse,' she told Phil, as he came out, closing the door. 'Or something.'

'Probably a vole. I told you – he's ruthless.' He looked round the field. 'Better leave him to it. Come on.' They walked back over the grass, and out to the lane. 'Feeling strong enough for a climb?'

'Of course.'

They walked down the lane. 'Tell me what you've been doing.'

She told him about the previous week, the rhythm of the children's days, broken now and then by visiting parents.

'Isn't that hard?' he asked her. 'For everyone?'

'Sometimes.' Her hands were in her pockets; she turned to look at him. 'What about you? What are you working on?'

'Something called "Birdsfoot". Don't know why I've called it that – the title came first, which isn't usual. It's full of percussion.'

'That's what we do with the children.'

'I know. I think it must have begun with you telling me that.'

'It must be very satisfying,' she said, as they rounded a bend, and drew back for an approaching car.

'What's that?'

'To have music at the centre of your life in this way – to be able to draw everything together with it – I don't know –'

'Everything's music,' he said, as she stepped off the verge. 'You just have to listen, that's all. Like now, on a walk – it's all around us.'

Despite her work, despite her own long involvement with music and painting and dance, and with helping the children to enjoy these things, there was a part of Nesta which instinctively withdrew from such statements. She said nothing.

'No? Too sentimental? Too New Age?'

'Perhaps a bit. Perhaps a musician would think like that, but –'

'It's true, though,' he said seriously. 'It's a gift, it's a craft, but just you listen, now.' He turned on the lilt; she smiled.

She listened – to their footsteps on the lane, and in the tussocky grass, as they entered a field on the right, to their breathing as they climbed a hill, to the cries of sheep and birds and running water when they reached the top and stood looking out over the valley. The wind blew Phil's pale hair over his face; he brushed it away, and smiled at her.

'See?' He held out a hand. She did not take it.

'Not yet?'

'Not yet.'

She did not know whether she was making too much of this: to take his hand could be just an easy acceptance of a growing friendship which might, or might not, become more. Not to take it, to say 'not yet' implied something already serious, already in the process of becoming important, waiting only for a touch to say: Yes, now, I will give myself to you –

And that she could not do.

Take your time, said Hal, as he used to say to the children. No rush. You'll know if it's right.

Phil's hand was back in his pocket. The wind blew his hair over his face again, blew the cries of the sheep and the birds all around them. Nesta looked out over the hills across the valley, at the clumps of bare trees, the churches and chapels; the farms where the sheep had been brought down to the lower fields, for lambing. She looked along the course of the winding river, which in the endless January rain had swollen and risen and threatened to flood: her first taste of a wet Welsh winter, the cottage windows lashed and shaken all one terrifying night, the track an almost impassable sea, car wheels churning the mud as she left thankfully for Cadair in the morning. She'd parked on the top after that.

She said: 'I can't believe I live here now.'

'You must miss London. I don't just mean –'

'No. I know.' Nesta considered. They walked on. 'I miss my friends,' she said, 'but I haven't been back to see them. They haven't been here. We write. We phone each other. The same with my parents, and – and Hal's mother. I haven't seen anyone.'

'Not even at Christmas?'

'No. I was up at the Hall.' They were coming down the hillside again. She said: 'Sometimes I think I'll go down on my free days, just get in the car and go and see everyone, but so far I haven't. I'm sure I will, I know I will, but –'

'Not yet.'

'No.'

The ground sloped steeply, and was uneven. It told on the knees, especially if you weren't used to it. They stopped and sat down for a breather. Phil rolled a couple of cigarettes. He said: 'Do you know why? Why you're resisting?'

'It isn't a mystery,' said Nesta, smoking. 'I closed a door there: it was very deliberate. All that illness, and decline, and grieving –' She stopped, shaking her head. 'It was too much, just – too much. I made a decision, to change my life. I changed it: I came here. Now –' She was tugging the tough winter grass. 'Now I suppose I can't bear to go back. I suppose that's the truth.' Stalks came away in her hand. She said, looking out across the valley, 'I didn't expect that to happen, but it has.'

Phil sat listening. He said: 'I'm sorry, Nesta. I shouldn't keep asking you things. It must stir everything up again –'

'It's all right. It's getting better.'

'Is it?'

'In some ways.' The grass was damp; she got to her feet. 'So,' she said, seeing his diffident concern, realising again how young he was, how difficult he must find such circumstances. 'So. Here I am in Wales. Let's go.'

They walked on down the hillside; below them, Phil's cottage was a featureless square, his van and her car two specks beside it.

He said: 'Nesta –'

'Yes?'

'I –' He stopped again. 'No. Never mind.'

Far above them, a buzzard was wheeling: she watched it, as she often did now – something else which had become a regular feature of her life, like the visits of the farmer. Things were taking shape.

'Go on,' she said to Phil. 'Say it – it's okay.'

'Only – I'm not going to rush you.' He looked at her, and then away. 'There's plenty of time.'

'Yes. Yes, I know. Thanks.' She felt a quickening of relief.

They walked on. Above them the buzzard rose and fell.

That night, Nesta had a dream which shocked her. She dreamed that Hal was walking away from her, down their old street, in Camden. He walked past parked cars, beneath the street lamps. It was dark, and every time he passed one of the lamps he disappeared.

'Hal?'

She was walking after him, trying to hurry, but her feet were like lead and her legs were dragging.

'Hal?'

He came out in the light of a lamp far ahead of her, he did not hear her, he did not look back.

'Hal!' She sank to the ground and began a long crawl down the street, as if that would help her, as if she could reach him now. A cat crossed the pavement, carrying something: she looked, and saw a baby hang from his mouth, small and white and bloodied. No, she said aloud, no, no.

She felt herself struggle to the surface, where part of her knew she was dreaming, she heard her own voice saying, It's Phil, with a mouse, that's all –

Then she sank back down into the dream again, drawn down as if she were drowning, seeing the baby, its little arms flailing, little feet kicking wildly; she heard its tiny cry – help me help me –

'Ha-al!'

She was standing in the sitting room of the cottage. It was night, there were candles. Hal leaned against the fireplace. He said coldly: 'You must do whatever you want.'

'But I don't want anything. I only want you –'

He turned away from her.

She said: 'Where is our baby? We should have had a baby –' She heard herself weeping. 'Hal, Hal –'

She woke, and the pillow was soaking.

She sat up, hearing a cry.

'What –' She struggled out of bed, stood shaking.

Outside the window of the night-watch bedroom the valley was silent and dark. A low lamp glowed on the table, low lights glowed all along the landing. Along the landing she could hear someone crying and calling –

'Yes –'

She was on night-watch. One of the children. Dominic. A nightmare. Yes. She drew a deep breath, and went to calm him.

He bit her and scratched her, and would not be calmed.

'Sssh, sssh –'

She struggled to hold him, as Hal used to hold the children, steady and strong, but Dominic was stronger, and he yelled. Other children were stirring. Nesta thought: I can't manage this –

She held him and held him, murmuring and whispering into his coarse dark hair. At last he stopped. She rocked him and rocked him. At last he slept.

Nesta crept out of the room and along the landing. Down in the hall the grandfather clock ticked steadily, then sounded slow deep notes. It was three o'clock in the morning. She went back to bed. She lay in the glow of the lamp, breathing deeply, but she could not sleep. She listened to the sounds of the children, the murmurs and moaning, the snores and uneven breathing. She thought about her dream, which had been a nightmare. She thought: I have held everything together for so long, and now – She began to cry again, quietly, dreading another call from the children. She fell at last into a fitful sleep, waking at daybreak, with the birds.

She lay for a few minutes, watching the light seep into the room, then she got out of bed and went quietly down the broad staircase, into the flagstoned hall. The clock struck six. She pushed open the door of the office, where the telephone was. Books lined the walls, and photographs of children. Nesta lifted the phone. She dialled Phil's number. It rang and rang.

'Hello?'

His voice was thick with sleep.

'It's me,' said Nesta, her stomach like water. 'I'm sorry to wake you.'

'Nesta. Are you all right?'

'No,' she said, hearing the birds beyond the window. 'No, not really.'

'Had a bad night?'

'Yes.' She took a breath. 'It's not like me to make phone calls at this hour – I'm sorry, I just –'

His voice was no longer sleepy. 'Nesta – you don't have to say sorry. You can phone me any time. Tell me what's wrong.'

She said: 'I've held everything together –'

'I know, I know that.' His voice was filled with tenderness.

'And now –' She wanted to tell him about the dream, she began to tell him, and then she thought: No, not yet. Around her the house was stirring, she could hear children waking, and somebody coming down the stairs, probably Jonathan, going to make tea. The day was starting. She began to feel better.

She said: 'When I'm off duty – next weekend – will you come to my cottage and see me?'

'Yes,' said Phil. 'I'll bring you some music. Would you like that?'

'Yes,' said Nesta.

Pritchard came over, to look at the ewes. Edward heard the trailer pull up in the yard, and went out to greet him. Pritchard jumped down, threw away the end of a roll-up, told the dog in the cab to stay. The dog, much bigger and older than Tarn, sat panting, turquoise eyes taking in everything.

'Morning.'

'Good morning.' Edward held out his hand. 'Good of you to come.'

Pritchard shook his hand briefly. Tarn came bounding down towards them. He took no notice. Edward fondled her head. 'Quiet, now.'

'Still young, isn't she? Need to keep her down still.'

'She works well.'

Pritchard looked about him. He was a small, thin man, with a map of broken veins on his nose. He wore a cap.

'Done a bit of work.' He took in the new slates on the farmhouse roof, the corrugated roofing on the barn, the patched-up doors on the outbuildings. 'Spent a bit.'

'On materials,' said Edward, feeling like a loaded Londoner. 'I've done most of the work myself.'

Pritchard grunted. He walked towards the barn.

Edward found he was following, instead of showing him round. 'I've cleared this out a bit,' he told him, as they came to the barn doors. He lifted the latch, heard something skitter away. They stepped into the airy quietness. Tarn went straight to a corner, tail beating madly.

'Rats won't do your lambs any good. Best leave her in here for a couple of nights.' Pritchard strode over the concrete floor, looked around him. 'Got a good space,' he conceded. 'Bit different from last time I saw it. Don't suppose Evans had shifted a stick in here for ten years. How much did you get for the tractor?'

Edward told him fifty pounds, from the dealer in Ledbury. Pritchard grunted again. He measured the hay bales stacked up in the corner, running his eye up and down them. Tarn, in the corner, was going wild with excitement. There was a sudden squeal.

'That's it.'

'Go on,' said Edward, nudging her to the door with his foot. 'Go on, take it out.'

But she wouldn't, and he threw it out after her.

Pritchard took a last look round. 'What about pens?'

'I thought I'd use the bales,' said Edward, returning. 'Unless they take up too much space.'

'They will do. How many ewes did you say?'

'Eighty. Eighty-five.'

Pritchard measured the floor again, pacing it out, spacing the width of a bale with his hands. 'Never do it.' He pulled out a handkerchief, and blew his nose violently. 'Never,' he said again. 'Let's say you have ten in a pen, that's enough. Couple of empties for trouble.' He shoved the handkerchief back in his pocket, lifted the peak of his cap and scratched. 'You can hire metal pens if you're short,' he told him, pulling the peak down again. 'Back of the market they do them, know where I mean?'

Edward knew. He would go in this week.

169

'Mind you,' said Pritchard, as they left the barn, 'I don't suppose Evans ever thought to bring all his ewes in for lambing. A few, of course, the ones giving trouble, but mostly they were left out to get on with it. More natural, less risk of infection. This your first time?'

'Yes,' said Edward. 'Except when I was a boy.' Tarn raced towards them. 'What have you done with that rat?' he asked her.

'Over there by the pump.' Pritchard nodded towards it. Edward glanced across, saw stiffened grey fur, a gaping mouth. They walked up the yard towards the back gate. He tried to tell Pritchard something about his boyhood, and Northumberland.

'My grandfather – he knew sheep well. He taught me a bit.'

Pritchard made no comment. They came through the gate and round to the back field. The morning was cold and grey, just a thin ribbon of sun here and there in the cloud. The hens, let out early, picked their way over the grass; the ewes, as always, lifted their heads and began to move up the slope, bleating anxiously. Tarn slunk towards them. 'Wait,' said Edward. He stood next to Pritchard, who was casting a practised eye.

'Not a bad-looking lot. They do well, the Half-breds, good sound stock for lambing. Often have twins, expect you know that.'

'Yes.' Edward looked out at them all, feeling an unexpected rush of pride. 'I want to bring them indoors because it's my first,' he said. 'Keep them together, keep it as simple as I can. And at night – I'll be on my own.'

'Quite a bit you've taken on.' Pritchard glanced towards the pen in the far right corner, where Edward had done the vaccinations. 'Could bring a few down,' he said. 'While I'm here. Have a look at them.'

'Okay, Tarn,' said Edward. 'Bring them in.' She was off in a flash, panting and eager, racing over the grass. He and Pritchard walked down to the pen, and Pritchard held the gate. Edward left him, bid Tarn bring down six.

'Come on – come on – ease up, that's it –' He whistled high: Tarn's ears were pricked and ready.

Pritchard stood watching by the pen. 'Un, dau, tri, pedwar, pump, chwech,' he said, counting them in as Edward and the dog shepherded the ewes towards him. He held the gate open for Edward, followed him in, clanged it shut.

'You were counting in Welsh?' asked Edward.

'Only for your benefit.' Pritchard winked at him. Edward smiled. Outside the gate Tarn sat with her tongue lolling, glancing now at the hens. 'Leave them be,' he told her. He watched Pritchard holding a ewe by the fleece of the neck, running his other hand over her, feeling everywhere.

'Not bad. Let's have another.'

The next one he frowned over. This was the one Edward had marked. 'Twins here.'

'And maybe another?' asked Edward.

'Maybe. I see you've marked her.' He let her go. 'Un, dan, where's the next?' He frowned over that one, too. 'A breech for certain, this could take a while.' He knelt down behind her, parting the fleece. The ewe stood patiently. 'Good girl.' He eased in a couple of fingers; she shifted. 'Steady.' He drew them out again. 'Better mark this one, keep an eye. Had any prolapses?'

'No, not yet.' Edward pulled out the can from his pocket, gave a burst of scarlet spray, stood back.

'You will have. Need to check them every day.'

Pritchard examined the last three. He looked in their mouths. 'These two are yearlings, have to keep an eye. She's a broken mouth, she's all right – years of experience, they'll be out like peas. Mind you, you can never be sure. Best to plan for the worst.' He let the ewe free. 'Right then.'

'Want to see any more?' asked Edward, his hand on the gate.

'No, that'll do for now. Better be getting on.'

'Got time for a coffee?'

'Got time for a tea,' said Pritchard. The ewes trotted out of the pen. The two men strode back down over the field.

'I know you'll be busy with your own lambing,' said Edward. 'I'm sure I'll manage here. It's just –'

'That'll be all right,' said Pritchard. 'If I can't come, someone else will. Cheaper than the vet. You'll know if you need him.'

'Thanks.'

They came to the back door of the house, and wiped their boots. Edward showed him through.

He could feel the man's silence as they walked down to the kitchen; noticing, ahead of him, the passage at the front, laid with rugs, hung with pictures, the door to the library open, a glimpse of bookshelves. He showed him into the kitchen, pulled out a chair.

Pritchard sat down. He took out his tin of tobacco, and rolled a cigarette. Edward found him an ashtray, put on the kettle. Pritchard sat smoking. He took in the orderly feel of the room, the clean domesticity of it, the cookbooks, the prints on the walls. The clock

171

ticked steadily: its case was polished, the glass gleamed. He smoked, still with his cap on.

'Don't suppose Evans would know himself here now.'

Edward made tea, and set the pot down on the table. He said: 'Londoners. I'm afraid he might hate it.'

Pritchard shrugged. 'We're getting used to Londoners. At least you're here in the one place, working it. It's second-homers I don't much care for.' He drew on his roll-up. Edward glimpsed yellowing teeth, and a gap. He poured out two mugs of tea. Pritchard stirred in three spoons of sugar. 'Here on your own?' he asked.

'I've bought it with a friend,' said Edward lightly. 'You might remember, you saw him once, when we first came here. He came to the market –' That had been last spring. They had driven out to the town on market day, taking a look. Edward had felt at home, amongst the men and the trailers, the pens and the noisy animals, prices chalked up on a board. Rowland had watched him, amused. Across a couple of stalls Pritchard, their new neighbour, had nodded towards them from his group of farmers, and carried on talking.

Now he shook his head. 'Can't say I do.'

'Well.' Edward drank his tea. 'He's mostly in London, he's not here that often,' he said carefully, feeling Rowland, a stranger to the local farmers, become for a moment a stranger to him, too. Who was this friend who lived in London, whom no one knew? 'He's a singer. Rowland King. I remember our land agent recognised him – he's on the box sometimes.'

'Is he? And you live here just the two of you, do you?'

'When he's not touring,' said Edward, lifting the teapot. 'He's mostly just up at weekends –'

Pritchard drained his mug. Edward could feel his gaze upon him. 'Plenty of singers in Wales,' he said, putting the mug down. 'Not that I'm one of them.' He pushed his chair back. 'Well. I must get on.'

'Of course.' Edward rose with him, indicating, at the kitchen door, the passage down to the front of the house.

'I can remember it pretty well,' said Pritchard, carrying his boots over the rugs. He did not give a glance towards the stairs, or the upper floor of bedrooms. He passed the book-lined study, made no further comment.

He knows, thought Edward, as they came out to the yard. He knows and he doesn't like it. How could he? He said, changing the

172

subject, giving him a let-out: 'I thought, if you were busy – I might ask Phoebe Traherne for help. Do you know her?'

Pritchard frowned, pulling his boots on. Down in the cab, his dog was barking.

'The gardener?' he asked, making his way towards the trailer. 'Over in –'

'Penglydr.'

'That's it. Whatever put that thought into your head?'

Edward laughed. 'She just seems fit for anything.'

Pritchard gave a grunt. 'I suppose she might do. Wouldn't ask the daughter, mind. She's a bit –'

'I'm getting to know her,' said Edward. 'She's a rather fine poet.'

'Is she now? Takes after her father, then. Plenty of poets in Wales, too. Not that I'm one of them, either. Well. I must be off. Thanks for the tea.'

'Thank you for coming. I'll try not to bother you.'

The dog leapt up and down in the cab. 'He can smell that rat,' said Pritchard, climbing in. 'Right, then.' He slammed the door, started the engine, backed towards the pump. Edward stood watching as he turned, and drove out through the open gate to the lane.

When he had gone, he walked over to the rat, and looked down at it. The nose was full of blood, the lips drawn back in a grimace over long yellow teeth. Edward picked him up by the stiffened tail and crossed the yard to the lane. He threw him out into a hedge, knowing that this kind of thing was what farmers did, what his grandfather would have done, not giving a second thought; knowing the place was well rid of him. He still didn't like it.

He whistled for Tarn; she came running; he hugged her.

'Think I'm a bit soft,' he told her. He looked at his watch. Half-past eleven. Rowland would be – Where would Rowland be?

Indoors, he rang the flat, and left a message on the answerphone.

'I miss you,' he said. 'I'll try you tonight.' He hung up, dialled the number again, just to hear Rowland's voice.

Nesta stood in bare feet on the polished floor of the chapel. The children were resting after lunch: soon they would be brought over. For a little while longer this smooth empty space was all hers: she held out her arms before her, spread them wide, held them high above her head. Light fell in shafts through the narrow windows; rooks flapped about in the trees on the smooth expanse of lawn beyond; clouds moved over the distant hills.

Nesta spun round in the silence, hearing her feet on the wood, the faint harsh cries of the birds, muffled by glass. There was a tape recorder, but she did not use it; there were boxes of shakers, bells and tambourines, but she did not go to them. She bent and stretched and clapped her hands, she moved wherever she wanted to move, in a dance without music, with only the sounds of her feet, her hands, her quick light breathing, the ceaseless cawing of the rooks.

Well. All that was a kind of music.

'*Everything's music. You just have to listen, that's all* – '

Nesta stopped dancing. She lay on the floor. She felt her heart racing, slow down, grow steadier. She stretched out her arms and legs, she drew them together, she lay with her hands behind her head, her ankles crossed. She gazed up at the high octagonal vault of the ceiling, bone-white and graceful, pierced with glass. When the sun was high, eight shafts of light came streaming downwards, crossing on the empty floor. The first time she saw this, last September, she had thought: If I believed, that would look like a sign of the grace of God.

She closed her eyes. It was the middle of the week. The broken night watch on Saturday, her terrible dream, had left her exhausted, but she had recovered, three solid nights of sleep behind her, and days too full with the children to allow much thinking. Now, in a breathing space before the next night watch, lying alone on the chapel floor, she did have time to think, and the dream came back to her. She thought: it was about betrayal. I feel I am betraying Hal, or am about to betray him: that is why he has left me. And he has left me: now we never talk. I have no sense of him beside me.

She could hear voices, beyond the chapel door. The children were coming over, wheeling and staggering, calling out. She heard one of the little ones, high-pitched and babyish. She thought of the tiny baby held in the mouth of the cat, shrieking and flailing, and she thought: we wanted a child so badly. Illness and death betrayed us both.

For a moment longer she lay there, contemplating what the future might hold. Then the voices of the children drew closer, and she got to her feet and went to welcome them, pulling open the chapel doors, letting the light pour in.

It was Friday evening. Edward had driven out to the market town, and made arrangements. He came home with piles of hired pen railings rattling about in the back, more on order for the next week.

He carried them into the barn. Tarn followed, sniffing hopefully in corners by the bales.

'You'd better stay out here tonight,' he told her. Already it was growing dark. He went to shut the hens up; she followed, chasing. 'Leave them!' When would she learn? Back in the house he fed her, and then he led her out again, down to the barn, and gave her a pat and left her, closing the heavy doors. For a moment there was silence; then he heard her coming towards them. She whined, she pressed her nose to the gap; he could see it, could sense her puzzlement. 'Stay there,' he told her. 'Make yourself useful.' He walked back up the yard, took his boots off, had a last look round. Already the stars were out. He went inside, closing the door on the sudden barking.

The house felt horribly empty. He put on some music, had a beer. He sat listening to the Consort's recording of Victoria's *Requiem*, which last Easter they had sung in four Wren churches, then taken to Dublin. This Easter, they were bringing the *St John Passion* to Hereford Cathedral, to celebrate a new recording, part of a country-wide tour. More time apart.

'*Libera me, Domine, de morte aeterna . . .*'

'Deliver me, O Lord, from everlasting death . . .'

Edward got up from the table. He opened the door to the passage, he climbed the stairs. He put on the same recording up there, too, up in Rowland's music room, so the whole house was full of him. He walked up and down on the landing, seeing the stars prick the evening sky at the window, and the sky grow dark and deep.

When the music ended, he switched the lights on. He went downstairs to the telephone, rang the flat. Rowland answered. Edward was shaking.

'It's me.'

'Hello, you.'

'Rowland – please.' He could not make light of it. 'Did you get my message?'

'That you missed me? Yes. Was it you who phoned afterwards, and didn't speak?'

Edward felt himself blushing. 'Yes.'

'What is it? Everything's all right.'

'Is it?' Edward pulled the telephone over to the table. He sat down, trying to steady himself. 'It doesn't feel all right. It feels like a hell of a long time.'

'I know,' said Rowland. 'It does for me, too.'

'Does it?'

'Yes. I've just said so.'

Edward smiled. 'What are you doing?'

'Well,' said Rowland, 'I've just come in. It's raining, I've had a shower, I've poured out a drink. I was just about to phone you.'

Edward sat listening. He pictured the Barbican apartments, and rain falling on to the well-kept gardens, past the white moons of the lamps. He pictured it falling on to the lake, the fountains, trickling down the acres of glass between concert-goers and the terrace. He saw the restaurants, lit up and busy, heard the clink and clatter, the tuning-up in the concert hall. He saw Rowland, coming home to all this, taking the lift, coming along the covered walkway, taking out his keys; entering the small, well-kept apartment, hung with good pictures, and heavy curtains, full of light and warmth. He saw him undressing, to take a shower, flinging his clothes on the double bed where they had spent their first night together, standing there naked and heavy –

He said: 'Rowland, I love you.'

'I know,' said Rowland. 'I love you too.'

Edward closed his eyes. He said what he had not been able to say for weeks.

'I want to make love again. I want you, I want you –'

'Well,' said Rowland, and Edward could feel the warmth in his voice, his smile. 'And when would you like this to happen?'

'Now. Now.' He covered his face.

Rowland said: 'It's the rush hour.'

'What does that mean?'

'It means I couldn't be with you before ten. Maybe eleven.'

'Are you serious?'

'Well, perhaps half-past ten.' Rowland was laughing.

'I mean – are you really coming? Tonight?'

'I hope so,' said Rowland. 'Yes? Would you like that?'

'Yes. Yes! But what about tomorrow – how long can you stay?'

'The weekend. That's what I was going to ring you about. So – shall I come up now, or leave it till tomorrow?'

'Come up now,' said Edward, flooded with happiness. 'Come up now.'

'Put something in the oven. On second thoughts, don't bother. See you later. Yes?'

'Yes. Wonderful. Yes.'

He put down the telephone. He got to his feet and heard himself give a great sigh of relief. He looked round the room. The kitchen, the house, and everything in it felt drawn together again: reconnected, recharged. The deep steady tick of the clock, the cries of the sheep, settling down for the night, the ceaseless background hum of the generator: everything had life and meaning.

There was only the dog, barking down in the barn. That wasn't right.

He went outside again, unlatched the doors. 'Bugger the rats,' he told her. 'You belong with us.'

She danced beside him, leaping to lick his hands. They entered the house together; she went to her basket, he ran a bath. He lay there thinking of the night ahead. How could he have doubted? How could he have feared?

He ran more hot water; the bathroom was filled with steam. He thought: That was our first difficult patch. I was right to say nothing. It passed. I knew it would pass. He reached for the showerhead, washed his hair.

Getting out, getting dry, he thought of all the things he would tell Rowland, afterwards, lying together so close and deep. Of the rains, and the talk in the village of Edward Traherne. Of visits to the vet, and getting all the ewes done; of Gillian's visit, her rapturous reading, into the winter light.

He thought, coming out of the bathroom in his dressing gown, followed by clouds of steam, walking along the passage: She is rare, she is something to cherish. In Rowland's absence I have taken much pleasure in her company.

'There,' he said aloud, going into his study, hearing the formal phrase in his head, 'how she refines me.' He switched on the light, he looked at the table, the books on the shelves. He pulled out the volume of Herbert, he went to sit down. For a moment he thought of them both together; her thin high voice in the quiet room, her eyes, when she raised them, like stones beneath water, looking away in her terrible shyness.

'It is an affliction,' he said aloud, as he so often said things aloud now, living alone in a remote Welsh farmhouse, with only a dog for company. And then he forgot her, settling himself by the window, waiting for the sound of the car in the lane, the headlamps, and Rowland's return.

Nesta sat waiting for Phil. She had said goodbye to the children at Cadair, and told them she would be back next week. Maureen stood at the door and waved, tears pouring down her cheeks. Nesta ran back and kissed her. 'Not long,' she said. 'Not long.' She had driven home yawning, watching the clouds thin out, and a weak February sun grow stronger, edging the furrows with pale light. She saw a pheasant. She saw a fox, trotting away down a field, his heavy brush dark behind him. Well: that was something. That was her first.

She stopped in the village and bought her provisions in the general store, greeting people who had become familiar, and some she had never seen before. She drove back to the cottage, took her bags out, closed the car doors, taking in the silence, and then the sheep. Good to be back.

She walked down the path, looking about the garden for signs of spring. Snowdrops beneath the apple trees, aconites bright at the foot of the hedge. She unlocked the door on a pile of letters.

Nesta made tea, and laid a fire. She unpacked her shopping, put on her washing, she went upstairs to her bedroom, and smoothed out the Indian bedspread. She ran a bath, she lay in it, drinking her tea, unwinding, swishing the water with her feet, washing her hennaed hair. She lay back again, looking at all the photographs from her life with Hal; so easy, so intimate, so close and free.

The bathroom was full of drifting steam.

'Hal?' she said quietly. 'Hal?'

The steam drifted up to the ceiling, and disappeared.

Nesta sat up in the bath and the water fell shining from her. She dressed in clean clothes, rubbed at her hair and combed it, put in her silver earrings. She lit the new-laid fire. Then she lit a stick of incense, and rolled a cigarette, and sat in the corner of the sofa by the window, smoking, reading her letters from London, waiting for the man she would take as her lover.

Yes?

Yes. Because he was young and strong and careless; because she admired his music; because, on the telephone, he had been tender to her. Because, in his way, he was beautiful, even though it was not quite her kind of beauty, as Hal's had been; because of all these things, and because, after illness and grief and widowhood, she needed a man again, even though something told her, deep within: This is not, not truly, the man for me.

She heard his car at the top of the track; she saw him come bumping down to the field gate, and park behind her car. She rose from her corner by the window, and went to greet him.

'Hi.' She stood at the open door of the cottage and watched him click open the garden gate and come down the path towards her, with his long easy stride, his bag on his shoulder.

'Hi.' He smiled, he looked round, taking in the sloping garden, the rough grass and apple trees, the hives, the unkempt hedge. 'This is nice.' He reached her, he kissed her cheek, touched an earring. 'I didn't know you kept bees.'

'I don't. I don't know what to do with them. I've never even seen them.'

'My grandmother kept bees. Pots of Welsh honey. Let's have a look.'

'Is it safe?'

'Just a peep. They're sleeping.'

'Not for much longer, it's almost spring. We might disturb them. Anyway –' she made a gesture – 'you haven't even seen inside.' She looked up at him. 'Mind your head.'

He followed her through the open door, bending down at the lintel. The two of them took up almost all the space before the narrow staircase; he followed her into the sitting room, stooping again. He straightened up, looked around him. 'This is nice, too.' He took in the crackling fire, the crowded fireplace hung with burnt orange and glinting glass, the ancient sofas draped with bedspreads, the low table crowded with books between them, the piano, pushed up against a wall. He glanced at the photographs, and then away.

Nesta thought: perhaps it's too much for him, now he's here. And the bedroom – all those photographs upstairs –

I should have taken them down –

I couldn't do that –

'Well. Let me take your jacket. Tea? Lunch? A sandwich?'

'A joint?' He stood looking down at her, filling the room. He dropped his bag on the sofa. 'Or does that still feel –'

'Can I think about it?' Nesta took his jacket and hung it next to hers, on the back of the front door. She moved into the kitchen, ran water into the kettle. Beyond the window the sheep were grazing steadily, scattered all over the field. She thought: Perhaps that's what he needs, in the strange house of a widow, full of photographs. Perhaps it's what I need, too. Not so much fun on your own, but I'm not on my own. He's here. She switched on the kettle, and heard it come gently to life. She thought: But getting stoned is another surrender, especially after so long. I don't think I can –

She went back into the sitting room. He was looking at the photographs; he stepped back, and blushed.

'Oh, Phil –' She moved over towards him. 'It's okay. I'll show you them properly.' She looked up at him, towering above her, the top of the light fair head not so far from the ceiling. 'How tall are you?'

'Six-two. And a bit.' He touched an earring. 'And you?'

'Five-six. No bit.' They were standing very close. 'And how old are you?'

'Twenty-seven. And you?'

'Older.' She shook her head. 'I'm thirty-three. Thirty-four at the end of September.'

'That makes you a Libra,' he said after a moment. 'And I'm a Leo. Do they go together?'

'I wouldn't know.'

'Another old load of baloney?'

'Yes.' She could hear the kettle click off; she moved away from him. 'I have a choice of herbal teas and I have builders' tea. Which would you prefer?'

'Builders',' he said firmly. 'Herbal teas are a load of shit.'

That did make her laugh.

'Okay, quits.'

She went back into the kitchen, made a tisane of rosehip for herself and a pot of builders' tea for him. She could hear him moving about the room, she heard him go over to the piano. She carried back tea on a tray and saw him, because it was natural for him to play, it was everything to him, lifting the lid, running his fingers over the keys.

Someday I'll find you, moonlight behind you,
All of our dreams will come true –

He saw her face, he froze. She froze. She came into the room again, and put down the tray on the table.

He said: 'His piano.'

'Yes.'

'Shit. Shit. Oh, Nesta –'

'It doesn't matter.'

'I don't know what I –'

'It doesn't matter. I understand. Completely. I want you to play.'

'It wasn't his song. Please tell me it wasn't his song.'

She shook her head, sinking on to the sofa by the window. 'No. But it is the kind of thing he –'

By the light of the silvery moon –

She covered her face.

He said from the other side of the cramped little room: 'His photographs. His piano. I shouldn't be here, Nesta, we haven't a hope. He's everywhere.'

'No,' she said sadly, unable to look at him. 'No, no he isn't. He's gone.'

He came to sit beside her. His arm went round her, and she leaned against him, smelling clean hair and a clean cotton shirt beneath his sweater. She drew a long breath and let it out again.

'I'm sorry.'

'We're both sorry,' he said, stroking her hair. 'What were you sorry about the other morning? On the telephone. You said you'd had a dream –'

'Yes.' She shook her head, feeling his chest against her cheek, and light soft hair as she moved. 'Later. I'll tell you about it later.'

He went on stroking her hair, he touched an earring. 'Everything can come later,' he said. 'I told you – there's plenty of time.'

'Yes. Thank you.' She thought: He is nicer than I ever imagined, or gave him credit for. She straightened up, reached for the tea. She said: 'Well. Do you want to look at these photographs?' She nodded towards the mantelpiece. 'Get it over with.'

'Don't say it like that. I want to see them, if you want to show me. But first –' He got up, went across to his bag on the chair. 'Even if we don't have a joint, I must have a cigarette. Yes? And you?'

'Yes.' She was standing up by the mantelpiece, lifting the photographs down. She said: 'The last person to see these was Gillian Traherne. She found it difficult, too.'

'She finds a lot of things difficult, I would imagine.' Phil pulled out his tin of tobacco. She sat down beside him, the photographs on her lap. Their backs were to the window; light fell upon them.

'That fire needs another log on it.' He was rolling up deftly.

She looked. 'So it does.' She threw on a couple, sat down again. He gave her a roll-up, she gave him the photograph of Hal and the boy Gerald, staggering towards his open arms. Phil looked at it in silence, smoking. He gave it back to her. She gave him the one of her and Hal on the sofa in their old flat, their arms around each other, their feet bare, everything cluttered and young and careless. Hal already thin. Neither of them noticing. Phil gave the photograph back to her; he drank his tea. She gave him a photograph of her parents, next to one another in their garden, her father in shirt sleeves, her mother in glasses, smiling at her in the sun.

He looked at it as carefully as at the others. He said: 'Are you close?'

She said, realising a truth she had not been fully aware of: 'I haven't been close to anyone since Hal died.'

She put back the photographs, nudging a square of white against a candlestick. Gillian's invitation.

'Look,' she said. 'It's still up here.'

'What's that?' He stubbed out his cigarette, rose to look. He took the card between long fingers, carefully, as he had taken the photographs. 'That was nice. Have you seen her since?'

'No. I think about her, but there hasn't been time. Next week, when I'm off duty – I think I'll go to see her.'

He nodded. He looked along the crowded mantelpiece. A thread of incense fell to the hearth. There was a silence.

'Are you okay?' she asked him. 'Was it okay – seeing the photos?'

'Yes.' He rubbed at his face, pushed his hair back. 'I think I'm a bit –' He looked round the room again, he looked out of the window, at the trees and beehives. The fire crackled. Everything else was still.

She said: 'Are you hungry? Shall I make us something?'

'No. No, thanks. Unless you – I couldn't eat anything yet.'

'No. Nor could I. Well –'

'Well.' He reached up his arms and spread them wide; he touched the low beams; he held out his arms towards her. 'Well, Nesta.'

They looked at one another. She moved towards him. Their arms went round one another, she lifted her face for his kiss. Light soft hair fell over her face, his mouth was warm and soft. She thought: I will always remember this moment, and then his tongue was opening her lips and she could think of nothing.

They drew apart. He held her face between long fingers, he kissed her again, softly, and then again. He took her hands, he led her to the sofa by the piano. They sat down with their backs to it, facing the window. Out in the garden, a blackbird began to sing.

'Just the right note,' said Phil. 'As it were.'

'As it were.' She leaned against him. He picked up her left hand and stroked it. His fingers ran lightly over her wedding ring. He touched her face.

'All right?'

'Yes.'

'Do you want to talk?'

182

'No.' She turned to him. 'Kiss me again.'

He drew her to him, his mouth covered hers and his tongue parted her lips again, going deep, going everywhere. She felt herself open, as if to the sun. She held him and held him, she gave herself up to this sweet exploration, tender and new. At last they drew apart.

He leaned back, his eyes closed, his arm along the back of the sofa, his hand on her shoulder, steady and warm. She moved away, she sat looking at him, at the length of him stretched out before her, his feet beneath the table.

'Phil?'

'Mmm?' He opened his eyes, he smiled at her, lazy and soft. She thought of the moment in his cottage, the first time she had gone there, of how they had fallen asleep together, and woken together, as if they had been making love. 'Mmm?' he said again.

'What are you thinking?'

'I'm not. I'm just being.' He stretched, long and beautiful, a sensuous cat. Like Abraham –

She covered her mouth.

'Hey – hey.' He sat up, full of concern. 'What? What are *you* thinking?'

'Nothing.'

'That isn't true.' He reached for her hands, he searched her face. 'Something came in there –' He frowned. 'Your dream. Yes? Let's hear about this dream.'

She shut her eyes, she covered her face again. 'It was horrible –'

One thing to lie by herself in an empty chapel, feeling the light stream in. Nothing was asked of her then, that she had not done many times: being with the children, doing what she did best.

But now –

Phil put his hand on her lap. 'I think you should tell me.'

She told him. She began to cry.

He listened. He held her.

When she had finished, she got up, the tears still pouring down her face.

'I'm sorry –'

'Not sorry.' He felt in the pocket of his jeans, he gave her a handkerchief. 'Please.'

'Please,' she said, with a watery smile, and blew her nose. She gave him back the handkerchief. 'I think I'll just –'

She went out, into the kitchen. She ran the cold tap and splashed her face, over and over. It was early afternoon, the sun was out. The sheep were enjoying it, she could tell, watching them move across the field, so heavy, so ready to lamb. She turned off the tap, she dried her face on a teatowel. They hadn't even had lunch. She went out, found him standing at the open door of the cottage, his back to her.

'Phil?'

He half turned, held out a hand. 'I think we need some fresh air. Let's have a look at those hives.'

They climbed the rough grass beneath the trees. The blackbird flew up and away.

'He'll be back,' said Nesta.

She could feel, even in a week, a change in the garden: the snowdrops and aconites, the hedge, and bulbs poking up in the grass. She hadn't known what to expect out here.

'It's going to be a mass of daffodils,' said Phil. 'Fabulous.'

'Yes. I was just thinking that.'

They came to the beehives, touched by the afternoon sun. They stood before them, listening. Not a sound. Phil let go of her hand, stepped towards them.

'Careful –'

'It's okay.' He bent down, listened again; he lifted the lid. Nesta drew back. 'Come and look,' he said. 'Just for a minute.' She went forward cautiously; he took her hand again. 'See?'

She saw. Innumerable tiny bodies, tightly packed, wings folded, silent and striped and still. She glimpsed the comb, its parchment waxiness, she saw innumerable folded legs and feelers. A breath of wind passed over the open hive; there was, just perceptibly, a stirring.

'Put it back!'

'It's all right, it's all right.' He slipped the lid on again, made sure it was firm. 'There. Interesting?'

'Very.'

'I'll help you make the honey. Yes?'

'Yes. Thank you. When?'

'Not for months.' He drew her to him again, he stroked her back. The wind touched the long rough grass, and it rippled in the sun. 'I'll help you cut the grass, too, if you like.' He kissed her hair. 'Feeling better?'

'Much.'

They walked round the garden, looking at everything. It was cold, but not too cold. A pair of chaffinches flew in and out of the hedge. They sat on the grass and watched them.

'What shall we do now?' asked Phil after a while.

They smiled at one another, in perfect understanding.

'You said you would bring some music.'

'I have.'

'Do you want to play it to me?'

'Not really. Not yet.'

His arm was round her, she leaned against him again, looking down at the cottage, where they would make love. She thought of herself this morning, just a few hours ago, sitting there waiting for him, of her sense that she had made a deliberate choice, even if it might prove to be the wrong one. Well. Perhaps it wasn't so wrong.

She thought, feeling open and vulnerable in ways she had not anticipated, sitting there smoking this morning: If this isn't right, I might not be able to bear it –

She thought: he's young, he should go on being young and careless and deep in his music. Nothing else. Not yet.

She said: 'Phil?'

'Yes?'

'There's something I have to say. Before – before we go back to the house.'

He looked at her, his eyes half-closed against the sun. 'Go on.'

She looked at the rippling grass. She said: 'I'm a serious person, I think. I don't take these things lightly.'

'No. I didn't think you would.'

'And – this isn't the kind of thing one should say, I don't think. Not – not at this stage of the game.'

'Say it.'

She said: 'I do want a baby one day. I have to say that.'

There was a silence. She looked at the ground. Then Phil said slowly: 'I know that, Nesta. Of course I know that. You don't need to tell me. No, that's not true. Of course you need to tell me.'

'And?' She pulled at the grass, tugging it up in handfuls, like a grazing animal.

'And we'll have to think about it,' he said. 'Mmm?'

'Mmm.' More grass, great clumps of it.

'Look at me?'

She looked. His face was open and fair and serious. He said: 'Nesta, I don't know how much I can give you. I know I'm very drawn to you. I think we are meant to be lovers.' He looked away. 'I think I would be very wrong to say more than that yet.'

A tractor was coming along the lane. It stopped at the top of the track, and turned down.

'That's the farmer,' said Nesta. 'He's come to feed the sheep. Listen.'

They heard the sheep bleating, loud and long, they saw the tractor cab pass the top of the hedge, bumping downwards towards the gate.

'He's not used to seeing visitors here.'

Phil got to his feet. 'Should I move my car? Will he be able to get through?'

'I expect it's all right.'

But they walked back down through the apple trees, towards the garden gate. The farmer jumped down from his cab, leaving the engine running. He had pulled up behind the two cars; his dog leapt down after him, and peed in the hedge. The farmer nodded to them both, going round the back to the trailer, heaving down a bale.

They watched him carry it through the field gate, and the ewes come gathering round.

'He comes every day,' said Nesta.

'That must be nice.'

When the farmer had finished, he walked back towards them, whistling for his dog.

'This is my friend Phil Dryhurst,' said Nesta, over the gate.

He nodded. 'Nice to meet you.'

They watched him slowly reverse tractor and trailer, up the rutted track, blue smoke puffing from the chimney. He sounded the horn at the top, and raised a hand. Then he was chugging away.

Nesta and Phil were still at the gate. It was colder now, and she shivered. His arm went round her, they walked back along the path to the door.

'We were talking,' he said, as they reached it.

'We were.'

He stooped to enter behind her. They came into the sitting room, where the fire had burned down low. The last thread of incense fell in the draught of air. Everything smelt of ash and sandalwood.

'Well?' he said gently, his hand on her shoulder. 'What do you think? If you want me to go now, I will. Did I say all the wrong things?'

She stood before him; her arms went round his waist. 'No,' she said, looking up at him. 'You said all the right things. What else could you say? Everything's moved very fast – I didn't expect it. I –'

He bent to kiss her. 'And you don't want me to go?'

186

'No,' she said, hearing the last of the logs fall to pieces, into the heap of ash. 'I want you to stay.'

Halfway up the narrow dark staircase she turned to him, stricken.

'Phil –'

'What?' He stood below her, half-laughing. 'Now what?' Then he saw her face. 'What, Nesta? Tell me, go on.'

'In the bathroom.' She was filled with desire and distress. 'In the bathroom there are lots of photographs – I can't bear to move them – I don't know what to do –'

'Oh, darling.' He came up the narrow stairs beside her. 'You don't have to move them, you don't have to do anything, that's enough worrying now –' He kissed her, up against the wooden panelling. 'There,' he said softly. 'Everything's all right.'

Then he carried her up to the top of the stairs, to the tiny landing. Her bedroom door was open. Inside, he put her down, and looked around him.

Nesta turned on the electric heater, and closed the door. She drew the curtains. There was the sound of the metal hooks on the rail, then the room was full of shadows.

They stood in the middle of the old flowered carpet. She took off her silver earrings, and gave them to him; Phil took them, and crossed to the cheap varnished chest, putting them carefully on top with the muddle of others that lay there. He sat on the blue-painted chair beside it, and pulled off his boots. He looked at the low broad bed, with its Indian bedspread, smooth and soft. He looked at the photograph of Hal, which stood on the table beside it.

How could she have forgotten that –

Because it was always with her, part of her, something she had never needed to think about –

She went slowly over, picked it up, and took it to the chest of drawers. She opened the top drawer. There. The wood was warped, and she had to give it a push to close it.

'You don't have to do that,' he said, so quietly into the quiet room.

'Yes I do.' She closed her eyes again.

'Yes, of course you do. Nesta? Are you all right?'

'I think so.'

'We still don't have to – we can just be.'

She crossed the room and stood before him. They looked at one another, and did not speak. Then he took her hands.

'Did ever two lovers have such a beginning?'

'I expect so.'

'Are you sure you are ready?' His features were blurred with desire and affection.

She said: 'Phil, you are a dear and lovely man. I'm as ready as I will ever be. I think you are right: we were meant to be lovers. Shall we stop talking now?'

He smiled, his long sweet lazy smile. He drew her to him, he kissed her. In silence they undressed one another, and their clothes fell like ghosts to the floor.

Late in the afternoon she woke beside him. He was deeply asleep, his cheek pressed into the pillow, his hair all over his face. She lay watching him for a long time, hardly moving. The room was almost dark, just enough dusky winter afternoon light to see him by, and soon it would be gone.

At last she slipped out of the bed. Her dressing gown hung on the back of the door; she pulled it on, and crept out to the bathroom. She peed, she washed. Then she switched on the light. Hal was everywhere.

'Hal?'

I told you I didn't want you to mourn for ever –

'Hal!'

She went to the photograph of him sitting on the edge of the bath, waiting for it to fill. The water gushed, his curly head was bent over the paper, his dressing gown fell open, his foot swung.

She lifted the photograph down from the wall and kissed it. Then she put it back.

Darkness fell, and the winter moon rose high. They woke again, feeling hungry. Nesta put on her nightdress and dressing gown and a sweater on top; Phil got dressed again. They went downstairs to the unheated sitting room. He laid a new fire, she cooked. They ate, listening to his music. It was full of the sound of bells and birdsong.

'It's beautiful.' She rolled cigarettes, curled up in a corner by the fire. 'You must come to Cadair, you should be with the children. I'm sure you could do something good.'

'I could try.'

He played it again, looking at her from across the room.

'How are you feeling, Nesta?'

'I'm feeling content,' she said. 'And fortunate. And you?'

'Pretty much the same.'

They climbed the narrow stairs and into bed. In the long moonlit hours of the night they made love again.

Just before they fell asleep, she said: 'You know what you should do.'

'What's that?' He was yawning, drifting, almost gone.

'Get in touch with Rowland King. You're so good, I'm sure he would help you.'

'Mmm. I could send him a tape, I guess.'

'You could phone him,' said Nesta drowsily.

'He'll be ex-directory.'

'Edward won't be.'

'Who? Oh, yes. Can't remember his surname.'

'I can,' said Nesta, trained to remember names. 'Edward Sullivan. He'll be in the book.'

It was evening. Phoebe sat by the range, working on her tapestry. She drew up fern-green strands of wool, she pushed up her glasses, counted squares. Almost finished. Two years of winter evenings; at Easter it would hang in the church. She snipped off the green, rethreaded the needle.

The tapestry featured a Cross: plain gold on simple blue; a border of clambering hedgerow flowers: honeysuckle, dog roses, poppies; cornflowers from the garden. At the base, a profusion of ferns grew round tall clear capitals: PENGLYDR CHURCH 1995. Phoebe felt in her box for the last skein of gold. Beside her the coke in the range moved and shifted down. Getting low again, time for another scuttleful.

'Gillian?'

Floorboards creaked in the room above. Phoebe waited. Silence fell.

'Gillian!' She threaded the needle, squinting; she snipped the skein. The fuel made another movement. Dammit. She set aside the tapestry, picked up the empty scuttle and took it outside. The house light shone on the bunker; she bent down to scoop out the rattling coke and was seized by a sudden spasm of pain. She drew in a sharp breath, waited, tried again. Too much lifting. Dammit. Gillian would have to –

The pain sliced like a knife through her lower back; Phoebe dropped the scuttle. She stood bent double. She heard herself groan.

'Gillian!'

Gillian, whose window overlooked this side of the house, made no answer.

Phoebe, with enormous difficulty, straightened up. She crept round the side of the house, clinging to brickwork and ivy and windowsills. Little by little, step by step. That was it. She stood at the back door, and called again, weakly.

The faint scratch of a mouse. The smell of wood and the earthy potatoes, in their paper sacks. Phoebe inched into the house, and along the passage past the kitchen. She reached the foot of the stairs.

'Gillian –' It was a groan. Ridiculous.

Up on the landing the door opened. Gillian came out. She stood at the top of the stairs with the light from the open door behind her, a shapeless silhouette of old jumper, lace-ups, long drooping skirt.

'What's the matter?'

Phoebe could go no further. She leaned against the banister.

She said, with difficulty, and a little laugh: 'I seem to have put my back out –'

Gillian looked down upon her. Low-watt lighting illuminated the wild hair.

'Would you like an aspirin?'

Sunday afternoon, the light fading. Edward walked up the field to shut the hens up, Tarn at his side.

'Go on, then, go and get them.'

She raced round the hedgerow.

'Gently, gently –'

They came out flapping and squawking, he counted them in.

'Un, dan, tri –' How did the rest of it go? Some of the birds were already in the pen, already roosting in the henhouse. He checked them all, loving everything about them: the smell, the rustling in the straw; the throaty sounds they made as they hopped up to the nesting boxes and cocked their heads from the perches and settled down; the fat soft featheriness of them, head on one side and a sweet crrck crrk. He felt in the boxes. Three eggs, two brown, one white, smeared with mess and a clinging feather. He slipped them into his pocket: Rowland could take them back with him. How very satisfactory.

'Good-night,' he said, as he always said. A murmur, a settling. He had always known he loved sheep: the pleasure he took in the hens was a bonus, something it would be nice to share with a child. Hard not to think that, from time to time. Well. Too bad. He shut up the henhouse, he shut up the pen. He stood looking down on the farmhouse, watching the dark fingers of cloud draw in over the roof, hearing the sheep all round him, seeing the lights so safe and bright. A light in their bedroom, where Rowland was packing, where everything had been put right again between them. A light on the landing, and down in the kitchen, where he could hear the phone. Could no one leave Rowland alone for a moment? Always, there was someone from London, something to ask.

He walked down the slope of the field again, whistling for Tarn to follow; he saw through the lit-up window Rowland come into the kitchen, pick up the phone, and engage in conversation. Rowland was always in conversation with someone, he always had been. In London the phone had never stopped. At first Edward had loved it: being a part of the buzz, the arrangements; he had felt privileged, drawn in, proud to take messages, to be the one who gave them. After a while it had become irksome, too much. Part of the point of buying the farm was to get away from all that. Now what did they want?

He had reached the back door; he stood pulling his boots off. He could hear Rowland laughing, saying no, no, that was fine. He went inside. Rowland's bags stood in the corridor. 'Bye, then,' he said. 'I'll look forward to that.' The phone clicked. Edward went into the kitchen.

'Who was that?'

'That was Phil Dryhurst,' said Rowland lightly. He was slipping his Filofax into his bag. 'Remember him?'

Phoebe sat up in her high iron bed and smoothed the green counterpane. She looked at the square plain room, at the wallpaper, faded and peeling. Spring sunshine streamed in through the open window, the curtains blew in the morning breeze. A perfect day for planting.

'Bloody hell,' she said aloud.

Footsteps along the landing. Gillian, with a tray. Weak tea, blackened toast. No butter.

'You forgot the butter.'

Gillian looked at the tray. 'Sorry.'

'When you bring it,' said Phoebe, 'could you be kind enough to bring me the wireless? And my tapestry.'

Gillian went to the door.

'And the box that goes with the tapestry,' Phoebe said. 'The scissors, all the wools.'

'Where are they?'

'Where I left them. With the tapestry. Next to the range. You know where they are. Have you stoked up?'

'Yes,' said Gillian.

'Thank you.'

She sat back and waited. Downstairs the letterbox banged.

When Gillian returned, she had forgotten nothing. 'Well done,' said Phoebe. 'I'll be up and about again tomorrow, I'm sure of it. Perhaps even this afternoon.' She shifted on the pillows, and winced. 'What was in the post?'

Gillian gave her the electricity bill and a letter from Oxfam.

'Give them something at Christmas and they never leave you alone. I don't know how they got my name in the first place.' Phoebe put the letter on the bedside table, and winced. 'Nothing for you?'

'No,' said Gillian. 'Do you want anything else?'

Phoebe looked at her. 'What are you going to do today?'

'I'm working on something new,' said Gillian, looking out at the fresh wild sky.

Phoebe lifted the mug of weak tea and bit her lip. Whatever had she done to herself? 'You'll ruin your eyesight,' she said. 'Really you will.'

Gillian went to the door. 'Call me if you need anything.'

Phoebe said: 'Your birthday – tomorrow's your birthday.'

'I know.'

'I was going to get you something today. I'm sorry –'

'It really doesn't matter,' said Gillian. 'Really. I hope you feel better soon.'

'Thank you.' Phoebe turned on the wireless. *Start the Week*. How they went on.

Along the landing, Gillian closed her door.

12

Phoebe and Gillian received a visitor. It was the middle of the morning, the middle of the week. Phoebe was up and about again, but not herself: she could do nothing in the garden but look at things; she felt drained and irritable. She was down in the kitchen, which after three or four days of Gillian's attentions had a disordered and displeasing air. She moved about slowly, picking things up and putting them back where they should be: cups, cutlery, newspapers, teatowels. The kettle was on the range. Even to lift and fill that was an effort. A car drew up in the lane. Footsteps. The knocker fell once, twice.

Now what? 'Gillian?' Even to call was an effort. She had been calling for days. She moved slowly out to the hall, and along towards the door. Little by little. The knocker fell again. 'Coming!' snapped Phoebe. The catch was stiff; she winced as she tugged at it.

'Yes?'

Nesta, silver and bright in the porch. For a moment Phoebe could not begin to place her. Then she remembered.

'Oh, hello.'

Nesta was full of apologies. 'I'm so sorry – you're not well.' She took in the lined face, the strain, the unkempt hair.

'I'm perfectly well,' said Phoebe. 'I've just done my back in, that's all. Come in.'

Nesta followed her into the hall, with its patterned tiles and darkness. Gillian's old tweed coat hung on a stand with a mildewed mirror, next to a mildewed map. 'I'm sorry,' she said again, 'I should have telephoned. I had some free time, I just drove over –' Her earrings glinted, her voice was light. Upstairs a door on the landing opened.

'Please don't apologise,' said Phoebe. 'You're a welcome distraction. Come and have a cup of tea.' She moved towards the kitchen, saying into the darkness, 'Your friend Nesta Frank is here.'

Nesta looked up to the top of the creaking stairs. Elaborate stains of damp decorated the wallpaper. Gillian came slowly down, in a drooping skirt. It was the first time Nesta had seen her in a skirt, the first time she had seen her for weeks.

'Oh, hello. I thought you might be –' Gillian broke off, blushing deeply.

'Someone else.' Nesta smiled up at her.

Gillian smiled back, descending. 'It's early in the year for visitors.'

Nesta felt as though she had come to a museum, out of season. She had a vision of stuffed birds in dusty cases, which crumbled to bits if the air got in.

'You were writing,' she said. 'I've disturbed you.'

'I was thinking,' said Gillian. 'I expect I should have been doing something else. My mother –'

'Come along,' called Phoebe.

They walked down the tiled passage. Nesta saw a door to her right, which was closed. 'That is a kind of sitting room,' said Gillian. 'Or study. It was my father's study. We never use it. Well – I go in there sometimes.'

At the end of the passage was a dark place with a tongue-and-groove door to the back. 'That is the larder and store room. This is where we live.' She nodded towards the left. Nesta went into a spacious kitchen. Clothes hung on an airer over a range. Yellowing newspapers lay on a chair. There was a sewing machine in a corner, a moquette chair between the sink and the range, where a kettle had come to the boil, its lid banging up and down with the steam. 'I can't pick the damn thing up,' said Phoebe.

'I'll do it.' Gillian crossed the room.

'Careful.'

'I'm being careful.' Water spluttered into a green enamel teapot. Nesta saw enamel saucepans on a shelf, yellow and green and pockmarked with chips. Everything looked as if it had been bought in the 1950s. She looked at the windows, one to the lane, where her car was parked on the verge, and one to the back, to the garden.

'Well done.' Phoebe was watching Gillian. 'That'll do.'

Gillian replaced the kettle. 'It'll boil dry,' said Phoebe. 'Move it to the back.' Gillian moved it to the back. She stirred the tea in the pot with a dessert spoon and put the lid on; she carried it over to the table. 'Thank you.' Phoebe turned to Nesta. 'Do sit down.'

Nesta sat, facing the garden window. Light was streaming in, on to a pile of books, and bills on a spike. Outside, she could see the bright spring sky and the trees coming into bud. She saw a dove.

'How lovely. I didn't know you kept doves.'

'They're mine,' said Gillian. 'I'll show you.'

'We'll show you round the garden,' said Phoebe, slowly putting out mugs. 'I need to get out and about. Not very good at being cooped up.'

'My mother is never ill,' said Gillian.

'I'm not ill. I've just put my back out.' Phoebe tried to lift the teapot. 'Dammit. You'd better do this.'

'Backs can be dreadful,' said Nesta, watching Gillian pour from a height.

'I do wish you wouldn't do that,' said Phoebe. 'Do you take sugar, Nesta?'

'No, no thanks.' Nesta felt in her shoulder bag. She thought of Phil, who took sugar, whom she had not seen for twenty-four hours and whom she would see tonight. She would tell him about her visit here. She felt the brush of his hair on her face, and his long smooth body against her own. She felt as though he were living in her bloodstream. She pulled out her tin of tobacco. 'Would you mind if I –'

'Smoked?' said Phoebe, watching her. 'I'd really rather you didn't.' Nesta put the tin back. She drank her tea.

'What is it you do again?' asked Phoebe.

They walked down the herringbone paths. Nesta, hearing sweet sounds behind her, turned to look back at the dovecot. The birds were walking in and out, in and out, over and along the ledges, into the arched dark entrances, heads cocked, eyes bright, lifting white wings in a fluttering cloud, out over the garden, down to a scatter of grain. Croo-croo, croo-croo.

'Soon they'll be laying,' said Gillian.

'How lovely,' Nesta said again. She thought of the pigeon, a soft smudge of grey in the snow at Christmas. How long ago that seemed. Now everything was changing. Perhaps there should be a dovecot, up at the Hall. There should be: the children would love it.

'Of course originally,' Phoebe was saying, 'as you know, they were kept for eating. Bred for the pot.'

'Doves?'

'Of course. For the lord of the manor. They lifted the squabs from the boxes. The great dovecots had nesting boxes for five or six hundred birds. Made of stone.'

'Well,' said Nesta. 'I never knew that.' She followed Phoebe down the garden, looking about her. Everything was coming up. Gillian had moved away from them, and was pacing about in the rough grass down in the orchard, her hands in her cardigan pockets. The fresh March wind blew over everything. Pale green catkins danced.

'Oh, that's better,' said Phoebe, swinging her arms. She pointed things out as they walked, naming shrubs still woody and bare, pruned right back. Daffodils and narcissi were everywhere. Nesta talked a little of her own garden, the apple trees and aconites, the hives. 'It sounds very nice,' said Phoebe. 'Now that is a *Corylopsis*.'

'A what?'

'A *Corylopsis*. Nothing now, but it will look well in a week or two. Needs that nice sheltered spot. Lots of little yellow flowers.'

'And what are these?' Nesta stopped beside clumps of grey-green flowers, nodding like bells.

'Hellebores. *Helleborus corsicus*. Hardy evergreen perennials. Very useful. You're not a gardener.'

'No. Not really. In London we had a small garden, but we were so busy – we just put in easy things like bulbs.'

'Yes. Very nice for a few weeks, but then of course they do tend to look a bit dead and gone.' Phoebe stopped, easing her back with the flat of her hands.

'I can't remember – are you divorced?'

'No,' said Nesta. 'I'm widowed.'

'Oh, dear, I'm sorry. Gillian didn't mention it. Well, of course, she –' Phoebe looked at Gillian, pulling up clumps of dead reeds by the pond, taking them across to the bonfire. 'No children?'

'No,' said Nesta.

But now I have a lover, she thought, filled with his touch, their new delight in one another.

'Well,' said Phoebe, 'you are still young.'

'Thank you. Yes, I –' She stood watching Gillian, carrying reeds. 'You were also widowed young, weren't you?' she said, answering Phoebe's brisk directness. 'How old was Gillian when –'

'She was three,' said Phoebe. 'Three and a half. Too young to remember it.' Wind blew in the trees, the clouds were racing. 'Well. Now I will show you the kitchen garden.'

They crossed the garden to the dry-stone wall and went through the gap. Heaps of cloches and manure stood in corners; the air smelt earthy and rich. Phoebe conducted Nesta round seed beds and cold frames and espaliered fruit trees. Little sharp shoots were everywhere.

'This is the onion bed, and this the potatoes and carrots and swedes – all the root vegetables. The brassicas are over there.' She looked at Nesta. 'Cabbages and so on. I do all my gardening organically, I always have, long before it became the thing. There is nothing to beat the taste. Where do you buy your vegetables?'

Nesta thought of Saturday visits to Safeways in London, and of the small, expensive, film-wrapped packages sold in the local shop. 'I'm afraid I probably go to all the wrong places.'

'Never mind. Now you can come to us. Much nicer, much more reasonable.'

'Thank you.'

'No need to thank me, it is how we make our living. We'll be busy soon, just coming up for the season.'

Nesta followed Phoebe up and down the paths. Beyond the wall she could see Gillian, dreaming, the wind in her mass of hair, coming loose. She thought: I have never seen anyone quite like you.

'This is the herb garden.'

Nesta looked down at a brick bed divided into eight. Last year's parsley and fennel, rosemary and sage and mint were cut back and just coming into new leaf. It was perfect.

'What I would like,' she said, visited by a sudden inspiration, 'would be if you would come over to Cadair and teach the children. They do a little gardening already, but if you were to come – I'm sure you could teach us all a lot.'

Phoebe considered. 'I'm not sure I'm terribly good with children. Especially children who –'

'Well. Will you think about it? I feel a bit of a new broom up there – I've invited a friend to come and teach music.' Nesta stopped, remembering. 'Of course – you met him, the night of the reading. Phil Dryhurst – do you remember him?' He's my lover, she thought, feeling a sweet twist in her stomach.

'Not the singer. No, of course not, that was Rowland King. That was rather an excitement, I must say. I believe he's doing a tour at Easter, there was something on the radio, I believe he's coming to sing in Hereford Cathedral, and over in St David's. One of the Passions, I think – did you hear that?'

'Yes,' said Nesta, recalling what Phil had told her of the phone call. 'Anyway – I should be so pleased if you would consider coming to Cadair one day.'

Phoebe snapped broken shoots off a flowering currant. 'I'll see. Well now –'

'How are you feeling?'

197

'Oh, much better. I'm sure it's being out here, and the exercise. It's absolutely no good giving in to these things, half of it's all in the mind. If you give in you're done for.'

They had come to the gap in the wall. Nesta stood looking out over the fields beyond the hedgerow, and the hills beyond the fields. Racing clouds and sun and wind were everywhere. She felt a rush of happiness.

'God, it's so beautiful here.'

'Isn't it.'

Gillian was standing down by the pond. In the clearing she had made in the circle of reeds fresh shoots were visible, tender and bright. Her hair caught the light, her hands moved, gesturing. Nesta stood watching her.

'I think I'll fetch a fork,' said Phoebe. She walked up the path to the house. The doves were everywhere. They flew down the garden, down towards the pond. They perched in the branches of the ash tree, they courted and preened.

Nesta walked over the grass.

'Gillian?'

Gillian jumped, and turned towards her.

'I came to see you, and I've spent all the time talking to your mother.'

Gillian smiled. 'That happens.'

'I'm sorry.'

'It doesn't matter.' She looked up at the doves in the trees. 'Aren't they perfect?'

'Yes.' Nesta observed her serenity, her radiance, here in this heavenly quiet place, away from the world.

She said: 'I'm going now. Will you come and visit me? Up at the school?'

'Yes,' said Gillian, alight with the coming of spring.

Nesta stepped forward and kissed her. 'I'll see you soon.' She walked up the path to the house, and round to the greenhouse, where she could see Phoebe, moving along the slatted shelves.

Down by the pond, Gillian stood motionless. The spring wind ruffled the stillness of the water, the doves cooed, the clouds were illumined with joy. Gillian stretched her arms in her old loose cardigan and raised them up to God.

Lov is the true Means by which the World is Enjoyed. Our Lov to others, and Others Lov to us. The very End for which God made the World was that He might manifest his Lov . . .

'Thomas Traherne,' she said aloud. 'Edward Traherne. Gillian Traherne. Edward Sullivan.'

Above her the doves were so tender and white, murmuring to one another.

Nesta said to Phoebe, tapping on the glass: 'I'm off.' Phoebe did not answer. Nesta looked at her. She stepped inside. The air was warm and close. Phoebe was holding on to the slatted shelves, a fork on the floor beside her. She was grey.

'What is it? What's wrong? Let me help you –'

Beads of sweat stood on Phoebe's forehead. 'I'm all right – I don't know –'

Nesta saw suddenly how thin she was, truly how thin, how her sweater and shirt hung off her, how loosely her trousers hung. She felt an old chill run through her.

She said, knowing she would meet resistance: 'Phoebe, you're ill, you must go to the doctor. I'll take you, I'll take you now, if you like –'

'I'm all right,' said Phoebe. 'Perhaps I'll just –'

Nesta helped her into the house. Phoebe leaned upon her.

A river of sheep poured into the farmyard, swirling this way and that; the morning air was full of their bleating and blaring, of Tarn barking, Edward's shouts.

'Come on, come on, away to me there – Tarn! Get them over! Steady, steady –' He banged the field gate behind him, came down amongst the crowded bodies with his crook, seeing, at the far end, ewes pressing up against the gate to the lane, and Tarn darting round them, guiding them over towards the barn.

'Good girl, good girl, that's it.'

There were ewes at the door to the house, ewes crowded all round the pump, moving towards the hedge which bordered the lower field. For a moment Edward stopped, and surveyed his flock, the last time he'd see them all out of doors for weeks, the sharp spring sun and swift clouds moving light and shadow over the mass of fleece, the speckled faces, yellow eyes. It was Hardy, it was the drovers' roads of Wales, it was his grandfather, up in the hills of Northumberland, the fields marked out by the dry-stone walls, guiding the ewes with his dog Ben –

Edward looked up at the running sky, and down at the swirling mass of ewes, and wondered, as he had wondered first thing this morning, if he were being foolish to bring them all in, when it felt set fair, and the forecast for the next few days was good. Should he not leave them out in the fields to get on with it, as shepherds had done for generations? The worst of the winter was weeks gone, there would be no snowdrifts, no lost ewes and frozen lambs, perhaps no rain-soaked nights. He could have managed out there – was he doing all this just to recreate a childhood memory? He heard his grandfather's voice, up in the windswept hills, feeling the first stinging drops of rain: 'Better inside, have them all together, keep them under your eye. Things can go wrong so quickly.' He heard the vet, in the market town: 'If there's a way of dying, sheep will find it.' He felt Pritchard's eye upon him, assessing his inexperience, his foolhardiness; he saw himself out in the darkness of the fields at night, with only a dog and a lantern, struggling with a difficult birth, making a Godawful mess of it, losing lambs, failing horribly –

'Tarn! Here, girl!'

He moved amongst the thick heavy press of them, down to the barn where the pens stood ready and open, where Tarn, in a couple of nights on her own, had surely put paid to the last rat. Perhaps he should have brought the ewes down in small batches, perhaps it was folly to have half the flock down at once –

He thought: You are losing your nerve, and you have not even begun.

He pulled at one of the doors of the barn, bid Tarn guard, guard, stay there at the front. Then he drove in four, six, eight, nine, ten, closed the door with his crook, ran about guiding them into the nearest pen.

'Go on with you, go on, in there now –'

The rustle of straw, the bleating, the smell of them all. Clang of the gate. That was one lot. The ewes stood about, and stared at him. One moved into a corner.

'That's how they start,' said his grandfather, pointing one out. 'She'll find her own patch, she'll be restless, won't know whether to stand or sit, you'll keep an eye on her then but she'll take her time –'

Edward stood watching. The ewe moved up and down in the straw, looked about her.

He went for the next batch.

Lunch was a sandwich, long after two. He ate it walking back down the yard, not wanting to stay in the empty house any more than he need to. Tarn was flaked out by the pump, enjoying the soft spring sun on her coat. Much warmer this afternoon, as the forecast had promised, but the clouds on the distant hills had grown darker. Forecast or not, you could never be sure: at this time of year things could change in an hour. He'd been right to bring the sheep in, he could feel it now, crossing the yard to the barn doors, hearing the rustle, the movement of feet, sensing the steadiness of it all, everything safe and contained and ready. He threw down a couple of pieces of crust, watched sparrows fly down from the roof and squabble.

Inside, he walked up and down the pens, feeling better than he had done for days. The ewes had settled down now, had found their places, stood cudding calmly, moving quietly about in the bedding. The air was full of the smell of straw, of oily fleeces, fresh droppings, old brick, dusty beams. The chirrup of sparrows came from the yard; he heard Tarn give an enormous yawn. The sun streamed through the open doors.

Edward leaned over a pen. He caught a young ewe by the neck, stood rubbing her bony head between the ears. The ears went flat; she shifted, he let her go.

'It's all right, girl, I'm not going to hurt you.'

He walked up and down again, looking at them all. Tonight he'd ring Rowland and tell him they were in.

Every time he thought of Rowland he felt a stab of unease. He realised he was trying not to think of him, that each time he hoped the uneasy, unsettled feeling would have gone, it never had. He hoped that thinking of the long powerful hours of the nights they had spent together, taking one another again, calling their names in the darkness, would reassure and restore him, and overcome the memory of what had followed, in their last moments together, but it didn't.

'*Who was that?*'

'*Phil Dryhurst – remember him?*' Rowland slipped his Filofax into his open bag. He looked – how did he look? Lit up. Inwardly delighted. Closed-off and concealing.

'Yes,' said Edward carefully. 'I remember.'

'He wants me to listen to a tape. I told him to send it. If it's any good we might meet up next time I'm here.' Rowland was moving around the kitchen, looking for things, not looking at Edward. He picked up a thriller, his glasses, a couple of tapes. 'Where are my keys?'

201

'Under the paper,' said Edward, watching this performance. 'There – sticking out.'

'Oh, yes. Thanks. Good. Right, then –'

'You must be off.' He hadn't meant it to sound provocative, but it did; it did, he could hear it.

'I must.' Rowland swung the keys on his middle finger, frowning. 'Don't sound so –'

'I'm not. Sorry. I didn't mean –'

'All right, let's not make a thing of it.' Across to his bag, dropping his stuff in, doing the catch. Edward stood watching him, feeling everything start to go wrong.

'Right.' Rowland picked the bag up, flashed him a smile. 'Don't look so stricken. Got to go some time.'

Edward said: 'Rowland, for God's sake –'

'What? *What*? What's got into you?'

'Nothing.'

'Doesn't sound like nothing. Come on, we've had a good weekend, haven't we?'

'Yes.' He pulled himself together. 'Yes, it's been wonderful, thank you –'

'I wanted to come.' Rowland patted his arm. 'Remember that. Where's Tarn?'

'Somewhere.' He followed Rowland out of the kitchen. 'I left her out in the field.'

'Tarn? Tarn? Here, girl.' Rowland opened the front door. It had grown dark. The stars were out. He whistled across the yard. 'Tarn? Come and say goodbye.'

Edward thought: this scene is a part of a pattern, now, part of the rhythm of our lives – the evening sky, the waiting car, the kiss. Down to the gate, the lane, away to the waiting city. Me going back to an empty house. I can only do it if he is – if we are –

A whimper, a sound at the back gate. Tarn, squeezed under it, was racing down the yard and round the house towards them. Rowland bent to embrace her.

'Goodbye, goodbye, you silly dog. Wag wag wag, I know. You look after your master now.'

Here we go again.

Edward waited. Rowland straightened up.

There was, perceptibly, an awkwardness.

Edward did not say: Rowland, you are my one beloved. You

are the core of me: I cannot live without you. I cannot live with betrayal, or the fear of betrayal –

He said: 'Thanks again.' He moved towards him. 'Really.'

'Stop thanking me. Thank *you*. It's been lovely.' Rowland held out his arms. Edward moved into them.

He said, but did not say: I want you again, I want you now, I shall always want you –

They kissed, their mouths warm and dry. Edward moved closer. Rowland drew back.

'I love you,' said Edward.

Tarn looked up at them, and began to bark. 'She doesn't want you to go, either,' he said lightly.

'Right, then.' Rowland slung his bags in the boot. He got in the car and started the engine. Edward felt the weekend, and all it had contained, drawn out of him, as if he were giving blood, as the car turned away from the house and moved down towards the open gate.

'Goodbye!' He raised his hand, and the repeated scene unfolded once again: the winking tail lights, the sound of the horn, the turning into the darkened lane. And gone, gone.

Edward walked down to the gate and closed it. He leaned upon it. He thought of the rush of hope and happiness he had felt just forty-eight hours ago, when Rowland drew into the yard, coming home, coming home. He thought of the passionate night that had followed: the darkness, the two of them, hour after hour.

'I love you, I love you. Yes, yes –'

'Like this?'

Like that. And like that. Falling asleep as the hours of the night ebbed away, and the stars and the sweet spring sky grew pale.

He thought how those hours had been robbed in a moment. A phone call. A look. No use pretending it hadn't been there.

'Tarn?'

She was out in the hedgerow, nose deep, paws scrabbling.

'What have you got there?'

She whined and whimpered.

'Come on.'

Whatever it was got away. She followed him; up to the gate, the house, the lights. He thought how the lights had seemed just now from the back field: so bright and safe. He fought against feelings of loss and apprehension.

*

Edward came out of the quiet barn, into the afternoon sun. The sparrows flew up and away. He crossed to where Tarn lay dreaming, he bent to pat her warm coat.

'That was a busy morning. Did a good job there.'

Now what? The last few days, perhaps, before the first lamb came. Wouldn't be much of a Now What then, wouldn't be a moment. He straightened up again, looked down the yard to the lane, to the sloping fields and valley beyond. A mist of new green, the first hint of blossom in every orchard, every garden. He thought: I'll go down to Penglydr, call on Phoebe and Gillian, have a look at the garden. I'll talk to Phoebe about the lambs.

His spirits, already soothed by the morning's activity and accomplishment, rose with the prospect. He felt for his keys, he whistled for Tarn.

Phoebe sat in the chair by the range, sipping water. Nesta telephoned the doctor in the market town. A locum would come when he could. Before the evening surgery. Was it certain that Phoebe could not –

'Certain,' said Nesta, looking at Phoebe's grey sweating face, hearing an involuntary moan. The telephone stood on a pile of library books and catalogues on a corner of the dresser. A handmade calendar hung on a hook on the wall. Greetings from Penglydr Church. There was a line drawing of the church, and a text for each month. The text for March read: 'The Kingdom of Heaven is like to a grain of mustard seed, which a man took, and cast into his garden, and it grew and waxed into a great tree.' Nesta thanked the doctor's receptionist and put the phone down.

Phoebe said: 'There hasn't been a doctor in this house since I don't know when.' She rested the glass of water on the worn wooden arm of the chair. 'What a lot of fuss.'

Nesta went over to her. 'How are you feeling now?'

Phoebe shook her head. Some of her colour had returned. She felt in her pocket, wincing, and drew out a large man's handkerchief. She wiped her face. 'A little better. I really don't know what –' She looked up at Nesta. 'You must have things to do.'

Nesta shook her head. 'Not today. Last week was very busy, and I'm on duty again tomorrow, but I've got nothing on now till this evening –' This evening she might lie before the fire in her cottage, and Phil might lie above her, while his music played –

The early afternoon sun came in at the window. She could hear the doves, and Gillian's footsteps, coming up the path. She said: 'But perhaps you'd prefer me to go. Gillian can –'

'Gillian can do nothing,' said Phoebe, putting the handkerchief back. 'It is fortunate you were here. Anyway, I'm feeling better now. I think that was just a turn, you know, I really don't think it was anything much.' She was talking more steadily, recovering herself. 'I really don't think I need a doctor.' She passed Nesta the glass. 'If you could just take that, I think I'll –' She made to rise, she sat down again, groaning.

Gillian came in. 'Oh. Hello. I thought you'd gone.' She looked across at Phoebe. 'Are you all right?'

Phoebe was doubled up in the chair. Nesta knelt swiftly beside her, murmuring words of comfort. Phoebe was sick on the floor.

Edward drew up at the house. Another car was parked on the verge across the lane: he hesitated, wondering if perhaps he should have telephoned, if he would be intruding. Well. He was here now, he needn't stay. He pulled right into the hedge, giving plenty of room for passing traffic, and got out, leaving Tarn in the cab.

'Wait. They might not want you, leaping about.' He crossed the lane, hearing birds, feeling the wind on his face, blowing down from the hills. He looked up at the sky, at the sun, fitful now, about to disappear amidst gathering cloud. He remembered his only visit here, late on an autumn afternoon; his first sight of Gillian, poking a bonfire with a stick, watching the rise of frail smoke, watching the fall of yellowing leaves on the still water of the pond.

'It is the altar of the garden.'

He had spent most of the time talking to Phoebe, but it was Gillian's words he had remembered.

He opened the gate, entered the darkened porch; he knocked.

Sounds of activity came from within. He heard a voice: 'Is that the doctor? That was quick –' and footsteps hurrying along the hall. This was obviously not the moment.

He stepped back, ready to make his apologies.

The door was opened by someone who was neither Phoebe nor Gillian. For a moment they looked at each other in incomprehension. Then –

'Nesta.'

'Edward.'

'I've come at the wrong time. I'm sorry – I was just calling –'

'Yes,' said Nesta. 'So was I. Phoebe's ill. I've phoned the doctor, but –' Her silver earrings glinted in the sun: against the darkness of the hall behind her she was an arrow of light. 'I'd better go back to her.'

'Yes, yes of course. I'll be off. Give them my best –'

Movement in the shadowy hall; footsteps along the patterned tiles.

'Nesta? Is everything –' She saw him, she stopped; in the dancing sun at the door he could see how deeply she blushed.

'Gillian. Hello. I came to see you, I'm so sorry to hear about your mother.'

'Look,' said Nesta, moving aside, 'we can't all stand here. I'll get out of the way.'

A sound from the kitchen. She flew.

Gillian stood in the hall. Edward stood in the porch at the open door. The afternoon sun came and went on the pattern of tiles between them.

'I must go,' he said gently. 'I'm obviously in the way. Unless there's anything I can do to help –'

'I don't know,' said Gillian. 'I don't know what to do, I'm not very good at –'

He took in her confusion, the distress, the fading blush, the drooping clothes.

She said: 'It was such a beautiful morning.'

'I know. I've been bringing the sheep in to the barn. How long has your mother been ill?'

She shook her head. 'She put her back out, a few days ago. Now she's been sick.' She made a gesture. She looked quite lost. 'I don't know what –'

'Oh, dear. Poor Phoebe. Poor Gillian.' He moved towards her, put his hand on her shoulder, wanting to comfort her. 'I'm so sorry. What can I do?'

She looked up at him; he could feel her tremble.

She said: 'It's so nice to see you.'

'And you.' At the far end of the hall the back door stood open, he could see now, beyond the place where they kept tools, and sacks of potatoes. He caught a glimpse of the garden, of daffodils swept by the wind; he saw a dove. He said, letting his hand fall, moving a little towards the beckoning light: 'I've only seen the garden in autumn, do you remember?'

'Yes,' said Gillian. 'And today it has been –'

Sounds from the kitchen. Nesta came out. She said: 'I think we'll try to get Phoebe up to bed, I'm sure she'd be more comfortable. Gillian, do you think you could –'

Edward stepped forward. 'Can I help? Or would that be –'

'I don't know,' said Nesta. 'I think we can manage, she's looking a bit stronger. Gillian –'

Gillian followed her; Edward, automatically, followed them both.

The kitchen smelt of disinfectant; ancient curtains moved in the wind at the open windows. Phoebe was huddled in a chair by the range. She looked up as they all came in, and saw him.

'Hello. Quite a party. Isn't this a joke?'

Edward smiled at her. 'I was going to ask you to give me a hand with my lambs. What have you done to yourself?'

'God knows. Bloody nuisance. What lambs?'

'My lambs,' he said again, going over, kneeling down beside her. 'I've got eighty-five ewes in my barn, and I don't know how I'm going to manage them all.'

'Neither do I,' said Phoebe. 'I'll come and have a look.'

'Your colour's coming back,' said Nesta.

'Is it? I feel like Exhibit A. Where's that glass of water?'

Nesta passed it. Phoebe drank.

'Better, now. Don't know what all that was about.'

'Do you think you'd like to go up and lie down?' asked Nesta. 'Before the doctor comes?'

'Doctor? I'm sure I don't need a doctor, I've caught some wretched bug, that's all. If you can just give me a hand –'

Nesta took one arm, Edward the other. Together they lifted her. Phoebe groaned.

'No, no –' She leaned upon them, greying again. Gillian stood at the table, watching, her hand to her mouth. 'What are you staring at?' Phoebe snapped.

Slowly they moved along the hall. Sun and wind danced in and out through the open doors. At the bottom of the stairs they stopped, and looked up.

'What do you think, Phoebe?' Nesta asked. 'You can have a good rest once you're up there.'

'I hope we're doing the right thing,' said Edward, feeling Phoebe's bony arm on his, feeling her unsteadiness. 'Patients aren't supposed to be moved – isn't that right?'

Phoebe groaned. 'Don't talk as if I'm not here. That is after an accident.' She looked up at the stairs, so broad and steep. 'Let's have a go now we've got here.'

Slowly they took the first two treads. Phoebe was moaning. They stopped.

'I'm afraid I can't –'

'I'll carry you,' said Edward. 'May I do that?'

'Oh, bloody hell.'

'Careful,' said Nesta. Her face was white.

'It's okay.' Edward touched the thin mottled hand. He hadn't seen Phoebe since the reading. Everything about her had changed: in a couple of months what was lean and spare and filled with energy had become frail and thin and enfeebled. How had this come to pass? 'I've been heaving sheep about all morning,' he said cheerfully. 'I'm sure I can manage a slip of a girl like you.'

Phoebe grunted. 'Lot of nonsense.'

He put his arm around her; Nesta released her; he lifted her lightness and weakness and carried her easily, up the creaking dark stairs towards the sunlit landing.

'Light as a feather.'

Nesta followed them, her hand on a banister which had once been beautiful, smooth and polished.

Down at the bottom of the stairs Gillian watched the ascent to heaven, leaving her to burn.

Phoebe lay on her iron bed, the counterpane spread over her. Her shoes were beneath the chest of drawers: to undress had been beyond her.

'That's enough – that's it.' Nesta fetched water from the bathroom. The mirror was mildewed, the lino cracked. Worn white towels hung on a wooden rail. She looked out of the window as she ran the tap, seeing the beauty of the windswept garden again, the play of the sun, the beat of wings. She took back the glass of water and took in Phoebe's thinness, beneath the quilt. She thought: I am the only person here who knows.

Edward was standing at the window, looking out over the garden. Everything was blowing about: the doves, the daffodils, the trees. Sun and shade passed over the hills. He saw how in a few weeks everything Phoebe had laid out and planted would be in leaf, in flower, how the garden in summer must be a rich and heavenly place, full of rustle and light and shade, smelling sweetly at evening. He thought: I must come here more often. He saw Gillian, coming out of the back door, walking slowly down the paths. Doves flew after her. He turned at Nesta's footsteps.

'Well done.'

Nesta gave Phoebe the water. Phoebe sipped, and lay back.

'That's better. Nice to lie down.'

'You're not feeling sick again? Is there a bowl –'

'I'm not feeling sick. Where's Gillian?'

'Out in the garden,' said Edward. He moved to the bedside, took Phoebe's hand. It felt as if he had always known her, as if they had always known how to talk to one another – without depth, but not without meaning. 'I must be off.'

'Must you? Will you go and fetch Gillian for me?'

'Of course.' He bent to kiss her. 'Get well immediately, understand?'

'I'll be up and about tomorrow. Just need another day. Thanks for the lift.'

'My pleasure.' He straightened up, smiling at Nesta. 'Goodbye. Nice to see you again.'

'And you. How's Rowland?'

'He's well, he's in London.'

Phoebe said: 'Rowland? Rowland King?' And then: 'Of course, I'd forgotten. You share a house, you mentioned it at Gillian's reading. Must be marvellous sharing a house with a singer.'

'Yes. Yes, it is. Well. I'm off.'

Nesta watched him. They bid one another goodbye again. Then he left, creaking along the landing and down the stairs. She turned back to Phoebe, and glanced at her watch. 'The doctor should be here soon.'

'I don't need a doctor,' said Phoebe crossly.

'Yes, you do.'

Phoebe looked at her. 'I'm sure you have things at home you want to be getting on with.'

Gillian was walking down towards the pond. She pulled off a twig as she passed a lilac tree, and bent it, to break it in two. Everything was in bits and pieces. The twig was pliant; beneath thin bark was a pale young greenness, full of life and moisture.

She tore it in two, then begged forgiveness. She came to the pond, full of fresh water from the winter rains, ruffled by the wind. Bright new shoots grew round it; soft pussy willow and trembling aspen blew. She stood there, she covered her face. Above her the doves spoke tenderly to one another, but she –

'Gillian?'

Her hands fell; she turned at the sound of his voice.

'I'm sorry,' he said, so gently. 'I'm disturbing you, you're distressed.'

'I –' she cast about her.

'I'm just going,' he said, observing the nervous movements of her hands, her distracted manner. 'Phoebe would like you to go up.'

He had taken her in his arms, he had carried her up the dark stairs –

'How is she?' Gillian asked of the trees.

'I think she's feeling much better now she's in bed. And the doctor will be here soon, I'm sure.'

'My mother does not believe in doctors.'

'No, I know. She likes to be self-reliant. But still – I am sure he will put her right. And if there is anything I can do to help, you must tell me. I'll always come. In between lambs, anyway.'

'Thank you.' Gillian looked down at the water.

Edward looked up at the courting doves, following one another along the smooth limbs of the tree, stopping to kiss, beaks locked, heads going this way and that, turning to walk back again, to flutter up and come down again, to murmur and coo and begin again. The wind blew, the air was fresh, Gillian looked so robbed and bereft.

'What is it?' he asked her.

She could not answer him.

'Your mother is ill – she was sharp with you – your beautiful morning is taken away –'

Gillian felt his hand on her arm, just a moment, a touch – the coming of spring was everywhere: in the wind, in the grass, in the rippling water –

'You were writing?'

'Thinking,' she said at last. 'Working something out –'

'Something new?'

'Yes.' She could not look at him.

'And now it has gone?'

There was a silence between them, though all around were the cries of the rooks, the conversation of doves, the bleating of distant sheep.

'Things come and go,' he said, as much to himself as to the singular spirit beside him. And then, directly to her, 'I'm sure it will come back to you. When it does, will you let me see it?'

'Yes.' She turned to look at him, and felt all that had fallen in pieces made whole again, set back in place by his voice, his gravity. 'Yes, yes, I will.'

'Good. You're looking better. Now I must go.'

They walked through the orchard, they walked up the herring-bone paths.

Gillian thought of her room, her desk, a consecration.

Edward had gone. Nesta, at Phoebe's insistence, had gone. Phoebe was rested, back in command. Gillian stood in her mother's bedroom, at some distance from the bed. The light was fading, the afternoon drawing in. It was beginning to feel cold again.

'I think you had better close the window. Just at the bottom.'

Gillian crossed the room. She pulled down the window: it rattled and banged.

'That sashcord needs mending,' said Phoebe. 'Replacing. Look how it's frayed. And filthy. Filthy. The whole house needs cleaning, from top to bottom. As soon as I have everything sown and planted –' Her hands moved on the counterpane, white and thin. 'Come here,' she said to Gillian's back.

Gillian turned from the window. 'What?'

'I want you to cancel this doctor. He's only a locum, anyway, Nesta told me. What do they know? I'm feeling much better already. Absurd to have him come all the way out here.'

Gillian stood there, her back to the fading light.

Phoebe said: 'I spoke to you harshly this morning.'

'It doesn't matter.'

'I was feeling unwell. And peculiar. Strangers in the house.'

'Not exactly strangers.'

'Well. People we don't know very well.'

'They were trying to help.'

'They did help. I don't know how we should have managed. But still – not the same as family.'

Gillian looked at her. Behind her the rooks in the farmer's field could be heard in the trees, through the half-closed window, settling for the night. It was a sound she had heard all her life, going deep in her childhood. The wings of Phoebe's reproaches beat through her childhood, dark and fierce.

Phoebe said: 'Cancel the doctor. Then you could make me a cup of tea. Tomorrow we can get back to normal.'

Outside a car drew up in the lane. Sounds carried far in this country quietness: even here, at the back of the house, they could

211

hear the door close, the footsteps, up to the porch. Then came the knock.

'Dammit. Too late. Oh, dammit to hell.'

'What shall I tell him?'

'He'll have to come up. Now that he's come all this way. Never mind. I'll deal with him.'

The knock came again. Gillian went to answer it.

'My mother's upstairs. She's feeling much better.'

'I'll just take a look.' The doctor came in with his bag, young and busy. Gillian closed the door on the darkening lane. So many visitors, all in one day. She showed the doctor upstairs, switching on low-watt lights; she left him and Phoebe to greet one another, not knowing, in any case, what to say next.

'Go and put the kettle on,' said Phoebe, as she closed the door.

Gillian went downstairs to the kitchen. She filled and put the kettle on, closed the windows, drew the curtains. She stood at the table, feeling the house draw round her again: worn, full of holes, familiar. When the doctor had gone, she would give Phoebe tea and go to her room, the poem within her released to the page, ready to send to him, ready to give.

The doctor examined Phoebe, and then he examined her again. He was young and ambitious and thorough: he ran his hands over her sunken abdomen and small breasts, wrinkled like apples too long in the dark. He asked a lot of questions; he asked her to sit on the side of the bed, observing the difficulty she had in all that movement: sitting up, turning, moving her legs. Her head hung, and her hair stuck out. He ran his hands down her back, he asked her to stand, and turn, and his cool young fingers ran along her spine: up and down, up and down, pausing, returning, moving over her lower back. Phoebe groaned. Rooks cawed from the field.

The lamp by the bed made the rest of the room look darker, the windows black. He let her lie down again, and took her blood pressure; the puffer made gasping sounds, the column of mercury climbed and stopped. He wrote down the figures, he went to his open bag, lying on the rush-seated chair in the corner. He took out a syringe, in a sterilised disposable bag.

'I think while I'm here, I'll take a little blood, if I may –' He opened the sterilised bag.

'Blood?' said Phoebe. 'I've put my back out, I don't need a blood test.'

'I think if you don't mind –' He turned her arm, swabbed a place in the hollow of her elbow, deep within sinewy tendons; he tugged at frail flesh round the vein, and spoke of a hospital appointment, for the result. In went the needle, deep, deep: up came the blood in the tube. Phoebe turned her face to the window, listening to the farmer's rooks, and the sweet beat of wings as the doves flew back to the dovecot. She felt herself distance herself: from a stranger's touch, a vile needle, the pain in her back, which, with all that poking about, had returned to trouble her.

'Well done.' The doctor withdrew the needle, transferred the blood to a test tube, wrote on the label. 'Right, then.' He put everything back in the bag, he carried the chair across the creaking floorboards and set it down on the rug. He sat down beside her, he cleared his throat. Light from the bedside lamp shone on to the tapestry, the pile of library books, the dust, the mended sheets.

'Well?' asked Phoebe.

The last light had gone from the sky. Gillian saw the young doctor out of the house. The wind which had blown all day across the valley was growing stronger; it blew through the trees across the lane and the branches creaked.

'I'll be in touch,' said the doctor.

Gillian did not know what that meant. She switched on the outside light and stood in the porch, watching him cross to his car, and sling in his bag. He switched on his headlamps, he drove away.

She stood looking at the empty lane, the darkness, the tossing trees. She closed the door on the coming of night and took tea up to Phoebe, leaning against the pillows.

'What did he say?'

'Nothing. He talked about tests. Lot of nonsense.' Phoebe took the teacup; her hand shook. 'Draw the curtains,' she said. 'Let's have the radio on.'

They drank their tea listening to *Kaleidoscope*. Someone in London took them to an exhibition at the Barbican.

'I'll be back in a minute,' said Gillian, wanting to get to her room, her fountain pen.

'Take this cup,' said Phoebe. 'I don't want any more.' She lay back against the feather pillows, lumpy and thin. Someone was talking about a concert in Sarajevo. She tried to concentrate.

The words which the doctor had spoken beat about the room like birds, dark and trapped and shrieking.

13

In a corner of the pen the ewe moved restlessly, this way and that. The bedding rustled, she turned about, lowered her head and raised it, walked up and down. Edward stood watching, Tarn at his feet.

'This is it,' he told her. 'She'll be the first.'

Outside the barn the sky was already dark, pricked by the first stars. The wind blew through the trees along the lane, and the door propped open banged against the stone. He looked at his watch. Half-past six. The bulbs wired up along the rafters shone steadily, but there were still shadowy places, like the place where they stood now, up at the far end. The other sheep shifted about in their pens; the ewe he'd been watching lay down, and then, with difficulty, got to her feet again. This was her second year of lambing. She looked across at him, turned away.

'What do you think?' he asked Tarn. 'Shall we leave her in peace for a bit?' He moved along the pens again, checking each one. The animals cudded steadily, the air smelled of droppings and hay and the fresh spring wind across the fields. A hint of rain in the air: as he and Tarn came out a few drops fell on the yard. He closed the barn doors, walked up to the house, made tea, fried sausages, listening to the rain begin to fall harder, against the back windows. He drew the curtains, ate quickly, drank hot tea. Tarn sat waiting for scraps. He tossed her the end of a sausage, wiped his plate round with the last of the bread and got up again, draining his mug.

'OK, let's have another look.' He felt like the ewe herself, up and down, turning about, waiting for something momentous. Rain fell fast at the door: so much for the forecast. He pulled on his jacket, hurried down to the barn again, picked up the bag of twine and knife and arm-length rubber gloves and spray.

The ewe was lying down in her corner; at his approach, she got

214

heavily to her feet again, giving a broken bleat. 'All right, girl? Anything happening?' She had a look about her, something he would not have been able to describe but which told him at once of a change. He pulled open the pen gate; bidding Tarn stay he hung the bag on the railing, moved slowly across to her, talking quietly. The ewe stepped quickly away, ears back: he saw a torn membrane limp on the straw: the water sac, passed while he'd been away from her. 'It's all right, it's all right –' He reached out and took hold of a handful of fleece: again came the urgent, broken bleating. 'Steady, steady –' He looked down, parting the fleece beneath the tail: the ewe tossed her head, made a sudden short sound and he saw it: the first glimpse of a dark wet foot, and another, which disappeared.

'Come on, come on –'

The ewe heaved, and moved in the straw, and pushed. Edward, kneeling, patted her side, looked again, searching for the rounded bluntness of the nose, which should be between the forelegs, the lamb crouched up like a diver, ready to take the plunge and gasp. Should he wait, should he feel inside . . .

'Let her get on with it for a bit.' His grandfather, patient and experienced. 'See how she goes, now, see how she goes.'

Edward knelt in the bedding and watched and waited. All round him was the rustle of straw and the sound of the rain, drumming on the roof, splashing on to the yard. He let these steady sounds soothe and calm him, glancing across at Tarn, watchful and obedient, feeling the two of them, in a Welsh barn miles from anywhere, wait for the moment of birth.

The ewe made a sound, and then another. She stretched herself, and pushed, gaping with strain, and then Edward, looking, saw the three black shapes of foreleg feet and slimy nose between, in perfect presenting position; he heard the ewe's quick pants and pushing, and saw head and soaking black ears and fragile legs come forward with a squelch, and the whole sodden lamb fall on to the straw and lie there, all tight wet curls and dark wet head and trails of blood and yellow muck and a thin little ribbon of bleating as the ewe, within moments, turned to her newborn and licked and licked.

Edward got to his feet and moved aside for her. He thought: I'll phone Rowland, and then: no, not yet. He wanted no flicker of unease or distraction to cloud this moment, and he stood watching the extraordinary transformation he recalled from boyhood: an animal passive and timid, craving the company and identity of the flock, made through motherhood fiercely individual, licking and snickering, cleaning the slimy tight curls, the half-shut eyelids, clogged nostrils; nudging and nosing the trembling lamb on to endless lanky legs, talking, encouraging, bringing to life.

'Good girl, clever girl.' He took a step towards her, with the can of spray. The ewe stamped her foot and lowered her head and glared at him. He reached for the lamb, lifted it by the forelegs, gave a burst of spray on the navel and trailing cord, essential against infection. Then he lowered the lanky body down into the bedding, and moved quietly away through the straw, watching the lamb struggle up again, and butt and search for the teat, and find it, tail wriggling wildly as it sucked and sucked.

Tarn, at the gate to the pen, sat whimpering. Edward went over, and stroked her sleek dark head. Across the barn came new sounds of shifting about. He glanced around, saw two ewes turning and pacing, restless and unsure. He went to check them: one was the twin breech he'd marked with Pritchard. Not so easy. He went back to the birthing pen and unhooked his bag. The lamb was curled in the straw like a cat, full-bellied, drying out, sleeping. Behind it the mother had pushed out the afterbirth, a full bloody sac in which Tarn, at a distance, was taking an interest.

'You can let her have one or two,' he heard the vet saying, out in the market town in the middle of a downpour. 'Best no more. But clear them up and get rid of them, burn them or bury them. Otherwise you'll have germs and infection going through that flock indoors like I don't know what.'

Edward pushed open the gate. The ewe glowered at him. He pulled on a long rubber glove and bent down to scoop up the mess and shovel it into a carrier bag; he dropped it out at Tarn's feet. She gulped it in moments. The ewe sank down beside her new lamb and began to lick again.

Rain fell hard on the roof. Tarn followed Edward, going from pen to pen, checking each one of his flock.

The twin-breech ewe had a long, difficult labour. By ten, Edward had seen another lamb born without help: a black-faced, white-coated male who stood up within moments on strong black straight legs, a good two pounds heavier, by the look of him, than the first, still asleep at the mother's side. By midnight, the twin breech was pushing and straining, passing a single water sac and then a trickle of blood which made Edward anxious.

He stood there watching her, debating whether or not to phone Pritchard, decided against it, felt he'd done wrong. He shepherded her to a pen on her own, pitying her evident distress as Tarn nosed her along the straw-lined channel and into a corner. 'Poor old thing.' He pulled the gate to, and knelt beside her, feeling all over, slipping a glove on, slipping his fingers inside. Gently, gently. He felt the slippery bones of the bent legs of the first lamb, moved along the wet length of the tail. He'd read the breech-delivery pages in the lambing books over and over, knew from them and the vet that he'd have to ease each leg backwards, and be ready to tug at them both, with great skill and care, guiding them out to the entrance. Sweat stood on his forehead, he heard himself breathing heavily.

'Don't know if I can do this.' He slid out his fingers again; the ewe panted. He cut off a length of baler twine, he fetched her a fresh bowl of water from the tap in the yard. The rain had stopped, but the wind was high. It was very cold. I did the right thing, bringing them in, he thought again, taking the bowl back to the barn, closing the door behind him. The ewe kicked the metal bowl into the straw, and moved away. He stood back watching her again. Too late for a phone call to Pritchard, in spite of what he'd said: not after midnight, not for the first time. He bent down, felt inside her again. If he could do this, he could do anything. He couldn't do it. He tried to tug at a single leg, and it would not come. The ewe gaped, shifted painfully. He got to his feet, pulled the glove off, went out again, up to the house.

The kitchen was warm and comforting. He dialled the vet, got the emergency number from the answerphone, given by a nice-sounding girl with a Welsh accent. He dialled the emergency number. It rang and rang. He stood gazing at the calendar sent at Christmas by the agricultural feed merchants in Ruthin. A Border Leicester ram gazed back at him. Nobody came to the emergency number. He put down the phone and went out again, into the barn where the ewe was gasping.

Nothing else for it. He knelt behind her, tried again. Tarn lay waiting, bored now, her head on her paws, eyes closed. Edward felt inside, and grasped a foot. He held it between his middle fingers, felt with finger and thumb for the other, held them fast. He tugged, sweating, and lost them. He tried again, cursing. He remembered his mild-mannered, quiet-spoken grandfather cursing, kicking a bucket out in the yard after a week of broken nights and a lamb lost. He'd never heard words like that before. 'Mind your tongue with the boy,'

217

said his grandmother, taking in the washing. His mild-mannered grandfather growled at her, and now Edward growled, feeling the pointed sharp feet slip out of his rubber-clad fingers again, and draw back.

Once more. One more time. He drew out his hand and flexed the cramped fingers; he wiped the sweat from his face with his sleeve, he tried again, he caught both slithery feet and held them and pulled, his other hand, grasping the fleecy back, giving him leverage. He pulled and pulled and the ewe jerked away and moved forwards, pulling him sharply so that his jaw hit her back, and his teeth clamped down on his tongue; he yelled, and the feet slipped out of his grasp. He spat out blood, felt tears start to his eyes.

'Oh, bleeding fucking everything.'

He got up, left the pen, paced up and down, wiping his mouth, waiting for the pain to subside. He went out to the windswept yard again, drank from the tap, came in again, tied the ewe up to the rail and started all over again. And did it. He did it. The two little feet were brought out to the entrance; he held them with one hand, felt for the baler twine with the other, tied them and drew them, inch by sweating and trembling inch, slowly slowly, the tail limp and dangling, the ewe groaning, until the slimy wet body came, speckled and bloody, and then the head and forelegs, and the lamb lay breathing so feebly in the straw, just a flicker of life in the tiny rise and fall of the belly. The ewe turned round, and sniffed, and turned away.

'Come on, girl, come on now –' Edward untied her, turned her, let her move her poor head up and down. He moved the newborn lamb towards her, she sniffed again, she made a low whickering sound, and began to lick.

Thank God. He sank to a bale in the corner, let his head drop between his knees, let tears come freely. The sweat poured down him, growing cold. Tarn came up beside him, nosing at his cheek. He wiped his face, put his arm round her; she leaned against him. 'What about that, then? Just got to do it all over again now, that's all.'

He gave himself and the ewe time to recover. Then he began on the twin.

At half-past three in the morning he closed the barn door on the ewes and the newborn lambs and walked stiffly up the yard. The sky was windswept and clear, emptied of rain, and stars were everywhere. Tarn trotted beside him. He heard an owl. He thought: I did it. They're safe. Inside, he tugged off his boots and sent Tarn to her basket. He climbed the stairs, pulled his clothes off, left them lying in a heap on the floor, as if in the urgency of lovemaking.

He pulled on his pyjamas, shivering, and got into bed, but his mind was racing. He lay in the darkness, and the struggle played out before him again; himself and the animals, all through the long painful hours of the night.

Four lambs.

He turned on the pillows. Tomorrow he would ring Rowland and tell him. He would ring Phoebe and Gillian, see how things were. He closed his eyes, and the barn and the struggling ewe swam again before him. Then he saw Phoebe, frail as a bird, carried upstairs in his arms to her bedroom, while Gillian, lost and excluded, waited below.

Another bright windy morning. Phoebe was up and about again. She drank tea in the kitchen, had a fried egg for breakfast. She put the appointment card into her bag, took her keys from the hook. Gillian hovered.

Phoebe went slowly outside, and climbed into the van.

Gillian followed. 'Shall I come with you?' she asked through the window.

'No,' said Phoebe. 'What would be the point? It's not as if you can drive.'

'But it's family,' said Gillian. 'You said I was family.'

Phoebe was in pain, and in no mood to argue. She started up the engine, reversed out into the lane. 'I'll be back for lunch,' she said, as Gillian walked alongside. 'If you want to do something useful you can strip the beds and get the washing done. It's a nice blowy day.' Birds were everywhere, the first hawthorn blossom starred the hedge. Down towards the village the church clock began to strike. 'I feel better already,' said Phoebe. 'Do me good to get out. I'm so sick of that bedroom. Right, I'm off.'

Gillian stood in the lane, blown about. 'Good luck.'

'It's only a check-up,' said Phoebe, and drove away.

The church clock finished striking nine. Gillian watched Phoebe as far as the corner, where she sounded two sharp notes on the horn. She walked up and down. The only times she had ever been to the hospital were as a visitor, accompanying Phoebe with gifts of fruit and flowers: once to Huw Williams, after his operation, and once to Gwen, after hers. She had not known what was wrong with either of them, and hadn't asked. It had never occurred to her that she or Phoebe might ever be patients, and lie in a row. She walked along, looking at the ground, felt a couple of bitter little lines take shape, and begin to grow. She called them 'Next of Kin'.

The lanes were moist and green and bright: spring grass along the verges, new leaf in the hedges and trees, the first shoots of corn in the wet ploughed land beyond the gates. Blossom foamed across the valley; rooks were everywhere. Phoebe came to the main road, slowed and turned left, wincing as she changed gear. She drove on, the traffic building up around her.

It was market day. The town was busy with shoppers. Large women in anoraks trailed toddlers in and out of Spar and Marks & Spencer; small men in flat caps came out of Ladbroke's throwing down tickets and cigarette butts. The traffic crawled. Phoebe, the windows wide open, could hear from a distance the shouts from the cattle market, the clanging pens, the lowing and bleating. She gave a thought to Edward Sullivan, who seemed nice enough; when she got back she would phone him, ask how he was getting on with the lambs, perhaps drive out there, see what he'd done to the place.

Her spirits lifted; she passed the street market, down beyond Drovers Alley. Bright nylon overalls swung from the railings; teenage girls picked through racks of cheap skirts and black leggings. Phoebe drove past Reg's Veg, which she'd supplied for years. On her way back she'd stop and have a word. Another day or two and she'd be back to normal, spring vegetables boxed for collection, trays of bedding plants out at the front, the blackboard chalked up and visitors calling. By Easter she'd have the tapestry done, the church flowers planned. Lilies for Good Friday, as always, waxen and stern; bowls of primroses, little jars of violets, sprays of forsythia amongst the daffodils. Nice to have Easter late for once, with plenty of everything.

Phoebe stopped at the traffic lights and the pain ran all the way up from her foot to her neck. Oh, bloody hell. She drove on slowly, out to the Brecon road. Bloody stupid place to put a hospital.

The wind blew over the car park. It felt like a half-mile over to the plate-glass doors. Phoebe stopped to let through a mother and baby, sucking on its bottle in its spaceship pushchair. She walked to reception, was given directions, was asked to sit and wait. She sat and waited, and though early for her appointment was not summoned until she had been there an hour. She rose with much difficulty, was led to a cubicle, was left there with another smile.

Phoebe, groaning, changed into a blue cotton gown. She sat on a narrow wooden bench at the side of the cubicle, hearing people come and go and chatter. She waited and waited, getting cold. When at last a teenage nurse arrived, she bit her head off.

Gillian stood at the kitchen sink, at the open window, her hands deep in soapsuds and soaking sheets. The morning sun played on the bubbles: she scooped up a handful and blew them gently out through the window, iridescent, glinting, floating out over the garden, vanishing. And another shining cluster: there, and there. The doves rose and fell on the air; Gillian plunged her hands into the water, and drew up the wet white sheets and pillowcases.

The bag of clothes pegs hung on a hook by the back door. She took it down, and carried the heavy load out along the paths and into the orchard, smelling the blossom: white, opening, innocent. She hung up the great dripping sheets on the line, fastening them tight with the wooden pegs; she strung up the pillowcases, one by one, at ill-considered intervals. When she had finished, she stood amongst the windswept boughs, watching the steady drip to the grass, the drift of fallen petals. The wind took the clean wet cotton and blew it back and forth: it flapped, in its wetness and heaviness, but the wind knew no resistance and the sheets began to move more freely, shaking off their burden of water, making great slapping sounds, spraying the grass, and Gillian, watching, raised her arms in renewed abandon-ment, the sickroom blowing away with harsh words on the rushing morning, the viciousness of 'Next of Kin' torn into shameful pieces, burned in the range.

'*You were writing? I'm sure it will come back to you. When it does, will you let me see it?*'

Yes, yes.

She would drink in the wild spring wind and return to her consecration: at the desk, at the open window, the white sheets of paper lifted by the airy currents of spring, held safe by the stones of Bryncarnedd, ancient and wise.

Gillian left the billowing cotton, and walked up the garden, watching the doves.

The wings of a dove that is covered in silver wings, and her feathers like gold –

221

There. It was given to her, out of the Book of Common Prayer and on to the feathery wind. She entered the darkness of the house, climbed the stairs to her bedroom. The dust blew gently over the floor, the curtains moved at the open window. White paper waited, love consumed.

The consultant bid Phoebe sit down at his desk. He went through her name and address on the front of the file, her date of birth.

'So you're sixty-six this year.'

'I am. Most of the time I feel thirty. Today I feel over a hundred. I am not used to being kept waiting like this. It's bad enough when you're well, but when you have put your back out –'

The consultant listened, and made his apologies, turning pages.

'Has anyone come with you today, Mrs Traherne?'

'No.'

He looked at a form. 'Your next of kin –'

'My daughter. We share the house.'

'So she'll be there when you get home today? Or is she at work?'

'She has never worked.'

The consultant made a note. He asked if Phoebe would climb on to the couch. She did so, groaning, helped by the teenage nurse.

'That's it, up we go –'

Phoebe glared at her. The consultant asked if she would have any objection to students coming in, to observe the examination. She said that she certainly would. The nurse stood beside her, and took her hand. Phoebe took it away again. The consultant felt all over her abdomen. He asked her to do things – to lift her legs, to breathe deeply. She did them, moaning.

'This is ridiculous!'

'Nearly done.' He prodded and tapped. He helped her turn over, and felt all down her spine.

'Right, that's it, thank you. Come and sit down.'

She was helped off the couch, she sat at the side of his desk. Beyond the consultant the sun streamed through slatted blinds at the plate-glass windows. The rays made the functional room look tolerable. One or two plants stood about; there was a Monet poster. Phoebe looked at its corn and poppies and girls in straw hats, as the consultant talked carefully to her. There ought to be a ban on the Impressionists. Put them away for a decade or so. Over-exposure in Woolworth's. Soppy and sugary. She might drop a line to *Kaleidoscope*.

'Mrs Traherne?'

Phoebe looked at him. The consultant took off his glasses, and laid them on the file. 'Did you understand what I was saying to you?'

'I'm afraid I was miles away.'

She drove away slowly, calling, as bidden, at the chemist in the High Street, to get her prescription. She parked on the double yellow lines. To hell with it. Inside the chemist's she sat on a hard plastic chair and waited, while silly girls bought tampons and condoms and evening primrose oil. She could have told them just how much use *that* was, all refined and factory-made and tarted up in expensive packaging. Lot of nonsense. As for the condoms – where were their mothers? Disgraceful. She argued with the pharmacist about the wait for the prescription, then bought Gillian a cardful of hair-grips. She picked up her packets of pills.

The pharmacist looked at her.

'Do you want to take a couple now, Mrs Traherne? I can get you a glass of water.'

'Don't be ridiculous.'

Phoebe went out to the van. There was a ticket beneath the windscreen wipers, a warden walking away. Phoebe shouted at her, but it was no use. She took the ticket back inside the shop.

'There,' she said to the pharmacist. 'You can pay this. If I hadn't been kept waiting I'd never have been given it.' She went out again, borne on a tide of rage. She drove away through the traffic, and out to the main road. The packets of pills rattled about in their paper bag on the seat beside her. After a while her rage subsided. She slowed down, taking the turn-off carefully, coming into the lanes again, smelling the rush of spring again, seeing the blossom everywhere and the thick white afternoon clouds sail over the valley, the glinting sun on the winding river.

Well.

Now what?

Oh, bloody hell.

Phoebe drew into the verge, by a field gate, and switched off the engine. She sat listening to the birds, the quietness, a distant tractor. She looked at the field, which soon would be filled with corn, and edged with poppies, not soppy, but unbearably beautiful. Her hands, resting on the worn steering wheel, began to tremble, and she could not stop them. She rested her head against the rim, feeling an utter, unknown exhaustion. Horrible words beat about her again, brutal and implacable. Carcinoma. Chemotherapy. Morphine. St Mary's Hospice, staffed by nuns. Not very long.

The wind blew over the fields, so fresh, so free. Phoebe leaned on the steering wheel and wept.

'Are you all right?' asked Gillian. 'What did he say?'

'Nothing. He gave me some pills.'

'What for?'

'Painkillers. Stop asking questions. I've bought you some hair-grips.'

Gillian looked at them. 'Thank you.'

The kettle was on, the kitchen floor had dried. She had made an effort, and tidied up.

'Did you manage the washing?'

'Yes. It's been perfect weather.'

'I'm glad to hear it. Perhaps after lunch you could help me put clean sheets on. I might have a rest.'

Unheard of. Gillian fetched bread and cheese and last autumn's chutney.

'Surprised there's any of this left.'

'It's the last jar.'

'I'll make a bigger batch this year,' said Phoebe. 'Will you get me a glass of water?'

Gillian ran the tap. Phoebe pulled out silver-wrapped pills from a packet.

'They're *huge*. Horse-pills.'

Phoebe unwrapped two, with trembling fingers. 'So long as they do the trick. Bloody stupid foil, how are you supposed to manage this?' She managed, she broke them in two, she swallowed. 'Ugh. Ugh! Right, then, let's have lunch.'

After lunch she felt better, slowly climbing the stairs without help, directing operations in the bedroom. Gillian flapped the sheets about, spread them over a threadbare underblanket. She punched up the lumpy pillows, and shook out the blankets. The room was full of fluff.

'That'll do,' said Phoebe, taking her shoes off. 'Just the eiderdown now.'

She climbed slowly beneath it, reaching for her tapestry, turning the wireless on. A man was talking cheerily. 'Why they moved *Woman's Hour* to the morning I'll never know.' She turned it off again.

'You've said that for years,' said Gillian, at the door.

'And no one has ever given a satisfactory answer.' Phoebe lay back on the pillows. The horse-pills were doing the trick.

'*Mrs Traherne? Do you understand what I'm saying to you?*'

Bloody man.

Well. So long as the pain went away. So much to do. She closed her eyes. She slept.

At the end of the afternoon, as the light was fading, Phoebe took a mug of tea down into the garden. She walked along the paths between the flowerbeds, making mental notes. The horse-pills had helped, there was no doubt about it: the stiffness and pain had eased away; she felt calmer, rested. Wouldn't do to take too many of the damn things, but for now, while she got her bearings, made her plans –

She felt in her waistcoat pocket for notebook and pencil. She put down the mug, made jottings about the herbaceous borders; geraniums reverting to pink, she recalled; time to put in some blue cuttings again. Lupins and hollyhocks and foxgloves all threatening to take over, needed thinning. Needed some more fritillaries, some spotted snake heads – they nodded so nicely, always went well at the gate. Campanulas, white and blue. Rue and cotton lavender, lavender and thyme along the borders – nothing much to do there, except cut back the wretched rue, perhaps, where it went yellow and rusty underneath.

She came to roses, beautifully pruned, though she said it herself. The hybrid teas were flourishing; nice to put in a couple of new ones, perhaps. She might get in touch with David Thorson in Norfolk. Might even tell him.

No.

Wouldn't tell anyone. What was the point? Nothing anyone could do. Gillian would have to know, of course, but not yet. As for the chemotherapy –

A trickle of fear ran cold down her spine.

Phoebe walked on through the garden. Clouds gathered over the farmer's field, over the hills. The rooks were settling. Everything was just as it always had been. She walked through the orchard, smelling the blossom, feeling the air grow cold. The billowing sheets were dry. She unpegged and folded them up in the dusk, the fine open-air smell of them clean and refreshing. She thought of the lavender bags in the cupboards, the linen all mottled with damp. Time to get everything out in the air, out on the line again, under the apple and damson trees.

She carried the pile of sheets through the garden, seeing the pond grow dark, hearing the beat of the doves, coming home to roost. The vegetable garden she'd leave until tomorrow. She turned, and walked back to the house, pausing at the back door, looking down over it all.

Thirty-six years.

The dusk was closing rapidly now. She thought of the chill November evening when they had come here, saw herself standing at the window at the back, on the rotting flowered carpet, looking out over a wilderness.

Her wilderness, waiting for her touch.

Edward phoned Phoebe a day or two later. She said she was fine.

'Much better. The hospital gave me some horse-pills. Obviously saw me coming.'

Edward laughed. 'You certainly sound on the mend.'

'What about you? How are those lambs?'

'I've got six,' he told her. 'Delivered a twin-breech on the first night.'

'Did you now? Can't think what you wanted my help for. Still, I might come over and take a look, when I've got this place back into shape.'

'You do that. How's Gillian?'

'Gone for a walk.'

'Give her my love.'

'I will. Thanks for phoning.'

'Oh, by the way,' he said, feeling himself dismissed, 'The Consort are singing the *St John Passion* in Hereford Cathedral at Easter. And at St David's. You might be interested –'

'I know all about it,' said Phoebe. 'It was on the wireless. Andrew McGregor announced it. Felix Pettit conducting.'

Edward smiled. No flies on Phoebe. He asked if she wanted tickets – he could get two for her and Gillian.

'And my friend Bron Morgan,' said Phoebe. 'She's musical. We could make up a party. Give me the dates again.'

Edward gave them.

'I think perhaps just Hereford, you know,' said Phoebe, writing them down. 'Not sure I'm up to driving all the way over to St David's just yet. I suppose you'd better get a couple of tickets for Ted and

Gwen, while you're at it, they like to be in on things. Right, well – that's something to look forward to.'

Nesta rang Phoebe, who said she was much better. She mentioned the horse-pills, and said she was drinking herbal teas. She mentioned the concerts in the two cathedrals. Nesta, curled up on the sofa with Phil, on her last night off, listened and asked if Edward might be able to get her a ticket, and if she could bring a friend.

'Phil Dryhurst,' she said, stroking his hand. 'I think I've mentioned him, and you met – he came to Gillian's reading.'

'Oh, yes,' said Phoebe without interest. 'I'm sure you can bring who you like, it's just a question of letting Edward Sullivan know how many.'

'OK, I'll do that. And you're really feeling better?'

'Much better thanks. Well – goodbye.' Phoebe rang off with a click.

'Gillian? Edward Sullivan rang. He sent you his love.'

'Oh. Thank you. Thank you. How are you feeling?'

'Fighting fit. Do you want to go to a concert?'

Nesta rang Edward, and asked about the tickets, and the lambs. She asked what he thought about Phoebe. He said that he thought she was making a good recovery.

'I'll go down there again, when I've got a moment. I'm up to my neck with the lambing –'

'Yes, of course. And I have to go back to Cadair tomorrow. Anyway – if you could get me two tickets: would that be all right? I'd like to bring Phil Dryhurst – remember him?'

'Yes,' said Edward, watching the night draw in, feeling his pleasure at the prospect of the concert drain away. 'Yes, I remember.'

Nesta put the phone down, and leaned against her lover.

'That's fixed, then,' she said, with a twinge of unease.

Phil stroked her hair, and drew her closer. The fire blazed; outside, in the garden, daffodils blew in the evening wind. 'That's good,' he said. 'You're brilliant.'

'I only made a phone call.' Nesta got up, feeling the draught blow through the cracks in the door. She drew across the blanket, she said: 'I'll make us some supper.'

'No, you won't. You're going back to work tomorrow. I'll cook. Yes?'

He kissed her; he went to the kitchen. It felt as if he had always been here. Nesta sat down again, rolled a cigarette. She thought about Edward, and Rowland, and Phil. She thought of the change in Edward's voice, before he rang off.

She thought about Phoebe, also dismissive.

'*Much* better, thanks.'

She drew on her cigarette. She thought: I don't believe a word of it.

'You've gone very quiet.' Phil came back with a bottle of wine, and two glasses. 'Come on – what are you thinking?'

'Nothing,' said Nesta, telling her first lie.

And why? she wondered, drinking her wine by the fire, while Phil banged about in the kitchen.

Because I am happy again, and just at the beginning. Because I don't want to talk about death any more, or illness, or grief. When Phoebe needs me, I'll go to her. Not yet. Please, not yet.

And Edward? And Rowland and Phil? Let's see how we go, let's not make a drama. Nothing has happened. No reason why it should.

The fire crackled. Nesta sat drinking and smoking, watching the flames, thinking of the long sweet hours of the night ahead.

Dusk had fallen; Hereford Cathedral was packed. Gillian followed her party down the aisle. People in suits and print dresses pressed about her, chattering. There was a tuning up, a trailing of cables, a testing of microphones. Candles stood on every window ledge, there were flower arrangements.

'Much too dressy,' said Phoebe, with a sniff. 'They look like something out of *Good Housekeeping*.'

'You do it ever so much better,' said Gwen, alongside. 'Mind you, it's nice in a way. Grand, if you know what I mean.'

'I do.'

They had parked a few hundred yards away, walking through the crowded streets towards the cathedral, seeing the BBC van outside, and people streaming in. Edward took charge of the party, greeting everyone, talking lambs with Ted.

'Thirty-five so far. Doing pretty well.'

'What about tonight?' asked Ted. 'I'm surprised you've left them.'

'I know.' Edward was looking exhausted. 'Well – it's only a few hours. I couldn't miss this. My neighbour Pritchard was kind enough to say he'd look in.'

'Just as well. A lot can happen in a few hours.'

'Don't go on at him.' Gwen was looking in shop windows. 'He's done very well.'

'Thanks. I'll just have to keep my fingers crossed.' Edward gave Phoebe his arm as they made their way amongst the Easter tourists.

'Still looking a bit peaky, if I may say so.'

'Nonsense. If Rowland is with the choir I hope I'll be able to talk to him afterwards.'

'I'm sure you will.' He turned to where Gillian was bringing up the rear. 'All right?'

She nodded. He watched her: an unpenned calf amongst the crowds, ready to bolt, and cause havoc.

Nesta and Phil were coming separately, picking up their tickets on the door. Gillian watched Edward leave the tickets with an attendant, a girl with shiny fair hair and a velvet band and little pearl studs in her ears. She flashed a smile up at him, showing perfect teeth. Gillian, as they proceeded, observed Edward's unending politeness, and kindness and charm: to her mother, and their friends from the village; to this bright empty girl on the desk beneath the posters; to herself, as she brought up the rear.

'All right?'

She nodded, and looked about her: at the stained-glass windows, the mighty vaulting.

A spinster of the parish of Penglydr, brought over in pony and trap to the city where Thomas Traherne was born, son of a poor shoemaker. Here she might marvel, as he had done, at the sights and sounds of the great cathedral, where a concert was to be given at Easter, marking the Passion of Our Lord –

'Gillian,' said Phoebe. 'Wake up.'

She followed them all to their seats.

'Those are for Nesta and her friend,' said Edward, indicating two by the aisle.

'That limp young man,' said Phoebe, and he laughed.

'I'm told he's a talented musician.'

Phoebe snorted. She sat between Bron and Gwen; Ted, beyond them, helped Gwen with her cardigan. Gillian found herself between Phoebe and Edward, who passed along programmes. Everywhere was the rustle of pages, spectacles taken out of their cases, the smell of glossy paper, and flowers and candlewax.

'Tenebrae,' said Phoebe with satisfaction, putting her spectacles on. 'Just as it should be.'

Gillian looked at her programme. Her arm brushed Edward's as she turned the page: he smiled at her; she felt herself burning.

'What do you think of it all?' he asked her.

'I don't know yet.'

'No, of course not. I just mean –' He made a gesture to embrace the whole cathedral – 'all this.'

'I prefer simplicity,' said Gillian, longing for cool stone and reverence.

He nodded, watching her. 'Of course. Just so. But I hope you enjoy it – they're very fine, the Consort. And – I'm glad you're going to hear Rowland.'

'Is this what your London life was like?' she asked him.

'Yes. Yes, I suppose it is.' He hesitated. 'This isn't the moment, but one day I want to tell you a bit more about London, and – and Rowland –' He broke off, turning.

The choir were coming in, led by their conductor: a procession along the south transept of evening dress and swishing satin, portfolios of music, gracious smiles. Applause filled the cathedral, they bowed, and took their places. Everyone waited.

Edward looked at his watch again. 'Nesta's late –'

'She's here,' said Phoebe, nodding towards the aisle. 'With that limp young man.'

Edward rose to greet them. Nods and smiles ran all along the row.

Gillian watched glinting Nesta being greeted with a kiss: once, twice on the cheek. Nameless and terrible feelings ran through her. She watched Edward and Nesta's new friend shake hands, and then an uncharacteristic awkwardness in Edward, as they all took their places again, and Phil sat down next to him, brushing back long fair hair. Edward looked at his watch. He turned to Gillian.

She did not know how to read his expression, but something there made her think suddenly of Bethan, her distant childhood friend, who in the treacherous wastes of the school playground had been loyal and kind. Her own burning feelings now were all at once of no consequence: she looked at him directly, knowing he was troubled, and said simply:

'I'm glad I came.'

'Yes,' said Edward. 'And I'm glad you're here.'

They smiled at one another, and everything dissolved within her.

*

The candles, one by one, went out; there was a hush.

> '"O mighty love, O love beyond all measure
> That bids Thee walk this way of sore displeasure!"'

Phoebe sat listening, watching intently the figures before the altar, the movement of candlelight and turning pages, the upraised baton.

> '"Thy will, O God, be alway done
> On earth as in the courts of Heaven..."'

A fine concordance of voices. She listened as she was accustomed to listening at home, on the wireless, waiting to learn more, from the announcer in the interval: of the period, the circumstances of composition, the performers. Over the years she had learned quite a lot. Of course, it was the *St Matthew Passion*, more often played and performed, which she knew better, and indeed preferred. The *St John* was so very dark.

> '"Ah! my soul, what end awaiteth thee?"'

Phoebe tried to listen as she usually listened, and found that she could not: she found her concentration came and went, like the flickering candles; that King's extraordinary voice was drawing her far away from appreciation and into the realms of feeling and fear.

> '"Who, who then will stand beside me?
> Shall I stay, shall I wait to see Rock and mountain fall to hide me?"'

Phoebe closed her eyes, she bowed her head, her hands clasped over the programme in her lap.
I, who have never believed –
Where did that line come from? Some tortured Victorian, no doubt. What on earth made her think of it now?

> '"Oh heart, melt in weeping and pour out thy dolour..."'

That was Katherine Pettit, the conductor's wife. Phoebe tried to concentrate on the beauty of the soaring soprano voice, but the words laid claim to her: she found herself sinking into a pitiless place, wherein was no garden, nor music nor bird. She tried to think of death as she had always tried to think of it: simply part of a cycle. The body died and was buried, and gave something back to the earth. That was a kind of renewal. That was the end of it.

> ' "Then waking from that dark abode
> Mine eyes shall see Thee face to face
> In boundless joy, O Son of God,
> My Saviour and my Throne of Grace." '

Phoebe tried to find comfort in Bach's richness and tenderness and certainty, and could not. She tried to find somewhere within her a pinprick of light, of belief. There was nothing.

She opened her eyes. Up at the altar the candles were burning, bright and clear. Everything was here, now, upon this earth: so much to cherish, so much to do.

I don't want to die, she thought wildly, clasping one hand against the other. I don't want to die.

'Returning you now to the studio in London –'

A roar of applause.

They all crowded round him: he greeted each one.

'Gillian – lovely to see you again. I did enjoy your reading. Phoebe, I'm sorry to hear you've been ill ... Nesta – I hope you enjoyed it ... Phil, we must talk ... Bron, Gwen, Ted, we met at Gillian's reading, I think, how nice to see you...'

Around them, the rise and fall of excited voices, the rustle of evening dress, laughter, the musicians putting away their violins and violas, wiping their faces with handkerchiefs; talk about having a drink, a meal, catching the last train back to town.

Gillian, shrinking against a wall, observed all this, and observed Rowland King, moving from one to another, greeting, making introductions, extending invitations.

'Felix and Katherine, you're staying with us, we arranged it, no, I insist – that's all right, isn't it, Edward?'

'Of course, of course.'

Crammed between a pile of coats and a double bass, Gillian looked from one to the other: from Rowland, exuding warmth and openness, everyone's friend, to Edward, taller, quieter, standing back out of the limelight. She saw Rowland put his arm, for a moment, around Phil Dryhurst's shoulders, and make an introduction to the conductor, and to someone from the BBC. She saw Edward turning to Phoebe, asking if she wanted to sit down, and Phoebe's brisk refusal, and movement towards Rowland, where the action was. She saw Nesta, laughing, and Ted engaging one of the violinists in conversation and Gwen drawing Bron's attention to black, backless silk.

It was very hot. It was crowded and airless. Gillian saw Edward smiling down at Nesta, saw her interested, animated response, her ease and grace, and beauty, as she looked up at him. Unspeakable feelings possessed her, the moment of intimacy in the cathedral vanished and torn away –

Gillian pressed her way through the crush, and out to the brightlit passage. She hurried past departing musicians, vergers and hangers-on, all deep in conversation, into the mighty vaulted airiness of the nave, where she leaned against a cool stone pillar, gasping.

Around her people were making for the doors; technicians wound up lengths of cable, packed up microphones. Chairs by the altar were being stacked; the girl with the velvet hairband was walking along the seats, picking up programmes, laughing at somebody's joke. She glanced curiously at Gillian, and then away. Someone invited her out for a drink.

'That would be fun.'

And when He had made a scourge of small cords, He drove them all out of the temple . . . And said unto them that sold doves: Take these things hence; make not my Father's house an house of merchandise . . .

Gillian walked from her pillar, and sank into a seat in the shadow. The sins of the world were come into the house of God, and she did not count herself blameless. Terrible feelings ran through her, and she was afraid. Where was her poetry? Where did she belong?

A spinster of the parish of Penglydr, brought into the city, where her head swam and she shrank into nothingness.

A wider world.

She longed for the sanctuary of silence.

'Gillian?'

She looked up: he was standing beside her, grave and concerned. 'This is too much for you.'

'I am afraid I can't – I'm sorry –'

'There is nothing to be sorry for.' He sat beside her, he rubbed his face. 'We're leaving in a few minutes, anyway. I must get back to my lambs.'

'Yes, yes, of course –'

He watched the technicians, the banging about.

'You said you were going to tell me – about your life in London –'

'Yes. Yes, I will. But not now –' Again he looked troubled. Then he said slowly: 'Anyway, I'm glad I left. If I hadn't left London I wouldn't have farmed, and I've always wanted to.' He turned to her, rested his hand on her arm. 'I shouldn't have met you, Gillian. You know what I thought, the other night? Before the lambing?'

She could hardly look at him. 'No.'

'How rare you are, you and your poetry. Something to cherish.'

The clatter around them, the voices and footsteps and scrape of chairs fell away. There was only this shining, timeless moment. She said, hardly breathing,

'Edward, I –'

And then all the others were round them, making a noise, bright and careless.

'Come on,' said Phoebe. 'Time we were off.'

Cars in the farmyard, visitors for the night. Edward, before leaving, had made up the beds in the spare room; he had put in a roast, in the slow oven, laid the table, opened a couple of bottles to breathe, put on the outside light. Now, as they all got out in the starry darkness – Rowland and Felix and Katherine Pettit, and Nesta and Phil, who were, at Rowland's insistence, joining them all for supper – and as car doors slammed in the quietness, he said:

'I'll be with you all in a moment. You go ahead.'

'Oh, but we must see the lambs,' said Katherine, pulling her coat around her.

'Perhaps we'll disturb them,' said Nesta quickly, seeing Edward's face. 'We don't want to interfere –'

'Not much you can do to disturb a sheep, surely,' said Rowland, and Phil gave a laugh.

Edward felt a wave of pure irritation. He said: 'Look, I don't want to fuss –'

'But you will,' said Rowland. 'Come on, chaps, let's leave him to it. Come and say hello to Tarn.'

'Who's Tarn?' asked Felix, following him up the yard.

Rowland unlocked the front door and was greeted by a frenzy. 'This,' he said, laughing, embracing her. 'Yes, yes, wag wag wag, and I'm glad to see you, too.'

'Oh, but she's *sweet*,' said Katherine, as they all went into the house.

'What a wonderful place –'

'You should have seen it – Edward's done miracles –'

Their voices faded, the door closed. Edward went back down the yard, and into the barn.

Oh, the blessed sweet smell of the hay, the sound of the animals, moving about. In the dim light he walked along the pens, checking and greeting. He could smell milk, and wool, and droppings in the straw; he looked at his dear beloved flock, the ewes staggering up to their feet in the bedding, the lambs fast asleep. A rustle, a bleat. All safe and sound, nothing new. He counted them all: thirty-four, thirty-five, thirty-six ... He yawned, walking up to the far end. He stopped, seeing something different.

A ewe stood with her head low, watching him. An air hung about her, something at first indefinable.

'Hello, girl. What have you got to show me?'

He crossed to the pen, talking quietly. He saw her lamb in the hay beside her, so small, so still –

'Oh, no.'

He leaned on the railing, looking at it, a white-faced, black-legged little one, smeared with blood. Not a breath, not a twitch. He looked at the mother and met her yellow stare. She lowered her head again, she made a long low sound.

Until now Edward would not, even after all his close acquaintance with the flock, have said it was possible for any sheep to be so expressive. But it was there, in everything about her: grief, anger, loss. A creature set apart.

He made to open the pen, and take out the dead lamb, but she stamped her foot, and he left her to stand over it, cold comfort, while all around her came the soft sounds of snickering, drinking, peaceful breathing in sleep.

'Bound to lose a few,' said his grandfather gently. 'Never known a lambing without a few gone, even inside.'

But he hadn't been here. He shouldn't have left them –

A sound at the door.

'Tarn –'

She was over beside him, he knelt to hold her close, he wept.

'You're mine,' he said, into the thick warm coat. 'You're mine, stay with me, stay.'

Distant laughter came from the house.

The Thursday of Holy Week.

Phoebe had finished the tapestry. She and Gwen, and the vicar up a ladder, hung it on the northern transept wall.

'I'm privileged,' he said, climbing down.

'And doesn't it look *lovely*?' said Gwen, when he moved the ladder.

'It doesn't look bad,' said Phoebe, standing back. Cornflowers and larkspur and fresh young ferns grew at the base; dog roses and honeysuckle clambered round the sides. The Cross on the simple blue of the sky was straight and plain and gold, the lettering fine.

PENGLYDR CHURCH, 1995

'Really puts us on the map,' said the vicar. 'I'll work it into the sermon.'

'So I should think,' said Phoebe.

Early on Good Friday morning she came back, this time with Bron, and an armful of lilies. They cut them and arranged them in tall green containers; pollen coated their fingers.

'You're not looking well,' said Bron bluntly. 'Not at all. What did they say at the hospital?'

'How do you know about the hospital?'

'Word gets about.'

'So it would seem.' Phoebe straightened up from beneath the pulpit, her hands at her back. 'They gave me some pills and I'm doing nicely. Now, then, where have I put the scissors?'

She came back on Saturday morning, with heaps of daffodils and narcissi, primroses in wet newspaper, a cardboard box of washed jam jars.

'You're not looking brilliant,' said Gwen. 'Hope you don't mind me saying so, Phoebe, but you mustn't overdo it. We're none of us getting any younger.'

'Stop talking drivel,' said Phoebe.

On Saturday morning, Gillian walked up to the letterbox. She stood by the humming telegraph wire, watching the ripple of wind in the wayside grass; she lifted the white enamel plate in its scarlet frame. Up and down, up and down, click click click. She felt in her pocket, she drew out the envelope.

She slipped it in.

There.

It fell to the bottom, the poem within.

To Edward –

On Tuesday he would receive it.

She walked up the hill of Bryncarnedd; she laid a stone. She stood on the hilltop letting the wind blow through her, reciting her lines. Above her the buzzard spread his wings.

Easter morning. Bells rang all through the valley. At dawn it had rained, but now the spring sun shone everywhere: over the blossoming orchards, over the wet grass and tender shoots of corn, in and out of the clouds and all down the winding river.

Gillian stood in the congregation, next to Phoebe. She looked at the tapestry, illuminating the whitewashed transept wall, full of the holy blue of the sky, the gold of heaven. She breathed in the gentle fresh scent of the flowers from the garden, the familiar smells of polish and wax and wood and prayer books. She heard the sweet low notes of the organ, the murmur of the people all around her, the summoning bell. She heard the footsteps of late arrivals, a cough.

She turned; she saw him, standing at the back. He saw her, he smiled. The church was full of his presence, filled with the presence of God.

In the quiet congregation, waiting for the vestry door to open and the service of Resurrection to begin, Gillian went through her poem, deep within.

To Edward.

She wrote of a cell, a single bell, the door of the convent opening, a choir of air. The hours of the night were ending: dawn broke, dew on the grass. Birdsong soared into the holy sky, and a nun in white robes, in bare feet, unveiled, ran over the soaking grass towards the racing river. White robes streamed out behind her, she came to the grassy, reed-filled banks, she took off her garments. Shaven head and straight white body. A baptism in the gold and silver morning: lark ascending, dove descending, sun on the corn. She drank in the water, she drank in the sun, she held out her arms to embrace the world. World made holy, woman made whole, wind in the boughs and whispered vows, a gasp as she knelt in the icy water, and was upraised: a woman transformed by love, at last set free.

The coming of summer

14

Late spring rains fell throughout the valley, and the river brimmed.
When they had fallen away, there followed fine high days of sun, and
the water, swift and clear, showed the flat round stones of the
riverbed, worn to smoothness. Waving weeds were anchored by
them, emerald bright; fish flickered in and out, glinting, and hid in
the shallows, drawn out at length to leap for the fishermen on patient
afternoons.

'Very nice,' said Gwen, as Ted laid out perch and bream on her
kitchen table. 'Might take one of those up to Phoebe. She's looking a
whole lot better since Easter, don't you think?'

Ducks were nesting, all along the banks; coot and moorhen darted
in and out of the reeds. The perfect curves of the swans drifted
downriver; they clambered out on to the marshy fields on the far side
of the bridge, nesting amongst tall grasses, in pairs long together,
revisiting old haunts. They hissed at passing walkers, beating huge
wings in the sun.

All through the Easter holidays children played on the bridge,
dropping stones, racing sticks. They knelt on the banks and peered
up at the smooth, echoing arch, at the dancing reflections of the sun
on the water, dappling cold grey stone.

'Coo-ee!'

'Coo-eee . . .'

'Listen to that.'

'It's nice here. We could have a den down here.'

'You come away,' said their parents, when they saw where they
were, so close to the racing water. 'You keep away from the banks,
understand?'

'Only playing.'

'Well, play somewhere else.'

They trailed them away to the shops.

The cows were let out from the covered yards behind the milking parlours, where they had stood all winter. They came out farm by farm in procession, all through the valley, into the rich spring fields: Friesian and Charolais, Limousin and Hereford. For weeks, as the rushing air carried the smells of the new season across the yards, they had been restless and edgy at milking, one or two liable to kick, and turn dangerous. They stayed till they'd finished the last of the silage. Now they were free.

Phoebe, working slowly in the vegetable garden, heard them come into the farmer's field, stiff and slow after months on concrete. She leaned on her rake and looked over the dry-stone wall. The cows gathered speed, they tried out a run, they trotted up and down, lowing, stopping to snatch at the hedges, bending to tear at the long moist grass. At the rear, one or two were limping badly: she saw a Friesian hobbling on three legs. A nasty infected foot, from a winter's standing on concrete.

'Poor old girl.'

She watched them all settle, taking up the rhythm of the season again, long grassy hours between milking and milking, day after lengthening day. The farmer followed them, checking. He lifted his cap.

'Nice morning.'

'Lovely,' said Phoebe. She pointed to the hobbling Friesian. 'She's not looking too good.'

'She'll do. Takes a while, but she'll do.' He scratched his forehead. 'Well. Better be off.' He leapt, suddenly, out of the way of a frisky heifer. 'Get away with you!'

Phoebe watched him go back to the gate, and had a little laugh. Then she took up her rake again, making her way slowly along the paths. The horse-pills were stronger, a new prescription. They seemed to be suiting her well: she felt stronger, no doubt about it. And the herbs were helping, no doubt about that, either.

She renewed her acquaintance with Culpeper, taking the worn volume down from the kitchen dresser and up to bed, reading a section before she put the light out, or if she woke again. Many of her nights were broken, now: Culpeper, like a tisane, was soothing in the small hours.

These are my choicest secrets, which I had had many years locked up in my own breast. I gained them by my constant practice, and by them I maintained a continual reputation in the world...

                                                            Nicholas Culpeper, 1654

Phoebe pushed up her glasses, and turned the pages. She looked up Cancer, in the index, and found a reference to Yellow-flag. Well, there was plenty of that, it was all round the pond in the summer.

The Yellow Water-flag, or Flower-de-Luce
  This grows like the Flower-de-Luce, but it has much longer and narrower sad green leaves ... The root is long and slender ... It usually grows in watery ditches, ponds, lakes, and moor sides, which are always overflowed with water. It flowers in July and the seed is ripe in August. It is under the dominion of the Moon ...
  The distilled water of the whole herb, flowers and roots, is a sovereign good remedy for watering eyes ... spots and blemishes about the eyes ... The said water fomented on swellings, and hot inflammations of women's breasts, upon cancers also ...

Have to wait until summer. Plenty of other things in the meantime.

Each evening Phoebe picked leaves off dried bunches hanging in the pantry, and made a tisane: dill for digestion, to restore her appetite; also varieties of mint. Camomile to help her sleep, and once the nettles had sprung up she would take them for iron. Nettle was excellent, one of the nine plants the Anglo-Saxons considered sacred. Fool of a consultant, murmuring about low blood-count, and possible transfusions. A good jug of nettle tea, that was the answer.

Phoebe moved slowly through the garden. Over the wall, Gillian, set to weed, was weeding, moving a hoe about in hopeless fashion.

'You have to get down on your *knees*,' called Phoebe. 'How many times have I –'

Gillian nodded, and dropped the hoe.

'Prop it up, don't just leave it lying there!'

Gillian propped it up.

Phoebe returned to the herb garden, where she was sowing new seed. Herbs were the thing, you could spend a whole career on them, probably make a fortune, too, now they were all the fashion. It was not often that Phoebe felt herself part of the swim, and never that she cared about being there, but now she stood considering a number of possibilities: more at the gate, more taken into the market, where Gillian might have a stall. Advertisements in the local paper: why not? She stooped to pick up a packet of fennel, drew in her breath at the pain, straightened up slowly, taking no notice. Never give in: give in, and you were done for. She looked at the packet. Fennel. Now there was something she'd always been fond of. Loved the leaves in salads, enjoyed the stems in stews. She opened the packet, trailed the falling seeds along the neat prepared row. Lines from Longfellow, and a distant schoolroom where they had actually learned something, came to mind as she bent down slowly, patting the earth.

'The Goblet of Life' – she heard herself reciting, up before the class, long before the war. Good God, where had the years gone?

> *Above the lowly plants it towers,*
> *The fennel, with its yellow flowers,*
> *And in an earlier age than ours*
> *Was gifted with the wondrous powers,*
>   *Lost vision to restore.*

Phoebe sowed another row of it, biting her lip against the pain.

Gillian received a letter, but it was not the one she was waiting for. She carried it up to her room.

'Breakfast,' called Phoebe from the kitchen.

Gillian closed the door of her room and leaned against it. Each morning she watched and waited for the post. Catalogues came for Phoebe, and Nesta sent a card, inviting them both to Cadair. A mid-morning knock at the door brought Gwen, with a fish, which they ate for supper, neither with much appetite, picking out the bones.

Visitors had begun to call. Phoebe wrote up the blackboard, and put it out at the front. Money was coming in.

There was nothing from Edward. Not a knock, not a card, not a phone call.

Gillian did not know what to think. Terrible fears possessed her. She gardened, and did what she was told. In the lengthening evenings she walked up the lanes and across the fields.

In a lowering and sad evening, being alone in a field when all things were dead and quiet, a certain want and horror fell upon me, beyond imagination. The unprofitableness and silence of the place dissatisfied me, its wideness terrified me...

That was Traherne, who through prayer and meditation had

managed to find something also of Hope and Expectation, comforting him from every border.

Gillian, in the empty fields, lifted up her arms, and tried to pray, and find comfort. She went home to her desk, and could not write.

Now there was a letter. The Mandrake Press, on a good white envelope. She took it to her desk. At first she could not understand it.

There was to be a reading by Mandrake poets at a forthcoming festival of the arts. Montgomery, in autumn. Among those appearing the editor was proud to include ... He would be honoured if she would join them ... A wider audience ... press and radio coverage ... He looked forward to hearing from her soon.

Gillian read it through again.

'Breakfast!' called Phoebe, faintly from the kitchen.

Gillian put the letter in the drawer of her desk, and closed it.

Downstairs Phoebe was drinking herb tea from a mug.

'You should try some of this, it'll build your strength up.'

The lambs were out. Edward drove his flock up the yard, pen by pen, whistling and calling. By some miracle, and by constant checking, he had, overall, lost only two: the little one after the concert and one who had died in the womb. He'd had to go to the vet for that one.

'She'll need a Caesarian, she'll die otherwise, no two ways about it,' said Pritchard, when Edward phoned for advice. 'Can you get her up in the back of your Land Rover all right?'

'I don't know.'

'Give it a go. I'm here if she won't budge.'

He gave it a go, setting an offcut of roofing up against the open tailgate, pushing and shoving the ewe up the makeshift ramp. Tarn barked, enjoying this. The ewe was terrified; he felt like a brute.

'Go on, go *on* –'

Her feet stamped and slipped: she came down again backwards, and refused to move.

'Oh, bloody hellfire.'

But if the sheep had taught him nothing else they had, in the lambing, taught him patience. He took hold of the canvas rein at her head, and led her and heaved her, the ramp sliding about so that they both almost fell to the ground. 'Come on Tarn, get her up here!' Tarn raced round the foot of the ramp, the ewe stumbled, he put out an

245

arm to grab hold of the side and made it. He crouched down, tugging at the tossing white head: with a last heave she was up there, huge in the back, panting. He tied up the canvas rein, bid Tarn come up and lie down with her, saw her terrified yellow eyes as the dog came near, and whistled Tarn out again, up to the cab.

He drove all the way to the market town in a sweat, checking the mirror every few yards. The ewe swayed about in the back, bleating. On the road he passed a lorry full of sheep, ears and noses and blank yellow eyes pressed against gaps in the slats. He thought of the protests at Shoreham, the wild-eyed calves and shouting drivers, the woman who had died beneath the wheels. He asked himself, hearing the stamping feet in the back: Why am I doing this?

Then he came into the town, with its press of traffic, and familiar cries from the market, and drove down to the vet, wiry and matter-of-fact, and got caught up in the everydayness of farming again, where animals were animals, and cash, and survival. The ewe came slowly down the ramp, more afraid to come down than go up; he led her up the path to the back door, where the veterinary nurse let him into a room which stank of disinfectant.

'She'll be fine, now, don't you worry.'

He signed a form, he gave the ewe a pat. He left Tarn in the cab and went out to the town and the shops, with a couple of hours to kill.

He bought a paper and sat reading it over a mug of coffee in the café by the covered market, which today was empty, save for one or two regular workers, sweeping the pens out, leaning on the railings for a cigarette. He thought: In a few weeks' time I'll be bringing my own lambs down here, and again felt a spasm of sadness and self-doubt: Is this what you really want to do? Raise lambs for slaughter and supermarket shelves? Shouldn't you have thought about this before? He folded back the paper, read the music reviews, read about Rowland's appearance in York.

A singer who grows in stature with every season – a rendition of the St John Passion *from a choir which under Felix Pettit's sensitive and sometimes inspired direction was approaching, in the Minster performance last night, something like perfection. I urge you to –*

Edward put down the paper. He paid for his coffee and walked round the empty pens. Stalks of straw blew here and there; sparrows were pecking up scraps and grain. A man in overalls was carrying pen partitions to a corner, stacking them up against a wall. He nodded to

Edward, made a remark about the weather, and yesterday's prices, which hadn't been what they should be. 'This is my first year,' said Edward, hearing his own English accent. He explained about the ewe up at the vet's: for a couple of minutes they exchanged farm talk.

'Well, better get on.'

They nodded to one another again. Edward paced about, the paper tucked into his pocket. The review had unsettled him, as everything about Rowland unsettled him now. He thought, with an hour or more to kill, of everything he had been managing not to think about, during the hectic lambing. Of why Rowland had not phoned last night from York, when he had said he would, nor this morning, when he might have done. Of why their phone calls, which used, on tours, to be loving and constant, had diminished to a weekly exchange of news. He thought, in particular, of the evening after the Hereford concert, the crowded kitchen, the talking and laughter – post-performance unwinding, but more than that: a charge in the atmosphere, in Rowland's demeanour, as he poured wine, made jokes, told anecdotes, listened attentively to Nesta's talk about the school, was attentive to each one of the guests as they talked and ate and admired the house – managing, somehow, in all of this, never to look directly at Edward, to distance and diminish him with every lightly barbed remark.

'Edward's gone terribly quiet. Haven't you, Edward? Are we intruding on your rural peace?'

'I've lost a lamb,' he said flatly. 'Sorry –'

'Oh, how dreadful –'

'Oh, what a shame –'

Nesta and Katherine were all concern.

'It's okay. Just that it's the first –'

'Bound to lose one or two, I should think,' said Rowland, uncorking another bottle. 'You've done well so far.'

'I know, but –'

'No use getting over-emotional. Have another drink. No? Nesta? Phil, what about you? That glass looks dangerously low to me. That's it, good man. What did you think of our friend from the BBC? Camp as a marquee, of course, but brilliant. I want to send him your tape.' He sat down again, turning to Felix. 'I want you to listen to this, as well, now you're captive. Quite a talent.'

Nods and smiles and enquiries and Phil's blushing deflection and pleasure. Edward and the lamb forgotten.

He walked up and down the empty market, watching the

squabbling sparrows, looking out over the hills beyond the town, beyond the sprawling light-industrial estate, and the new brick houses. He thought of the silence between him and Rowland, later that night, when Nesta and Phil had said their goodbyes, with promises of renewed contact. Felix and Katherine had gone up to bed. He cleared the table, he put things in cupboards, plates in the sink.

'Leave it,' said Rowland, yawning. 'Stop fussing about.'

Edward put down the tray of glasses and looked at him. Rowland looked away. 'I'm off to bed,' he said, giving another, elaborate yawn. 'I'm bushed.'

'I'll have to check on the lambs again.'

'No problem. See you in the morning.' Rowland went out, taking a bottle of mineral water from the fridge.

Edward sat down at the table, his head in his hands. After a while he finished the clearing up, and went out to the barn. The grieving ewe stared at him, and in his own distress he could hardly bear it. He checked the others, found all was well, went back to the house with Tarn beside him, turned all the lights off.

He climbed the creaking stairs to the landing. The spare room door was shut. The door to his and Rowland's room was shut.

He pushed it open, slowly, carefully. He went in hardly daring to breathe. Rowland was utterly quiet. No one slept as quietly as that, and especially not Rowland, when he'd been drinking. Edward took his clothes off, dropping them one by one to the floor. He moved towards the bed. Rowland yawned enormously, and turned away. Edward got in beside him. They lay like sarcophagi, side by naked side. Moonlight came through the curtains at the tiny window.

'Rowland?'

'Don't start.'

Edward looked at his watch. Time to go back for the ewe. He walked through the empty market, back through the lunchtime shoppers in the town, stopping to replenish stocks for one. He carried the bags back to the surgery, was greeted by Tarn with rapture. He paid the bill; he and the vet and the nurse got the ewe up the ramp.

'She'll be a bit sore, but I've given her an injection to keep the worst away. Keep a close eye; I'll come out to check the stitches, or you can bring her back if you like.'

'You come out,' said Edward, and gave a brief description of the morning's struggle.

The vet laughed. 'You did well. Right, then, I'll be up on Wednesday. Ring in the meantime if there's any worry. All the rest doing well? No mastitis?'

He shook his head, closing up the tailgate. 'So far so good.'

'Not bad for a first-timer.'

'I was guided by my grandfather,' said Edward, feeling for his keys. 'Right, I'm off. Thanks a lot.'

He drove home again, checking the bemused ewe in the mirror, taking in the changes in the valley, the drifts of fallen blossom, the fullness of the clumps of oak and ash, coming well into leaf now. Lambs were everywhere; good to see the cows out, too. The landscape was full of life again; soon his own lambs would be out in his own fields, the ewes grazing, the lambs growing fat. At least he'd got something right.

And now he drove the flock up the yard, pen by pen in the morning sun, the lambs trotting after the ewes, skittish and playful in the new fresh air, desperate when they lost sight of their mothers.

'Baaa-aaaaaa!'

'What a noise. It's all right, there she is – Tarn! Tarn! Get that little one over –'

She was everywhere, she was all round them, filled with excitement at working again.

'That's it, that's it–'

He drove them all on through the open gate, up to the back field. Now, for the first time, he was using the field to the side of the yard as well, right at the end of the lane, a great spreading acreage bordered by trees, sloping down and away from the farmhouse, with a stream: a lovely place, a new place to spend time in and enjoy, before they all went up to the hills again after shearing. Edward felt the nagging unease which now was almost always with him, lift and dissipate, like late autumn mist from the fields.

He spent the morning moving from barn to fields, pen by pen until at last he drove the final few up to the lane field, darting to catch stragglers out of the hedge, through the gate and on to the new pasture, on to the windswept view. The folds of the Black Mountains grew smaller and bluer, fading towards the border, and distant cities. Hereford. Worcester and the Malverns. The Cotswolds. London.

The plan had been that he should go down to London, to hear the end of the *Passion* tour in Bartholomew the Great, just a walk from the Barbican.

Not now. Not unless he was asked.

Edward walked over to the dilapidated complex of pens near the far right of the field: four or five gated folds for shearing and dipping. Gates hung off rusting hinges, rails here and there had fallen or rotted: all were in need of repair. Right: that was the next job. He turned back to the field, saw the spread of the flock, and crows moving here and there amongst them, stabbing the ground. He saw a ewe limping, hobbling over the tussocks of grass, and frowned. He hadn't noticed her before.

'Tarn?' He whistled her up; she held the ewe close by the gate, her lamb beside her. Edward bent to look at the lame back leg, and saw an abscess the size of a fifty-pence piece. Flies buzzed round it. He drew in a breath. 'Better take you in again, give you a shot.' He picked up the wriggling lamb and the ewe bleated anxiously. 'Come on.'

He opened the gate and she followed him, Tarn on command at his heel. 'Good girl.' He stroked the lamb's bony head, tugged at the long soft ears. Gangling legs were folded into the crook of his arm, tight swollen belly against his chest. He ran his fingers over the nose and the lamb took hold and began to suck. He felt a consuming tenderness, walking down the lane towards the farmhouse, hearing the wind sigh, the trees in new leaf rustle above him. A thrush flew swiftly out of the hedge: he stopped and looked, saw a nest deep within, a still bright eye in the hawthorn. He drew back quietly, walked on, thinking of fledglings darting in and out, of the martins and swallows returning, any day now, nesting under the farmhouse eaves, swooping everywhere.

Edward thought, stroking the warm tight curls of the lamb's white coat: But who can I share all this with? Rowland won't give a damn for a nest, not the way things are between us now. He thought of him with an ache which was more profound than anything in the last few months. They had been everything to one another. How could they have come to this?

He saw, ahead of him, rounding the bend, Gillian, pushing a bicycle up the lane. She was wearing an old print skirt and a jumper; her hair was tied back with a cotton scarf but escaped at the front in wiry tendrils. Her face was flushed, and she had not seen him: she turned towards the open farm gate and he saw her stop, and stand there, watching the house.

A girl on a bike, solitary and strange. That was how he saw her then, as if he hardly knew her, and he remembered thinking that months later, when everything had changed.

'Gillian?'

She leapt: a terrified animal, shying away.

'Tarn! Heel!' He walked on down the lane towards her, holding the lamb to his chest. Everywhere were the cries of the sheep, the birdsong, the wind in the trees. His mind had been full of Rowland, and longing, and loss. Now he took in Gillian's evident distress, and embarrassment, her crimson cheeks, her wild hair damp from exertion.

'Well,' he said, reaching her, stroking the lamb, smiling a greeting. 'This is a nice surprise.'

She looked up at him, gripping the handlebars; she gave a hesitant smile at the sight of the lamb, stepped out of the way of the limping ewe.

'I am disturbing you –'

'Not at all, I'm delighted to see you. How is Phoebe?'

'Much better. I haven't come to talk about her.' She spoke directly, looking away from him.

'Well, then –' he made a gesture towards the open gate. 'Come and have some lunch.'

Gillian said: 'Edward –' and he heard the despair in her voice, and put a hand on her shoulder, shifting the lamb.

'What? What is it? You can tell me, surely –'

'My letter.' She looked at the ground, her hands clenched on the bars. 'The poem –'

He was bemused. 'You sent me a poem?'

'Yes. Yes!' She looked up again, her face on fire. 'You didn't receive it?'

He shook his head, casting a mental eye about the kitchen, the clutter, the magazines and music.

'I posted it at Easter, on the Saturday. You should have had it two weeks ago –'

She turned the front wheel, away from the gate. 'I must go, I should never have come here –'

'Gillian. Please.' He reached for the handlebars. 'I must see to this ewe,' he said gently. 'And then we shall look for your letter.'

Inside the yard, she leaned her bicycle up against the wall by the gate. She followed him into the barn, and stood watching as he and the dog drove the hobbling ewe into a pen. He set down the lamb beside her; Gillian watched its fierce butting beneath the fleece, the frantic tail. The barn smelt richly of sheep and hay; dust motes swarmed in the sun pouring through the open doors, and through gaps in the brickwork. The dog nosed about in the empty pens, then went outside and drank from a puddle beneath the pump.

Edward said: 'I have to go into the house, for an antibiotic. Will you come with me or wait here?'

'I'll wait,' said Gillian, planning her flight into Egypt.

He touched her arm. 'Don't go away.'

She waited, leaning on the railing, watching the ewe and her lamb, listening to the eager suckling in the quietness, to the chirrup of birds in the yard, to Edward's footsteps, going up to the house. The dog finished drinking, and lay in the sun. Gillian walked up and down the gangway between the empty pens, her heart pounding. A chaffinch flew in at the open doors and perched on a rafter. It cocked its head, small bright eyes discerning her every foolish thought. The lamb finished drinking: it moved from the mother's side, unsteady and bloated; it sank to the bedding and closed its eyes; the ewe lifted the lame back leg and watched Gillian's nervous movements. Sweat poured down her; she wiped her wet hands on her skirt. She would go, now, and leave him to search alone for her poem; she would wait for his response in the sanctuary of her room, with its dust and brokenness.

Footsteps came back down the yard: Edward entered the doorway, and the shaft of sunlight was fractured and then made whole.

'No sign of your letter, I'm afraid. You'll have to help me look for it.' He carried a foil sachet; he opened the gate to the pen. 'Here, girl, this'll put you right.' The chaffinch chirped, and let fall a dropping. Edward looked up. 'Hello, when did you arrive?'

To each bird of the air and to each of his animal kingdom a kind word, a touch. Gillian watched him kneel beside the sick sheep, tear open the sachet and remove an ampoule, slip the cap off the sharp and shining needle and hold it up to the light. 'Here we go.' A hand on the fleece, a prick; the ewe shifted abruptly and was still. Edward steadily plunged in the fluid, into the trembling flank. 'That's it.' He patted the broad back. The ewe moved away, and bleated; Edward came out of the pen, dropping the empty ampoule into his pocket. He smiled at Gillian, touching her arm again. A river of longing and fear ran through her.

'Right then. Let's go.'

The sunlight was dazzling as they came out. She followed him blindly up to the house.

In the kitchen Edward lifted piles of newspapers and magazines. He opened drawers and looked on the mantelpiece. Gillian stood trembling.

He said: 'If you sent it on the Saturday, and it came on the Tuesday – what were we doing, then?' Long fingers moved amongst cards and china on the dresser shelves. 'On Tuesday Rowland went back to London . . . I was up half Monday night with the last of the lambing, that's right, and I slept late, so when the post came he would have brought it in . . .'

She said, her voice sounding high and strange: 'Edward, it really doesn't matter – please – I must go now –'

'I hope you kept a copy.'

She did not answer. Edward moved to the sideboard, beneath the clock. It drew breath, and struck the hour, a single deep chime. Then it resumed its steady tick.

'Ah,' he said suddenly. 'Here we are.' A row of books was propped against the wall beneath the clock, without bookends. The last two had fallen: from beneath them he produced a bill, a postcard, and Gillian's letter. He glanced at the postcard, he frowned at the bill. 'That's from the feed merchant.' He dropped them both on the table. 'Now, then –' He felt in the drawer for a knife.

Gillian said unsteadily: 'Edward – read it later – when I have gone – please –'

He looked at her. She felt the blood drain from her.

He said: 'Gillian, you know how much I admire your work. I'm sure I shall like this, whatever it is. Stay and have some lunch with me, after your long ride. You'll be keeping me company. Then we can read your poem together. Yes?'

Gillian knew nothing at all about men. She did not know how to refuse a man. She was in love: she felt herself imprisoned.

'Yes,' she said, white as the envelope he so carefully propped up against the jug of spring flowers on the table. She sat as he bade her, she watched him put out bread and cheese, run water, make a salad. She felt, as he did these things, a quickening of hope amidst her fear: he would not want her to stay unless –

Her poem would release his declaration. And then –

Beyond the open window the hens looked enquiringly at every

blade of grass, stepping hither and thither, clucking of this and that. Gillian took what was passed her, and tried to eat. She gave news of her mother, was drawn into calming conversation about eggs and lambs and gardening.

Beyond the open window clouds blew over the sun. The wind blew over the field: fresh, free, unaccountable.

They took their coffee into the library. Edward brought the letter. He pulled out a chair for Gillian; he settled them both at the table. He put on his glasses, he picked up a paperknife; he looked at her enquiringly:

'You don't want to read this to me?'

She shook her head, gazing once again at the place in the table where someone once had gouged at the wood, over and over, angry and bored. The window here was open, too, to the yard, and the smells of the hay and sheep drifted into the room with the scent of the new spring grass. Down by the pump the dog made a sound in her sleep.

Edward slit open the envelope. Gillian felt herself rent in twain. He took out the poem, he read the dedication.

'This is for me? Thank you.'

Gillian gazed at the table and the blood throbbed through her as he began to read, pulsing at her throat, her temple, beating against her ribs.

A nun, unveiled, running through the dawn-wet grass towards the rushing river – Lark ascending, dove descending – Woman disrobed, naked, adoring – Into the icy water, gasping, upraised – Wind in the boughs and whispered vows – Baptism, rebirth, rapture – Naked and virginal, pierced by the sun, by desire – Transformed by longing, by love set free.

Edward laid the paper on the table before him.

There was a silence, long and deep. Gillian felt the rush of blood roar in her ears, as if the whole world must hear it, as if a great river had borne her upon it, sweeping away everything known and safe and certain, whirling her into mortal dread. The table with the gouged-out place swam before her, her nails dug into her palms like the nails of the Cross –

A blasphemy.

She said out loud, her voice shaking: 'Forgive me –' She covered her face.

Edward said gently – oh, with what tenderness and gentleness he addressed her – 'Gillian. Dear Gillian –' He touched her agonised hands, the lightest brush. 'Look at me?'

She could not move. The room with its quietness and new, terrifying knowledge, pressed upon her, held her a prisoner: exposed, discovered, naked.

'Please.'

Slowly she uncovered her burning face. She dared to look at him, trembling on the brink of hope, craving his tenderness, his touch –

She saw only sadness and regret.

He said: 'Gillian – I am so very sorry. There is something I have been meaning to tell you – something important. I should have told you a long time ago, but the moment has never seemed right. It is I who must ask forgiveness –'

He was steady and grave, and concerned; Nesta, so lovely, so glinting and bright and generous, so lonely in her widowhood, swam before Gillian's burning gaze as she listened to Edward pour pity on her own misplaced, unrequited feelings, saying quietly that he must explain –

The telephone shrilled through the house.

'I'm sorry – excuse me – I must –' He rose and strode out to the kitchen. Gillian heard him say, as if he were falling over himself, 'It's you – thank God. Listen: can I phone you back?'

She rose from her chair. Her legs were like water; her body streamed. She made for the door, for the passage, the yard, the air on her face; she began to run, blinded once again by the sun. Down by the pump the dog stirred; she rose at Gillian's wild approach and came towards her, tail beating.

'Leave me –' Gillian's voice was taut, and barely audible. She came to her bicycle, leaning half-dead against the wall; she wrenched it to life and bestrode it, weaving wildly out of the gate, pedalling as if from pursuit by the devil, turning down to the bend in the lane, the wind in her loosened hair streaming out in a cloud around her as she raced away, between hedge and illimted field and gate, and on through the valley, beneath the aching barrenness of the hills, the great mocking emptiness of heaven.

15

Nesta and Phil lay in one another's arms. It was Sunday: church bells rang. Nesta woke, and beheld Phil's sleeping face. Strands of hair had fallen across his cheek: she stroked them away and he stirred but did not wake. She lay listening to the bells, to the cries of the lambs from the field behind the cottage, to blackbird and sparrow and thrush all around it, up along the track to the lane and in her garden, where the daffodils were over but where the hedge showed tendrils of wild honeysuckle, and the grass beneath was full of primroses. She listened to Phil's steady breathing on the pillow beside her and turned to look at the bedside clock, next to an empty space where Hal's photograph had stood.

Eight o'clock. By twelve she must be at Cadair. Phil stirred, murmured, drew her close to him, kissing her forehead, her eyes, her mouth: soft, sleepy imprints, full of warmth and tenderness. She ran her hands down the warm firm length of the body she had begun to know so intimately now, as he knew hers: a sweet familiarity which still, each time they began to explore one another, held the prospect of discovery.

He parted her legs, his fingers slid into her. 'How can we live for four days without this?'

Birdsong rose and fell at the open window; Nesta felt herself open like a flower with his caress: steady, generous and knowing.

'Yes?'

'Yes – yes –'

He opened and entered and filled her; she lay spread beneath him and he looked down upon her, steady and direct. The bed creaked, the bells for Communion rang a last peal and fell away. There were only the lambs, the blackbirds in the garden, the sounds of their own bodies, tenderly seeking one another, over and over, beneath the rustling sheets.

'I was right,' whispered Phil above Nesta, as he drove slowly into her, and slowly out again, prolonging and sure.

She looked at him, held on the crest. His hair fell over her, brushing her face; they moved in an unspoken harmony of restraint and longing.

'Yes?'

'We were meant to be lovers.' He came in again and she heard herself moaning, and closed her eyes. 'You were meant to lie beneath me – and above me – and all around me –'

Restraint became abandonment. The room was filled with their cries.

Nesta drove over to Cadair, and the morning was green and bright and rustling: young hawthorn, alive with quarrelling bluetits; sharp corn; trees full of nesting rooks. Below her, rushes grew all along the riverbank: she could see Sunday fishermen, and walkers out in the hills. Lambs were everywhere, scattered like snow; cattle were grazing, or gazing from gateways as she drove past. She wound down the window and the light May breeze blew into her; she slipped in a tape and the music filled her. 'Listen,' she said aloud. 'Listen to this –'

Pipes blew, gentle and breathy and mysterious; in came the soft hollow drum, in came a line of percussion, ringing and pure. And then the piano, a refrain so lovely that Nesta, driving over the hills, beneath the waving trees and down towards Cadair's creeper-covered stone, found herself in tears. Phil's hands ran over the piano; she felt them stroking her, holding her face, drawing her close to him, opening her; she felt his mouth cover her mouth, and then move everywhere, she saw the two of them, deep in the hours of the night, consuming one another –

Consumed now by the beauty of the morning, by the sadness of parting and the aching minor chords of the piano, Nesta drew into a passing place in the narrow road and let herself weep freely. Caution and doubt and hesitation had all been swept away: she wanted only to be with her lover, and feel him inside her again.

The music flowed through her, the morning rippled all round her, everything joyous and new. And sitting there in a parked car, in a quiet lane in Wales on a Sunday morning, immeasurable miles from the pain of widowhood, Nesta recalled a conversation with her therapist, deep in the grief of the past.

Her therapist was a big quiet man in his fifties, with grown-up children. He was not an analyst, nor did he simply reflect Nesta back to herself; he answered her occasional questions about his own life as one human being to another, and she felt that he cared about what happened to her, and that she should recover, and no longer need him.

Their conversations were held in the basement consulting room beneath his house in Primrose Hill, where he sat filling a generous armchair and Nesta sat slender and sad in another. Bars had been fixed to the window frame after two break-ins: they were painted white, and tubs of shade-loving plants stood on the flagstones outside. Up on the pavement, footsteps went past, and voices carried.

'They have their own lives,' said the therapist, watching her. 'It's you I want to hear about.'

Nesta talked about her life, and how she felt she would never stop grieving. Often she wept. Sometimes they sat in silence. He never pushed her, and since this secluded basement room was the only place where she felt she was not being pushed to get better, and move on, and leave Hal behind, Nesta left these quiet, thoughtful sessions feeling rested and restored. Perhaps she gained more from them, and from his calm acceptance of her, than from any other. But sometimes they talked: unhurried, uninhibited conversations, in which she felt free to say anything.

It was one such occasion, towards the end of their time together, which she remembered now.

'I'll never love anyone else.'

'You might.'

She shook her head. Footsteps came and went on the pavement past the railings.

'Not the way I cared about Hal. Never like that.'

Someone was moving about upstairs; the telephone rang and was answered.

She said: 'I'll never have a family.'

'You might. I hope you will.'

He smiled at her, steady and kind. Nesta began to talk about how she felt she would never have a lover again, how so far love and sex had been indivisible, and that since she could not imagine loving again there lay ahead now only an empty bed, and barrenness.

Her therapist listened, and waited until she had finished. Upstairs the front door opened and closed, as someone in his own, long-tended family left the house. The session was almost over. Nesta sat back in her armchair and closed her eyes.

'I think sometimes,' said her therapist, considering and slow, 'that sex is not always the consummation of love. I mean it can happen the other way round. Sometimes love can begin with a touch.'

Nesta opened her eyes and looked at him.

'Do you really think that?'

'With the right person, yes, I think so.'

'You think I should go to bed with someone and see if I fall in love?'

'I don't think you should do anything for a long time,' he said gently. 'I think you should do only what you want to do, and when you want to do it. You heard what I said. You might want to bear it in mind, that's all.'

And now, three years later, high on a Welsh hillside, the valley spread out below her and the memory of her lover's touch coursing through her, Nesta remembered his words, as clearly as if he were talking to her now. She thought: I took Phil as a lover when he was only a friend – a new friend, even; we hardly knew each other. And now we are passionate about one another. We are intimate and close and full of longing, and Phil was right: we were meant to be lovers.

And I am in love.

I am astonished.

The music had ended. Nesta wiped her eyes, and looked in the mirror. A woman blurred with emotion looked back at her. How vulnerable she was now.

She started the car; she drove on down through the valley.

Nesta drove into Cadair through the lower gate, and parked behind the house, by the stables. She stood in the yard for a few moments, breathing in the air from the hills, collecting herself. Then she carried her bag through the back door, hearing the lunchtime clatter from the kitchen, the rattle of a trolley, out in the hall. She greeted Claire and Jon: outside the office she checked the duty rota, and signed herself in.

The house felt quiet, with none of the usual weekday activity. The front doors were open, and many of the children outside in the sun, wheeling themselves along the smooth paths towards the gates, or sitting beneath the trees with Sadie, who was reading a story. The chapel doors were open, too, after the Sunday morning assembly, which visiting parents attended. She saw Steven, whose parents never visited, in there now, wheeling himself round and round in the open space while Martin stacked chairs away. She put down her bag and went over.

'Hello, you two.' She stood in the doorway.

'Hi, there,' said Martin. 'You're looking good.'

Steven stopped spinning. He made an inarticulate sound, banging his hands on the wheel. A long stream of saliva dangled from the corner of his mouth. Nesta took a few steps forward; she signed, 'Hello, Steven,' and held out her arms.

Steven grunted.

'Come on, what are you waiting for?'

She stood there, her arms outstretched. Martin stacked chairs; children's voices came in at the open door.

'Steven?' signed Nesta. 'Come on, darling, my arms are getting tired.'

'Go on,' said Martin, turning from the chairs. 'Don't keep a nice girl waiting.'

Steven spun round and away. Nesta crossed the smooth wooden floor and sank beside him.

'Are you cross with me?' she signed. 'I'm sorry I've been away. I've missed you, too.' She felt in her pocket for a tissue, and wiped the rope of saliva away. 'There. That's better.' She took his hand, and held it. Steven's hands were twisted and stiff: on his right he could move two fingers, on his left the thumb and middle one. It was the left she held now, stroking the hard swollen joints, moving the thumb back and forth in a teasing little rhythm.

Steven looked lopsidedly down at her. His hair stood in dark, untameable tufts from a bony head; the lower lid of one of his brown eyes drooped.

'Hello, Steven,' Nesta signed, and took the thumb again.

Steven made a sound, and then he smiled. Open happiness lit his clouded features, his right hand waved up past his head and down again, over and over.

'He-rrow. He-rrow.'

They hugged one another: Nesta so fluid and warm, Steven so stiff and cold and difficult.

'There,' she said, kneeling beside him. 'Now we're friends again. It's almost lunchtime, I'm starving.'

Martin had finished the chairs. He came and stood over them, a tall, loose-limbed man in his forties, a Buddhist, who had given up mainstream teaching in Leeds, retrained and come to live in Cadair six years ago.

'What a touching sight. All right now?' Steven waved, and jerked his head. 'Good man.' Martin sat down beside them. 'What about you, Nesta? You're looking –' He studied her face. 'Not quite so good? Been crying?'

'A bit.'

'Anything I can do?'

'No, thanks, I'm all right. Just rather – overcome.'

'Well. You take your time. Nothing to rush for, we're all glad to see you.'

'Thanks.' Nesta smiled at him. 'It's nice to be back.' For a while they sat there in silence, Steven above them making gnomic sounds.

'Let's go,' said Martin, rising. He held out a hand, and she took it, getting to her feet. The three of them went slowly out of the chapel, walking and wheeling, seeing the others come up from the garden, children and therapists and visiting families. Maureen, hand in hand with her parents, saw Nesta and swung their arms up and down. She called out, in her strange deep voice:

'Mummerdad! Mummerdad!'

Nesta went over to greet them. 'I'm just going to wash and brush up. I'll join you in a few moments.' She picked up her bag from the hall, and climbed the back stairs to the upper floor. In her bedroom she splashed her face with cold water, and brushed her hair. Then she stood for a moment, hearing the everyday sounds of the house downstairs, thinking of the afternoon ahead, taking her own group of children out to the lanes, returning for tea, seeing them, later, all safely to bed. Night watch was not until Thursday: tonight she would go to bed early and sleep, chaste and single again. The prospect felt restful. Tomorrow there was a staff meeting; on Tuesday Phil was coming over to observe the children in a music session.

And then we shall see, thought Nesta, considering the two halves of her life anew. This would be the first time Phil had seen her at work; it would be his first time with the children.

She went to the window, and looked out over the yard. Swallows were nesting beneath the eaves of the stables: she watched them come and go, feeling the passion and turmoil of the morning begin to fade, leaving her calm again. I did right to come here, she thought, hearing laughter from deep within the house. Whatever becomes of me now, I do have a place here.

She thought of her therapist, steady and wise in his basement in Primrose Hill, watching her try to recover.

'Nesta?'

Someone was calling: Martin, down at the bottom of the stairs.

'Coming.'

Swallows swooped up to the eaves; the sunshine of early summer was warm and fresh. Nesta went out of the room, along the broad landing; she went down to lunch in the refectory, taking her place at the table.

Phil came over for lunch on Tuesday. He parked by the stables and Nesta, who had been waiting all morning for his arrival, went out to greet him. The sun was bright and the sky clear; someone was sawing in one of the stable workshops.

'Hi.' Phil had climbed out of his beat-up van; he stood watching her approach across the yard, his back to the sun.

'Hi.' Nesta walked towards him, shading her eyes in the midday light. This morning she had woken early, and lain wondering about his arrival and presence here. How would Phil react to the children? How much would his reactions matter to her?

The intensity of her feelings for him had not diminished, although she felt calmer and stronger, soothed just by being here, and getting on with things. But lying wakeful in her single bed this morning, listening to the birds, she felt herself begin to approach turmoil and unease again – filled with excitement at the prospect of seeing him, and also anxious: that they should not, in a different and important setting, be disappointing to one another.

The chorus of birds grew full and intricate. Nesta lay trying to remember if she had ever experienced such anxieties and apprehensions with Hal. It had been he, older and more experienced, who had introduced her to the children she had come to work with, and he had done so with such ease and generosity that she had felt few qualms about her relationships with them, and none about him. From the beginning they had been at ease with one another, slipping from colleagues to friends and from friends to lovers as if there were simply no question about it.

I knew from the moment you walked into the place – so calm and clear –

I was so nervous –

Of course you were. But you were in charge of yourself, even so. You knew how to be. That's what I liked –

In six years together they had never had a real difference, and rarely quarrelled. Perhaps it was all a bit unreal, thought Nesta, turning the pillow. No doubts, few arguments. We just loved one another, that's all: we were lucky. Until Hal fell ill. That was pretty real.

The sky was growing lighter. Nesta reached for her tobacco tin. It was wrong to make comparisons, foolish to anticipate disappointment. She got up and went outside to smoke as the dawn began to break above the hills.

And now, walking across the stable yard in the sun, seeing Phil move towards her, tall and graceful, she felt simply a clear delight.

'You found us all right.'

'I did.' He bent to kiss her, his arms went round her. 'How are you, Nesta?'

'Fine,' she said, aware of the sawing from the stable workshops, gently disengaging herself. 'I suppose we'd better not make too much of an exhibition of ourselves.'

'Sure.' He stood looking around him, at the darting swallows, the plain grey stone, the open back door to the house. 'What happens now?'

'Shall I show you round? Lunch won't be long. You can come and meet my group.' She led him round to the front, where the lawns fell away to the tall iron gates. Down beyond the trees a petrol-powered mower sent up a spray of cuttings; someone in the chapel was playing the piano.

'Who's that?'

'Probably Claire – I'll introduce you.'

They walked along the path; Nesta indicated the refectory windows. She told him about the art room, the indoor pool, for hydrotherapy. 'I'll show you it all later.'

'And this was once a convent?' asked Phil, looking at the children beneath the trees.

'It was. The chapel was built in the sixties: I think it was commissioned to try to give the place new life, put it on the map, as it were. But it didn't work – the community was dwindling. The Order made the place over to the school in the early eighties.'

'And where did the nuns go?'

'I don't know,' said Nesta, seeing Maureen come lurching along the path towards them. 'Where do nuns go? Into another community, I suppose.'

'Like moths,' said Phil, looking at the white octagon of the chapel roof. 'Where do moths go in the winter?'

'They die.'

'All of them?'

'This is my friend Maureen,' said Nesta, stopping. 'Maureen, this is my friend Phil.'

Phil collected himself; he held out his hand. 'Hello.'

Maureen squinted up at him through her thick round glasses. She was wearing a pink and blue viscose print dress with a belt, which her parents had brought on their visit: a garment which made her look as though she might be working as a counter assistant in a small-town draper's in the fifties. She planted her sandalled feet square upon the path and took Phil's outstretched hand.

'Howdo.'

'Hello,' said Phil again. He shifted his shoulder bag, and made to remove his hand.

Maureen lifted the hand and placed it against her cheek. She held it there, and began to caress it, in short, slapping gestures.

'Okay, Maureen,' said Nesta, after a moment or two, and signed to her: 'Stop now, please.'

Maureen lifted Phil's hand away from her cheek and turned it over. She cradled it carefully, examining the palm. She was breathing heavily, after a cold. She lifted the hand and clapped it on and off her open mouth. Deep sounds came and went.

Nesta looked at Phil, who was letting her do all this. Exuberant Mozart came from the chapel windows.

'Okay, Maureen,' she said again. 'Shall we go and listen to the music now?' She touched her arm.

'She's making her own music,' Phil said, unperturbed. 'It's like –' He disengaged himself from Maureen's grasp, and squatted down before her. He put his own hand over his own mouth, and made Red Indian noises. 'Like this. Yes?'

Maureen stared at him. She looked up at Nesta. The bell rang for lunch.

It was two o'clock. The children had eaten, and rested. Now they were in small activity groups all through the house and garden: painting and clay-modelling in the art room, carpentry in the stable workshop, swimming and hydrotherapy in the pool. Nesta sent Phil to take a look at all this in his own time, while she settled her group in the chapel.

'Come and join us when you're ready, all right?'

'Sure.' He touched an earring, moved away down the corridor

towards the art room, where Martin was kneading clay. 'Anything I can do?' he asked him.

He fits in, thought Nesta, observing Phil's entry to the art room, remembering his easy demeanour at lunch, in a situation which not all first-time visitors to Cadair handled as naturally, though most did their utmost to appear unruffled by feeding tubes and drool. Gillian, clearly, had found it disturbing. But Phil had sat at the table, passing and receiving dishes. He had not spoken much, but she sensed him taking things in, taking his time, in much the same spirit as most of the people who worked here: unhurried and patient.

Nesta walked alongside Steven, who was wheeling himself stiffly through the chapel doors. Beside them, Nadine walked small and straight and silent. Every now and then she brushed away something invisible. Maureen was pushing Rachel, who was rocking energetically back and forth in her chair. 'Careful,' said Nesta, seeing them through; she bent to check Rachel's strap. Claire came in with Dominic and Robert, holding their hands. Dominic did not want his hand held. He broke away the moment they were inside the chapel, and made for the box of instruments by the piano. He picked out a tambourine, and flung it across the floor. It skidded over the polished surface, coming to a halt beneath a pile of chairs with a clatter.

Dominic leapt about. 'Well! Well!'

Maureen shouted, and slapped her legs.

Robert, cocooned in a deep inner silence, wavered over to a window, and stood looking out. His mouth hung open, his arms hung by his sides.

Nesta asked Dominic to fetch the tambourine. He went to the pile of chairs and heaved one off. He put it on its back and skidded it across the floor.

'Dominic! That's dangerous.' Nesta got up from the circle. Claire began to play, something quiet and soothing. 'Thank you,' said Nesta. 'Dominic, come and sit with us properly.'

Eventually everyone was settled, with something to play.

'Okay,' said Nesta. 'Well done. Now today –' In speech and sign she told the children that a friend was coming to hear them play, and perhaps make music with them. 'Shall we take it in turns now?' she asked. 'Let's listen to each other. Steven? What are you going to play for us?'

Steven lifted his stiff and twisted hands. He banged against a tambourine with jerky gestures, sometimes missing it; his head hung to one side. Inarticulate noises accompanied the banging.

'Well!' said Dominic.

'Sssh,' said Nesta. 'Thank you, Steven, that's lovely. Who wants to play next?'

One by one, as Claire continued her quiet improvisations, they went round the group, and Nesta watched them, each child so vivid and individual: deeply passive, or capable, like Dominic, of wild disruption. Rachel's dark head hung low, and it was hard for her to raise it. She rocked, she ground her teeth, her arms lay limp on her lap. Of all the group, she was the one least able to lift and play an instrument: Nesta had given her a drum; she tapped it, and it lay in her lap; she stared at the floor beneath heavy eyebrows.

Next to her, Robert moved elaborately slowly, gazing down at the instruments before him, requiring endless prompting to pick one up and do something with it. At length he had chosen a shaker. He put it in his lap, and left it there, gazing straight ahead of him, gaping. Maureen loved the music. She had lost interest in picking at Robert's sleeve, and had chosen a triangle, which she held straight out before her, tapping and listening to its reverberating ring. It was hard to get her to stop and listen to Nadine, so small and afraid, a tiny dark reed of a child, who had only joined Cadair six months ago. She sat on the edge of her chair, brushing air before her, over and over, shrinking from contact. Nesta had helped her to choose a shaker, but that frightened her. She tried to go back to her chair, but took, in the end, a string of bells, which she shook timidly, and which Dominic tried to snatch.

'Sit down,' Nesta told him. 'Let's hear you now.'

Dominic, tense and thin and urgent, beat on his drum. 'Yeah yeah yeah yeah yeah yeah yeah YEAH!'

Claire went on playing. Nesta looked round at her group.

A wind had swept over their faces: she often thought this. It was as if a great dark movement had brushed all these children one way, like corn, or rippling grass, when it might have brushed them another: had it blown back, you could have seen the child beneath, the child who was meant to be, or might have become, were it not for a gene, a chromosome, an accident at birth.

The afternoon sun fell in eight shafts from the windows high up in the roof. The door of the chapel opened, and Phil came in, closing it quietly behind him.

'Hi.' He stood there observing it all: the circle of children, the falling light, the piano, gentle and slow. Claire turned; Nesta beckoned.

'Hi.' She rose to greet him. 'Would you like to bring a chair and join us? Or do you want to watch for a bit?'

He crossed the floor towards her. 'I'll watch, if that's all right.'

'Of course. Just let me introduce you.' She led him back to the circle. 'This is my friend Phil,' she told the children. 'You've met him already, haven't you, Maureen? And he was with us at lunch. Phil, this is Nadine, and Steven...' She went round the circle. Dominic leapt to his feet.

'Well! Herrow!' He held out his hand, and squeezed Phil's violently.

'Hi.' Phil smiled down at him, dwarfing everyone, all long straight legs and long straight hair, which he brushed away. 'Okay –' He made a gesture. 'Carry on – please.' He took himself away from the group and greeted Claire; he squatted down on a windowsill, his shoulder bag on the floor beside him.

'Right,' said Nesta. 'Now we've each had a turn, let's all play together, let's make a great big noise, and then go very quiet. Shall we try that? All together, pick up your instruments – Maureen, can you help Steven, please; and Claire, do you want to play something loud and strong?'

Stern chords sounded; Dominic, Steven and Maureen rattled and banged.

'And stop!' said Nesta. 'Sssh, sssh, go quiet as mice – Now, let's hear you, Maureen, all by yourself. Can you play that triangle very soft and slow? Can you see how it sounds like that?' She was signing to all of them: soft, quiet, slow, slow, slow. For a moment or two she was very aware of Phil, observing all this, and then she began to relax, re-engaging with the children, absorbed in helping them to play, or clap, or try to beat out a rhythm in time to Claire's music on the piano, where she had changed to a clear simple tune they had all heard many times.

'Yeah yeah YEAH!' Dominic picked up his drum and ran with it to a corner. Steven in his wheelchair grimaced and made harsh sounds, like a squeezebox. Nadine perched on the edge of her chair and dropped her string of bells. She wrung her small hands in anguish. Robert, very slowly, got to his feet. He stood in the middle of the circle, gazing up open-mouthed at the ceaseless dance of the dust motes in the sun.

'Well,' said Nesta later, walking with Phil to the stable yard. 'What did you think of it all?'

'I don't know yet.' Phil put his arm round her shoulders. 'I'm going to go home and find out.'

She leaned against him. 'Aren't you going to tell me anything? You've been so calm and laid-back – it almost feels you belong here.'

'Yes. I was worried – but somehow it wasn't as difficult as I thought. There's a good atmosphere here.' He stopped on the cobbles and stood looking down at her. 'You know what I'd like to do? I'd like to try one or two things with your music group. How would you feel about that?'

Nesta thought of Rachel's lolling head, and grinding teeth, and Steven's immobile fingers. She thought of Dominic, hurling and shouting, and Robert, impenetrably silent; of Nadine, endlessly trying to brush something away, and Maureen, filled with enthusiasm. She thought of herself in the car on Sunday morning, moved to tears by Phil's music, and the memory of his touch.

'I'd be glad,' she said, 'I'm sure you'd be good with them.'

'Well – I could try.' His mouth brushed the top of her head. 'Anyway, we'll talk about it. I suppose I'd better go now.'

'Yes, I suppose you had.' She reached up and kissed him. The afternoon sun was warm, and swallows were everywhere. She thought of her cottage, her bedroom, the curtains drawn in daylight. Phil's arm went round her: she saw herself spread out on the creaking double bed, saw him kneeling naked before her. A shiver ran through her. 'I'll see you on Thursday,' she said, 'I can hardly wait.'

'Nor me,' said Phil, stroking her back. 'And I must tell you – I've heard from Rowland King.'

'Oh?' Nesta drew away, to look at him. 'And?'

'He rang me on Sunday evening, from London. His tour's finished, and he wants to come and see me, to talk about the tape. He's got some ideas.'

The sun was warm, and swallows were everywhere. There was every reason for Nesta to feel happy: at the prospect of being with her lover again, and the prospect of his success. But it seemed to her then, as she thought of Rowland's sleek, plum-coloured car bumping slowly over the grass towards Phil's cottage, in the quietness of a summer evening, that the cries of the darting birds were unnaturally loud and shrill: as if one of their flock had been seized by a cat, and the others, too, were in mortal danger.

16

The evenings were lengthening, the grass growing lush. Overnight, the fields were full of buttercups, the lanes cloudy with cow parsley. All along the river ducklings and young coot and moorhen scooted in and out of the rushes, grown dense and tall. The swans, too, had hatched their broods, and come lumbering back to the water with them, sailing downriver past the fishermen.

Edward sat in the library, writing a letter. The front door of the farmhouse was open to the yard, where Tarn was taking the air. He could see, when he looked out of the open window, the sun slipping slowly down towards the spine of the hills across the valley, where the tiny figures of walkers were just visible, making the most of a fine end to the day. Swallows and martins swooped low across the yard. They had nested everywhere: in the outbuildings, on beams in the barn, in the eaves of the house: he was woken each morning by their insistent chatter, had already found fledglings, half-naked and bulging-eyed, fallen to the concrete.

> *My dear Gillian,*
> *I am sorry I left you so abruptly in the middle of your visit, and I was very sorry to come back and find you gone. Thank you for coming; thank you for your poem, which is beautiful, and which I was honoured to receive. But Gillian: as I began to try to tell you then, there is an aspect of my life which makes it impossible for me to return your loving feelings, much though I have enjoyed your company...*

He stopped, and thought.

Intermittent bleating came from the end field, where the lambs were growing fat; he checked them each day, and was halfway through mending the pens, but the urgent activity of the spring was over. Until shearing and dipping began, there was time to walk, and read, and consider.

This aspect is something which I have wanted to talk to you about, but
I have always felt protective towards you. Your life in this remote and
lovely place, and your own temperament, has meant perhaps that you
have been very sheltered: I was afraid that what I had to tell you might
shock or disturb you . . .

He felt her presence, burning and intense beside him. He saw her
stand at the leaded window, reading as he had asked her to do, in the
pale winter sunlight, her voice wavering nervously, then growing
strong.

We must find you an audience – a wider world awaits –
A world in a grain of sand. My place is here.

Here, in the border country of Wales, or here, at his side?
Had he been obtuse, all this time, not to realise what she felt for
him?

If I did wrong in this I hope that you will one day be able to forgive
me, and I hope very much that our friendship, which I have come to
value deeply, will be able to continue . . .

Rooks were coming home to roost in the trees in the end field,
kicking up a din in their ragged nests. He stopped again, listening,
looking out of the open window. A long, beautiful evening stretched
ahead. In Rowland's absence he might, had things been different,
have been able to imagine few things more pleasant than to walk
down to Penglydr, and up to Phoebe and Gillian's house, to sit and
enjoy the summer garden, the doves, the view of the hills. He realised
that the prospect of losing this, and losing Gillian, was, indeed, sad
and painful. And yet – he still shrank from telling her the truth, to her
face or in a letter.

What I have to tell you, dear Gillian, is that I am homosexual, and
that Rowland King and I share this house not simply as friends but
as lovers . . .

He stopped, as he had broken off this letter before, several times.
Rowland and he were not lovers, had not been since that one
weekend before the lambing. They seemed to have reached an
impassable divide of silence, which he no longer knew how to breach,

and where were they to go from here? Rowland telephoned: the calls felt dutiful. He had not been here for weeks, and although, now the tour had finished, he had rung to say he'd be up soon, Edward no longer felt inclined to open himself to rejection. If Rowland wanted him, he must make the first move. If not –

If not, then how were they to proceed?

How was he going to bear it?

Edward reread the letter. He reread Gillian's poem, as passionate a declaration as he had ever made. He thought of her, sharing uncommunicative days with Phoebe, working up at her desk or out in the garden, doing what she was told to do, waiting to hear from him.

He tore up the letter. He rose from the table and went to shut the hens up. Then he took his keys and whistled for Tarn and went walking.

At the bottom of the lane he might have gone straight over towards Penglydr, but he didn't, he climbed over a stile on the left, and struck out across the fields, his dog close behind him, sniffing for rabbits, of which there were plenty, out in the evening sun, though they bolted at his approach. He walked on through the valley, down towards the winding river, to the broad low banks where cattle wandered and went to drink.

The evening was calm and still. Edward stood watching the fishermen, casting their lines, and the widening ripples as here and there a fish broke the surface. A flock of ducks, settled amongst tall grass on the bank, flew up at the sound of the dog and flapped anxiously into the water, disturbing everything. Then it cleared again.

Edward moved on, his hands in his pockets, whistling now and then for Tarn, nodding to one or two walkers, coming home. He thought of his return, in a while, to the empty farmhouse, and he knew that the reason he was not writing to Gillian was because his own loneliness was now too deep: that until he could put things right with Rowland he had no emotion or generosity of spirit left for anyone else, and if that meant hurting her, it was just how it had to be.

The sun slipped further towards the hills. The air was growing cooler. He stopped to turn back, saw a fisherman pack up his rod and stool, calling it a day. Swans came drifting downriver, large and heavy-billed. Edward frowned, trying to place them in the book of birds he'd bought soon after he moved here. Whooper swans, that's what they were, and there was something about them, some melancholy and poetic myth he couldn't recall.

He walked on, trying to think what it was, and then, seeing another pair, floating like ghosts on the darkening water, he remembered. They took the souls from the dead.

Now that the evenings were longer, Nesta's shifts at Cadair sometimes did not end until eight o'clock or later, after the children were in bed. In autumn and winter, and early spring, she had stayed on overnight even at the end of an afternoon shift, not wanting to drive across the valley and arrive home in darkness. One thing to be there already, as evening fell: to put on the lamps, light a fire and draw the curtains, her sense of belonging established through a day or half-day of domestic activity; quite another to arrive in the silence of dusk at an empty, unlit cottage.

But with the change of the season any feelings of apprehension had gone: as the day sank into the river, and the sun melted into the summer sky, she drove up through lanes thick with cow parsley and rosebay willow herb, looking down over the sloping stretch of fields, at the cows returned from milking, lying down here and there as shadows lengthened. She thought of her garden, where the apple trees were in full leaf, the first small hard fruit just visible. Phil had cut the grass. She had planted geraniums in tubs outside the door: forget-me-nots had appeared all along the path, and clumps of foxglove, up along the hedge, and several flowers whose names she had no idea of. She must go and see Phoebe, who had not answered her card, any more than Gillian had done; she must buy boxes of cuttings, and seek advice, and see how much help Phoebe needed, in her undeclared illness. She knew she was putting off this visit, wanting, still, to cherish an unclouded happiness.

So Nesta, on these early summer evenings, drove through the hills after work with her window down and sometimes singing. Rabbits hopped into the hedgerows, the smell of grass and manure blew in at the window, thrushes and blackbirds sang. She drove past the Feathers, where the door stood open, where she and Phil sometimes went for a drink; she slowed for the ducks, who ventured across the road for scraps put out by the publican's daughter, crossing back again to the pond behind the hedge, dense with rushes and full of nests. Once, as the sun was sinking, she saw ahead of her a whole line of ducklings, following their mother across the road. She slowed right down; she stopped the car and got out to watch them. They panicked, as the mother was panicking, lifting small wings at the sound of her, peeping wildly as they raced for the safety of the hedge. Swallows swooped low in the road ahead, she heard the splash of the mother duck, the tiny ones that followed; messes were splattered all over the tarmac; she drove on slowly, keeping a watch for stragglers.

On evenings like this, if she did not drive out to Nant-y-Coed, Nesta sat out in the garden, reading or writing her letters to London, waiting for Phil to come over for supper. Sometimes she was home in time to see the farmer, who checked his flock morning and evening, after milking. They had pleasant, neighbourly conversations: about the hedge beginning to overgrow the track, and whether or not the council hedge-trimmer would be down this week; about his lambs, and the ills that sheep were heir to: maggots and ticks and fly strike; and how he always hoped to get the shearing done before the Three Counties Show, but usually didn't.

Nesta thought of Edward, during such conversations, and of the lamb he had lost, on the night of the concert: how he had made light of it, and how the conversation, largely controlled by Rowland, had soon moved on to other things. But she had seen how deeply Edward was distressed, and had been aware of his quietness, all through the meal. She sensed that the death of the lamb had touched something else: for weeks afterwards, rejoicing in her newfound happiness, she had pushed this knowledge to the back of her mind, not wanting to face what lay behind it.

On the afternoon of Phil's visit to Cadair, when he had told her of Rowland's phone call, the memory of that Easter evening came rushing back to her, as they stood in the sunlit stable yard and the twittering swallows flew everywhere, loud and shrill. She saw, as Phil embraced her and told her his news, Edward's white face at the dinner table; she saw Rowland glance away from him, directing his gaze upon her and Phil – charming and attentive to each of them, but seeking, she knew, Phil's response, not hers.

She and Phil had said goodbye to one another, out in the stable yard at Cadair; he had driven away, waving from the window of the van, and she had waved in answer, as if all were as it should be. But walking back across the yard, smelling the summery air from the hills, she saw once again the hard bright coldness of the evening of Gillian's reading, the glittering snow in the lanes. She recalled the warmth of the pub, the evident interest which Rowland had taken in the new arrival.

She thought of the first afternoon she had spent with Phil, out in his isolated cottage, the rain falling, the fire crackling, the miracle of King's voice when she heard it for the first time: hairs on the back of her neck rising, though she knew nothing of such music.

'*You do realise he liked the look of you?*'

Phil's lazy sweet smile.

'*Really? I'm pretty easy about these things...*'

How easy? Nesta had wondered. She wondered again, this early summer, as soon as she knew that Rowland was coming up from London – not inviting Phil out to Tremynydd, but driving all the way over the valley to Nant-y-Coed, giving his valuable time to a young, unknown musician, taking the turn-off, making his way down that lonely, unvisited lane. She had said nothing.

And again: they were out in her garden, three or four days before Rowland was due to visit. It was late afternoon. The bees, who had emerged from the hive in the middle of April, were humming about in the foxgloves. Phil had cut the grass two days ago, and a small heap of cuttings lay up by the hedge in a corner, next to Nesta's growing compost heap.

'Is that okay?' Phil asked, as she walked round everything, tugging up weeds here and there. 'About Rowland?'

'Of course. I do hope it goes well.'

She stopped, and stood watching the bees, of whom she had been so fearful and who now gave such pleasure. All this new life in the garden. Buzzing came from deep within a foxglove flower: the bee came out dizzily, thick with pollen. Phil's arm went round her; he drew her to his side; she closed her eyes. A bit late to start raising questions now, when it was she who had suggested Rowland King in the first place.

'*I suppose he could help you –*'

'*Yeah, I suppose he could.*'

That was on that rain-soaked winter afternoon.

'*You know what you should do. Phone Rowland King.*'

'*He'll be ex-directory.*'

'*Edward won't be. Edward Sullivan. He'll be in the book.*'

That was here, on their first night together, the moon at the window, their clothes strewn all over the floor. Whatever had she been thinking of?

Nesta walked over to the compost heap, and dropped her handful of weeds. She brushed away the earth from her fingers, and said nothing, only: 'Shall we go and eat now?'

'Or shall we go to bed?' Phil, at her side again, turned her to face him, hard against her belly.

They went to bed. All doubt was vanquished as he came into her.

And afterwards, as they lay murmuring to one another, she thought: After all, I have only been wanting the best for him; I still want that. To raise anxieties now is absurd. More than absurd: insulting. Phil is here; he has said: We were meant to be lovers. What more do I want?

It was only much later, waking at an indeterminate hour of the night, going sleepily into the bathroom for a pee, that she felt, once again, a shiver of anxiety. The early summer moon was approaching the quarter; the light at the window was bright in the darkness; it had grown cold. May was always an unpredictable month. Nesta drew her dressing gown around her; a splinter of light from the moon touched the photograph of Hal, sitting on the side of the bath, head bent over the paper, as the water gushed. She touched his dark hair, his hollow cheek. She thought of the hours of love she had spent with Phil, and how her happiness now had blotted out not Hal, but the pain of widowhood, until she had almost forgotten it.

Was that betrayal? To have found such delight with a man and a body so different, to feel – yes, it was true – passion as powerful and fulfilling as anything she had ever felt?

Nesta stood in the night-time quietness of her cottage, which a year ago had been a place quite unknown to her, and thought: I am as much in love as I have ever been in my life. I cannot pretend otherwise. And if I were to lose this now –

She thought: The truth is, that if you have once lost everything, and known such grief, you really want only one thing: never to feel it again.

I give all I can to my work. Beyond that, deep down, my only concern is myself. To shield and protect myself.

And when Edward's face, white as a ghost at Easter, floated before her again, a mirror image of her own fear of lost happiness, she blotted it out, as she had blotted out the pain of widowhood, and crept back into bed with her lover, her arms about him, curled up against him, thinking: Nothing else matters but this.

And so she said nothing: not then, in the coldness of the night, nor in the days that followed. She did not speak of her own fears, nor of her fears for Edward. He must look out for himself.

The fine weather lasted. Yellow and purple vetch, and creamy-gold honeysuckle, clambered over the hedges; dense undergrowth in the ditches was shaded by clumps of nettle, and the mighty spreading leaves of giant hogweed. Poppies blew on the verge, and bordered the cornfield; clover and misty-blue scabious and harebells were everywhere. The spiralling, burbling call of the curlew began soon after dawn; at noon the dizzying song of the lark broke the stillness. Flocks of lapwing flew over the hills and came down in the peace of the evening, feeding for hours on insects, amongst the grazing cattle.

Rowland, in the middle of May, came up from London, arriving in late afternoon. He did not stop in Penglydr, nor take the turning out up to the farm. He looked at the map and drove out fast across the valley, over the river, skimmed by swallows, and up towards the hills again. Pipes and percussion and a melancholy line of piano accompanied this last lap of his journey: music he had listened to many times and now heard again with particular intensity. He came, as Phil had said he would, to the sign for Nant-y-Coed; he took the turning, driving more slowly now, taking in the corn, the poppies, the scent of grass blowing in at the open window, the isolation. He switched off the tape, seeing, right out in the middle of a field, what must be Phil's cottage, set down and forgotten, miles from anywhere.

The car was full of silence; then he heard the birds, and distant bleating. He saw rooks, beating over the field, he saw the still deep shadows of the trees bordering the lane on the left. Shirts hung out on a line; a van had been parked in the shade. He drew up before the open gate; sweat trickled down from his armpits as he looked towards the cottage. Sun gilded the windows, a cat lay asleep on a sill. How warm it was.

Rowland drove through the gateway. He glanced in the mirror, and saw someone wilful and determined, a man whom he had not seen for a long time, but who he now recognised had never gone away, had always been there, waiting. He wiped away sweat. He drove slowly over the bumpy ground, stopped, and switched off the engine.

The front door of the cottage opened.

Rowland was given a beer in the kitchen, where flies were buzzing round a cat dish on the floor. Phil, noticing a fastidious glance, picked it up and put it in the sink.

'Sorry about that – I've been working, I forget about things.' He turned the tap off, brushed back long soft hair, looked at Rowland standing in the middle of the room. 'It's nice of you to come – I can't really believe I've got Rowland King drinking beer in my kitchen.'

Rowland smiled. 'I'm glad to be here. If life hadn't been so hectic I'd have got in touch properly a long time ago.' He looked around him: at the ancient fridge, humming in the corner, the stone sink and bucket beneath, the painted cupboard on top of a chest of drawers. 'Well. If ever there was an unfitted kitchen, this is it.'

Phil laughed. Sun came in at the open window, flies flew out on a current of air. A small enquiring sound was made from the passage, and the cat walked in. 'Hi, Abraham, I thought you'd put in an appearance. He heard his dish,' Phil explained. 'Mind if I feed him?'

He opened the fridge, spooned tinned food into the clean dish. 'There you go.' He set it down again, and chucked the spoon into the sink. 'You've got that brilliant dog, haven't you?' he said, watching Abraham eat. 'I'd like a dog myself, but I don't suppose Abraham would.'

'He's very handsome,' said Rowland, finishing the beer. 'How old is he?'

'Four, I think. Are you four, Abraham?' Phil looked back at Rowland; he saw the empty glass. 'Still – you haven't come all this way to talk about my cat. Can I get you another?'

'You can. Thanks.' Rowland watched Phil get a beer from the fridge. His movements were graceful and unhurried; he seemed at ease, though he must be on edge.

'Here you go. And then do you want to come into the other room? That's where all the music is.'

'Lead on.' Rowland poured the beer into his glass. 'You're not having another yourself?'

'I'm all right for a bit – I haven't had a long journey.' Phil ruffled his hair, and brushed it back again. 'Right then. Follow me.'

'Will do,' said Rowland, lightly touching Phil's arm.

They crossed the few steps of the hall. The sitting room, having a window on to the back as well, was warm and close and sunny. Rowland stepped over wires and looked out over the hills. 'Very nice. How long have you lived here?'

'Ages.' Phil indicated an armchair by the fireplace. 'How long have you had Tremynydd?'

Rowland made a dismissive little gesture. 'Oh – coming up for eighteen months?'

'It's a lovely place. This is a bit more basic, as you can see. Did you stop in there on your way?'

Rowland frowned. 'No, no, I didn't.' He took a seat in the armchair, leaning back. 'I haven't come all this way to talk about Tremynydd, either. It's you I'm interested in. You and your music. You're rather gifted, you know. Do you know?'

'Well –' Phil perched on the arm of the other chair. A long leg swung, crossed over another. 'Thanks. I'm glad you like it.'

'Good.' For a moment Rowland said no more. He sat drinking his beer, taking his ease, just watching. The promise of an extraordinary sunset lay beyond the open window to the back, beginning to melt into summer clouds, turning crimson and gold. Just the first touch. His eyes travelled back from the dissolving sky to this small, crowded room; they travelled over Phil, long, lean and well-made, swinging his foot, brushing his hair away, blushing. Waiting for Rowland to speak.

'Do you mind me looking at you?'

'No. No, I –'

'You're rather beautiful,' said Rowland slowly, 'as well as gifted. I'm sure you must know that, too.'

Phil looked at him. There was a long moment of silence. It was broken by the cat, coming across from the kitchen, stepping neatly over the yards of flex, and general clutter.

'You know you're a handsome beast, don't you?' said Rowland lightly, stretching out a hand. 'Why don't you come and say hello?'

Abraham sniffed the outstretched fingers. He stopped, considered, then made a leap. Rowland shifted; Abraham walked round and round him, kneading his belly, purring hard.

'He likes visitors,' said Phil, getting up from the arm of the chair.

'So it would seem.' Rowland stroked the broad smooth head; he ran his hand down over the long striped body, as Abraham finally made his choice of position, curling into Rowland's full fleshy belly, closing his eyes. 'That's a good cat.' He went on stroking him, over and over.

Phil was at the piano. He played a few melancholy minor chords.

'That's what I was listening to in the car.'

'Yeah? You've probably had enough of it, then.'

'No. Go on. I've come here to listen: I'm not going to say anything else for a bit. Just play for me. Anything you like.' Rowland made a gesture: to embrace the piano, the keyboard, the tapes and CDs.

'Give me an idea of the range. Talk me through it all. Then we can discuss things.' He leaned back, the cat falling asleep upon him.

'Okay.' Phil went on playing: a haunting line began to develop, became more complex. 'I wrote this in the winter,' he said quietly. 'For my friend Nesta – remember her?'

Rowland nodded. 'I do. Is she a friend or a lover?'

'A lover,' said Phil steadily, his hands moving over the keys.

Rowland said nothing. He thought of the glittering cold January evening when Phil, after Gillian Traherne's reading, had waited to introduce himself. In the months which had passed since, and in the meeting at Easter, the impact of his beauty had not diminished, but deepened.

The room was full of Phil's music, his languid grace. Beyond the window, blood-red fingers of the sun slipped into darkening cloud.

How had he waited so long?

The last piece was drawing to a close. Phil, at the piano, was playing something new. 'This is what I'm working on now. I don't have a name for it yet. It's still a bit tentative – I'm not quite sure where it's going.'

His fingers touched the keys; a quiet line sounded in the room, full of sadness and longing. Phil was humming softly over it, pausing now and then to think, and take a new direction. The shadows in the room grew deeper; the sun had sunk low. He reached up to a lamp on the piano; now his hands on the keys moved in and out of a pool of light. Rowland watched them, so slender and strong; he watched the lamplight catch strands of soft hair as Phil moved this way and that, pausing, repeating the refrain, so yearning and deep.

'Well –' he broke off abruptly. 'I guess that's it.' He looked at his watch. 'God, I've been playing for ages, you should have stopped me, you must be wanting to get on –'

'Not in the least.' Rowland moved in the armchair, dislodging the cat. He rose heavily, crossing the little room in a couple of strides; he put his arm round Phil's shoulders, as he stood uncertainly by the piano. 'I wouldn't have come here if I hadn't known you were good, and now you've confirmed it. Well done.' He moved to the keys, he began to play, picking out the refrain of the last piece, hesitant at first, then with more certainty.

'Very nice – not there yet, needs more depth, I think. But it's on the way. When you've developed it I feel sure it'll be interesting.' He stopped, and turned. 'You've never written anything for the voice.'

Phil shook his head. 'I had a thought about that a week or so ago, with some children –' He broke off. 'But that's another story. Other than that I've never even considered it. Are you suggesting I should?'

'Not necessarily. Just making enquiries.' Rowland looked out of the window. The field was sunk in darkness; the last line of light rimmed the hills. Behind him, Phil, suddenly, was turning on lamps: one in a bottle on the mantelpiece, another small reading lamp by the armchair. 'Oh.' Rowland turned back to him. 'Is that necessary? I was rather enjoying the mood.'

'Just that one can't actually see.'

'True. Now – I must use your bathroom after those beers.'

'Sure. It's out here, at the back –' Phil showed him the door at the end of the hall. 'Can I get you another? What about something to eat?'

'I'm really not hungry, thanks. Anyway –' Rowland patted his belly. 'I have to watch this. I'll be back in a minute.'

He walked up the narrow passage, hearing Phil let the cat out. When he came back, he saw that a quarter-moon was rising over the fields at the front; Phil's hand was on the lintel, and he was bending this way and that, long hair falling, long straight back and legs stretching and flexing.

'Very nice,' said Rowland, coming up behind him. He touched the well-made shoulder, so young and hard. 'You must be tired.' The scent of the summer grass came in at the open doorway. 'Why don't we get a breath of fresh air for a minute? It's going to be a fine night –' Rowland stepped out, gazed up at the stars. 'I hardly notice the sky in London. Look at that.'

They walked over the rough ground. 'And the silence,' he said. 'It always takes me a while to get used to it. I don't suppose you even notice it.'

'No. It's part of me, I guess I need it now. I'm often playing, and anyway – music is about silence as much as anything else, isn't it? Pauses, intervals, moments of tension: they're just as important.'

'Of course. Everything is in that tension. I do like your last piece; it's so full of feeling, like all your work.'

Phil did not answer. Their feet crushed the long summer grass, lit by the rising moon, and the air was full of it.

'What a lovely place.' Rowland stopped, and stretched out his arms. 'It's simple, and peaceful –'

'No more peaceful than Tremynydd.'

'But you have it all the time.'

'Is that what you'd like? Is that the plan? That you'll come and live here with Edward one day?'

Rowland gave a little laugh. 'I don't think I'm quite ready to be pensioned off yet – I really haven't thought that far.' He touched Phil's arm again. 'It was you I was thinking of – having this perfect peace to work.'

'It hasn't exactly made me a fortune –' Phil broke off, watching the hedge. 'Abraham's caught something, look.'

Moonlight silvered the long grass: the dark shape of the cat could be glimpsed, briefly, making a dash for it, something small and limp dangling from his jaws.

Rowland stood watching: then walked on. Phil, turning back to him, said hesitantly: 'I don't suppose you feel like singing –'

'Now?' He smiled. 'A special performance?'

'Sorry – I suppose it's a bit of a nerve.'

'Not at all.'

'It's just the idea of it – Rowland King. Not just drinking a beer in my kitchen, but singing in my field. Well – my rented field. Rented kitchen too, come to that.'

Rowland looked at him; tall and young and talented; diffident but determined. Out in the middle of a field in the moonlight, asking him to sing . . .

'What did you have in mind for this performance? Do you have a particular favourite? Or perhaps I flatter myself – why should you know the repertoire?'

'I know quite a bit of it.'

'Even though you don't write for the voice.'

'Even though. I have wide tastes, I always have done. The first time I heard you sing –' Phil stopped, and shook his head.

'What?' Rowland asked quietly. 'What happened the first time you heard me sing?'

'I had gooseflesh all over me,' said Phil. 'I was nineteen, I was into electronic stuff, it was all I could think about. Then someone at college who was into classical music – he played me some Schubert one night.' He looked at Rowland and then away. 'I suppose that was the beginning of my education, really – broadening my range, or something. I thought you were extraordinary. I still think that.' He stopped. 'Sorry. You must have people go on to you like this all the time. I don't know what I'm thinking about, asking you –'

'People don't go on to me like this all the time, and anyway, you're rather different. You've just given me enormous pleasure, I admire your work: I'm happy to sing for you. Why don't I sing you some Schubert now?'

Rowland moved away on the grass; darkness and silence were all around them. There was only the moon, the first pale stars, the lights from the house across the field. He drew a breath: a big, heavy man, in the middle of a darkened field, miles from anywhere.

Phil stood listening, and a prickle of delight lifted each hair on the nape of his neck.

> '"Du bist die Ruh der Friede mild
> Die Sehnsucht du unt was die stillt...
>
> You are rest and gentle peace,
> You are longing and that which stills it.
> To you I consecrate, full of joy and grief,
> My eye and heart as a dwelling place."'

Rowland was pacing over the grass, pausing to translate, and give a smile. His voice, so noble, so powerful, explored each phrase, rose higher, rang out through the first dark hour of the night.

> '"Come into me and silently close the gate behind you,
> Drive other griefs out of my breast.
> Let my heart be full of your joy.
> This tent of my eyes lit solely by your brightness –
> Oh, fill it wholly."'

The words hung in the summer stillness, and slowly faded.

He stopped, he smiled, he held out his arms.

'Christ.' Phil stood rooted to the spot. 'That was –'

'I'm glad you liked it.' Rowland stepped towards him, he gave him a hug. For an entirely timeless moment, he felt the softness of Phil's hair against his cheek, the roughness of the cheek beneath, the strong hard bone. Then he released him, with a little laugh, and patted his shoulder. 'You're a good audience.'

Phil was flushing; he brushed the hair off his face; he did not speak.

'Not just singing in your field but taking you in his arms,' Rowland said easily. 'Come on, it's getting cold. Let's go back to your studio, or sitting room, or whatever you call it. They walked towards the open door, the lights. 'You're the one we're supposed to be talking about – I'm not just here for the beer.' Rowland put his arm round Phil's shoulders once more; Phil drew away.

'No?' No answer came: he looked, he saw Phil's face a blur of emotion. 'Phil? I haven't upset you, I hope –'

Phil made a gesture which might mean anything. 'I suppose –' he cleared his throat. 'I suppose I'm quite churned up, that's all. It's taken me a bit by surprise.'

Rowland felt a quickening of desire and longing so powerful that for a moment he was overcome.

'Oh, Phil –' He did not touch him, just then he did not dare. 'Come on,' he said carefully. 'Perhaps we're both a bit churned up. Perhaps I will have that beer after all. Then we must talk properly. Mmm?'

Phil made no answer. There was a movement, and the cat came slinking past them; it disappeared into the darkness. The night air had taken on the chill of May, always an unpredictable month. Rowland followed Phil towards the lights of the cottage.

They sat with their beers on either side of the empty fireplace. The lamp on the mantelpiece shone on Phil's head as he leaned back, long legs stretched out on the rug; behind him, the uncurtained window was black.

'Well, now,' said Rowland. 'Your future.' He smiled. 'We have a number of options. I've given your tape to one or two people, as you know – Felix Pettit, our conductor, and the BBC producer I introduced you to after the concert in Hereford. Simon Land. You remember him?'

Phil nodded, listening.

'Felix, like me, is really an early music man,' Rowland went on, pleased to feel himself now as impartial and professional as he would be in giving advice to anyone. 'He doesn't know a great deal about contemporary work, but he does have taste, of course, and he did quite like what he heard. Simon Land's more to the point: he's steeped in contemporary stuff, interested in people like Philip Glass.' He shifted in the chair, watching Phil chew at a hangnail, nervous and intent. 'I have to say that Land's tastes on the whole are pretty austere – I think he found you a touch too sweet, to be honest. "Has charm, lacks depth." Sorry. But still – you're very young.'

Phil bit off the nail and gave a shrug. 'And you can't please everyone.'

'Quite. And one should never try to. But you do have something original, there's no doubt about it. And Land did have one useful thought.' Rowland reached for his beer; he drank slowly, sensing Phil's tension and hope. 'Nothing happens overnight,' he said firmly. 'I'm sure you know that. I don't want to raise false hopes. But Land mentioned a man called John Kirkby, no relation to Emma, who's launching a new label. I think that's the answer for you, you know. Somewhere small and innovative and hungry. Kirkby's looking for interesting new work, he has a good background – I've a feeling he may be our man.' Rowland put down his beer. 'I'd like to send him your tape, with a personal recommendation. How does that sound?'

Phil gave a smile of dazzling sweetness, and stood up. 'It sounds bloody fantastic.' He took a tobacco tin from the mantelpiece, and opened it. 'I'm really sorry,' he said, lifting out papers, 'I know you don't like it, but –' He was rolling up quickly, his fingers trembling. 'I've held off for hours – would you mind very much?'

Rowland sat watching him: his nervousness and beauty. He felt a new stirring of desire.

'I'd quite forgotten you smoked.'

Phil lit a match; he inhaled deeply. 'I held off after the concert, when we came back to Tremynydd for supper. God knows how, I was so on edge.'

'Were you really?' Rowland leaned forward. 'I hope you're not on edge now.'

Phil threw the match into the fireplace; he drew on the roll-up again. 'Christ, that's better.' He looked down at Rowland; again, he gave his slow sweet smile. 'Of course I'm on edge. I'm also – like I said outside – churned up, I suppose.' He looked away. 'And this John Kirkby guy – I'm really grateful.' He moved towards the window, and stood looking at the darkened pane, smoking intently. 'It's funny – you go on and on doing your own thing, saying you don't mind not getting anywhere, there's plenty of time and all that, and it's bullshit. As soon as you have a glimmer of hope, you realise –'

'What's that?' Rowland asked, free now to take in the sight of him, tall and dreamy. He pictured an upper room in darkness, the stars and the quarter-moon at the window; he pictured Phil standing before him, naked and grateful and aroused.

'You realise how long you've been holding on, keeping your real feelings down, pretending it doesn't matter. You realise how much you want it: to make it, to be there.'

Rowland sat very still.

'It's just an introduction, Phil. I wouldn't be doing you any favours if I said it was going to be easy.'

'Sure, sure.' Phil turned from the window. 'I understand all that. But even so – you've been very kind, it feels like a break.' He moved away from the window; cigarette smoke hung in the air. 'I'm sorry about this,' he said, moving back to the mantelpiece. 'Why don't –' He lit another match; he lit one of a bundle of joss sticks, which Rowland had not noticed before, standing in a jam jar. After a moment or two a pungent scent began to take possession of the room. 'That better?' Phil drew on the roll-up again; he sank into his armchair. 'What I really need now,' he said, with his lazy sweet smile, 'is a joint.' He stretched out, relaxing again. 'Still. I don't suppose that's your scene. It isn't even Nesta's. Seems it's a pleasure I'm destined to enjoy alone these days. Never mind.' Another pull on the cigarette. 'Thanks again.'

Rowland had finished his beer. He sat in the sagging armchair, in the smoky, sandalwood-scented air, drinking in Phil's long, languorous body, stretched out in the chair before him. It was a very long time since he had been in a room full of incense, or thought about the sensuous sharing of a joint, or been to bed with anyone except Edward, who seemed at this moment to be part of another lifetime, almost forgotten. For months all desire had been eclipsed except in relation to a drift of hair, slender musician's fingers, a long, languid young body arched beneath him. Now – he felt himself on the brink of conquest.

Phil went on smoking. They smiled at one another.

Rowland said slowly: 'It's entirely my pleasure to help you. I hope I've made it clear: I wouldn't be here if I didn't think you had talent.' And it was true: he believed it was true. Not just a body, but a young musician. Someone who'd worshipped his voice for years, ever since the first time he heard it; someone who'd asked him to sing in a field in the darkness.

For an unexpected moment, Rowland was afraid. Perhaps this was dangerous. Not just a fuck in the dark, but the beginning of something he had not expected to feel again, something new and all-enveloping, leading towards the abyss.

Phil registered the intensity of the gaze upon him. He sat up again, flicking the end of the roll-up into the hearth.

'Rowland, I –'

'What?' Rowland leaned forward. 'What, Phil? Say it.'

Phil hesitated, then looked away. 'Nothing.' He made to rise, to escape a feeling in the smoky, scented room which was suddenly almost palpable.

'Wait,' said Rowland. 'I don't think it was nothing,' he said slowly, and knew that the moment had come.

In his youth the darkness he had always known lay deep within had given him secret, narcissistic pleasure: now, seeing Phil's real unease, seeing his lean young body tense with emotion, recalling sleepless hours of the night spent wanting him, Rowland knew only that he had to have him, no matter what followed for either of them, and his blood raced.

'Phil,' he said quietly. 'Listen to me. Don't be afraid. I want to tell you something. I'm sure you know what it is. Mmm?'

Phil did not answer. He made to rise again.

'Look at me. Please.'

Phil looked. Rowland held his gaze and saw, as he had glimpsed in the moonlit field, a real confusion, a meeting of longing and fear.

'I want you,' he said, and his voice was quieter still. 'I've wanted you from the moment I saw you. You're gifted and beautiful and I want to help you. I also want to take you to bed and fuck you all night, and I think, deep down, you want that too. Yes?'

The room was full of the scent of incense, the small pools of light. Beyond them, beyond the black, uncurtained windows, lay the silence and darkness of the fields: empty, isolated, unvisited.

Rowland waited.

Phil leaned back in his chair. His slender, beautiful fingers covered his face, and long soft hair fell over them.

'Phil?' Rowland asked softly. 'What are you thinking?'

Phil lowered his hands. A thread of the joss stick crumbled and fell; Rowland was filled with the urgency of desire.

'I don't know what to say.' Phil reached for his tobacco tin; he turned it over and over; at last he looked up. He met the renewed intensity of longing in Rowland's eyes, and turned away again, opening the tin. His hands on the packet of papers shook.

Rowland leaned across the narrow space between them; he touched the graceful trembling fingers.

'Don't be afraid.'

'Stop it.' Phil took his hand away; he rolled a cigarette, lit it and drew deep, chucking the match away. 'I can't think.'

Rowland sat watching him. 'Then shall I tell you what I think?' Phil did not answer. 'I think you've denied something all your life.'

Phil shook his head. He made to speak. He stopped.

'You're thinking of your friend Nesta,' said Rowland. 'Your lover. You're thinking of people, I don't know who – girls in the past, I'm sure there've been plenty. But creative people are complex, Phil, it's in their nature to be divided. There's a darkness, kept hidden. There's a shadow, walking alongside. Don't tell me you've never felt that.'

Phil was smoking, listening. 'I don't think I –'

'If you haven't, then there is something missing in you.' Rowland looked at him closely. 'Perhaps that is still what is missing in your music, why it has charm but lacks depth. Because there's a side of you that's denied, or unexplored. Something you don't want to acknowledge, or are afraid of.'

Phil flushed. 'That feels –'

'Unkind? Too close to the truth?'

'It feels manipulative,' said Phil, and he got to his feet. 'I don't like that.'

For a moment Rowland was taken aback. Then he recovered himself, rising too. 'I didn't intend –'

'Didn't you?' Phil moved away from the narrow space between them; he brushed back his hair in a quick, angry gesture. 'What did you intend, then?'

Rowland felt his heart begin to hammer. 'Well, well.' He tried to steady himself. 'It seems I really have touched a nerve.'

'Yeah, perhaps you have.' Phil looked straight at him. 'I don't need you to come here and tell me what's creative and what's not, and how if I went to bed with you it would be good for my music, thanks. That's crap, it's the oldest, most disgusting cliché I ever heard.'

'Phil. Please. Listen.' Rowland tried to steady himself. 'Whatever my feelings for you, I wouldn't be wasting my time on someone I didn't think was worth it. I've said that already –'

Phil was pacing, smoking. 'It stinks. It stinks like blackmail.'

'Don't be ridiculous. Of course it's not.'

'Isn't it? I'll push your second-rate music if you let me fuck you. What's that, then?'

'Oh, Phil. Come on. I'll help you anyway. All I meant was –' Rowland moved towards him; he put a hand on his arm.

Phil shook him off. 'Don't touch me, okay?'

'All right!' Rowland's self-control snapped. The evening, and all his hopes for it, so long imagined, had slipped from his grasp: he felt

287

the smoky, poky little room press in upon him; the incense was cloying and thick. He fought to regain his control; he began to cough.

Phil, who had picked up his tobacco tin again, dropped it back on the chair. He moved to open the window: cool night air came in, and the soft hollow note of an owl sounded, far across the field. The two men looked at one another; smoke drifted out into the darkness. There was a long, difficult silence.

At length Phil said slowly: 'Can I ask you something? Where does your own shadow lie? What walks alongside you, Rowland, that sets you apart as an artist?'

Rowland stood at the open window. The two breathy notes of the owl came again: he could not escape the memory of Edward: walking across the darkened farmyard last autumn; lying in his arms in the whiteness and stillness of their bedroom last winter, as the snow fell past the window.

'*A white Christmas. You even managed that.*'

'*Of course. The barn owl's next.*'

'That is a very good question,' he said to Phil at last.

And one which no one had ever asked him: not the tutors or lovers of the past, nor his colleagues and friends in the Consort, nor Edward, to whom he had been as close as to anyone. He tried to remember the last time anyone had challenged him, on anything other than a musical technicality; he looked across at Phil, younger and less worldly than anyone he had dealings with these days, for whom Rowland had been an idol, for whom he could open almost any door in London, but who, unlike anyone else in the circle of admiration which had so long surrounded him, had told him to go to hell.

'And?' asked Phil.

The air coming in at the window was growing cold. Early summer nights could be treacherous. Rowland saw the dark shape of the cat, making his way down the field again, the hunt still on. He closed the casement; he leaned against the frame; he said thoughtfully:

'It's a serious issue. And actually, Phil, you're right to be angry.' He stopped; he stood thinking, picking at loose flakes of paint on the wood. 'I do believe in the notion of a shadow,' he said, letting the flakes of white fall to the floor. 'A shadow or a watcher: there's some kind of deep duality in most creative people. That's hardly a new idea. I also believe that sexuality is –' He moved away from the window, he spread his hands. 'A continuum. Not something immutable. Interest and desire can grow, or ignite, with different people, men and women, all through your life. I find that creative in itself, but some people are afraid to face it. And perhaps –' he looked at Phil again – 'perhaps that really is true of you, Phil. I do sense that it could be. What was wrong of me was to make the link between your work and your life in the way I did. You're young, you're just at the beginning of your career. To speak as I did then – it was unforgivable.'

Phil, listening, had let the fragile cigarette go out. He lit it again, and stood smoking thoughtfully.

'Well. Thanks for saying that.' He flickered a smile. 'You still haven't answered my question.'

'Haven't I?' Rowland suddenly felt very tired. 'I think I have.' He sank into the battered chair again, rubbing his face. 'You've just seen the dark side, Phil. Someone ruthless and cruel, who has to get what he wants. Does that make me an artist? I don't know. I do know that not many people have seen it, but you had a glimpse. And the guts to tell me to fuck off.' He closed his eyes, exhausted. 'Good for you.'

Smoke and incense had drifted out through the open window; the last grey thread of the joss stick fell. Phil put his cigarette out in a saucer; he crossed to the piano. Rowland, defeated and weary, lay back listening to a few almost arbitrary notes, the kind of half-tune a child might pick out, questioning and uncertain.

'The only artist I know,' Phil said seriously, 'other than you, is Gillian Traherne. She's the real thing.' His fingers moved over the keys. 'What kind of darkness does she have, I wonder?'

Rowland did not answer. He heard Phil playing a line he recognised, and realised he was going back to his last piece: the most recent, most haunting, filled with an unequivocal sadness.

'Shadow at my side,' Phil said, half-ironically, continuing to play. 'Do you think I should call it that?'

Rowland shook his head. He went on listening, as the room took on the coldness of the summer night; he no longer felt the urgency of desire, but something more profound, and more disturbing. Moments of knowledge had been given to him in a cramped room: he was on dangerous territory. What he could feel for Phil might be complex and all-enveloping; terrible pain could be attendant upon this. He thought again, listening to the music grow darker and more passionate, of how Phil had been the only person ever to stand up to him: an unrestrained anger, which had to be respected. He thought: in ten years' time, this will be a man to reckon with.

The passion diminished, the music grew calmer; the sea was still again, lit by a sailing moon. Rowland felt deeply moved.

'Saul and David,' he said, as Phil drew towards a conclusion, certain and sure, and he opened his eyes and saw the light on the fall of pale hair, on the long, perfect fingers, the yellow keys.

The music ended. The room was very cold. Phil turned to smile at him: ironic and forgiving and direct.

Rowland thought: This is the beginning of a hopeless passion.

He had that one moment of perfect clarity.

Then he rose, and held out his arms, and Phil said: 'Rowland. I think you should go.'

He drove out fast across the darkened valley. Here and there lights shone from lonely houses; the sky was full of stars, and the river glinted. Rowland raced over the bridge at Penglydr, and down through the village. People were drinking in the pub; he glimpsed the bar, the winking mirror, a few familiar faces. He thought of the winter snow, the icy sky, the moment after the reading: turning to see a young man at the door, framed against the light from the stairs, tall and languid. The first flicker of interest. He drove on, leaving the village behind, speeding through the lanes. The fields stretched out on either side in the starlight, a rabbit froze in the road ahead. He slowed, he sounded the horn. Eyes shone in the headlamps, huge with terror.

'Go on, you bloody fool.'

He drew closer; the horn pierced the silence. The rabbit suddenly bucked, and made for the hedge. A gleam of white tail, then it was gone. Rowland changed gear, and came to the sign for Llanfonen.

Ahead lay the farm, where Edward was aching to see him.

Rowland pulled up at the sign, put his head in his hands. This was the moment, the turning-point: here, he could retrieve what was slipping away; he could take Edward back, embrace the future –

'Rowland? You didn't say you were coming.'

Lights in the house, and a face full of longing –

'No,' said Rowland aloud.

He could not do it. Phil's smile, his integrity and grace, and his refusal all swam before him. Later, perhaps, he could return to Edward. Now –

He let down the handbrake, he drove past the sign. Darkness lay all around him. He raced towards the road to London.

17

Gillian scrabbled in cardboard boxes. She took out desk drawers, turned them over and shook them. Papers lay strewn across the floor; a naked bulb burned into them. She knelt, coughing in the dust, and sorted them into piles, roughly dated.

The darkness of the summer night enclosed the house; the bell of Penglydr church struck the hours. Gillian picked up her poems and laid them out upon her desk, weighting them down with stones. Her breathing came fast and her cheeks burned.

Once I wrote this –
and this –
and this –

They lay in the order of composition, some long dead and some still breathing: written in pencil, in pen; typed out and re-typed; rejected, accepted; published in little magazines, published in the Sunday papers – once, twice, damp and yellowing, three times, four times, a long time ago. Letters from publishers, compliment slips: try again, keep writing, sorry not this time, space precludes, this one I like, these are of interest, yes, yes, yes . . .

The magazine from the Mandrake Press. The invitation from the Mandrake Press. A forthcoming festival of the arts. A wider world.

You are inspired –
I am in love –
The sacred winter light.

Gillian stood at her desk and breathed in dust and pressed her hands to her burning cheeks. Her poems and papers lay before her, roughly arranged: a circle enclosing a childhood, a church, a river; the tick of a bike and the sound of a bell; a grille in a convent gate. Illimted fields of orient gold and the white of winter lay upon the pages; voices wove in and out of the dust: a poet on an old recording, dry flat voice on cracked black vinyl; a poet up at the bookshelves, taking down volumes, reading aloud:

Lov is the true Means by which the World is Enjoyed. Our Lov to others, and Others Lov to us . . .

The volume closed; a smile to a child in an armchair, a sleeping doll. Back to the desk. The scratch of a pen, a pause, a consideration. The long tear of a sheet from the pad, a crumpling. A ball of white cast out of heaven, into a hearth full of soot.

Gillian stood at her desk, and a sea of white lay round her. Scraps and scrunched-up balls – the floor was full of them, weeks of single lines and half-lines, torn into pieces, rent in twain. Here on the desk was the work of a lifetime: some of it crumbling, dust to dust, but amongst it the living nerve of poetry, full of tearing linen, the unwinding spool of the thread of life, lapping starlit blackness; holy blue shone through the pages; angels stood at the four corners of the earth, holding the four winds of the earth; a pathway led to God.

And now –

A woman disrobed, naked, adoring –

A door swung shut for ever.

Gillian stood in a foaming sea; she walked up and down her creaking floorboards, all through the hours of the night. Her body burned and her hair sprang out around her; her nails dug into her palms.

'Edward. I cannot write. I cannot write!'

The church bell tolled the hours. Three o'clock. Four.

The door at the end of the landing opened. Footsteps into the bathroom, painful and slow. Running water, the bang of the pipes. Footsteps out, and along the creaking landing; a pause at the crack of light.

'Gillian?'

Gillian stood stock still, and closed her eyes.

A knock. She did not answer. Phoebe quietly opened the door.

'Gillian!'

Her eyes flew open.

Mother and daughter, in ancient dressing gowns, stood facing one another. Gillian beheld a woman older than time: shrunken, sunken, wispy and mottled and mothlike. Phoebe, feeling her illness tug her across the divide, saw a feverish, febrile creature, wild-eyed, staring from a sea of litter.

'What do you want?'

'I heard you – I couldn't sleep. What on earth are you doing?'

All down the long dark tunnel of her childhood.

'Nothing,' said Gillian, burning. 'Leave me alone.'

Dawn was beginning to break, the birds to sing.

Phoebe went back to her room: slowly along the threadbare runner, hands on the dado, the balustrade.

Gillian switched off the naked bulb. She sat at her desk as watery light filled the room. The poems on her desk lay where they were bidden, weighted down by stones.

'Edward,' she whispered.

The sun rose, the sky was streaked with gold.

Gillian waited: for the hum of the milkfloat, and for the postman's van, winding up from the village, changing gear on the flat, pulling up outside the house. A bang on the letterbox, a square of white on the mat.

Her name, his writing.

The sky grew lighter, the milkfloat came rattling. She heard the chink in the porch.

The sun rose higher. She waited for Phoebe to start the day.

Phoebe went past the door again: down to the kitchen, without a word.

The post van drove past the house without stopping, picking up speed, and was gone. Gillian put her head in her hands. She pictured the van pulling up at the box on the telegraph pole, far up the lane, serving the scattering of farms and houses. Scarlet box against the hawthorn, hum of the wires.

The wind had rippled the wayside grass, she had stood there at Easter and slipped in her poem. The buzzard soared through the fresh spring sky; she had climbed to Bryncarnedd and stood there reciting her lines –

And now he had no more to say to her.

Not a line, not a word.

Clouds were gathering over the hills: the summery morning was changing, rain in the air. Cool air came in at the window, the poems struggled beneath their weight of stones.

Gillian bowed her head, enduring the crucifixion of silence.

Nesta walked round her garden, feeling the threat of rain. The morning had promised more fine weather: already there was a change, a coolness, gathering cloud. She should go in, pack her bag, drink her coffee, be ready to go. She put off this moment, watching the bees come and go in the foxgloves, sailing out over the hedge. She thought of the children at Cadair, the days ahead; she thought of the night which had passed, mostly sleepless; of the telephone call which had not come in the morning; the telephone call she had not made.

The door to the cottage stood open: she could see, from here, the phone on the windowsill. She walked round and round her garden, her hands in her pockets, smelling the grass, the lavender, listening for the sound of a van in the lane, a slowing down at the top of the track, feeling the first drops of rain.

She thought: If Rowland has taken Phil from me –

She thought: If Phil has betrayed us –

She could not finish these thoughts.

Rain fell. Coldness spread through her. She thought of all the things to sustain her life if Phil had abandoned her: the children, her colleagues, the rhythm of the days. She thought of Phoebe, whom she had neglected, and of Edward, who would need every friend he had. She thought, as the rain fell in earnest, and she made for the open door: But I could not stay here. Not after this.

My new home. My refuge.

She felt a wave of anger.

A blackbird's alarm call, up in the apple trees.

She stopped at the door, she turned.

A van at the top of the track, bumping down to the field gate, pulling up.

He strode towards her, easy and smiling; he held out his arms.

Anger dissolving, rain and tears.

Inside, they embraced on the sofa, by the empty fireplace, warming one another. Rain fell against the windows, steady, unending.

'I love you,' said Phil, for the first time. He took her hand, he lifted it to his lips.

'And I you,' said Nesta, her fingers moving over his mouth.

They kissed, softly, over and over; they drew apart and leaned against the Indian bedspreads, watching the rain.

'I guess this is it,' said Phil.

Nesta said carefully: 'Phil – you're so young – you may not want – it may not be right –'

He turned to look at her.

The rain fell and the river rose; the grass grew lush and the rushes tall. The rain blew away and the summer was established: long hot days when the cows made slow procession across the fields, moving from patch to patch, grazing, resting to cud in the sun, slowly rising, moving on again, heavy with calf. They swayed to and from the farms for milking; cars slowed down behind them, and the lanes were splattered with cowpats.

All through the valley the farmers were drenching and shearing and dipping. Edward rang Pritchard, rang round the list of names he was given: he made a date for the shearers, a date for the mobile dip. Each day, twice a day, he checked his flock: lifting the stubby tails and looking for clusters of eggs. Fly strike. If he failed to find it, the hatched maggots could eat a sheep alive in a matter of days. Already he had missed one, and found a rotting carcass, right down at the bottom of the sloping back field, the eyes pecked out by crows or magpies, black head twisted to one side, black feet stiffly stretched towards the sky. He felt sick, going back to the house for a spade to bury her. Two days later he found a lamb caught overnight in the fencing wire he'd put up all along the hedge: he raced for his cutters, and released it, shaking with relief as he watched it bounce away, crying for the mother.

'If there's a way of dying, sheep will find it.'

He thought of the words of the vet again, as he walked every day amongst them all, his dog beside him, a bag of vaccine or a drenching gun against worms in his jacket pocket. He checked them for sheep scab and ticks, he trimmed their feet and checked them, too, for maggots, the cause of foot rot. He was busy, and anxious to get it right; to see his first lambs through, his ewes fit for tupping, then up to the hills again: a rhythm established, a flock growing strong.

He began to feel part of the farming community: a novice doing a decent job, asking advice, paying his bills. His savings were dipping; he did his accounts and knew he would have to go to market, no matter what the wrench, to recoup even some of the cost of winter feed, the vaccines, the shearing and dipping, the fencing and roofing and pens. Never mind what he'd spent on the house.

The house, in high summer, had all the windows open. It smelt of the first cut of hay, from Pritchard's place; of hens and cows and ripening corn, of earth and buttercups, manure and flowers and wool – a rich grassy scent blowing all through the valley, the kind of smell which if you drove up from the city, and opened the car door, would hit you smack in the face. Walkers stood drinking it in: on the hills, where the bracken grew dense, on the footpaths, where burdock and cow parsley brushed their legs. Dragonflies hovered above the river; midges hung over the lanes at evening.

Edward, in the evenings, the last check made, sat out on a chair in the yard, reading, with Tarn at his feet. Hens clucked in and out of the barn; the swallows and martins were everywhere, darting in and out, their nestlings grown to scrawny fledglings, the fledglings, survivors of the first, awesome flight, swooping low, growing sleek. Edward raised his head from the page and watched them; he watched the scratching of hens in the dust, Rhode Island Reds and Dorking Black, laying well, growing fat. He closed the book and went into the empty house, the quiet kitchen. The clock ticked, the radio murmured, he ate bread and cheese and sausages, salad and hunks of ham; he fed Tarn, and went to shut the hens up, taking renewed delight in them, and in eggs to take down to the village and leave for sale in the shop: a small, pleasing income.

He saw a sign on the shop door, an announcement of sheepdog trials. He made a note of the date; he drove out to the venue, half a mile from the village, a broad, open, twelve-acre field spread out beneath the lower slope of the hills. He had a word with Pritchard; he took Tarn out with a handful of ewes for practice. He put his name down.

The summer evenings stretched before him. He whistled for Tarn and went walking again: down by the river, watching the melancholy glide of the swans towards dusk; up in the hills. He stood looking out over the valley: towards Penglydr churchyard, full of lengthening shadows, up towards Phoebe and Gillian's house, windows glinting in the last of the sun, doves here and there on the roof.

He could not bring himself to visit.

Dusk fell. He walked home, praying to find the Peugeot pulled up in the yard. He dialled the flat in the Barbican. Rowland's voice on the machine.

I'm sorry I'm not here – please leave a message –

He buried himself in routine, and casual acquaintance; he climbed the stairs as the stars came out, and slept with his dog on the floor beside him. Melancholy and loneliness lay buried deep; he waited with diminishing hope for Rowland to phone without warning, to visit, to lie in his arms.

He wrote a long letter; he quoted Beckett, lines to die for:

> *If you do not love me, I shall not be loved.*
> *If I do not love you, I shall not love –*

He thought of Gillian, and her own poem to him – naked, upraised, adoring, baptised by the descending dove –

What should he do?

He kept her poem, slipped into the pages of her father's book.

He tore the Beckett into a hundred pieces; they fell like snow to the floor.

Phoebe lay in her high iron bed, and Gillian sat on the low wooden chair across the room. Her stomach was a black sea, tossing beneath an incoherent sky. Outside, the summer evening spread over the garden, the kitchen garden, the deep still pond. In the farmer's field the cows, returned from milking, stood beneath the trees; crows flapped over the hills.

Gillian twisted her hands back and forth.

She said: 'You have never loved me.'

Phoebe stirred on the pillow. Unwashed mugs and cups cluttered the table beside her. Her hair stood in tufts of white, her eyes were dark stones, reflecting nothing.

'That isn't true.'

Gillian's breathing came fast and light. 'That is how it feels. How it has always felt.' Sweat streamed down her, a river of fear.

Phoebe's bony hands smoothed the sheet, which needed changing.

'Gillian, I –'

'Nor my father,' said Gillian, clenching her fingers.

A current of air came in at the open window; dust drifted over the floor.

'That isn't –'

'He is never spoken of.'

Silence.

'You have not kept alive his memory.'

'I put up a plaque –'

'He deserved more than that. He deserved to be kept alive. His memory should have been kept alive!' She burned with anger.

Phoebe's head moved on the pillow; she sank beneath the covers. Her bones were like sticks and her mouth was dry.

'You see,' said Gillian, consumed by fire and water. 'You see. You cannot answer.'

Phoebe turned her head towards her. Everything was painful.

'Something has happened to you.'

Gillian rose.

'I am your mother,' said Phoebe.

Gillian laughed. A tearing of linen, rent in twain.

'What is it? Tell me –'

Young doves beat over the garden. They flew past the window, they settled on the roof. Soft sounds were everywhere.

'Nothing,' said Gillian, making for the door. 'I should not have spoken. I wish I had not –'

'Gillian –'

She stopped, she turned.

'Fetch me a drink. Nettle tea, there's a jug in the fridge. Or water. Anything. My mouth is –' Phoebe licked cracked lips.

Gillian left the room, and walked along the landing. Dust motes danced in the sun falling on to the runner: from the open door of the bathroom, the open door of her room, where heaps of white paper lay grieving.

She descended the staircase, she descended into hell. She walked along the dark tiled hall, stained with sin, and along to the kitchen, where flies flew up in alarm. Nettle tea, bitter and strong: into the last of the cups. The windows closed, the sink full of dishes, the chairs heaped up with clothes, milk going off in a pan.

She had not left the house for weeks.

She had not been to church since Easter.

I must walk, said Gillian, opening a window.

She took the bitter cup to Phoebe.

The therapist must believe in the individual goodness and value of each person she works with. She must work with a clear stream of their being, drawing energy from prayer . . .

Nesta sat in the office at Cadair, drinking tea and reading. An hour off-duty, the house book taken down from the shelf: not the log, not the record of meetings, but a loose-leafed file where everyone was free to make entries, to clip in a page with a thought, a quotation, an observation.

When the blind poke their own eyes they may see flashes of light . . . Children banging their heads are letting themselves know they are there . . . Terrible things happen in nature, nature is extremely cruel . . .

Nesta sat thinking, listening to the sounds of the house: wheel-chairs spinning and turning and locking; laughter in the refectory, where tables were being laid for an early supper; the hum of the chairlift down the stairs, swing doors swinging open and shut, carpentry and birds in the stable yard. A roaring from Dominic, racing along the corridor: inarticulate sounds from Steven, whom she loved, being wheeled across the hall.

People get better, and then they slip back... We are drops in the ocean, we are part of something bigger than ourselves...

Martin had made these entries, quoting from a television programme. *Everyman, June 1992*, he had written, *I'm glad I saw this.*

So am I, thought Nesta. *A clear stream of being.* She said it aloud. *Drawing energy from prayer.* Martin drew energy from meditation: he had told them this in the staff group. He meditated each morning and evening, sitting before an open window: a ritual, a rite.

And she?

Nesta finished her tea, and closed the file, slipping it back on the shelf. She thought: When I came here, I was drawing energy from a great struggle, a fight to survive. I look back now on my life then, and that is what I see: a pushing forward through grief, a refusal to go under, a determination to build a new life, to look outside myself. I drew strength from Hal's voice, deep within, from the knowledge of all we had been to one another.

She walked out of the office, across the worn flags of the hall, out through the wide open doors of the house, seeing the sweep of the summery lawns, the fullness of the trees. She walked to the chapel, which no one was using, and entered its whiteness and smoothness, lit by the high shafts of light from the octagon windows. She took off her shoes and spun round in the empty quiet, as she had done once before, before she and Phil had become lovers.

Music is everywhere, it's all around you –

She lay down, once again, on the polished floor.

And now?

Now I draw energy from love again, she thought, feeling the warmth of the sun on her face. I cannot pray, I shall never believe, but I have been blessed.

The twelve-acre field was set up for the trials with a complex of fences and pens and marker-sticks. Land Rovers were parked all along one side of it; the air was full of whistling and pipe smoke, and Welsh was spoken. Farmers came down here from all across the valley: an annual event, with raffle tickets, gossip, dogs kept up in the back with their tongues lolling, children racing about. Full summer clouds sailed over the hills, somebody spotted a hang-glider, drifting towards the river, and the children ran to look.

'Think he'll come down in it?'

'Hope he does.'

A gate on the distant side of the field held back each handful of waiting ewes, each dog, each farmer. They waited for a signal: a white flag held aloft, dropped suddenly. The gate swung open: in came the sheep, anxious and bleating, scattering, stopping, lowering their heads to graze. In came the dog, crouched low and moving rapidly; in came the farmer, with whistle and stick. On went the stopwatch: the trial began.

'Feeeeeh! Feeeeh!' The whistle, thin and high: 'Come by, come by, come by!' The calls, ageless.

The sheep trotted, panicking, from stick to fence: the stopwatch was out; farmers in caps stood smoking and watching and waiting their turn, their dogs held beside them, panting, watchful, ready to go.

'Away to me now, get down, get down –'

Edward stood by his Land Rover, drinking it all in. Beside him, Tarn was whimpering, straining with excitement.

'Quiet! You'll burn yourself out.' He ticked off the competition; he looked at his watch. He saw Ted and Gwen amongst the spectators, and went to have a word; he was introduced to grandchildren.

'Keeping well?'

'Very well, thanks.' He hesitated. 'How's Phoebe?'

'Haven't seen her for a bit. Expect she's busy – this is the time of year for her, always somebody calling. Mind you, she's usually in church, like Gillian. I must try and get up there. Like a raffle ticket?'

He bought a whole row, without taking in what the prize might be; he drifted away again, greeting Pritchard.

'Nice day for it.'

'Not bad.' Pritchard's cigarette clung to his lips; his fingers were stained with yellow. His dog, turquoise-eyed, barked from the back of the pick-up. Tarn strained at the leash.

'Tarn! Heel!' He tugged at her, hoping that over-excitement would not spoil her performance; not that there was anyone here who would care where they came in the trials, but on principle he wanted them both to do well. Next week the shearers were coming, men who'd been with sheep all their lives; he thought he'd feel less of a fraud, or a novice, if he and his dog had shown their mettle.

Number nine had his sheep up in the pen; his dog lay panting; a spatter of applause.

'Did well.'

'Not bad.'

Edward, number eleven, took Tarn out of the field, and along through the next to the gate on the far side. His ewes were there in a pen, brought down this morning, and watered. He strode over the ground, hearing the calls and activity behind the adjoining hedge, feeling nervous.

'I'm entering Tarn for the trials,' he'd told Rowland, in their weekly phone call.

'Well done.' Papers lifted on the desk, buses roaring past the window, summer in the city. 'It's baking here.'

'Why don't you come up? Everything's at its best – it would do you good –'

'I wish I could. Don't seem to be able to draw breath at the moment. Lined up for weeks.' Pages in the diary turned, voices came and went. 'Ring and tell me all about it. Good luck.'

To hell with it.

He waited, up by the gate, straining to see the flag. Tarn encircled the half-dozen ewes, back and forth, back and forth; the air was full of the smell of grass; his hand was on the latch.

There. The flash of white.

He lifted the gate, he held it wide, he whistled. The ewes went through nice and slowly, keep it steady, don't tire them before they've begun, good girl –

He strode out to the middle of the field, his crook in his hand, his animals beside him.

Gillian went walking. Out across the fields, stumbling over the tussocks and humps. She panted in the heat, and the sweat poured down her; cattle stared, and one or two young bullocks came towards her, in the field below Bryncarnedd. She shouted and waved: they shied away, eyes rolling. Sorrel brushed her bare legs, and sharp flints pressed into her feet. She climbed the stony path up the hillside, gasping, her eyes on the ground. Sheep bounced away on either side of her; the bracken was dense and would not yield when she stopped to break off a fan against the flies. Coarse, tough stems, refusing to tear away from the roots.

She came to the summit, she came to the cairn. A pair of buzzards rose above her, wheeling and searching, drifting on currents of summer air, high in the blue. They had been watching her all her life, they knew everything. They circled, gimlet eyes gleaming, invisible but intent.

Gillian stood by the cairn and fixed her eye upon it. She searched for her consecrated stones; she found them, one by one.

She took them out. She cast them out of heaven and down the hillside. They rattled like bones.

She lifted her arms to the uncomprehending sky and abandoned herself to weeping.

'Ease-up, ease-up, not too fast, steady, steady now –'

Summer clouds sailed over the hills, the field was all moving light and shadow. Tarn worked the ewes round the course and Edward ran beside her, stopping when she stopped, shading his eyes, watching the swift fluid flock of them, down to the first fence, and round to the stick, on to the second, a straggler trotting away towards the hedge –

He whistled, Tarn raced and held her.

'Lie down!'

He ran towards them, the sheep swerved away, Tarn growled, but he would not let her nip.

'Come on, come on, come on –'

Back to the rest of them, scattering now, hold them in tight, drive them on, down to the fence on the left –

'Come by, come by –'

He felt he'd been out here for ever, running and calling and whistling, sweating in the sun. A glance at his watch: already he was three minutes over time. Up from the fence and on between the markers, get them all through. Another one swerved, another followed –

'Tarn! Get on!'

She was round them in a flash, low on the ground and up again, driving them up through the gap, and round, down to the fold in the middle of the field where the gate stood open.

'Away to me now, go on, go on –'

His grandfather, out on the fells, training Ben up for the trials and winning, certificates stuck on the kitchen wall, splashing his face at the white stone sink, scraping his chair back. Ben at his feet. Sun at the window, everything right.

'Tarn! Get down there!'

The whistle piercing the summer air, men at the edge of the field, the sheep streaming into the pen, and the gate swung shut.

'That'll do.'

She lay at the gate to the pen, sides heaving. Across the field he could see a couple of nods exchanged, and knew he was in there, had not disgraced himself, his dog a decent animal, his sheep well kept.

He wiped his face, thinking of nothing but this moment.

Phoebe woke, hearing the front door slam. She heard the doves, crooning through a summer afternoon. The garden rustled, the air was sweet. She rose from her bed and crept along the landing. She descended the staircase, step by painful step, she crept along the tiles to the kitchen.

A glance was enough. Piles of clothes, and unwashed dishes, the sour smell of milk and flies all round the wastebin; cans on the table, roughly opened, left with food in. Cold cups of tea half drunk and abandoned, crumbs on the floor and dirt on everything. Wasps. Undoubtedly mice.

Intolerable.

She could not bear to look.

She shuffled past it all, out past the closed study door to the back, where herbs hung on a hook. The scritch of a mouse, the smell of sage. The fridge hummed fitfully in the corner. Phoebe opened the back door and the fullness of the scented garden greeted her. Lupin and lavender and rose bush; translucent iris, each year bluer and taller and more lovely –

She shuffled along to the bench.

Japanese anemones, paper white, stirred in a shady corner. Bees sucked in waving mallow, they buzzed amongst foxgloves and spreading hollyhock, in and out of wallflowers and lavender. Peonies were opening, drifts of lily-of-the-valley lined the paths, *Alchemilla* trailed over the brickwork – such a lovely thing, *Alchemilla*, holding the drops of rain like mercury, rolling and bright. Butterflies danced amongst white and purple buddleia, the fruit trees were leafy, the doves beat over the uncut grass, the pond was fringed with rushes.

Heavenly.

Phoebe tried to rise, to see what was what in the kitchen garden, but could not. She knew she should go to the greenhouse to check on the watering. She could not. She sat in the afternoon sun and the garden rustled, full of dappled shade.

She would stay here for ever.

Gillian found her asleep on the bench. She walked past her, down to the pond. She stood before it, gold with the melting sun.

'*Your mother is ill – she was sharp with you – your beautiful morning is taken away –*'

His hand on her arm, just a moment, a touch –

The coming of spring: in the wind, in the rippling water –

'*Things come and go – I'm sure your poem will come back to you – when it does, will you let me see it?*'

'*Yes. Yes.*'

She covered her face.

'Gillian?'

Phoebe had woken. Gillian walked up the path towards her. High summer, the fullness of June. Everything rustling and rich.

And she –

Her eyes were swollen and sore. She did not know where to look.

'The house is a disgrace,' said Phoebe, wincing as she moved. 'What on earth have you been thinking of?'

Edward stood in the kitchen and dialled Rowland's number. A sunset as fine as he had ever seen was lighting the hills across the valley. Even here, behind the house, the sky was glorious, streaked with gold. Soon he'd be driving his flock up the back field, across the dirt track behind it, up the lower slopes to the thick summer turf amidst the bracken, leaving them out there, shorn and free. And now –

The telephone rang in the Barbican apartment. His heart pounded.

Tarn lay in the sun by the open back door. Now and again her tail thumped. What a fine dog.

'Hello?'

His heart turned over.

'Rowland.'

'Yes?' A casual intonation, as if they'd just spoken, as if everything were settled and content, and they just had to tidy up an arrangement.

'We did all right in the trials.'

A pause. 'The trials.'

'The sheepdog trials. Remember? Tarn was brilliant. We weren't placed, of course, we were way over time, but we made a respectable showing.'

'Well, well. Very good. I'm glad.'

A silence. A glance at a watch: he could feel it.

He drew a breath. Tarn twitched.

'Rowland?'

'Yes?'

He had to say it. 'I can't go on like this.'

Silence. Out in the field the hens were clucking; a Leghorn fluffed up her feathers, deep in a dust bath. Sweet enquiring noises, everything here so beautiful, his half-dozen sheep from the trials spread out in the field again, grazing calmly. And he –

'What do you mean?'

304

Such a chill in that voice.

'You know what I mean. You're never here. I never see you. I miss you, I miss you –' He covered his face.

More silence.

'Rowland. What are you doing?'

'Now?'

'Now.'

'I'm just about to go out, to tell you the truth.'

'To do what?'

A sigh.

'To talk about a new recording. A possible new recording.'

'With whom?' He was racing and thumping, he no longer cared.

'A man called John Kirkby.'

Edward frowned. 'John Kirkby? He doesn't – he isn't sacred music, is he?'

'Did I say I was going to talk about sacred music?' Rowland was sharp. 'Stop quizzing me, Edward, I'm tired. I'll talk to you later, all right?'

'Rowland – please –'

A sigh. 'I'll talk to you later.' A shade kinder. Just.

'Okay.'

He put the phone down. He sat at the table, listening to the hens, the sheep, Tarn's whimper in sleep, watching the rays of the sun slip low.

The days were long and the weather fine but the nights, still, could be cold as death. A full moon rose, pale as marble, veined with blue: it hung in a sky the colour of mourning; the stars were a scattering of frost.

Phoebe sat up in her bedroom, rocking with pain. The bed was a rumpled sea of white: she could not bear the covers to touch her; she shivered when she cast them off. She lifted her emaciated legs, white as marble, mapped with the rivers of veins, and swung them round to the side of the bed, groaning. She doubled over her stomach, she lowered herself to the dusty rug, she crept to the chest for a jumper, she rattled and pulled out a drawer and found one, any old thing would do, and pulled it, shivering, over her head.

Horrible. Horrible scratchy heavy thing. Every cell on her skin rebelled against it, and still her teeth chattered.

We are cold, we are cold –
Hold, hold –

Who wrote that?

The room was filled with moonlight, a vixen's cry came from the field. Phoebe crept shivering to close the window: she saw from the casement the garden, her garden, silvered by the night. Still it was beautiful, even with the flowers closed in darkness. The boughs of the apple trees gleamed. Doves were roosting on the wall of the kitchen garden; bamboo canes leaned against one another, and the first shoots of runner beans twined over them.

The onion beds must be choking with weeds. No one had thinned out the lettuce –

Gillian –

Gillian was worse than useless.

She must go out there, she must get better, and put it all to rights –

Phoebe closed the casement window, and let the curtain fall. She crept to her bedside table and fumbled for pills. She took three; the packet was almost empty, she must drive into town again, visit that fool of a doctor, get more.

So cold, so cold –
We are old, old –

She crept into bed again. She could not lie down for the pain in her back; when she sat up it was worse. She did not know what to do with herself.

Sounds from Gillian's room: pacing and creaking.

Phoebe hunched up on her high iron bed, rocked backwards and forwards, rocking and groaning, all through the hours of the night.

Phil drove over to Cadair, leaving home just after nine. Dew was still on the grass, the hedgerows glistened as he wound through the lanes, meeting an occasional car, and once a milk tanker, climbing the hills beyond Nesta's cottage, making the descent through the valley. The sun rose, the river was bright, the corn was thick and yellowing.

He changed gear, turned a corner slowly, hearing a shift in the back of the van, where all the equipment for the day ahead was boxed up and covered in blankets: speakers, amplifiers, multitrack recorder, tapes and mike. The road straightened out, he picked up speed, singing.

Nesta was waiting in the stable yard. He drove slowly towards her, feeling everything settle, and fall into place.

'All right?' She came smiling to greet him.

'Fine.'

Their fingers met through the open window. The yard was still wet, still in shadow, the air quite cool. Together they unloaded the van; Martin came out to help. They carried the boxes over to the chapel.

Phil spent the first hour setting everything up, and Nesta left him to it, coming back once to see how he was getting on.

He was wearing a headset. He moved from recorder to mike, sliding knobs, pressing switches, his fingers conducting air. He did not notice her entrance, and for a moment she stood watching his complete absorption. Then he flicked a switch, and the chapel was suddenly full of sound: a string vibrated; two notes echoed one another as if in a cave; rain fell. He saw her, and lifted a finger, waiting, listening, raising and lowering the volume, breathing into the mike, moving to the recorder. He nodded, flicked a switch again, everything stopped.

The sun had risen higher: the chapel was full of the morning. Phil picked up a cylinder, and gave it to Nesta. It trembled inside as she took it.

'Turn it over. Hold it up and turn it over.'

She did so. Rain fell, swishing and soft and slow.

She turned it again, more quickly: it fell harder, pattering into the silence.

He smiled, taking off the headset. Strands of pale hair clung to the headphones.

'I love it,' said Nesta, thinking of Maureen's face, and of Nadine, reaching out into the air before her, thin hands plucking and searching, always in hope.

'The rainmaker. I bought two. A present.' He picked up another, resting on a table, and prised off the lid: he showed her the thin metal strips which fell, one upon another, like rain upon the earth.

Steven leaned stiffly towards the mike and addressed it. With his two good fingers he pressed a switch on the recorder, and the tape rewound. Another switch – 'Then the tape will make a loop,' said Phil, squatting down beside him. 'You'll hear the sounds over and over. Okay – off now.' Steven pressed the switch again, was guided to another. In moments his voice filled the room: low, hoarse, strong sounds, repeated over and over, making a rhythm. He jerked and twitched, listening.

'Now try this,' said Phil, guiding the hand like a bunch of twigs to the synthesiser. 'Do you want to hear loud music or soft music?'

Nesta, beside him, signed the question, watching Steven's lopsided face fill with interest and concentration.

'Loud,' signed Steven. 'Loud!'

'OK...' Phil turned the volume, Steven pressed a flat red key. Hoarse notes of a cello sounded. 'Like that? As loud as that?' Steven nodded. 'Do you think that sounds a bit like you, the cello? Shall I play your voice again?'

Steven's crooked smile grew broader; his hands shot into the air; he groaned.

'Lots of time, plenty of time –'

For minutes they went back and forth between voice and cello, listening, mixing down, listening again, lowering the volume. 'Just a little, yeah?' What emerged was so resonant and profound that Nesta, watching Steven's beloved and contorted face, the jerk of his dark bony head, his intent expression, found her eyes full of tears.

'Right.' Phil guided Steven's fingers to the deck again: one by one he pressed the switches off. 'Brilliant! Well done, Steven, thanks a lot, I think that's a really nice sound, don't you? Shall we listen to someone else, now?'

Steven jerked and said something, in his hoarse loud voice.

'You don't want to stop, do you?' Nesta signed. 'I know, it's been lovely. We'll do it again.'

She looked at her watch. Clearly, this was going to be something which would take days, not a morning, something empowering, transforming.

'You're a natural,' she told Phil, as he fiddled about on the deck. 'That was –'

'It was all right, wasn't it?' He pushed back his hair. 'Who's next?'

'Shall we try two? Nadine and Robert?'

Robert stood in his customary place beneath the dancing shafts of light, gazing upwards, gaping. Nadine shrank against Nesta, clasping her hand.

'Let's make a triangle,' said Nesta, gently guiding Robert to a chair. The three of them sat in the sun.

'See what you can do with this.' Nesta gave Nadine the cylinder; she gave Robert a drum, covered in thick leather. He sat hugging it, staring ahead. Nadine moved, and the rainmaker shivered; she jumped. 'Look.' Nesta showed her: she gingerly held it aloft. Down came the rain in silver sheets. A flickering smile.

'Yes! That was beautiful. Try it again. Turn it upside down – see?'

Nadine very slowly turned the cylinder over: the rain fell gently, a summer shower. Robert gaped, as if nothing had happened. Phil stood watching.

Nesta let Nadine swing the rain about; she knelt beside Robert, and lifted his hands. She beat them upon the drumskin: one, two, one, two, like a heartbeat. Down came the shimmering rain; in came the pulse of the drum. Phil, behind them, was playing about again. Robert was breathing heavily: Phil came across with the mike.

'Want to try this?'

They pushed back the chairs; Phil knelt down and Robert's breathing, so heavy and slow, was amplified into something hollow and mysterious, spirit of the falling rain, deep amongst the trees, heart beating quietly: one-two, one-two.

'Keep it up,' said Phil, passing Nesta the mike. He moved quickly back to the recorder, long fingers running over the switches, while Nadine held the rain aloft, and the rain-god drifted in and out, one-two, one-two, breathing like the wind.

Bang went the letterbox. A square of white on the mat.

Gillian shook as she came down the hall. She picked up the letter and her blood raced through her.

Her name –

The Mandrake Press.

She tore it open, raging.

Dear Ms Traherne, I wonder if you received my earlier letter . . .

She carried it down to the kitchen; a kettle was boiling for morning tea. Phoebe was lying in bed, dry-mouthed and demanding. Gillian lifted the lid of the range where the coke was filled; it was low and needed replenishment. Something else to be done. She picked up her letter, with its talk of festivals, and plans, and platforms, and tore it in pieces. She dropped them into the mouth of the furnace and watched them fall on the burning coals. They curled up, they grew black, they were consumed by fire.

Slam went the lid.

Gillian made tea, rinsing two mugs at the sink. Everything was full of mess and clutter. Phoebe was furious. She did not care. She carried the tray up the stairs, past the treacherous letterbox; tea overflowed from the spout of the pale green teapot, and the tray swam with it.

Phoebe did not notice. She tried to sit up against the pillows; she asked Gillian to help her; she shouted with pain.

'Not like that!'

Gillian stood back, enraged and frightened.

'How should I –'

'I don't know, I don't know –'

Somehow they managed. Phoebe sipped tea.

'Do you want me to call the doctor?'

'No.' The mug shook; she must go to the lavatory. 'I'm going myself, I'll have to. Need some more pills –' The mug shook harder, tea slopped all over the sheets. 'Oh, bloody hell.'

A knock at the door. Gillian, trembling, went to answer it.

He was here, he had come to see her –

'I hope I'm not intruding.' Nesta stood at the porch, radiant. 'I've been meaning to come over for such a long time –' She looked at Gillian, glaring from the door. 'How are you?'

'I'm perfectly well.'

'Well. Good. I –' She hesitated, wondering. 'And Phoebe?'

'She's going to see the doctor.'

'Today?'

'I don't know.'

Nesta looked at her: dishevelled and awry. She looked –

Something must have happened –

She said: 'Gillian, is everything all right?'

'Mind your own business.'

Nesta shrank.

'Gillian?' Phoebe's voice, weak from the upper floor. 'Who is it?'

'Nesta,' said Gillian, shaking all over. She made to close the door.

Nesta said quickly: 'Gillian please – I'd like to see her –' She stepped into the hall. The house stank. She coughed.

'Do what you want,' said Gillian, stalking away down the hall.

Nesta climbed the stairs. A sour smell of decay came from downstairs, a sickly sweetness hung in the air up here. She walked along the landing, past the closed door of Gillian's room, on to the open doors at the end. The bathroom. Phoebe's room.

'Hello?'

She took one look.

'Phoebe –'

An ambulance, racing through the lanes.

18

Nesta followed Phoebe to the hospital. Gwen came up to the house. She stood in the porch with a basket.

'Everything all right, love? Haven't set eyes on you for weeks.'

Gillian stood staring at her. Gwen took in tangled hair and red-rimmed eyes and clothes which needed washing.

'Everything all right?' she asked again.

Gillian shook her head. 'I'm afraid I haven't been keeping up with the housework.'

Gwen frowned. She took in the customary darkness of the hall behind, and then the smell.

'Gillian –'

'What do you want?'

Gwen was taken aback.

'I wondered how Mother was keeping?'

'Taken away.'

'Taken away?'

'To hospital.'

Gillian stood aside, with a gesture. Gwen walked past her, along to the stinking kitchen.

'Dear oh dear oh dear.'

She flung open the windows. She went to the back and unbolted the door. She stood breathing in the freshness of a summer garden on a fine summer morning; she saw the uncut grass, the dandelions. She shook her head.

'Knew I should have come up.'

A dove beat past her; Gillian came up behind her, and went straight round to the greenhouse. She stood stacking flowerpots, one upon another. The seed trays were full of gasping plants. Lobelia, alyssum and viola drooped. She picked up an empty watering can and held it upside down and shook it. Serve it right.

Gwen went back indoors. She stood for a moment, uncertain, in the kitchen, and then she set to work.

The telephone rang. Gillian stood in the kitchen, swept and scrubbed clean.

'Yes?'

'It's me,' said Nesta.

'Yes?'

'I'm sorry I haven't phoned earlier.'

Gillian waited.

'Phoebe's had some tests. She'll see the consultant later. She's sleeping now.'

Gillian looked at her watch. Afternoon sun warmed the field across the lane; upstairs, Gwen was Hoovering, banging about.

'What time will she be home?'

'Gillian – I think she'll be here for a little while.'

'How long?'

'Well – at least a few days. Are you all right? I feel bad about this, but I'm on duty this evening, otherwise I'd come back and see you –'

'Please don't trouble yourself,' said Gillian. 'An old friend of the family is visiting, as it happens.'

'Oh. Good. Well – shall I give you the name of the ward?'

'Just a minute.'

She found a pencil in a cup; she wrote down the name on a newspaper. 'Hopkins,' she repeated, and wrote down the direct line, as Nesta dictated. 'I shan't use that,' she said, 'except in an emergency. I'm sure they are busy. Hospitals usually are.'

'Yes, but –' Nesta stopped. 'I expect you'd like to see her. I could take you over –'

Gillian twisted the flex of the telephone. It coiled round her fingers, then leapt to freedom. Upstairs, the Hoover came squeaking out of Phoebe's bedroom and along the landing.

'Hello?' said Nesta.

Gwen knelt down by the socket next to the landing cupboard. Floorboards creaked. Gillian could hear her huff and puff. The Hoover began to roar. Soon it would reach her poetry, fighting for life.

'I must go,' she said. 'I have things to attend to.'

'I'll be home by lunchtime tomorrow. I'll phone you. Shall I give Phoebe your love?'

'Love is not so easily given,' said Gillian. She put the phone down.

*

'Gwen! Gwen!'

The Hoover devoured the house.

'*Gwen!*'

She panted up the stairs.

Gwen, driving along the ancient runner, saw a wild-eyed creature bearing down upon her.

'Whatever –' She switched off the Hoover in a hurry.

'Don't go in my room.' Gillian was gasping. 'You mustn't touch my room.'

'I won't go near it,' said Gwen. 'Don't you worry.'

She looked at Gillian, unwashed and terrible.

'Why don't you have a nice hot bath?'

'The furnace – the range – the boiler – everything is – nothing is –'

Gillian slumped on the stairs between heaven and hell, possessed by weeping.

The shearers came. The lane field was full of activity, Tarn beside herself with excitement, racing round the blaring ewes, driving them six at a time into the pens beneath the trees. The men worked steadily, clipping and shaving, and stamping with dye. Swathes of fleece fell aside and lay in the rich afternoon sun. The sheep struggled: new creatures, naked and bony and strange, lying upended, white legs thrashing the air, yellow eyes wide with fear. Edward, bagging up armfuls of greasy fleece, going with Tarn for the next half-dozen, was full of emotion. His sheep, manhandled by strangers, impersonal and rough.

He gave no sign of such feelings, opening the pen for each skinny batch, driving in the next. Released, the ewes ran faster than he had ever seen them, except at the trials, sweeping away across the grass and down the slope. Their lambs followed wildly, seeking and bleating; butting the dark teats, curly heads and laid-back ears pressing beneath pink scraped skin. Shreds of fleece clung here and there or dangled absurdly: the animals looked prehistoric, hideous, roughly stamped on bare rumps with scarlet letters. Within minutes they were grazing again, their shadows dark on the grass as the afternoon wore on.

The men took a break, drinking tea from flasks, smoking beneath the trees. Clouds of midges danced above the pens, flies were everywhere. Tarn sat with the men, her tongue lolling. Edward bagged up the last of the fleece and counted how many more to go.

'What time do you think we'll get to the back field?'

The hens were shut up for the day, clucking and fussing, then settling down in the boxes, still and bright-eyed.

The men wiped away sweat, checked watches.

'Another hour? Should be.'

Edward nodded, joining them in the shade. They spoke of the heat, and market prices, and the mobile dip, coming tomorrow. Thistledown drifted over the field. Tarn panted.

'She did well in the trials.'

'Thanks.'

They fell silent, resting and smoking. Edward sat watching his flock, stripped naked. It made little difference what time they moved into the back field, or what time the men packed up and went. He had nothing to do but follow this rhythm of the season, shearing and dipping and checking for foot rot; soon he'd be driving them up to the hills, and then the farm would be quiet again.

And then?

Thistledown drifted over the field. Rooks cawed in the trees. Summer was everywhere.

'Better get moving,' said one of the men.

Edward rose to his feet. He patted his legs: Tarn was up in a flash, beside him as he walked down the field again, his crook in his hand, the shadows lengthening.

The house was fresh and clean and sweet. Plates gleamed in the plate rack, saucepans shone on the shelf. Washing dripped on the line beneath the apple trees.

'There,' said Gwen. 'That's better.'

She sat at the table, drinking tea. Gillian, washed and pale, sat across from her, clasping a cup. Her hair was still wet from the tepid bath, and the last of the shampoo: it clung to her head, roughly towelled and drying slowly.

'What a business,' said Gwen. 'What a to-do. Poor Phoebe, I'll take you to see her tomorrow.'

Gillian did not answer. She could not leave her poems to die.

'And you must come down and stay with us,' said Gwen. 'Wouldn't that be better? Just until Mother gets home again?'

'I –'

'We'd be glad of the company, it's ever so quiet since Sally went. Mind, the children are always over, but there's plenty of room.' She

314

looked at Gillian. 'You do look peaky. You must have been worried sick – I wish you'd telephoned.'

Gillian sipped her tea. 'I'm sorry.'

'No need to be sorry. You finish that up and then we'll pack a few things and go home for supper. I'll phone for Ted to come and fetch us. You've got a key? Ted can come up and cut the grass tomorrow.'

Doves made soft noises through the open window. The scent of the garden was heavenly; she could hear bees. The sun was slipping low: soon it would sink into the pond, a font of gold speared by bulrush and reed. She would go down and stand before it, seeking the presence of God. Tonight, in the clean quiet house, she would write again.

She put down her cup. She said: 'You have been very kind. I'll be all right now. I'd rather stay.'

Gwen shook her head. 'I don't like to think of you up here on your own, love. I'm sure Mother would rather you were down with us. Come on –' she reached across the table, patted Gillian's bitten hands. 'Look at those nails – you've hardly got anything left. What a business. Come on, now, you fetch your things.'

'No.' Gillian took her hands away. 'You don't understand. I have to stay in the house.' She made a gesture, white-faced, eyes rimmed with sleepless circles. 'Everything is here,' she said unsteadily.

She stood by the still deep pond, where the sun was melting. Insects climbed the reeds and rushes; a dragonfly, brilliant and bulging-eyed, hovered and darted, on wings of gold. Water boatmen jerked across the surface; tiny ripples came and went. Somewhere in the dense secrecy of the reeds a frog was clambering slowly: Gillian could hear him, full of damp and solitude. He leapt all at once, an arc of joy in the sun: plop, he was gone, and the ripples widened.

Thistledown floated over the hedge from the farmer's field. The cows had returned from milking: they tore at the lush summer grass. The doves had come down for their corn on the path; they flew through the evening, white and gold and loving. Edward's name was everywhere, softly spoken.

Edward had broken her in two.

I shall purify myself, said Gillian, unto the still deep water. I have lost touch with God, and with holiness. The sacrifices of God are a broken spirit: a broken and a contrite heart. I shall seek humility.

The sun sank low; the evening and the water darkened.

When my mother comes home, said Gillian, we shall begin a new life.

Doves fluttered, white against gathering cloud. Gillian knelt, bowed her head, and sprinkled holy water.

She walked through the garden, full of dusk and moths.

Night fell. Gillian moved through the empty house. Lights burned. Beyond were pools of darkness. The silence pressed upon her: it rang in her ears. She listened for the scritching mouse, and heard her, deep amongst the sacks. 'You have been spared,' she said aloud. Moths bumped against the window panes. Floorboards creaked. The coke in the range, freshly filled and burning, shifted and sighed. Sounds which went deep, and lay within.

Gillian walked the empty house and listened for her poems, a broken urgent whispering. At first she could not hear them. Then they were everywhere – drowning beneath the tiles in the hall, where Gwen had washed and scrubbed and let water drip into the cracks. They spoke to her in faint, watery voices – save us, save us. The house was full of them: Gillian went everywhere, listening: unchecked, unquestioned.

She opened the door of her father's study, so long unvisited. The door stuck, then suddenly gave. Dust rose: Gwen had not touched this room. Gillian stood looking into darkness. She tried the light but the bulb had gone. Something skittered over the floor. Everything smelt of damp. Gillian stepped over the threshold. Boxes and unwanted furniture and things that got in the way were here: a study become a store-room, a lumber-room, a dumping ground.

Stars were at the window. Dark shapes of unwanted objects loomed. She stood in the silence, listening.

Papery voices.

The scratch of a pen.

Gillian climbed the stairs. She went to her bedroom, crossing the floor with its heaps of white. Voices were everywhere – write us, write us, save us from death.

She commanded them to be still.

She sat at her desk and uncapped her marbled fountain pen. She unscrewed it, and dipped it into her bottle of ink: it drank from the blackness, was filled, and full of longing. Beneath their weight of stones the poems waited, moaning.

Some things were male and some were female –

White paper lay beneath the fountain pen, waiting to receive his touch –

Gillian trembled and shook.

Edward, whispered the room, in its dust and brokenness. Edward, Edward, Edward –

Gillian lifted her pen. She sat with it poised above the waiting paper, and nameless and agonised feelings possessed her.

A woman disrobed, naked, adoring –

Full of desire and longing –

Transformed by love, opening to the sun, waiting for a word, a touch –

Come to me – enter me – pierce and fill me –

Cast aside, into darkness.

Gillian flung down her pen. Anger and grief made war within her, voices rose around her, beating and clamouring –

'I cannot write! I cannot write!'

Humility and holiness swept away.

The devil was in this room. The devil had taken and possessed her –

'I cannot write!'

Howling through the house.

Gillian flung open her door. She wept along the landing, into Phoebe's bedroom.

The bed was stripped, the blankets lay neatly folded. Everything was swept and dusted and cleaned away, books straightened, cups of bitter herbs taken downstairs and washed, the bedside table polished. The window was open a little: the night air was cool and perfect.

This was how everything should be.

Order and cleanliness. Everything cared for.

Gillian pressed her hands to her head. She tore at her hair, possessed.

'I cannot, I cannot –'

Moonlight silvered the room.

Gillian left it, howling.

All through the hours of the night.

Dawn broke. Gillian, in her heap of litter, lay upon her bed. She had slept and woken and slept again, burrowing into the lumpy pillows, craving oblivion. Now she woke again, and watched the summer morning fill the room, pale and pure and beautiful.

Exhaustion filled her. She lay waiting for Phoebe to begin the day.

She waited for footsteps, brisk as usual, for the rattle in the range, the kettle held beneath the running tap, the call from the foot of the stairs.

'Breakfast!'

She waited, listening to the music of the birds in the lane: full-throated, liquid, intricate, full of delight, and a great weight lay upon her, and she groaned.

At last she rose, descended the staircase, descending into hell. She filled the kettle, she filled the range, she went to the back of the house and opened the door to the garden. Everything was covered in dew. Fat speckled spiders hung in their silvery webs, the doves were awake and murmuring.

Just as it should be, said Phoebe.

Gillian went back into the house. She dialled the number written in pencil on a newspaper. The kettle was boiling, the lid lifting up and down. Steam was escaping, in frantic clouds.

'Hopkins. Staff nurse speaking.'

'Tell my mother –' said Gillian.

'Hello?'

'Tell my mother –'

She put the phone down, weeping.

Gillian went to Penglydr church, to seek salvation. A van was parked on the dewy verge. She left her bicycle down at the lych gate, and walked up the smooth grey path to the porch. Blackbirds and thrushes hopped amongst the graves. One or two sheep cropped the turf.

Gillian came to the heavy west door; she turned the handle. The choir of air, as she opened the door: she felt her heart quicken in hope. Into the sanctuary of flagstone and organ and streaming light. Piles of prayer books, echo of footsteps, wood and stone and tapestry; the spirit of God, streaming through stained glass on to font and gold Cross and pulpit, on to the Bible bound in black and clasped with gold, held on the back of the eagle, sweeping through the skies –

And what was this?

Cables, trailing over the flags. Cables up to the altar steps. A microphone. A man.

Phil looked up from the tape recorder. A cassette was rewinding, spinning in the silence.

'Gillian. How are you?'

Gillian glared at him. 'What are you doing here?'

'Just trying something out.' He switched off the machine, and

smiled at her. Streaming morning sunlight lit strands of hair. 'Sorry –
you were wanting peace and quiet.'

'I was seeking holiness.' Gillian, scarlet, stepped over the cables.
'What is going on?'

'Preparations for a concert. I've been working with some of the
children at Cadair – making music.'

Music was flutes and lutes and virginals –

An organ, mighty and magnificent, plaintive and slow –

Music had nothing to do with those children, gaping and banging
on tambourines –

Besides –

'We thought we might bring them down to the church one day. Let
everyone hear them.'

This is a church, not a concert hall, said Phoebe coldly.

'This is a church, not a concert hall,' said Gillian, raging. Her
hand, with its bitten nails, swept over the clutter, the mess, the
microphone. 'What are you thinking of? This is the house of God.'

Phil looked back at her steadily.

'I think the children at Cadair probably deserve that, Gillian.
What's wrong? You came to the Bach in Hereford, didn't you? That
was a concert, wasn't it?'

'It was a desecration,' said Gillian. 'It should never have been
allowed. Cables and microphones –' She clenched her hands and her
nails dug into her palms. 'I don't know what you are thinking of.'

Phil came down from the altar steps. He came towards her.

'Gillian – I'm sorry. You look – Do you want me to go for a bit?
Leave you in peace?' He hesitated. 'You came here to pray –'

'Mind your own business,' said Gillian. 'I have nothing to say to
you.' She turned towards the west door, passing the plaque to her
father. The memory of Edward, entering the icy church in winter,
filled and possessed her. She burned.

'I admire you,' said Phil quietly. 'Your work – you're an artist –'

Gillian was blazing. 'I do not need you to tell me that. Excuse
me –' She strode to the door.

Outside, a jackdaw was walking along the path. It flew up at her
approach and settled on the wall of the churchyard, watching her,
head on one side.

'Begone!' said Gillian. 'Begone, begone with you!'

She strode to the lych gate, covered in lichen, she seized her
bicycle. She rode away from the church, and down through the
village, greeting no one.

319

*

She rode out, far across the valley. On the hills she dismounted, panting with exertion, feeling the release of anger and tension in every footstep, her blood racing, her heart pounding, her hair spread wild about her. She was filled with energy and passion.

The sun rose and the river shone. Gillian climbed on to her bicycle again and pedalled madly. She freewheeled down the sloping quiet lanes, beneath a cathedral of arched and leafy branches, dappling the ground with sun and broken shade. The fields stretched away and the corn was ripening, orient gold. Larks rose into a cloudless sky, singing unbearably.

At last she came to the lane to Nesta's house. Ducks were crossing it, quacking and splattering, feathers all muddy. They cocked their heads, and a great big Muscovy drake stopped, and flapped his wings. Pendulous crimson flesh swung beneath his beak; he hissed.

'Out of my way,' said Gillian. 'Out of my way!'

She came to the top of the track. The car was parked; the door of the cottage stood open; inside it was cool and dark.

The mobile dip came first thing in the morning. They set up the tank wearing heavy overalls, standing well back as they filled it. The air had a strange, metallic smell: Edward, who had read in the papers of farmers making claims for nervous diseases, depression and wasting muscles, wore thick overalls himself, and rubber gloves, as the men did. He and Tarn drove the sheep one by one through the tank: they gasped and swam madly, eyes enormous. Once out, they dripped on the grass, then looked about them, bleating hard. Edward kept his eye on Tarn, reaching to grab her collar whenever she got too near.

Flies swarmed; it was very hot. Everyone sweated, wanting to get the job done quickly.

'Can't rush it, though,' said one of the men, as they broke for an early lunch at mid-morning. 'That's how accidents happen.'

They came down to the yard, scrubbing their hands beneath the pump. Edward brought beers from the kitchen; they drank in the shade of the barn, opening packets of sandwiches. Tarn lay beside them, loving it all.

By two they had finished and gone.

Edward stood with Tarn at the gate, raising his hand. He pulled off gloves and overalls, dropping them in a corner; he walked back up the lane to the field, walked round his shorn and disinfected flock. Thistledown floated everywhere, the sheep were noisy and unsettled.

He reunited a frantic lost lamb with its ewe, he waved his arm at the infernal flies. Time for a break and a shower.

He whistled for Tarn and went out to the lane again, shady and just a little cooler. A sound from beyond the bend ahead: a car, climbing the hill in the heat.

Rowland's car.

Edward felt his whole stomach turn over. He stopped, collecting himself, knowing that a visit like this, in the middle of the week, must be for a purpose.

Well. This was it.

Make or break.

He strode on down to the yard gate, and the Peugeot rounded the bend, and came towards him.

Nesta came to the open door of the cottage. She looked at Gillian in some astonishment.

'Hello. I wasn't expecting you.'

'You said you'd be here.' Gillian had leaned the bicycle up against the wall. She held a small plastic bag, a package. She proffered it. 'Something for lunch.'

'Oh. Thank you. Well – come in.' Nesta took this offering. She smiled at her, warm and tired and forgiving. 'Or perhaps we should eat in the garden – it's so hot. I've only just got home.'

'I am disturbing you,' said Gillian, shaking.

'Not at all. How's Phoebe –' She broke off, suddenly alarmed. 'Oh, Gillian – has something happened?'

'What do you mean?'

'Phoebe –' Nesta steadied herself, treading carefully. 'Have you rung the hospital?'

'Yes.'

'And?'

'No news,' said Gillian. 'But I am sure she is doing well. The house is made ready for her return.'

'Good. Well –' Nesta stood holding her package, looking out over the garden, full of the hum of bees. 'I think we should stay out here. It's much too nice to be indoors. I'll get us something to drink, you look –' She gestured at the bench beneath the window: Gillian sat down in her hot print belted dress, shoes and white socks. Sweat cooled on her face. She pushed her hair back, and looked straight ahead, at the hives, the apple trees.

'I've never seen you with your hair loose,' said Nesta, watching her. 'It suits you, it makes you look –' She trailed away in the face of Gillian's obdurate indifference. 'Well,' she said again.

'Something to drink,' said Gillian.

Please, said Phoebe.

'Please.'

Nesta put the package down on the bench; she went quickly inside, murmuring apologies. Gillian went on looking at the garden, the sun and shade, the pots of geraniums along the path, the spilling forget-me-nots. The grass was cut, there was the beginning of a vegetable garden, up in the corner. Canes were tied neatly, like a wigwam: runner bean plants stood at the foot, growing nicely.

So. This was where they sat, this the garden they were working on. This, at the end of the day, was where he came to lie with her –

Gillian trembled and shook.

'Here we are,' said Nesta. A tray, a chink. She set it all down on the makeshift table of planks and trestle. 'I must get a proper table, there never seems to be time. Anyway –'

They drank from tall glasses of fresh lemonade. 'That's better.' She picked up the package again. 'This is kind of you – and to tell you the truth, lunch will be pretty simple, I haven't shopped yet.' She opened the plastic bag.

She pulled out an ill-wrapped two ounces of Stork margarine.

'I'm sorry it couldn't be more,' said Gillian. 'Stocks are low.' She turned to look at Nesta, with her flat, yellow-green eyes, like stones beneath water.

Nesta, in the stillness and heat of the garden, felt something cold trickle down her back. She swallowed. The bees were everywhere, buzzing in the midday sun.

'Gillian –'

'Yes?'

Nesta said slowly, carefully: 'Gillian – tell me what's wrong. You're angry with me, I have offended you. I'm sorry. Perhaps –' she shook her head, trying to phrase it properly. 'Perhaps – you and your mother – I have intruded upon you. You must forgive me.'

'Why?'

Nesta shrank back. 'Gillian, please. You must understand – I have experienced a great deal of illness. And I am trained to – to –' She tried again. 'When I saw Phoebe I knew I had to –'

'Why do you keep talking about my mother?' asked Gillian. 'Everyone is always talking about my mother.' She was looking out over the garden again. 'When my mother comes home from hospital, we shall begin a new life. Everything will be as it should be, ordered and peaceful.' She spoke dreamily; she turned back to Nesta, suddenly sharp again. 'I have not come here to talk about that. I have come for quite a different reason.'

Nesta could hear the bees. She could smell the grass, freshly mown and drying in the sun. She was aware of these things, but only just: they came from a distance, and everything was concentrated into this heat, this moment, sitting full of fear on a bench in a garden in Wales, her life a long long way away as she waited, held by Gillian's flat green gaze, and fury.

'Edward,' said Gillian, and her voice broke.

'Edward?' Nesta was lost. 'Edward? What about him?'

'You,' said Gillian, and the sweat streamed down her. 'You –' she gestured at the garden, the open door of the cottage, the cool dark place within. 'You and he –' Her voice cracked asunder, fury and passion became a despairing cry.

Nesta sat gazing at her. Between them the ounces of margarine melted and dripped between the slats.

'Oh, Gillian.'

She picked up the package and dropped it into the shade. She held out her hands. Gillian drew back. Nesta beheld her: a woman on the brink of madness, a woman who perhaps had already crossed the border, deluded, disturbed, possessed.

She said gently: 'Gillian, listen to me.'

Gillian bowed her head, and listened, broken.

Nesta said: 'Gillian, Edward is homosexual. He and Rowland King – surely you –'

She said: 'Phoebe is dying. How could you not see – She may have only weeks –'

She said: 'Phil and I are lovers. We have been so for months. We hope to remain so. We hope to have a child.'

Gillian listened, and the world spun away from her, a tiny dark speck against the blinding sun, spinning and spinning, like the spool of the thread of life: unwinding, faster and faster, gone.

They stood in the shady kitchen, and the cries of the sheep and birds came in at the open window, carried by the summer breeze, a rich grassy scent blowing all through the valley.

Rowland said: 'Edward, this isn't working.'

Edward could feel himself go white.

Rowland said: 'It hasn't been working for a long time. It is my fault, not yours. I am not made for –' He gestured at the room, the house, the hens scratching peacefully over the field. He shook his head. 'For rural bliss. I'm sorry.'

Edward said: 'Rowland, please –'

He held the back of a chair so tightly his knuckles cracked. 'Please.'

'I'm sorry,' said Rowland.

Sun poured in at the open window, mellow and rich and content. Tarn, in her basket, thumped her tail.

Edward began to weep.

'Don't,' said Rowland. 'Please. Don't. I wouldn't make you happy. I have made you unhappy. We both know that. Better to wrap it up. I feel a bastard. I'm sorry.'

'No,' sobbed Edward. 'No, no, no.'

Rowland said: 'I'm going to get my things.'

'No! No! Rowland –' He kicked the chair aside, he moved, sobbing, towards him. 'I love you, I love you, please, please –' He took Rowland's arm, and the tears were pouring. 'Hold me, hold me –'

'Jesus.' Rowland's arms went round him.

Edward howled against him. 'I can't bear it – my life – everything – you're everything –'

'Edward. Please. Stop it.'

Edward drew a breath like the breath of a dying man. He shuddered, and drew back. He looked at Rowland, and everything swam. He said: 'Make love to me. Please.'

'No.'

'Please.'

'No.' Rowland made to move away; Edward clung to him.

'Listen. Listen. If you leave me –' His voice broke. 'If you are going to leave me – you can't go like this – you have to do it properly –'

'I'm trying to do it properly!' Rowland shook him off, and his face darkened. He moved to the door.

Edward blocked it. He said: 'Rowland, I'm begging you.' He spread out his arms. 'For everything we have been to one another – for everything. I cannot let you go like this. We must be together again, we must make it right –'

'We can't.'

'Rowland, you are my *lover*! You are my beloved. I need you. Please.'

Rowland covered his face. He took his hands away again, he paced the room. He said: 'Edward – if we make love again it will only make things worse. I'm not going to change my mind. It wouldn't work, it would be based on guilt and duty –'

Edward went whiter. 'Not on love.'

'No,' said Rowland. 'Not any more. Affection, yes. Enormous affection. And respect. You are the better person.'

'But.' He dropped his arms.

'But. I'm very sorry.'

The sun at the window struck the clock; the clock struck the hour. Three deep notes. The hens stepped over the tussocks of grass, this way and that.

Edward said: 'I'm not going to ask you if there is anyone else. I know there is.'

'Don't be too sure,' said Rowland.

'I don't want to know.' He wiped his face, he crossed the sunlit floor, he put his hand on his lover's lips. 'For all that we have been to one another,' he said unsteadily. 'We cannot say goodbye like this.' He swallowed, he moved to hold Rowland close. 'Make love to me. Please. One last time.' He bent to kiss him, he began to cry.

Rowland's arms went round him again.

They left the kitchen. They climbed the stairs.

Gillian took her bicycle. She wheeled it up the track. Nesta walked beside her. Thistledown blew.

'Let me come with you.'

Gillian shook her head.

'Phone me.'

Gillian did not answer.

They came to the top of the track.

'I'm sorry,' said Nesta. 'I had to tell the truth.'

Gillian climbed on her bicycle, and rode away.

The valley lay spread beneath the sun, everything open and exposed and hard. The river shone like glass. Gillian rode between the standing fields of corn, beneath the empty blue of the sky. Larks sang, and cars went past her. She rocked in the sudden swish of air, swerving towards the ditches; she rode on, right across the valley, down to Penglydr, where she did not stop.

She turned to the right, she dismounted, and pushed her bicycle up the lanes, towards Llanfonen, and up towards the farm. The heat

325

was intense, her bicycle ticked in the stillness. Above her the buzzard wheeled and soared. The buzzard knew everything; it had mocked, and told her nothing.

Gillian pushed her bicycle up the hill. She rounded the bend, she panted in the heat. She came to the farm gate. It stood open, and a sleek purple plum of a car stood in the shade.

She stopped, she waited.

The deep silence of the afternoon enclosed her.

She wheeled her bicycle through the gate; she leaned it against the wall; it rested gratefully.

Gillian walked across the yard and the dog came out to greet her, slow in the heat.

'Hush,' said Gillian, stroking the once-beloved head. She walked across to the front door, open to the warmth of the afternoon. She knocked, quietly, filled with terror.

No answer came. The dog flopped down in the sun.

Gillian knocked again.

She went quietly into the house.

Along the passage, with its rugs and pictures.

Past the sacred room of her reading, the polished table where they had talked to one another, where she had been exposed, humiliated, broken.

The quiet tick of the clock.

Sounds from the upper floor.

'Edward,' whispered Gillian.

Slowly she climbed the stairs.

Sounds from a bedroom, hoarse and horrible.

She crept along the landing and she shook.

She saw an open door.

She saw –

Nakedness and darkness and maleness and –

and –

Gillian swayed and shook like a tree in a storm.

She turned.

She flew.

She did not know how she reached her bicycle, how she crossed the yard and leapt upon it, riding away, the sun blazing, the buzzard high in the cruel heat, circling and circling, wings outstretched to the limits of earth and heaven, waiting to plunge to the ground and seize her, tearing her open, ripping her open bloody and raw and dying dying dying.

19

Nesta lay back in the pool and paddled away from the side. She raised one arm, and then another, unhurried and graceful, not going far, re-acclimatising herself to the heated water, watching the steady activity on the edge.

Martin was easing Steven into the hoist, talking him through: the lifting from wheelchair to plastic seat, the strap, the waiting water.

Steven made incoherent sounds. A drooping eye looked down.

'That's it, there you go.' Martin pressed a button: the hoist began to hum.

'Here I am,' said Nesta, swishing up alongside. She stood in the water and watched the slow descent, opening her arms in greeting. Above her, Steven jerked and twitched and flung his hand out. Stiff pale feet made a gentle splash; slowly the water rose around him, immersing long flaccid legs, shapeless belly, sunken chest.

The echoing pool was full of his cries. He jerked, he gave his twisted smile.

'Well done.' Nesta, beside him, unfastened the strap; she tugged him, buoyant and shouting out, away from the side, and the hoist and the chair, into the water's embrace.

Above were the ribs of the vaulted roof; beyond, the soaring sky.

Steven lay back in Nesta's arms. Blueness lapped gently round them; he floated, weightless and joyful.

Nesta scooped up water and splashed him: he thrashed about, laughing, and the water caught the sun and sparkled all over his white skin. A layer of gooseflesh rose, despite the warmth: Nesta lifted his jerking limbs and moved them, this way and that; she rubbed him and swung him round in the water. His drooping eye beheld her, deep and unswerving; she swished him back and forth, so safe and free. His bony head and tufts of dark hair were baptised and soaking; he grinned, he roared.

'Quiet,' said Martin. 'You'll disturb the neighbours.'

He stood on the side in his tracksuit and trainers, watching the two of them move up and down and the water rise and fall.

'You look better,' he said to Nesta.

'Thank you. I am.'

She lifted Steven's misshapen hands and he waggled his two good fingers. She moved the hands at the stiff and bony wrists, this way and that. Above them, through the vaulted glassy roof, the sun came and went in the clouds. The pool was full of his happiness.

And, less exuberantly, of her own. But the encounter with Gillian still coursed through her: the heat, the gaze like stones beneath running water, the cry of despair. The memory of Phoebe still coursed through her: white, shrunken, carried beneath a scarlet blanket, racing through the lanes.

'What are you thinking about?' asked Martin, trained to observe.

'Other people,' said Nesta. She lifted her legs, and swam away, bearing Steven with her.

Gillian sat in her father's study. She breathed in dust and must, damp paper, ancient soot. Boxes and bags lay all around her. Beyond the window, summer blew over the garden. The doves flew endlessly back and forth, feeding their young.

Gillian, by the tiled fireplace, sat in her armchair, in a lost and distant childhood.

Phoebe came home to die. She would not countenance a hospice, nor the hospital a moment longer.

She lay in the high iron bed, yellowish-white against the pillows, a nut in a shell, a scrap of a thing. Visitors came and went: Gwen, calling daily, with flowers and messages and trays and clean sheets and a mop; Ted out in the garden, cutting the grass, watering and potting on in the greenhouse, feeding the tomatoes. He hoed and dug in the kitchen garden, he brought boxes of vegetables – new potatoes and carrots and plump fresh lettuce – and trays of bedding plants out to the front. He took them down to the village, and into the market town; he kept accounts, and gave the book to Gillian.

'You take that up to your mother, that'll keep her spirits up.'

Gillian looked at the columns of figures, rising like smoke. A large brown envelope held receipts: they lay at the bottom, like dead things.

'How are you keeping, love?' Gwen asked each morning.

'Very well,' said Gillian.

The district nurse came each day to give Phoebe an injection. Phoebe shrank from the needle. Each day they had to search for a new, unbruised place, on disappearing flesh.

Gwen came up with a tray. Phoebe ate specks, and slept. The nurse went away, and left her number. Bron Morgan came up with a pile of books. Phoebe, a little stronger that day, slipped spectacles on to a bony nose and turned a page or two. A life of William Morris: expensive new hardback, a treat.

'You always had a good brain,' said Bron, perched on the rush-seated chair. 'Always a good enquiring mind. Just because you're ill, there's no need to give up reading.'

'My thoughts exactly,' said Phoebe. 'You're very kind.'

William Morris was so heavy he sank into her bones. After a few moments she had to ask Bron to take him away.

'Bloody nuisance. Try again tomorrow.'

She looked at Bron, her spectacles slipping down her nose. Her eyes were fading, the iris rimmed with white. 'Sorry,' she said. 'Nice of you to call.' She fell asleep, breathing unevenly.

Bron rose from the rush-seated chair and gently removed the spectacles. She laid them on the bedside table, on top of William Morris. She went to the open window, looking down on the garden. Bees buzzed amongst the clumps of creamy lupins; delphiniums and larkspur were tall in the sun. Down beyond the dry-stone wall Ted was weeding the onion beds, down in the orchard Gwen was pegging up a line of washing. Bron went to join them, passing Gillian's room, shut fast and silent.

Nesta phoned Edward, and had no answer. She phoned Gillian, to ask if she might visit.

'We're managing very well,' said Gillian. 'My mother is well cared for. She sleeps a great deal.'

'Might I – do you think she would –'

'She is seeing old friends,' said Gillian. She put the phone down.

The vicar came. He waited down in the hall.

'He's asking if you'd like to take Holy Communion,' said Gwen.

'Tell him to go to hell.'

Edward drove the sheep from the lane field into the yard, up to the track at the back of the farmhouse, and in amongst the hens in the back field. Over two days he drove the whole flock up to the hills, the sheep bleating noisily, Tarn working them out through the field gate, over the lower slopes, full of harebells and scabious and here and there wild mint. Rabbits sprang out from bumps in the ground and raced away. Edward climbed the track through the hills, where the tussocky grass became springy turf, and clumps of bracken were everywhere. The sky was hazy and high, and the heat intense. The ewes and their lambs began to scatter, cropping at fresh pasture; near the tops he left them to it, and stood with Tarn at his side, both panting, looking out over the valley.

Below, the farmhouse and the barn and buildings stood within the walled and empty yard: solid, grey, well kept and well proportioned. He could see the pump, he could see the place where Rowland used to park. Beyond was the lane; he could see the gate where they had stood the first time they came here, kissing one another in the freezing cold of a November afternoon, the wind whipping their faces, the buzzard soaring amongst the clouds.

Fields sloped away towards the river, full of grazing cattle. Beyond lay distant, unknown farms. Tractors rumbled along the lanes, cars and tankers climbed the hills and came down again, speeding away. The corn was golden, the trees full, the air alive with birds.

Edward looked out over this lovely place, which Rowland would no longer visit. Beside him Tarn had dropped to her paws, tired but watchful. All around were the quiet steady sounds of the sheep, brushing against the bracken, cropping the turf.

He heard his own breathing, he heard the endless river of dialogue, deep within.

You cannot – I cannot – but listen – please – Rowland, I –

He strode down the hill, sobbing, with Tarn beside him.

Now the sheep were away he had no need to busy himself in the fields. He could not stay in the house.

He walked and walked.

It was evening. The visitors had gone. Gillian sat on the low rush chair and listened to the conversation of doves beyond the window. The sky was fingered with gold. She twisted the button on her sleeve, back and forth, back and forth.

'Stop fiddling,' said Phoebe restlessly. 'It tires me out.'

Gillian stopped.

'You look terrible.'

Gillian did not answer.

'Did you eat, while I was away?'

'I –'

'What kind of answer is that?'

Gillian did not know.

'I never see you,' said Phoebe. Spasms of pain coursed through her. She moved on the pillows, she gazed across the room. 'All these people –'

The sun sank into the bank of cloud, piercing it with gold. Light of extraordinary beauty filled the room. A dove flew on to the windowsill. Gillian watched its transfiguration.

'Everyone says I'm dying,' said Phoebe. 'How are you going to manage?'

Gillian did not know.

Phoebe said: 'It isn't true. What you said to me. Before I went to hospital.'

'What?'

'You said I had never loved you. That isn't true.' She stretched out a skeletal hand.

Gillian stayed in the low rush chair.

Phoebe said: 'You were always difficult.'

Gillian bowed her head. A river of reproaches rose within her: remembered, half-remembered, dark and deep.

She whispered: 'I have not the strength –'

The last of the light had gone; the window was closed, the curtains drawn. The lamp at the bedside burned.

'My father,' said Gillian. 'Tell me about my father.'

'You know about him. You know all there is to know.'

'But he – But you and he –'

Phoebe, against the pillow, was feverish and damp. Her hands plucked the sheet. She said: 'Some people should never marry.'

'Then why –'

Phoebe tried to remember. Illness and exhaustion had sunk so deep within her she did not know where to put herself. Pain began to gnaw. It felt like a lifetime until the next injection.

'What? What did you say?'

'My father,' said Gillian. 'Why did you marry?'

Phoebe shook her head. 'He loved me – we were very different – I can't remember now –'

The pain began to bite and tear. She groaned.

'What shall I do?' said Gillian, rising. 'What shall I do?'

The pain began to claw, going deep, deep. Phoebe fought it,

gasping. She gripped the iron bedstead and the sweat streamed down her.

Outside a snowstorm howled across the fields –

The paraffin stove burned high and the room was bitter –

She clamped her teeth upon white sheets as the child within her fought to be born –

Help me – help me –

Edward, racing down to telephone –

Hour after hour of the whirling night –

The doctor – The baby girl in the crib –

Silence and stillness of snow on the fields, the sky an unearthly colour, everything changed –

Some people should never have children –

'Help me – help me –'

Phoebe was screaming. Gillian flew down the stairs. She raced to the telephone, dialled and dialled.

'My mother – my mother –'

Phoebe was screaming. She flew to her.

'She's coming, she's coming – what can I do –'

'Help me – help me –'

She held her and held her, brittle frail frame against her breast, smoothing the soaking white tufts of hair, rocking and rocking on the high iron bedstead, murmuring words from she knew not where:

'I love you, I love you –'

All through the hours of the night.

Dawn came. Phoebe was sleeping. The district nurse made tea and would not go.

'I'm phoning the doctor. It's not long now.'

They sat in silence in Phoebe's bedroom, watching the summer morning break behind the cotton curtains, listening to the birds.

Phoebe stirred. She opened her eyes and looked towards the window. Gillian rose, and drew the curtains. Phoebe made a tiny gesture. Gillian opened the window. Fresh air and the scent of dew on the grass came into the room. Phoebe gazed fixedly at the casement, the curtains, the morning sky.

A whisper.

They moved the heavy iron bed to the window, slowly, slowly across the floorboards, bringing it forwards away from the wall. They stopped. Doves beat past in the silence. A knock came at the front door.

'That'll be the doctor.' The nurse left the room, creaking along the landing.

Gillian sat on the side of the bed. She lifted her mother, slowly, slowly, and Phoebe, a thread of a thing, leaned against her.

The sun was rising, dew was everywhere.

Phoebe looked out over her garden.

Nesta knew, because she kept on phoning.

'Yesterday morning,' said Gwen. 'They said it was very peaceful.' She looked round the empty kitchen. 'I can't believe she's gone.'

Nesta phoned Edward. This time he was in.

'I am the Resurrection and the Life...'

The church was cleared of cables, filled with flowers: on ledges, on the altar, on the plain pale coffin beneath the chancel steps. The gold Cross was carried high down the aisle, and Gillian trembled and shook. Gwen was beside her; all around her all the people she had ever known were gathered. Phoebe's tapestry hung on the white-washed wall, long and blue and beautiful.

'He that believeth in Me shall not perish, but have Everlasting Life...'

Gillian, in a lost and distant childhood, stood at her mother's side as the rains fell away and they buried her father, deep, deep. A hand held her hand, out in the garden.

'*Mother?*'

'*Yes?*'

'*What is going to happen to us?*'

'*Nothing. Everything will stay the same.*'

Sun streamed through the bright stained glass. It lit the brass plaque with her father's name.

'Let us give thanks for the life of Phoebe Traherne, for her courage and endurance, and for her creativity...'

The coffin raised high by men.

She followed it, trembling. Faces turned towards her, and looked away. People were waiting at the door. Nesta, glinting and tender and black. Edward, white and hesitant. He held out his hand.

'Gillian. I –'

She could not look at him. She could not speak.

Down the smooth grey path to a grave, reopened. Footsteps behind her, quiet and slow. Birds here and there on the grass, sheep in a corner.

'He that believeth in Me shall not perish, but have Everlasting Life ...'

Down, down –

dust to dust –

A settling, one upon another.

And of his wife, Phoebe Traherne –

> *We are cold, we are cold.*
> *Hold, hold.*

People came back to the house, and then they went away. Gwen had done everything, Gwen and Bron Morgan and Gwen's married daughter: all the food, all the preparations, all the fetching and carrying and washing up. The house was full of people: the vicar, the vicar's wife, the people from the shop, from the Fox, from the village.

'Please come and stay with us,' said Gwen. 'You're ever so welcome, Gillian, you know that.'

'No,' said Gillian.

She stood at the gate and watched them leaving. She said she would see them tomorrow. She waved.

Then she went back into the empty house and climbed the dark stairs to the landing. She went to Phoebe's bedroom, and stood in the quietness.

She beheld the high iron bedstead, where she had been born, the mattress covered with a smooth white counterpane, washed and ironed.

She walked along the landing to her own closed room, and entered it. Dead poems lay everywhere. She beheld the dust and brokenness, the heaps of paper.

She beheld her life.

The sun sank low, and Gillian went walking. Out through the valley of the shadow of death and down across the marshy lowlands. Cattle lifted their heads and stared at her; wild swans rose at her approach, and beat out over the water. She came to the banks, to a quiet deserted place. Ducks swam in and out of the reeds; fish, now and then, broke the surface.

Dusk was falling.

Then Gillian, who could not swim, slipped down through the

rushes into the long drowning river of her childhood, into its cold embrace, and let it close over her, and fill her, until she was gasping, and borne away.

Edward, out walking with Tarn, looked down upon the river as the sun sank low.

He beheld –

In the dusk he beheld –

For a moment he stood there, unbelieving.

Then –

'Tarn! Tarn! Go on, go on –'

She looked. She raced down the hillside, and he raced after her, shouting.

My sister, my love, my dove, my undefiled –

She lay in his arms and the water streamed from her. He turned her on to the grass, turned her face to the side. Blue-white. His mouth covered her mouth, so cold, so cold, and he pumped and pumped, the dog barking wildly above them.

Water gushed from her, she spewed and wept.

20

My sister, my love, my dove, my undefiled –

The lanes were dark, and the air was bitter. The moon rose, silver and pure, glinting on the water, hinting at the outlines of cattle and sheep spread out over the fields, vanishing again. It was summer, but summer nights could be treacherous.

Gillian trembled and shook. She was sodden and squelching, exposed and broken anew.

'Edward –'

'Lean on me.' His arms went round her. 'Here.'

She was barefoot and filthy. She could not speak.

They made their way across the grassy lowland by the river. Cattle breathed in the darkness, looming round them. The dog ran quietly, nosing for traces of rabbit and mole. They came to a field gate, a lane. Gillian shivered and shook. The beginnings of fever coursed through her. Returning moonlight silvered the trees. There were the lights of distant farms; occasional headlamps swept the hills.

'We cannot walk all the way home,' said Edward. 'If a car passes – We need only speak of an accident –' Soaking trousers clung to him; he, too, was shivering.

He released her, opening the gate; the dog followed them, panting, her coat beginning to dry.

Out in the lane he drew her to him again: the woman from the wilderness, leaning upon him, half-drowned and terrible.

Gillian sank herself against the body of a man.

Nakedness and darkness and maleness and –

She drew away, shaking violently.

A car approached: he flagged it down, stepping out from the verge, his dog beside him. Gillian, on the wayside, in the headlamps, was a dreadful thing.

A window wound open, a radio quietened. A cautious greeting.

Out walking – the riverbank soft from the summer rains – she had slipped and fallen – luckily the dog –

Edward said what he could.

The farmer nodded. The dog made everything human: he took them in.

The house was in darkness, but the door unlocked. Edward switched on the light in the hall. Gillian stood listening for Phoebe. She trembled in the silence.

'Hot water,' said Edward. They went down the dim tiled passage to the kitchen. The range was alight, just. He rattled the coke and refilled it.

Tarn sank into a corner, her head on her paws.

Gillian sank into the chair by the range.

'You must have a hot bath, you must get warm quickly. Where are the blankets –'

'The cupboard on the landing – I think there are some –'

He made for the door.

'You must not go into my room! It is full of – it is full of –'

Dust and desolation and her longing for him –

She covered her face.

Gillian bathed. She lay back and the water and clouds of steam rose around her nakedness. She closed her eyes and exhaustion filled her, darkness and bitterness and cold swirled round her, dragging her down, down –

She opened her eyes again, on the bathroom of her childhood, on cracked white tiles, and cracked black flooring, a paraffin stove and drooping towels.

She climbed out again, dried and wrapped herself in her ancient dressing gown, creaked along the landing to her room. Her poems breathed their last in the darkness, seeking eternal life. She dressed in what clothes she could find, and left them. She descended the staircase. Phoebe was everywhere and nowhere.

The kitchen was full of light and warmth. The dog slept, the kettle boiled, there was the smell of toast. Edward had stood against the range to dry himself. He had made tea, in the pale green pot.

They sat at the table, as they had sat at the long polished table up at Tremynydd, reading and talking to one another in the quietness.

'You saved my life.'

He nodded.

337

'I did not want to be saved.'

His hand covered hers.

She gazed at the table of her childhood, at its rings and scratches and worn smooth places. The coke sighed and shifted in the range. Phoebe was everywhere and nowhere.

Tarn twitched and murmured.

Gillian said: 'You must be wanting to go home. To – to –'

'Gillian, there is no one at home. I think you should sleep, now. Tomorrow I think we should talk.'

Silence and warmth enclosed them. Her head drooped; she laid it upon her arms; wiry damp hair sprang out around her. She slept.

Edward carried her to the chair by the range. He covered her with blankets, put a pillow beneath her burning face. He switched out the light and stretched out on the floor beneath an ancient eiderdown. Tarn lay between them, dreaming.

Edward and Gillian walked round Phoebe's garden. Dew lay on the ground, doves were everywhere, the pond full of early morning light. Beyond the hedge to the farmer's field the cows, returned from milking, were tearing at the grass.

'So,' said Edward. 'Where shall we begin?'

> *In my beginning is my end …*
> *In my end is my beginning –*

Dry cracked voice on black cracked record, round and round in the loneliness of the past –

A whisper of memory, a voice in a lost and distant childhood; tall beloved man at the bookshelves, reading aloud, going back to the desk –

Tall spare woman out among the flowerbeds, working, working –

Come along, now –

No, not like that –

I love you –

They were nowhere and everywhere.

Gillian and Edward walked through the garden. They talked and talked.

21

The last of summer. A quiet, well-kept town had been invaded. Tents were set up in a nearby field, strings of bunting stretched across the street, the pubs were overflowing. The festival box and information office, operating from two tables in the back of the health-food shop, gave out fliers, press releases, photographs; posters and programmes lined the library walls, signed copies crammed the bookshop windows. The local press was here, and some of the nationals; local radio had covered all yesterday afternoon's events, and run a poetry phone-in; tonight a reporter from *Night Waves* would be interviewed by phone from the studio in London, describing highlights.

It was three o'clock. In a tent in a corner of the field, airless and packed with three hundred people, the Mandrake poets were finishing their reading.

Gillian sat on a folding chair and shook. Sweat poured down her; she beheld the desert of the platform, which she must walk across, whipped by the sun and the wind; she beheld the monstrous microphone. In the audience, programmes were fanned like the wings of birds. Children ran past the open entrance, shouting. The air was thick with the smell of bodies and beer and trampled grass.

The editor of the Mandrake Press was at the microphone: a small, bearded man to whom she had spoken twice: once on the telephone; once today, in a crowded pub at lunchtime. She had been introduced to other poets: a devilish lipsticked woman in a hat and sundress; a tiny man in glasses; a lecturer in Welsh. They had taken a table in a corner of the pub: they drank and drank, and Edward talked to them and she sat silent. Now, on the platform, exposed and trembling, she dared to glance once at the sea of faces before her.

The sea rose and fell. She was a bird on the swell of the waves, tossing beneath a frantic sky, lashed by the wind.

I cannot, I cannot –

She lifted oily wings and flapped across the water, she rose on the

339

roaring wind and beat away. Ocean and desert stretched out beneath her, she stretched out her wings and let the air bear her, weightless and free –

'And finally, with enormous pleasure, I should like to introduce a poet new to Mandrake, one with a distinctive heritage –'

Descended from Thomas Traherne – a father whose work had been undeservedly forgotten – an original, passionate, lyrical voice –

He turned from the towering microphone, and his face was full of kindness. From somewhere in the audience she felt Edward's certainty and belief reach out to her.

She rose, she shook, she walked across the world.

'This reading is dedicated to the memory of my father. It is dedicated to the more recent memory of my mother.' She drew a breath: 'My poetry draws on –'

The whispering paper in her room –

the rattle of stones on a hilltop, beneath the bruise of clouds –

the drowning rain and the rising river, the beat against windows, the beat of wings –

orient gold in the stillness of summer –

white and unearthly winter –

the holy light of dawn –

'Some of these poems have been with me for many years. Their roots go deep. Some are more recent –'

They rose from dust and brokenness, they rose from the dead.

They spoke, she listened.

Solitude, silence, the scratch of a pen.

I am writing again –

She began to read.

Within the church, the congregation waited. It was early evening, mellow light pouring in at the windows and open door. Phil was up by the altar steps, surrounded by cables and equipment, adjusting things. No one knew what to expect.

A stray gleam of sun struck the Cross, and Phoebe's tapestry. Then it was gone. People coughed, and glanced at watches; high on the tower the bell chimed six. They looked once again at their programmes.

The children of Cadair are proud to present –

Movement from the direction of the vestry. Wheelchairs came rolling out across the flags. Behind them, large and clumsy children staggered. Alongside was the vicar, divested of surplice, collared in white. Alongside were Nesta, and Martin and Claire; they took their places.

The vicar spoke a few words of welcome, Nesta and Phil exchanged a nod. She signed to the children.

They began to play.

Voices as high as the last of the wind – the beat of a drum, a breath, a sigh – the rain, falling endlessly – echoing voices – the ring of a bell –

Some of the music was made by the children, up in their circle beneath the altar steps: Nadine, a whisper of a child, radiant, making the rain come down; Dominic, beating a drum, wild with the deep hollow sound of it, roaring; Maureen, her hand beating against her open mouth, listening to the sounds that came and went. Some of the music was recorded, amplified, woven into something mysterious and new: wind chimes; Rachel's breathing; Steven's disjointed cries; Nadine, once, singing a thread of a tune, sweet and high and never to be repeated; Maureen, humming like a bee; Dominic, let loose amongst percussion.

The sounds became a symphony: living, once living, echoing through a church on a summer evening.

Only Robert, clothed in stillness, did not make a sound. He stood in the middle of the circle, open-mouthed, gazing at the light from the coloured windows, the dance of dust within.

Gillian, amongst the congregation, watched and listened, and the strangeness of her childhood lay upon her.

22

An afternoon in autumn. A gathering, beneath the trees in Nesta's garden. The fields around are harvested: acres of stubble lie gold beneath the sun, and lines of stooks cast shadows, deep and still. The last of the hay lies drying in heaps and the air is full of the scent of it, and full of the sound of bees. The hedges lining the track, and up in the lane, have grown dense and tall; sheep crop the grass invisibly beyond them. Every now and then there is the sound of a car, and sometimes a tractor passes, the top of the cab brushing against the hawthorn. Birds flit in and out of the garden, and sing in the trees: blackbirds and thrushes and finches, darting and bright.

The apples have ripened. A basket lies on the rug spread out beneath the trees; there is the last of a picnic, there is a dog, sleeping in the shade.

Soon the leaves and the rain will fall throughout the valley. Now, the light is rich and full and constant, bathing the fields, the garden, the gathering of friends.

Here is a single afternoon in the lives that lie ahead.

Two of these people are lovers, and one is expecting a child.

Two of these people love one another, and are celibate.

The air is so still, so still.

These moments are perfect.

No one speaks.

Acknowledgements

In the writing life of a book, and particularly, perhaps, in writing fiction, there can come a time when it feels as though everything within and around you is feeding into it: landscape, people and themes all finding their place, being drawn together; becoming, at last, a novel.

In the spring of 1995, I was driving on a Sunday morning through the outskirts of south London, half-listening to Radio Three, when sounds of an extraordinary and mysterious beauty filled the car. I gave my attention to the broadcast of a concert given by children from Brays Special School, in Birmingham, and realised that the children in *The Hours of the Night*, who already had a life on the page, in a book half-written, were waiting for this moment of discovery, and for liberation through music and the new technology. Next morning, I rang the programme's producer.

Paul Wright, the Education Officer of Sonic Arts, kindly put me in touch with Katey Earle, Head Teacher of William C. Harvey School, in Haringey, where a similar project of music with children with special needs was being planned. Here, in due course, I was privileged to observe the work of staff and children with Sonic Arts and the composer Duncan Chapman, culminating in a memorable concert performance in the Queen Elizabeth Hall. I should like now to pay tribute to the energy and creative vision of all these people, and also to Adèle Drake, of the Drake Music Project, and to thank them for letting me see and draw a little on their skilled, generous and inspiring work.

I should also like to thank Sarah Clark and Jess Curtis, who at different times gave me invaluable advice on other aspects of music.

For information on the life and background of the seventeenth-century poet Thomas Traherne I am indebted to *Centuries of Traherne Families*, by the late Vera E. Purslow, now published from Birmingham by her son, Duncan Purslow. Quotations from Traherne's own

Centuries are taken from the complete edition of his works edited by H. M. Margoliouth (1958).

I am grateful to Faber and Faber for permission to quote from T. S. Eliot's *The Waste Land*, 'Ash Wednesday' and *Four Quartets*. I thank the producers of the BBC Everyman series, and Phoebe Caldwell, for allowing me to quote some of her words from the programme *Moments of Love*, broadcast in 1992.

Music and poetry both play a large part in this novel, but so do sheep. I could not have written about sheep with any shred of authority without the long and helpful conversations I have enjoyed with our friends Roger and Sally Dickson, whose Herefordshire farm we have been visiting for some twelve years. I thank them most warmly.

For peace and quiet and an empty house to write in I am very grateful to Jane Beckermann and Mandy O'Keeffe, in whose homes outside London I now and then took refuge. I also thank David and Jane Howall, who kindly let me type upstairs in their house in London. For real typing, at top speed, for patient deciphering and intelligent questions, many thanks to Lynette Levine.

I should like to thank my agent, Jennifer Kavanagh, who has always had faith in this book, for all her wisdom, humour and friendship over the years; and my kind and generous publisher, Kate Parkin. Finally, Mary Loring has proven herself to be all that an author could wish for: endlessly attentive, inventive and encouraging – the perfect editor. Any errors here are mine alone.

And now, as always, I am grateful to my family, Marek and Jamie, who, with this particular book, have put up with more than the usual dose of abstraction.

Thank you both.